I0831705

Sanctum: Sands of Setesh

SANCTUM: SANDS OF SETESH

C.S. Kading and Tony Fuentes

SandDancer Publications

Phoenix

Based on the Creative Works in the World of Sanctum by Todd E. Filek

ISBN-13: 978-0578756981 (case bound)

ISBN-10: 0578756986

Cover design by: Rocko407

Library of Congress Control Number: 2018675309

Printed in the United States of America

Dedication

To Lord Todd Filek, without whom none of this would have been possible.

A very merry Unbirthday, Old Friend

Contents

Foreward

When I was 8 years old, I received two gifts that would shape my creative interests for a lifetime.

The first was a beat-up old briefcase full of comic books from my older cousin. The second was a hardback copy of condensed (and PG-13 edited, I would later learn) Greek myths from my father. I believe the second gift was an effort to counteract the first, but that went quite happily awry.

Two weeks after reading through both of my gifts, I wrote a fumbling but earnest child's story about Hephaestus repairing Captain America's shield (spoiler–Hephaestus used his wedding ring because he didn't need it anymore). It was the first real piece of writing I ever did, and it started a fascination with mythology and heroes that still drives me.

For the last 20 years, Sanctum has been my place to explore this fascination. A world where everything has already gone wrong, the heroes of old failed, and the surviving mortals and divinities must craft a new world with only scraps of what has come before. Saving the world is a fine crucible for heroes–but forging a new one? How would those heroes be different?

Exploring this question through Sanctum was an intensely private pastime. I sketched, I amended, I wrote through all the changes in my life. Sanctum was always there for depressed me, joyful me, or, on the occasion I created a few characters, what must have been a mildly intoxicated me.

The most public I ever was with my work was through one of the first online video game persistent worlds, but this was done piecemeal, under internet anonymity, and involved a great deal of compromise. So, Sanctum in its greatest detail returned to strict isolation in my head and my increasingly thick pile of notes.

A few years ago, I took some halting steps towards sharing this world with a group of close friends by translating it into a pencil-and-paper roleplaying game setting. I carefully shared bits and pieces, testing and judging reactions, parceling out more of the enormous enterprise Sanctum represented for me only after I was sure no one was laughing. But finally, this world, which had been clutched tightly and jealously to its creator's chest for two decades, had others living within it through their characters.

I was humbled to learn that two of those friends not only enjoyed what they saw but were inspired enough to write what expanded from a simple Google document into the novel you now hold. But my initial reaction was complicated–visitors to the world were one thing, but now others were creating, changing, and forging new ideas in a space that had always been mine and mine alone. I wasn't prepared for more smiths at the anvil, as it were. I am immeasurably fortunate that my friends understood and were patient with a grumpy old man's fear of the unknown.

As I read what they created, I saw that their patience was coupled with true talent and the same passion for exploring what it means to be a hero. The result of all their virtues is the extraordinary story you are about to read. It is a story that shares the moral I learned from its authors: None of us need walk alone on our journey.

– Todd Filek –

Introduction

Every faith has a story of how the world ends. It's hard-coded in their mythologies. But when the end of the universe actually happened, it was unlike anything ANY of them predicted. Those Divine beings who survived the Reaping crafted a place of survival for their people and ushered them to safety.

Gone are the once glorious civilizations of myth and legend. Gone are the heroes of ancient days: Hippolyta, Beowulf, Gilgamesh, Cleopatra, and Arthur. Their stories are the foundations of civilizations seeking to rebuild in the wake of destruction. Here are peoples of myth made real, some crafted from the clay of this new world; others pulled from the dreams and nightmares of the old. Human and Orc, Dwarf and Fae. Here, The Divine has taken a personal and vested interest in the Realm. These are the last of their followers.

For 5000 years the survivors of the Reaping have tried to reassemble some shadow of the former glory that was once their respective civilizations. Cultures war with one another seeking supremacy and control while their chosen Divine continue their ancient battles in the heavens still. The names they possessed when they came here have been lost to time; but their position and function... for those who have survived... remain.

All the while they watch the moonless sky for portents signaling that catastrophe has come once more.

Welcome to Sanctum

Prologue

She staggered onward, feet dragging through the white-hot sand that slowed her movements. Tiny particles of uncompromising grit rubbed against her flesh; beneath her breeches, inside the crevices of her armor, rubbing raw what was not already calloused or scabbed over from sun blisters. Her lips were parched and cracked; they had ceased to bleed a day ago. Her hair, once dark and voluminous, was sun-bleached and coated in the white dust of the uncaring desert.

The metal of her armor had proven to be merciless in its punishment of her. She had removed what she could and shoved as much as was possible into her pack. Now she wore only her hardened leather cuisses and vambraces. Arms and legs protected as best as she could, the rest of her formerly pale skin, which pants and gambeson could not cover, was now a ragged ruin.

She turned her green eyes skyward and then toward the horizon in an attempt to gain her bearings. Her right hand, wrapped in torn fabric, clutched at a small, broken compass that hung around her neck from a leather cord. The beast had said it was this way, the direction of her destination; but that had been hours ago. She released the compass and raised her hand to shelter her eyes, in an attempt to look for something across the vast, white, wasteland. The sands shimmered with the false hope of water and relief. She shook her head and braced herself. The love of her God would keep her going for a few hours more, surely; but without water, this could well be where her Quest ended.

One foot pulled free from the sand and placed before the other, by the strength of will alone, she continued her pained trudging. She crested the top of the dune, shaded her eyes, and looked outward once more. A shadow in the distance beckoned to her. A shape that did not quite blend in with its smooth surroundings. Could it be? The Temple? Her pace quickened with the light of Hope once more. She stepped forward.

The sand shifted beneath her, her right leg sinking more deeply than she anticipated. Her arms went wide in an attempt to regain her balance. The pack flew off of her shoulders, upsetting her weight ratio. She flailed, helpless in the sand, as her body tipped forward, out of her control. Her head hit the hot sand, filling her nose and mouth with grit and dry. She tumbled.

And then it was nothing but darkness.

~~~

He was uncomfortable.

The room was adorned with both polished gold and brass. Each bearing a depiction of his devotion. The images told the story of The Radiant Lord and his trek to Sanctum to bring the light to the darkness of the world. Each wall and ceiling piece told a different tale of the god and His exploits. Each was kept pristine so that the light caught from above was always bounced and reflected. The room was used when one needed to commune with The Radiant Lord.

As a child, Tulok observed many of the priests sit in this room, cross-legged and head turned up toward the solar window above. This was his time – he was no longer an Acolyte, but a full member of the priesthood. While he wasn't the first of his kind, he was the most recent Orc inducted into this local temple. The Solarium, in which he currently sat – was constructed with humans and dwarves in mind – not the massive frame that he presented. It was
~~~

one thing getting into the door, it was another to try to sit cross-legged in a very small room.

"The Radiant Lord never backed down from a challenge..." he said to no one.

Tulok closed his eyes and tried to settle in. Relaxing his shoulders, he breathed in deeply and raised his head up. The bright rays of the sun fell from the sky upon his upturned face and he could feel the warmth of god throughout his body. The room no longer felt small – but rather HE did as he let his body finally settle into place and reached out with his senses to the world around him. For a moment, he caught a flash of the Temple and the small village around it. He could sense every person that The Radiant Lord's light touched. He fell into the sensation even more – hoping that it would expand his vision of the world around him. He sensed the sand, the air, and...
There was a hideous howling noise of an animal – a cat?

He opened his eyes and looked around the room. There was no one there and nothing else in the room. He listened and there was no repeat of the wailing howl. There was nothing but the quiet sounds of the village and a few voices speaking down the hall. Slowly, he tried to get to his feet, but only managed to catch himself under his own robe which promptly tore. Tulok sighed and sat back down. He thought of how he got in the room and sat and slowly tried to reverse the process. In an almost comical fashion, he slowly divorced himself from the room and its doorway.

Stepping out into the light, he stretched his arms out to the sky in an effort to put his body back in place. It was then that he felt a tug on the waistline of his robe.

Laith was no more than 10 years old. Still a child, but mature enough to do chores and his duty to the Temple. The young boy stared up at the massive seven-foot being who seemed even taller with his arms raised in the air, "Father – there's a lady."

Seeing the boy, Tulok lowered himself down to a knee and smiled at the boy. The Orc was never sure how others took his smile, as it was accented by a pair of tusks that protruded from his lower jaw. "A lady Laith? Does someone in the village nee..."

"No Father, I saw her fall from the dune," the boy said, but quietly added, " I think she's dead," the boy said wide-eyed.

Tulok pursed his lips together and stood up, "Show me."

Chapter 1

She could feel the dampness of cloth on her body. It was dark and she could sense wet fabric on her face. Drops of moisture on her lips and on her parched mouth – water. She wanted more and weakly tried to move. She felt someone or something hold her down.

A deep, but the calm voice spoke to her in a strange tongue. She shook her head – her exhausted mind raced, trying to remember something of Reynard's lessons. The words repeated again, but then paused, "You need to take it slow," the voice said in the Trader's Tongue. "Too much water and you will get sick and feel even worse than you do now." She felt something lift up her head and water was slowly poured into her mouth. The body's greed overrode her common sense as she tried to take a normal drink. She coughed and almost gagged as her body was unprepared.

"I warned you..." the voice cautioned. Her head was lowered back on the bed. "Any more will not be good for you so you need to rest. Leave the wet wraps on your body, there are ointments mixed with the water that will help your skin heal," the voice said.

There was a pause. A slight hint of amusement flavored the voice, "Also...don't suck on the wraps, the ointment tastes worse."

She closed her eyes under the wraps and darkness came again.

~~~

She alternated between shivering and sweats; dreams filled with memories of ice-cold lakes and the unforgiving sun of the desert. There was pain. She cried out from her unconscious and bedridden state. Each time, just as she felt the crescendo of pain return to her wrecked form, there was a gentle hand and a soothing voice in the darkness. Deep and calming. It settled the healing nerves from their white-hot fury. She had no idea how long she remained in this state of semi-lucid trial; how many hours... or days...passed. In time both the darkness and heat hallucinations slowly lessened and her sleep became more restful.

She remembered reaching for the cloths that covered her eyes, only to hear that same deep, soothing voice speak out,

"No. You need to leave those on a little longer. Your eyes are sun damaged; they need time to heal, or you will be blind," the familiar voice said.

The prospect of perpetual darkness gave her pause. Such a state would invalidate her place and her path. How could she bear witness to the world, with no eyes to see? She nodded slowly in comprehension of the gravity of the situation.

"I... understand," her voice croaked and cracked. She wheezed and then coughed, clearing her throat. "How...how long?" she asked quietly.

"Resting? Almost a week's time," she felt one of the wraps being lifted slightly, "A few more days and you'll be able to wear your lighter armor without pain."

There was a shift under her head as she felt it lightly raise, "This is warm and tastes even worse than the ointments- but it will help your mouth and throat. The last of
~~~

sickness will pass after this." She felt something at her lips and she prepared herself to take a sip.

When she was a child, she remembered accidentally drinking stagnant lake water and being sick for days. At this particular moment, she wished for another taste of the lake water compared to what she was being given. She almost retched. Will, coupled with the potential for embarrassment kept her drinking. She coughed slightly after the last sip had been taken and she felt a pleasant warmness in her mouth and throat. She felt her head lowered back down,

"Rest a bit more and we'll have you back up soon."

Heavy steps walked away and were lost in the far-off sounds of chanting/singing, children playing, and other signs of village life. Wherever she was – her god ensured that she was alive.

She took a deep breath, inhaling and smelling the scents that surrounded her. She could not see her environment, but even now, in the state that she was presently in, she could bear witness.

Songs, unknown to her ears, but clearly reverent, echoed in the distance, sung in a key that she was not familiar with. She strained to listen, but could only make out bits and pieces here and there. Tones, repeated in cadence and unity. Prayer hymns? The scent from the liniment-soaked fabric filled her nostrils, making it more challenging to sort out anything else; but there was ...something... dark, musty, she could almost taste the thickness of it...incense...

She nodded and relaxed into the bed. The last of her weariness finally released as she accepted where she must be.

One step closed to her destination.

She closed her eyes and for the first time in months, relaxed into an unguarded sleep.

~~~

She was awakened by the sound of someone quietly whispering. Their voices were speaking in the same desert tongue. All she could do was listen.

"He says she's not from here..." one hushed voice issued.

"I could have told you that," another voice returned, *"Nobody walks the dunes wearing what she was wearing."*

They sounded young. She lay there, silent and still, and allowed them to continue.

"Where do you think she's from?" the first voice asked.

"Somewhere with water and trees, I'd guess."

"Like one of the Oasis?"

"Nah, even the merchants know what to wear and to travel at night and not midday".

The second voice sounded older than the first, but both were clearly young.

"Shhh!" the older voice chided. *"You'll wake her up, and then we'll both be in trouble!"*

"I'm sorry, Laith" the younger voice apologized.

~~~

It was difficult to say whether it was day or night, but she could see the weave of the cloth over her eyes.

She could see!

With cautious movements, she slowly started to move her right arm. There was soreness but no burning sensation on her skin. She felt the dampness of the healing wraps all over her skin. Reaching up, she lifted the bandage from over her eyes and slowly blinked. Her eyes slowly adjusted to the candlelight and darkness. Slowly moving, she turned her body to the side to look around. There were two other beds and a few chairs. A few shelves held what she assumed were more medicinals. Looking down at herself, she saw that her entire body was bandaged. There were stories that the desert people wrapped up their dead before burial or setting on the pyre. Was she that bad off when they found her that they pre-wrapped her? A question better left unanswered.

With a firm will, she began moving each of her limbs and cooed lightly as the soreness came in flashes as the muscles ached. She forced herself to sit up and turn her body off the bed. Planting two feet on the cold ground, she felt a sense of assurance. Seeing a pitcher on a table across the room, her mouth suddenly ached.

"You can do this...stand up, and walk four steps...take a drink. Simple, " she said to herself.

She stood and felt a wave of vertigo force her back down on the bed, "Okay, maybe not as simple." It was then that she heard the familiar heavy steps outside the room – the Healer! She turned toward the doorway.

Through the doorway came not a man, but the hulking frame of an "ORC!!" she shouted hoarsely. Her muscle memory caused her to leap from the bed into a fighting stance. Her hands balled up, ready for a fight.

The orc blushed and immediately looked down.

She paused and stared at the creature. He raised a hand and stuck out a finger at her, moving it up and down.

She relaxed her stance and looked down.

With the exception of her bandages, she was naked.

Slowly raising his hands in the air, he took a few steps toward the wall. He pulled a bundle off a shelf. Letting the bundle unfurl, it revealed a robe.

The orc held it aloft as he took a few cautious steps toward her, his gaze firmly fixed on her face. "I see you're feeling better," spoke the same calm deep voice.

There was both confusion and recognition in that voice. She furrowed her brow and narrowed her eyes, suspiciously. She broke eye contact briefly to glance at the table with the water pitcher. How far away was it? Could she reach it for a makeshift weapon if needed?

The burly orc's eyes followed her quick gaze. A familiar recognition of response came upon him, born of decades of mistrust and hatred from others. He sighed deeply, and waived the cloth robe in his massive hand once more, then cleared his throat, politely. "If not for your own modesty, then for mine?" he offered. Once again, the timbre and tone of familiar, and friendly actions washed over her ears, as her mind struggled with the scenario.

With a cautious and deft hand, she reached to snatch the unassuming cloth from his hand and quickly wrapped her agile figure in its comforting embrace.

"You're..." she began, her voice trailing off.

"Tulok," he paused and his posture straightened though not so much for authority, but for recitation. "I am Father Tulok, Devout of The Radiant Lord – Lord of the Skies, and Bringer of Light to the Ever Burning Sands." He relaxed and looked at her, "...and resident Healer of this temple."

Giving her space, he walked around her to the table with the pitcher. Picking it up slowly he poured water into a cup. With his forefinger and thumb, he picked up the small cup and held it toward her, "Thirsty?"

Looking at the Orc, she realized he was dressed in priestly vestments; an ornate sun medallion hung from his neck, etched with the symbol of The Radiant Lord – the All-Seeing Eye. He looked young – or at least what she considered young as he was clean-shaven. Could orcs grow facial hair? His head was shaved as well. Was this a priest thing? He was her healer? He was taller than any man and he held the cup with two fingers.

Slowly he moved the cup toward her, “It is still cool, but you should drink it slowly for now.”

Her face was a mask of both confusion and curiosity as she slowly reached for the proffered beverage.

“Thank you?” she replied, not certain herself if it were a statement or a question. She carefully accepted the cup and then raised it to her still parched lips.

This is new – a voice whispered somewhere in the maze of her mind as the coolness of the water broke the barrier of the dry that surrounded them.

Her eyebrows rose toward her hairline and her eyes widened with sudden and new insight into the situation before her. She coughed and sputtered a little on the water.

“Oh, sweet Wanderer’s beard...I am so rude!” she exclaimed, suddenly flustered and awash with her own embarrassment. “You... you saved my life...and I... here I am...” she began to speak, quickly and with flustered tones, “I’m just being so... I mean... I’m such an asshole...I mean...” her eyes looked skyward, “Oh please don’t be too mad at me..” she looked back at the big orc before her, “Avalon is very sheltered... you know...is why..” she gestured at herself and opened her mouth to continue, then stopped suddenly. She inhaled sharply. “Ohhhhh...guest right...hospitality...I’ve gone and made a mess of things...oh...I’m so sorry, I’m such an idiot...I mean...oh gosh...uh..” she shook her head in self-disappointment and looked back at the healer.

“Hi, I am Isolde.” She smiled brightly, hope filling her green eyes as she held out her left hand. She blinked, “Oh, sorry!” She took the cup out of her right hand with her left and extended her right hand in greeting. “Isolde duAvalonne, Knight Wanderer... um... hi.” She blushed.

In another light, his half-smile could have also looked like a snarl, but his red eyes said otherwise. She noted it was the first time she had seen 'kind' red eyes. Most creatures with red eyes tended to be the enemy, but this was different. He reached toward her extended hand and lightly grasped her forearm instead in an accepted greeting.

"You should probably have a seat," he said as he released her arm and pointed toward her bed. He reached out for a sturdy-looking chair against the wall and sat down. "So tell me Lady Isolde," he said acknowledging her title with a light sense of formality, "Were you lost or exiled to wander the desert?"

"Huh? Oh. Right." Isolde replied and took a step back to the bed. She sat down in an unceremonious 'flomp', seated in a wide stance as one familiar with riding horses. She winced slightly and drank from the cup, swishing its contents around in her mouth.

Tulok's eyes found a cross beam on the ceiling to stare at. He cleared his throat politely once more.

She frowned at his response and then took an assessment of herself. "Oh!" she nodded and readjusted accordingly, fighting with the cloth robe for a few seconds. It was clearly not a garment that she was accustomed to wearing. "How do you..." she muttered. "Ok... there!" she smiled at her simple victory and looked back over at Tulok. "Not exiled, oh my gosh no... though...I mean.I could see how someone might think that. I certainly don't *belong* here," she gestured wide. She paused, and considered her words, drinking from the cup once more and clearing her throat. "I mean...that's not..." she stumbled over her words, her voice cracking, as she realized that she may have given insult again.

She blinked quickly, assessing her words. Looking over at Tulok she replied more formally,

"I'm sure this is a very lovely region of the world for the people who have made it a home." She smiled and nodded, content with her assessment. She paused, for a few beats of a human heart.

Her shoulders slumped, she set the cup aside, and she leaned forward and placed her head in her hands, as she rested her elbows on her knees, "I'm sorry, Reynard, I'm messing this all up." she said to some unknown personage.

The priest ran his hand over the top of his head as one would combing through their hair. He let his shoulders drop and he cocked his head slightly to the side, "Let's try this again. We are two people in the infirmary on this very lovely evening. I am Tulok, your healer, not your host. You are Isolde, my patient who literally almost died, but by the Grace of our gods was found and brought to me. You are exhausted, tired, and probably hungry. However, you are alive and that is the most important thing to me."

He reached out and gently patted her knee, "Now, how did you end up in full armor while walking the desert? Is this a wandering knight thing?"

She slowly lifted her head from her hands at the kindness in the big man's words. Their eyes met for a moment. His were filled with patience and compassion, and hers were filled with thanks and hope, though red-rimmed from her own frustration.

At that moment, she seemed nothing more than a young woman, lost and alone in the world. The fact that she had been found in a warrior's garments seemed completely out of place and contrary to the visual evidence before him. She sniffed, and nodded, and sat up straight, regaining her composure.

"Undead." She replied simply.

Chapter 2

Tulok's right eyebrow cocked upward at that. "Undead?" he repeated back to her.

She nodded. "Undead... putting to rest the remnants of the final Quest of my Lord...may he rest in the peaceful arms of the Summerlands, and may he be found worthy to re-enter the Cycle once more." Her eyes glistened slightly in the candlelight at the words. She cleared her throat and wiped her eyes with the bandaged back of her hand.

His compassionate countenance was replaced with a look of harshness – though not aimed at her. He leaned back and for a moment and looked toward the window giving a view of the night sky. Turning back to his patient, "Start from the beginning, do not leave a detail out."

It was not so much a trigger to action, but rather it was the activation of duty that each member of The Radiant Lord's faithful adhered to. The Tenets of Faith that both priest and champion followed were very simple. *The enemy is always the greatest evil present. There is never a choice between lesser evils. Both must fall to the sword.*

The Undead, abhorrent creations of the Unsleeping Goddess were considered blight and plague upon the world. While the Priesthood of Risen Lady created and controlled their undead servants – there were cases when the undead got loose or the Necromancer was no longer in control. When that happened, The Radiant Lord's Children brought their Light to vanquish the Darkness.

She nodded and chewed on her bottom lip for a moment.

"Alright, but I am going to need two things first."

The big priest folded his arms across his broad chest. "Go on."

"The first... I'm really hungry...do you think we could do this over food, maybe a beer?" her stomach growled to punctuate the request.

Tulok's lips turned up in a grin that he struggled to control. He nodded. "Absolutely." he cleared his throat, still trying to evoke a formal appearance. "And the second?"

"Can I please have my pants?"

~~~

She frowned.

She looked around the small hall. There were at least fifteen children laughing and eating some sort of meaty game.

She looked down at her bowl of broth and sighed. She shifted in her seat – her pants felt awkward. They felt almost too soft, and the color seemed off. Then it dawned on her that they were clean. Someone had laundered and mended her clothing. Though there was an addition to each mended fix. Little Eyes of The Radiant Lord or a sun was added in the embroidered thread.

With thankful, albeit sad eyes, she slowly spooned her broth, feeding her empty stomach. Apparently in the desert, ale was a foreign concept. Here they had a spiced wine. It was strange as it felt cool going down but offered a light, pleasant sensation that one would get after a couple of tankards of ale. Several cups of wine would probably be dangerous, so she sipped it slowly.
~~~

She knew the broth was necessary, she just wasn't happy about it. The orc came back from the hearth with his own bowl and a plate of what looked like disks of bread. Sitting down across from her, she half expected to see his massive bowl filled with chunks of meat or something on a bone. Instead, it was more broth. He tore off a piece of some of the doughy disk and rolled it up. Dipping it into the broth he took a bite. Looking at her, he motioned at the bread. Following what he did, she tore off a piece and dipped it into the broth. While not meat, the flatbread gave the meal more substance.

Between bites, "So where does the story begin?" he asked.

"Right" She nodded and dipped the bread into the broth. She allowed it to soak up some of the dark liquid before pulling it away and lifting it to her lips. Broth dribbled down her chin as she ate. She wiped it away with the back of her hand.

"So... Ser Reynard the Swift...may his soul rest..." she added as she began, "I was his squire, back on Avalon." She paused as the flavor of the broth assaulted her taste buds. It was the first real food she's had in what she assumed were weeks. Her eyes widened and she looked at the bowl. "Hey, this is really good!" she exclaimed.

Tulok nodded from across the table. "Go on."

"Right," she nodded again. "So we were in Brede, that's a little wharf town in the northern...never mind" she waved it off and continued, "We were in Brede, we ran into a merchant who had recently come from this area of the world." She tore off a chunk of bread and dipped it once more, "Now...we don't get very many travelers from here. In fact, I'd only heard STORIES about the desert growing up, never imagined it would be anything like this."

The big priest nodded and nibbled on his bread and broth. "I never would have guessed," he commented.

"So, this merchant, he had this necklace that someone had asked him to deliver in Brede, something from this area, someone had paid for it ahead of time, it was supposed to be a big deal." Isolde continued, once more dunking her bread into the broth. More dribbles on her chin. She wiped them away with the palm of her hand. "But...the person who ordered it...had died before he could deliver it, so now he was trying to find their next of kin so he could complete the transaction. I mean...it was paid for by an advance against fall crops from the family, the family should get the item, right? At least that's how honorable merchants are where I'm from." she tore off a chunk of the crust and gnawed on it.

Tulok carefully continued to nibble on his bread and sip from his bowl, nary a droplet was misplaced.

"So, Reynard...may his soul rest...he offers to help the merchant find the owner of the necklace. Seemed like a simple enough task, right? Ask around, find out where the next of kin are, deliver the item, move along. Merchant gets to complete his deal, the family gets to settle their debts and not worry if someone was going to show up asking for a portion of their stores come Winter, and The Wanderer gets to see the sights as we knock about. It is a win for everyone involved."

She suddenly realized that the room was silent. The children were quiet and looking at her as well as a few other adults.

They were all listening.

They were all listening and looking at her.

She was a stranger here. A pale, dark-haired stranger from a land none of them had heard of. She was telling a tale of places that none of them had ever conceived.

Whether she wanted it or not, she had the audience's attention. She cleared her throat and took another sip of the wine.

Tulok smiled at her as he chewed. He motioned at her to continue.

"Oh boy..." she sighed.

She drank deeply from the cup, her eyes searching the faces of the youth who had all turned their attention to her.

"Right!" she exclaimed and set the cup down with a solid THUNK. The liquid sploshed a little around the rim.

"So... there we were..." she cleared her throat, her voice taking on a more commanding timbre. Tulok's right eyebrow twitched once more as he watched her. Without looking at the children she slowly rose from her seat. "The Brave Ser Reynard, on the coast of cold, Avalon, in the township of Brede, on the cusp of Winter..." She paused. She could feel the held breath around her. She suppressed a smile and waited.

"What happens?" one of the children asked. She was a small girl, Isolde guessed her to be about eight. Her dark hair was braided and coiled, and her sun-kissed skin glowed almost bronze in the lamplight. The girl struggled with the words slightly and frowned. Isolde realized that the children seemed to glean bits, but the Trader's Tongue was probably still being learned. She would have to improvise.

"What happened next?" Isolde asked the girl.

The girl smiled and nodded. Several other heads bobbed in unison.

"Well..." she stepped out from behind the table, swinging one long leg free of the bench seat and then stepping over with the other. She stood. Using her hands to gesture and pantomime her words, "We listened to the merchant, and from his tale, we gleaned that we needed to find a very specific family...in a very specific area of town." She continued. The knight's voice had changed now, from one of casual conversation to one designed to command the attention of an audience...albeit a young one.

"Where?" one of the other children asked.

She turned her attention to the young boy who had spoken up. "A very specific area...beyond the walls...and inside a sacred grove..."

She watched Tulok frown at the word. Her eyebrow rose a little in response, as she noted the confusion in the eyes of many of the listeners.

"Ah... right" she nodded. "And what is a grove you may ask..." she looked at the audience, several children nodded. "A grove is where there are many many trees, all gathered together, and there is a ...a... a clear space in the middle," she explained.

"Like an Oasis?" the first girl asked.

Isolde paused and thought. "Well... I mean... yes...and no..." She walked over and took a knee so as to be eye level with the children.

She continued to move, "Here in your desert, trees are very rare. An Oasis...is a place where there are many trees that surround a source of water...right?" She asked. Many of the children nodded, a couple of them inched closer to her. "Well...where *I* am from...we have trees ALL OVER the island...and some of those trees...and the areas they grow in... are sacred to our gods..." she paused as her eye caught the sun symbol that had been embroidered into her breeches.

"Like...like this place is sacred to..." she looked over at Tulok, "The Radiant Lord?" she offered.

The priest nodded, impressed.

Isolde nodded and continued. "The family that we needed to find ...was a very old family...from an ancient...uh...very old...lineage..." more children began to crowd around her. Isolde unfolded her leg from beneath her and sat down on the floor with them then. Tulok shifted his great weight and turned around on his bench seat. It creaked under him.

"Were they bad people? Why outside of town?"

"Oh no... nothing like that." Isolde shook her head. "They were a very honorable family, and they were responsible for keeping track of the history of the area."

One of the smaller children, a young boy, walked up to Isolde and stared at her. The child had green eyes, like hers. His tiny hand reached out and gently touched Isolde's face with all the innocence that only a child can own. Isolde could hear the whole of the group inhale simultaneously and hold their breath. The young knight smiled warmly at the toddler and then reached out to place her fingers on his face, she tapped next to his right eye with her left forefinger and then tapped next to her own.

The boy beamed brightly at her. "Same!" he said clearly and then planted himself firmly in Isolde's lap.

Isolde paused at that, her hands very carefully placed at her sides and away from her body as if the child were an exceptionally fragile item. The gesture, however, was interpreted differently by the throng of children before her; who interpreted the gesture as one welcoming a hug. Suddenly the foreigner was swarmed by small bodies, each reaching out to touch her, pat her, or hug her.

Tulok frowned a little and cleared his voice, and stood. "Now, children..." he began.

Isolde waved the big priest off as she proceeded to laugh and giggle with the children, her story forgotten for the moment, lost instead in joy.

~~~

The hall was quiet save for the small cooking hearth.
~~~

The Orc sat on the ground next to it watching the quiet embers of the fire. The wandering knight sat across from him on the bench, exhausted but happy. She couldn't remember the last time she played or told stories. It had been a very long time. In Avalon, she never seemed to have time of her own. Her training as a Squire and duties to the Realm had her traveling all over. A quiet smile crossed her face. It felt good to know that regardless of place – children still loved stories wanted to be carried to bed.

She had never been blessed with them, but it was said that The Wandering Lord bestowed dreams on children so they might reach for something more in the world. Stories and tales were the wicks to light their imagination. While not so much as a sworn duty, it was something that needed to be done to inspire the young – The Wanderer would be proud. Carrying two of the children in her arms was a test of her own body's healing. Something like that should have been simple. It wore her out, but it was worth it. What was more surprising was that she learned that all fifteen children were orphans of the temple. The children had either been left at the temple or their parents died and The Radiant Lord's Faithful took them in.

She looked at the orc across the way.

He was sitting cross-legged with his back leaning against the bench. This massive being had the responsibility of teaching and raising these children. He was more than their Father in Faith, he was the one they would look back on when they talked about their family and who raised them. She let out a deep sigh and closed her eyes. She would be taking away their father.

The happiness of the moment faded.

"If it was something as simple as taking a necklace to where it belonged, I wouldn't be here," she started.

Without looking at her, the orc just nodded his head.

He had been waiting for the rest of the tale. He must have the patience of stone, she thought.

"This is where things took a twist. The man's name was Nahem and he lived in the town Deneb-aal."

The orc gave a half-smile, "Home of the Water Fat."

"Huh?" she said quizzically.

He leaned forward and stoked the embers a little. "In the desert, there are two types of people – 'Sand Blooded' and the 'Water Fat'. Here in Tarf-qua, the people practice strict water discipline. From the young to the vulnerable, each knows the value and scarcity of water. So we conserve it by all means. In Deneb-aal, they see themselves as desert folk – but at the edge of the desert and a dozen town wells," he gives a slight laugh, "none of them would survive out here."

Isolde raised an eyebrow, obviously not sharing in his sentiment. "Are all the Sand Blooded this self-righteous?" Her tone was full of disappointment.

The orc turned to her; his look of surprise soon replaced with quiet shame. He was silent for a moment, "My apologies Lady Isolde. Please go on."

Shaming a priest, Gods! An orc no less. Wanderer forgive me. She ran both her hands through her hair. The embers crackled a little. "I understand. Every town that I have visited has had a sense of pride and that pride can distort itself or even get ugly. Far be it from me to tell you how to see the world. Just know to an outsider, it doesn't sound good."

Like you, stumbling over your insults last night She thought to herself.

The orc nodded and cleared his throat, "Deneb-aal is about five days from here. Based on the sun damage to your body, it looked like you were out there for more than a week."

She nodded, "Nahem was supposed to have lived there

but apparently he had died a year ago. What was even odder, the transaction took place three months ago."

Tulok ran his hand over his head and just nodded.

"So we decided to see if he had any kin within the town." She chuckled and shook her head, "Do you have any idea how hard it is to get information out of people out here? I mean, sure, information for information, the task for the task, but... what is the fascination with the little metal discs that everyone seems so fascinated with?" She asked.

Tulok's brown furrowed. "Metal...discs?" he asked.

She nodded "You know...the ones made from silver, or copper, or sometimes gold?" she nodded, a look of confusion on her face.

The orc's eyes widened and his eyebrows raised. "You mean...coins?"

Isolde shook her head and shrugged.

"Money?" he offered.

"Uh... I suppose?" she said hesitantly. "Reynard seemed to understand it better. He secured our passage from Avalon to the continent and made all of our travel arrangements. Your people want these metal discs for things, instead of favors, or items in kind, or tasks I guess?"

The big priest took a deep breath and held it for a moment, then exhaled slowly. The rumors were true. The people of Avalon did not use money for trade.

"Your people function on... barter...then?" he asked carefully.

"Ya, sure, I mean... I guess that's what you call it. I need a loaf of bread; I'll give you a dozen eggs?"

Tulok rubbed the back of his neck and shook his head, then rubbed his face with both hands. "Yes, that's barter...and... You are going to have a rough time with that out here."

Isolde frowned and scowled and looked away. "I was concerned about that. Reynard knew how it all worked out here...I... none of it really makes sense," she replied with a note of sadness.

Tulok pursed his lips in thought and watched the young woman struggling with her failings. "I will do what I can to assist you with this issue." he offered.

She turned her emerald green eyes back to his, they were brilliant with hope. "You will?!"

Tulok suddenly worried that he may have over-offered, "I...I mean that I will help you understand, and make certain no one takes advantage of your lack of knowledge." he replied carefully.

She nodded. "That would be terrific. I appreciate it!" she smiled warmly at him.

The big priest nodded and gestured that she should continue. "Go on with your tale?"

She nodded and thought, "Right... So.. It turns out that the local Magister in Deneb-aal was Nahem's brother. So we took the package to his home, hoping we might get somewhere with all of this. The Magister was happy to receive us, though admittedly he was very confused. His brother was laid to rest only a few months before, and he certainly did not remember seeing anything left outstanding in his brother's estate. Vanhem... that was the name of the Magister... opened the package and we saw our charge for the first time. It was an ornately carved beetle. He called it a Sacred Scarab?"

Tulok cocked his head to the side, "You were delivering a Sacred Scarab to a dead man?"

"Exactly – I mean...the transaction was placed about 3 months ago, and his brother had apparently died sometime before that, so...it was all very confusing," She agreed.

"I can see that." Tulok nodded. He shifted his position to give Isolde more of his attention.

She continued, "The Magister...Vanhem... explained that it was a powerful magical item, though he wasn't sure why his brother needed it so much as the family had the ability to acquire one easily enough. He thanked us for the delivery, gave Reynard a sack full of ..coins.." she said the word carefully, "As thanks for his efforts and sent us on our way." She took a deep breath and reached for her wine cup. Sadly, it was empty. She frowned and turned it upside down on the bench seat next to her.

"Well, that is when things turned bad," she began. Isolde closed her eyes and tilted her head toward the ceiling as she began to remember how things unfolded, "We were walking away – discussing whether we were going to return to the Island, or explore this new path we were on...and suddenly the air was filled with a horrible scream. We turned around and saw Vanhem falling out his front door, his body wreathed in green flame. He was screaming in agony. Ser Reynard invoked our Lord's Grace to try to save him, but it was too late. Whatever conjured those infernal green flames made it impossible to save his life. Vanhem managed to say one thing though, 'Silent One'."

Tulok inhaled sharply at that. Isolde looked over at him. "Did I say something wrong?" she asked.

"Are you absolutely certain that the Magister said Silent One?" he asked carefully.

Isolde nodded. "Very. Why?"

Chapter 3

Tulok pushed his massive frame into a standing position and held out his hand. "We will have this conversation, but not here. Come," he replied. His tone was not one that invited challenge. Isolde narrowed her eyes cautiously but slowly stood and followed the priest outside.

The dark desert sky greeted them both, the kiss of the breeze blowing softly across their skin. In the distance, the inky black of night was beginning to give way to lighter shades of violet, heralding the coming of pre-dawn. Tulok turned his gaze skyward a moment, tracking something, and looked back at the building. He took several deliberate steps away from the building and into the courtyard area until he was satisfied that they were no longer standing on holy ground.

"The Silent One... The Lord of Kush, a onetime rival of The Mighty Radiant Lord, Father of the Skies, Golden Life-Giver of the World, may His Light Never be Tarnished." Tulok intoned reverently. "There was a rumor that a Cult of The Silent One still existed, but I thought it was just that...rumor. If they are involved in this, then the Halsa needs to be made aware."

Tulok was met with a confused look on Isolde's face.

"The Hals..." he paused, "The priest above the other priests." he offered

Isolde blinked, uncertain of what to say. "I... uh...wow..." she stammered a little. Her dark brows knit together in confusion and thought. She looked at the sand for a moment, thinking, then turned her face up toward the towering hulk of a priest. "I never meant to bring theological chaos to your doorstep, Father." she apologized

Tulok's red eyes met hers. Seeing the earnest concern and regret there, his countenance softened. He shook his head and laid his hand on her shoulder in a gesture meant to reassure her. Isolde was not a small woman. Her stature rivaled that of many men, and despite having been the daughter of a local bureaucrat, her life had been anything but soft. She was not broad, but she was strong. A lesser being would have balked at the weight of the orc's hand upon them, but the young woman seemed to barely notice it as anything other than "normal".

"You have nothing to apologize for, Lady Isolde." his deep voice resonated in his chest.

"It is just Isolde." she smiled up at Tulok. "No titles anymore. Just... Isolde...for now," there was a sadness that flavored her voice for a moment.

Tulok frowned a little. Formality and form were part and parcel to the Faith, to be so familiar with another was... awkward.

Isolde watched the priest's face struggling with her request. She scrunched up her nose and pursed her lips as she chewed on the situation. *This is new* – a silent voice echoed somewhere in her mind. She sighed deeply, reaching up to pat Tulok's hand with her own. "Names and... titles...have responsibility ...and ... history... where I am from." She began. "Being a ...well..a Lady... means that I have land, and people that I am responsible for." there was a shadow of sadness once more across her green eyes. "That may have been true once... but... no longer." she cleared her throat and looked away.

The light of recognition graced Tulok's red eyes. He carefully pulled his hand away from the woman's shoulder. "Ah," he replied simply. "I did not mean to open old wounds..."

The tall woman shook her head and forced a smile and turned her gaze out toward the horizon. "I suppose it would be easier if they were old." She commented.

Tulok bowed his head slightly and tucked his thumbs into his belt. "You came from Avalon with your knight, but you are here alone now..."

Isolde nodded.

"How recently?" he asked simply.

The woman took a deep breath and closed her eyes, "Deneb-aal." she replied in a shaky voice.

The orc priest took a deep breath with those words. He nodded. "You've been alone...in a foreign land...in the desert...with no help or guidance, for over a month?"

Isolde smiled a pained smile and placed her hand over her heart. "I am never alone, Father. My Wandering Lord is always with my steps... even when I am lost in the wilderness..."

The priest paused for a moment in his reply and took a moment to actually *see* this strange woman from her strange land, standing alone in the pre-dawn's light, with The Radiant Lord's light barely kissing the freckles that danced across the bridge of her nose. Her conviction and the power of her Calling seemed to radiate from her very being for the briefest of moments. Like the warm and comforting sound of a beating heart.

He closed his eyes and nodded his head in understanding. There were many who bore the mark of their gods.

Sometimes they physically carried it, and other times one could sense it in their being. Something was special about this woman that her faith emanated in such a powerful way. He had seen it before in a few members of the faith and was even told he bore the same blessing by his own mentor – though he could not see it in himself. Perhaps that was the way of The Radiant Lord to ensure a humbleness of those who served him. Looking back at this woman, he thought, *The Wandering God truly looked after his own.*

Breaking his internal thoughts, he motioned her out of the courtyard and toward a different part of the temple. As they approached, she could smell an odd, but familiar scent. Turning the corner, she saw half a dozen large hawks in enclosures. The morning light finally broke on the horizon and she watched with a bit of awe as the birds all awoke at once and turned their heads toward the light. Even the large priest spun his heel and opened his arms wide with his head upturned. The dawn's light was blinding and powerful, and for the briefest of moments she thought she thought she saw something move within the light but it became too much to stare at. This was the entrance of a God whose very being gave the world light to guide themselves with.

Tulok spoke softly in a tongue she could not understand, but as she looked around she saw others standing in the morning light taking the same pose of oblation. All of them, young and old, spoke the quiet words to themselves as they welcomed the presence of their God who has visited them again.

Closing her eyes, she let the morning's warmth wash over her. When she was in the desert alone, she saw the sun as her daily torturer as she made her way. Now, she felt the other side of that presence. Like a father's embrace – she felt the cold within her melt away. She felt pleasantly lost in the moment until hawks began to squawk loudly, "Yes, yes – breakfast and then work!" said the Orc.

Tossing chunks of meat to each of the birds, the priest made sure that each was fed their breakfast. After the food was given, he pulled out a small slip of parchment and began writing on it. Once satisfied, he rolled it up tightly and tied it off with an odd-looking knot. He then reached out and pulled a pair of leather gloves off a hook and went to one of the cages where the bird was still eating. It did not pay attention to him as he reached in and opened up a small leather pouch that was secured on the bird.

Looking at each – she saw they were all outfitted with the same style harness. They were messengers. Depositing the parchment in the pouch, he slowly withdrew his hand and placed the other just below the bird's talons. The two stared at each other for a moment, but finally, the great hawk stepped forward and perched on his large forearm. Leaning towards the bird, Tulok whispered something to it and with a swing of his arm, he threw the bird aloft in the air. Spreading its graceful wings, the hawk began to flow towards the northeast.

"We are a small temple. Tarf-qua is one of a few settlements here. I sent Adio to the temple of Djad-aal. It is a few days from there, but it will take Adio a matter of hours. They will send guidance if not more help. If it is *Them*, then The Radiant Lord's Devotees," he paused and thought for a moment. "I think you would call them...Champions... when The Radiant Lord's Light needs to break through the chaos, it is the Devoted who Shine Brightly to bring His Justice. They will know what to do."

Champions were never something to balk at. Every faith in Sanctum had a group that acted as the Hand of their Gods. If the Devotees of The Radiant Lord were as the stories told – they would arrive in a blaze of light. Their movements would be quick and their justice merciless those that transgressed against the innocent.

The concept was exciting to think that she would meet one, and then she yawned.

Tulok raised his eyebrows in shock until he realized, "We have been up all night. You need to sleep. I can't have you falling asleep when help arrives." Moving forward, he led her back to the infirmary. The bed has since been changed and looked even better than she had remembered. Isolde sat on the bed and looked at the orc who was pulling down the shade.

"Rest, there will be questions to answer and more tales to be told. Your body is almost healed, but more rest will help that. I will wake you when they arrive."

Before she could say anything more, he left the room. The exhaustion of the day came upon her all at once as she laid back on the bed and closed her eyes. Outside she could hear a bell ring and the laughter of children. Then there was only darkness and dreams.

~~~

The descent into The Dreaming seemed different to her.

The normal sense of drifting slowly downward was replaced by a more direct dive; like a smith plunging a blade in a quench to harden the steel. Strange purple skies overhead, her awareness shocks into place. She is on the shores of a vast lake, utterly and impossibly still.

Gathered on the banks are four figures staring outwards towards the water, blades, and shields held in place as if anticipating an attack. The water remains still. She walks around silently, hoping to catch a glimpse of the defender's faces. Three men and one woman, all clad for battle in distinctive armors, but bearing familiar crests upon their shields.

She first recognizes The Wanderer, her Lord, but not as she has known him. The age is lifted from his visage; color in his
~~~

beard and a smooth, youthful forehead. The familiar stylized image of the Strange Beast appears on his shield. His eyes are fixed on the water.

Next, a young woman of small stature; seemingly incapable of supporting the substantial weight that her intricate green-grey armor must represent. Her shield bears the image of a two-headed Gryphon. The red diagonal slash across the icon is immediately familiar to her from her earliest studies. As the woman's steely blue eyes emerge from under the thick, black curls of her long hair, Isolde takes some measure of pride, knowing that she too is a woman and warrior.

Holding a massive bastard sword in one hand and bearing a small, round shield on a noticeably withered right arm is a figure unfamiliar to her. The small heraldic icon on the shield is an ornate silver crown on a blue background. The man wears a small circlet of silver on his bald head. His skin is pale and almost ghostly, giving his dark eyes even greater intensity as he stares outwards towards the lake.

The unmistakable dark complexion of the final figure reveals him as the mortal bother of The Wanderer, his companion and confidant. Only he looks away from the lake and into Isolde's eyes. His voice is slowed and soft.

"None of us knows what is in the lake. None of us will be the same after. We will forget."

He turns his eyes towards the lake in concert with his fellows.

"But the lake will remember what we do here today, long after we are ash and legend."

The four figures raise their swords as the waters crash and seize suddenly, a thundering cry emerging from its depths.

"Something always remembers."

Before she can turn to see what they face, darkness and undisturbed sleep returned.

~~~

He sat in his room and stared at the parchment. He had
~~~

read it five times already and with a sixth reading, it did not change the words. Several hours had passed when Adio had returned. The Hawkmaster sent one of the children to find Tulok and deliver the message. When the child arrived, Tulok asked if anyone had appeared or arrived with the bird. The child shook his head. The orc frowned and asked him to go see if anyone had arrived within the last ten minutes. Dutifully the child left and Tulok opened the message.

By the time the child had returned and reported that there wasn't anyone who had arrived, the priest merely nodded his head and continued to stare at the message.

Unto Father Tulok, Devout of The Radiant Lord –

Based on the story you have told us, we have confirmed the death of the Magister of Deneb-aal. This along with other reports in the region has led us to believe that the threat of a cult is real. As The Radiant Lord's Light – you are to accompany the Wandering Knight to the southern ruins of Ahsal and investigate further. Acolyte Amir will oversee the Tarf-qua Temple. The Radiant Lord has His Faith in you as you have Faith in Him.

May The Radiant Lord's Light Shine Through You

-Ahsom Ibris – Devotee of the Light Bringers, 2nd Order

He needed to talk to Isolde; their world had just gotten more...interesting.

~~~

A small crowd gathered in the courtyard, assembled in total silence. Tulok ducked his head to clear the doorframe to step outside and see what the commotion was all about. His great height afforded him a better vantage than many and he was able to see over the heads of the various residents of the area. The onlookers created a circle some twenty feet across, in the center of which was Isolde.

The foreign woman held what appeared to be a shortened broomstick in her right hand, which had been cut to
~~~

the length of a sword. Tulok tensed, his eyes darting among those gathered for the threat; but there was none. He turned his eyes back to Isolde, curiosity alight in his red eyes.

Left foot forward, she held the mock sword by the right side of her head, its tip slightly dropped. She stepped forward, blocking an invisible assailant, her arm following through and across her body, tip low, she leaned into the motion, twisted, and brought the strike back up with a backhanded slice. "Ox, guard, step, strike." Tulok heard Isolde chant quietly to herself as she readied a different stance.

Several of the children gasped in awe.

Tulok folded his massive arms across his broad chest, the hint of a smile tugged at the corner of his mouth. He watched as she moved through her training exercises. They were different from those the Temple taught; no doubt due to different weapon styles and cultural preferences. The medic in him also noted that she was still favoring her right knee and she was hesitating to fully extend her left arm. He would have to look at those when she was done, there may yet be damage there that had not yet healed.

As if on cue, Isolde suddenly dropped the weapon and grabbed her arm. "Ahck! Dammit!" she swore, shaking her arm out. Several onlookers gasped and stepped back. She looked up at them all, sheepishly blushing. "Uh...sorry about that.." she apologized.

Tulok took advantage of the break in the action to step forward. He clapped his hands together a couple of times, as he strode through the gathering. "That's enough for now." he called out, "Our guest and..my patient..." he said a little pointedly to Isolde, "needs to rest for a little bit, she's still recovering."

"Awwwwww" a collective complaint issued from the crowd...and Isolde.

Tulok cocked his head and looked down at the young woman, who looked back up at the big orc with a grin. He scowled at her, in mock irritation, "Off with you, young lady..."

"But... Father...." she teased and winked at the children.

He pointed back toward the infirmary. "March."

Chapter 4

Isolde hung her head, and slumped her shoulders, dragging the stick behind her, like a petulant child. She caught the eye of one of the smaller orphans on her way back in, they seemed concerned for her. She winked at them and grinned, in the shared secret conspiracy. The child's eyes brightened. Once clear of the fuss of the courtyard, the woman turned around and walked backward before the huge priest. She smiled and winced a little. "So...when are they coming?" she asked with a hopeful smile.

"Funny you should say that," he started and handed her the message. She took the parchment and looked at it with a raised eyebrow. Then she turned the page to the side, and again. Looking up at him, "What does this little bird thing mean?"

The Priest looked at her and then realized the message was written in Faith's written word, "Apologies – I forgot." He took the parchment back and read aloud the message to her. Afterward, he sat on a nearby stool. It creaked under his weight.

"Sooo..." he said in an uncharacteristic tone, "I guess I am the help." Over the last week with the orc – whether she could see him or not, gave her the impression that he was a being of confidence. Right now, there was uncertainty.

Where his head was high and back straight, this was not it. His shoulders were slumped as he looked at the ground.

"You probably should sit down, the way you favored your right knee said a lot. We need to...figure this out, yes?"

Tulok looked up at her, "Priests – while the backbone of faith, are rarely on the front line. It is not that I am unsure of being there – it is that...I...I don't know." He paused, "I apologize. This...this is new for me."

Isolde watched the slumped figure of the mighty man sitting before her. His countenance bowed; his certainty shaken. A feeling stirred in the core of her being, a memory of an Oath, a reminder of her Call. She stepped forward to reach out and placed her right hand on his massive shoulder. Then she knelt down and looked up into his face, and quietly intoned.

"*I am the light in the darkness, so shall I breathe life into embers and kindle that light, for unto me is given this charge – let Hope never falter in my presence so long as I draw breath.*" The words were sacred and filled with the faith of her people and her Wandering Lord. As before, a quiet power seemed to emanate from the young woman before him. She was no longer a simple, innocent woman, lost and alone in the wilderness. She was a beacon of hope in an ocean of despair. The orc priest gazed on her for but a few heartbeats, as realization slowly came to him. By The Radiant Lord's Light and Mercy, they had been brought together, two servants of differing faiths, united in cause, and complemented in calling. She was no Devotee of the All-Seeing Host, so she was not given the charge of retribution and cleansing. Yet still, the Light shone within her. This was not The Radiant Lord's scorching rays, but rather, The Radiant Lord's guiding hand. Tulok met Isolde's eyes as the dawning of understanding and appreciation for the foreigner came to him. Her gaze did not falter, her grasp did not waiver. As very few had in his life, she did not see a creature of ancient, bloodborne battles, hiding in the vestments of a priest, trying to convince them of his worth. Rather, she saw him for the truth that he was, a man of faith, called as she was.

An equal.

Isolde smiled warmly up at Tulok then, "Well, then...I am glad to have you at my side, Father Tulok, of the Devout of The Radiant Lord, guardian of orphans, and..." her knee made a slick popping noise, she winced a little, but held her place and his gaze, "..healer of broken knights..." she added through clenched teeth. She forced a smile, paused then "Ow..." her face scrunched up and she shifted her position. The inspirational visage fell away and was gone. Once more she was merely Isolde, broken and lost in the desert.

He raised his eyebrow and stood. A sense of confidence filled his face again, "Stay here, and get off that leg." He walked out of the room leaving his charge in the cool shade of the room.

Making his way back to the temple proper, he headed into the small archive. While not as grand and endless as some of the larger temples, Tarf-qua had an older & humble temple that the orc kept painstakingly neat. Scrolls divided by subject, era, location. Sandstone tablets stacked in closed shelves with thick cloth separating each. While The Radiant Lord was the Keeper of his faith, The Scribe – God of the Word and Knowledge was his inspiration for learning. Digging away through the reference section, he found his treasure.

Hurrying back to the infirmary, he walked in on Isolde pacing around on her injured leg. She was so focused on her movements that she missed the sound of his heavy footstep.

"I thought I told you to stay off that leg," said a voice in the entryway. Earlier she had played at being scolded by the orc; here her face quickly blushed and with a pivot of her good heel she sat back on the bed looking down. Walking inside he said nothing as he moved past her. Pulling the bed closest to her's, he spread out a large scroll that he'd been carrying. She looked up at the parchment and then her eyes became wide.

"There's a MAP!" She almost stood in excitement but grabbed the bed instead. "Of course you have a map. Priests are always bookwor...," she paused, "Scholars! Always scholars at heart."

He laughed. It was the first time she ever heard him laugh much less heard an orc laugh in amusement. "I will have you know I am a decorated bookworm. I was the first in my scribe group to master the Divine Word, and I have curated most of this temple's small but resourceful library to ensure we have this," he motioned proudly to the map. "I am THE Bookworm here good lady, and lest you forget it!" He chuckled, almost amused with himself.

Isolde rolled her eyes, "Well my dear bookworm, what do you have for us?". She appreciated his varied aspects. He was not just a devout priest or serious scholar, but probably a man who made faces to make the children laugh or instill faith in yourself when you felt it waning.

"That is Father Bookworm to you, at least until you heal up...which by the way we may need to speed up a little given our new direction." Slowly reaching for the arm Isolde had been favoring, he held it up slightly to examine. His hands weren't rough or soft but in that in-between place of someone who knew the value of hard physical work and book learning. He placed his right hand on the sun medallion and began to speak to air with his head raised up. She did not understand the words but they were similar to the morning, afternoon, and evening chant she had heard. Suddenly he started to glow with a warm golden light. It felt warm and her body became flush as if she were seated in a hot spring. The dull ache and pain in her arm and leg faded away. Though not completely gone, she did feel a greater sense of mobility return to the damaged limbs.

He took a deep breath and his posture relaxed, "While using The Radiant Lord's gifts are a privilege to use, I believe that as people, we want the body to heal naturally. I will do that again tomorrow before we leave and you should be fit to travel."

Flexing her arm and legs, "Thank you for the gift of healing." She looked around the room for where the sun sat on the horizon. She nodded in that direction, "Let Him know that He has my thanks."

The orc nodded, "I will. In the meantime, our journey will take us here," he pointed on the map to an image of broken blocks. "These are the ruins of Ahsal. It will take us ten days to get to the Iteru, cross, and then several more days to reach the ruins. There is a settlement or temple every three to four days along this path, but we should take at least two others with us. Travel during the day is dangerous so it is better to rest. We travel when The Radiant Lord takes His Eye to the other parts of Sanctum, but other desert denizens come out at night as well so it can be dangerous. I can petition one of the traveling merchant guards who have been to...," he ran his finger along the line denoting a trade route. "...Nahral," he gave a slight smirk and shook his head, "Of course."

"Something wrong?" she asked.

"No...no," he said carefully. "It is...," he paused thinking of his words, "we will have to be careful what we say and do in Nahral. It is a holding for the Sobekites. They are helpful people, but sometimes the cost...well, the cost is worth the services they provide. Though, some would argue differently. "

Her eyebrows wrinkled together, "They cheat people?"

Tulok shook his head quickly, "No, they cheat no one. They provide exactly what you ask for at a cost. There are stories that some will say they have been cheated, but I think it is because they did not fully understand what they were getting into. However, I digress – once we get there – we can do final preparations before we investigate the ruins to see what we can find."

She nodded, flexing her arm. "Sounds like a solid plan. So, what happens when we get there and the ruins are empty... or full... of cultists?"

"Well if nothing is there, we send a bird back and you and your Lord get to experience a comfortable way of desert travel that does not involve slowly dying in an unforgiving light. If there are cultists there," he looked down at his open hand for a moment. He closed it into a fist as he looked back at her, "then The Radiant Lord's Justice shall be dealt to those that have suffered at the cult's hand."

~~~

The long-bodied lizard danced quickly across the sand, darting from one outcropping to the next. It paused and carefully watched its surroundings. Front right foot and back left foot raised off of the hot hands to cool for a moment. It blinked twice and changed feet. Its tongue moved out of its wide mouth to moisten its right eye and it blinked again as a breeze gently blew across the dunes. A light dusting of sand coated the tan body of the reptile. It shifted once more, their head turning to glance around as it readied itself for the next section of its journey. A dark shadow passed over the creature. It froze momentarily, hoping that its natural camouflage would be enough to keep it safe from the unseen predator. Soundless and silent wings
~~~

brought death from the skies by way of sharp talons. The great owl swooped down and effortlessly scooped the lizard up in its claws, then soared off to alight atop the roof to the Temple Rookery, slapping the body of the lizard against the bricks and snapping its neck. The hawks in their cages below screamed at the interloper as it began its feast.

All across the village of Tarf-qua bodies began to stir and cooking fires were kindled. As the rays of the sun slowly faded behind the horizon, life began anew. Life in the desert was harsh and unforgiving. One slept and rested during the daylight hours and was active at night. This was not mandated by cultural or religious law; it was simply survival. Conserve energy and water where one could; because one never knew when there might not be more of either.

Children stirred from their beds in the Temple, bringing with them the sounds of laughter, tears, games, and all the sounds associated with large families.

From her bed in the infirmary, Isolde duAvalonne lay quietly, listening to the sounds of the Temple around her. If she closed her eyes, she could almost imagine that she was home. The sounds of a village around her in the dawning light of day, the smell of wood smoke fires, the clucking of chickens, adults scolding children for stealing sweets from the kitchen, bodies walking under windows, residents calling out greetings to one another. There was a momentary tightness in the knight's chest at the memories of the place she had left behind. Shores... and people...she may never see again.

That's because we buried them. They're all gone now. A quiet voice spoke in the back of her mind. *You have no home to go back to. This is your life now.* A moment of sorrow touched her. She took in a ragged breath.

"No!" she shouted firmly, and sat up, swinging her legs

over the bedside and standing. Her heart beat fast in her chest. She closed her eyes and shook her head. Her right hand reached for the small token strung around her neck. Her fingers closed over it, in quiet desperation.

"I am the light against the darkness..." she whispered.

In the distance, a soft chorus of voices began sunset chants as the rays of the sun disappeared.

"I am the light..." she closed her eyes.

Knuckles rapped on the doorframe. A familiar deep voice broke her thoughts. "Isolde? I heard you yelling. Is everything alright?"

She started at the interruption, dashing her hand quickly over her eyes and wiping them clear of tears. Clearing her throat, she nodded quickly. "Ya, I am fine, Father." she lied.

Tulok's brow furrowed deeply with concern. He stepped carefully into the room and over to the bed opposite hers. He slowly sat down on it. As all furniture seemed to, it groaned in complaint beneath the weight of the big man. Pursing his lips together he folded his hands between his knees and regarded Isolde quietly.

"If you need to talk to someone..." he offered, trailing off.

She shook her head, and then rolled her eyes toward the ceiling, and looked away from the priest. "You have already done so much..."

"Some believe that the burden of Faith is that it is as heavy as we make it. The trick is understanding that Faith has no weight, but lifts the soul. This leaves room for us to carry others who need a moment to stand free. So, in other words – healing the body is one thing, but helping a friend when I can who needs a moment when I can..."

"Are we then?" the woman asked as she continued to stare at the ceiling and avoid eye contact.

"Are we what?" the priest asked, watching her

She turned her green eyes back to him. Even without the glistening of unshed tears, he could see the sorrow weighing heavily on her. It was visible in her face and on her soul.

"Friends. Are we friends, Father?" the knight asked. It was a simple enough question for many; but what did it mean here?

"We have broken bread, shared a meal, told stories, carried children to bed, shared a dark conspiracy fraught with murder and evil, and we are about to embark on a journey that could be exciting or horribly terrible. Yes, I think that qualifies... it makes you more than my strange patient, and instead, you *are* my strange friend," he said simply.

The dark-haired woman looked over at him then and smiled a gentle smile, nodding simply at the response. "Thank you." she offered.

Tulok shrugged a little in response, "It is only the truth."

Isolde nodded and inhaled deeply, recentering herself, his words seemed to have been the balm her psyche needed at the moment. Tulok regarded her for a moment, as she did so. He then spoke in a low voice, "So, I am going to ask you again then... are you alright?"

This time Isolde did not evade the question. Instead, she shook her head in response. "No, not really," she replied, closing her eyes and rubbing the back of her neck.

Tulok nodded and looked up at her from his seated position. "Nightmare?" he asked.

She shook her head once more. "No, no, nothing like that...I do not often get those..." she waved it off, as she noted Tulok's surprise, "It is... a... Wanderer thing..." she tried to explain, and failed to do so. " Erm...hard to explain," she finally offered. Tulok nodded in acceptance for the oddities of her faith.

He watched her once more, her hand clasped around the token around her neck. "Warding something off then?" he asked and gestured at her.

She looked down at her right hand still wrapped tightly around the small metal item.

"Oh!" she exclaimed as if becoming suddenly aware of the thing. She blushed a little sheepishly. "Ya...I... guess so," she replied and finally released the item. She took another deep breath and sat down on the bed opposite Tulok. "Just homesick, I guess." she finally managed to say.

"Ahhh." He nodded appreciatively. Unclasping his hands, he leaned back on the bed, hands behind him, arms supporting his massive frame, in a more relaxed fashion. "I can imagine this must be quite the change for you?"

Isolde chuckled and nodded, leaning back into a similar position opposite the big man. She let her gaze drift toward the ceiling. "Indeed, that it is," she affirmed. She closed her eyes and relaxed a little. "I mean...this is all still very exciting...and new...and part of what I am supposed to be out here doing, to begin with..." she reasoned.

"And what would that be...exactly?" Tulok asked in curiosity.

Isolde sighed deeply and closed her eyes, "See the world and bear witness to its wonders, and share those wonders with my fellows, that our Lord may know Sanctum as the living and breathing thing that She is." Isolde offered. Her voice was tinged with both nostalgia and inspiration.

Tulok whistled low, "That is...that is quite the call." he commented.

Isolde nodded and looked back over at Tulok, "He doesn't often stick around in one place for very long." She frowned a little. "It has taken some getting used to." she said and considered her words, "It was easier back home, even when we went someplace new, there were still points of reference..."

He nodded. "While here, you have nothing...and no one." Tulok offered carefully.

Isolde shrugged a little, neither acknowledging nor denying the statement. A large sandaled foot reached across the divide that separated them and lightly tapped the toe of her boot. She looked down at the foot that belonged to the priest and then up to meet his gaze. He smiled gently and warmly back.

"Well, now...I guess... You have me." he offered.

The smile that he was gifted with lit up the entire room with joy, happiness, and hope. She sat up and moved to reach over to him then paused. "Ermmm...uh..." she stammered.

He blinked. "Is there something wrong?"

"Can I...is it...uh... do your people...hug?" she asked in an embarrassed tone.

Tulok chuckled deeply. "Well, I cannot speak for all of the Seteshi... but I certainly do." he opened his massive arms wide to welcome her. The young woman stood and allowed the Priest to fold her into his great embrace. She clung to him for a moment, relishing the contact and comfort that was offered, and taking inspiration from the shared exchange. She whispered into his neck, "Thank you, Tulok."

She felt the rumble of a chuckle in his chest, "Hugs are a kindness that is free and freely given from young to old – at least that is what I have been told." He rubbed her back and shoulders with his broad hand and then slowly released his hold. "The merchant train will be by soon and I will find out who is able to go with us. After that, I will take a volunteer from one of the devout who has experience in the trek as well. By the time I am done, the evening meal will be ready and I will join you in the hall."

He stood up and patted her less injured leg, "Oh...that reminds me," he paused "I know that it is customary for any warrior to ensure that they are ready for battle but," he walked toward the back of the room and over to a shelf. Reaching high above, he removed the make-shift bag that was her cloak. The outside bore Avalonian imagery, though its brilliant greens and blues had faded a bit with the sun's touch. Laying it on the bed across from her, he unraveled the bag to reveal her armor. "Metal armor on certain places of the body is easier to wear if you are used to the desert – otherwise it can lead to a slow death. I would suggest taking the pieces you feel are *absolutely* necessary for a fight and replace what you can with leather or hide substitutes."

She frowned a bit but nodded her head in agreement, "Yeah it was something I was thinking about when I was practicing outside. Oh! My sword! Do you..." she didn't finish as he also reached in and produced both her shield and the scabbard that held her blade.

"Look over what you need and let me know. I can see about acquiring what I can here or purchase along the way."

She had a slight look of confusion that quickly faded, "The money thing? I have the coins from Ser Reynard. Would that help?"

The Orc nodded, "With your permission, I will have it go toward any cost that the Temple cannot cover. I'm relatively frugal so your money will not be wasted." Then a stern look returned to his face, "Just because it feels better, does not mean that it is completely better. Treat your body kindly. Tomorrow we will not receive the same from the desert." The smile returned again to his face, "I will see you at mealtime," and left the room.

Chapter 5

Isolde watched the big priest leave. She wondered once again what it was that had brought an orc to the service of the Temple. She had heard the stories of the orcs, how they...along with the other civilized people of Sanctum... had been brought here to save them from the Reaping. She knew they existed. She'd even seen one or two in the past. Most of these had been traders, traveling with the heathens of the northern climes in Avalon. There, they were few, and none of them were as fastidious and well-spoken as Father Tulok seemed to be. The island of Avalon was remote and isolated from the rest of the realms of Sanctum. Some claimed that was by design, and that it was the will of the Gods to keep their people safe from the influence of others and preserve their heritage. Others, like Sir Reynard, and the rest of the Knight Wanderers balked at this idea; claiming that The Wanderer Himself was raised to the ranks of Ascension by throwing off the shackles of fear of the unknown and traversing the world on his mighty Quest. It was to honor His bravery, and echo that guidance of expansion, adventure, and the quest for the unknown, that the Wandering Knights had been formed.

She reached out and gently traced the heraldic crest that was embossed on the hilt of the weapon that Tulok had left her. The figure of a strange creature, rampant on an embattled field. The Questing Beast. The object of her Lord's endeavors, and that which had eventually earned him his elevation. Each Knight was expected to continue that Quest, and return home only at the end of their journey.

"But I have no home to return to now..." she whispered quietly as her fingers traced the heraldry. "Where shall I return once all of this is over?" she mused.

A sound outside the doorway drew her attention. Her eyes darted up and in that same direction, catching sight of a familiar face. A young girl, trying to hide in the shadows, and failing terribly. Isolde sat down on the bed, next to her gear, and waived the child in, patting the bedside across from her. "Well, I see you out there, you may as well come in." Isolde offered.

A timid little girl, wearing a long dust-colored shift padded into the room, her eyes on the floor. "I apologize, I did not mean to..." she apologized.

"Shhhh... none of that now." Isolde comforted and gestured to the girl. "Come on over here." Isolde looked at the girl, trying to get a better look at her face, "You are Shufi, right?" Isolde asked.

The girl turned her face up to the woman and beamed brightly at her. "Yes!" she exclaimed in an excited voice, clearly happy to be remembered.

"Well, Shufi, what can I do for you tonight?" Isolde asked politely.

The little girl, Isolde guessed her to be about seven, climbed up onto the bed across from the Avalonian and pulled her legs up underneath the hem of her shift. She picked at a loose thread as she spoke. "Are you and Father Tulok leaving?" she asked quietly.

Isolde took a breath and considered her words, careful

of how they might be received by young ears. "Father Tulok and I have... a mission...that we need to complete together." she began. "That...mission... will take us both away from the Tarf-qua for some time, yes."

The little girl frowned a little. "How long?" she asked plainly.

"I wish I could tell you, Shufi," Isolde replied.

"Is it a secret, is that why you can't say?" she asked, turning curious eyes toward the strange woman.

Isolde paused for a moment before giving her answer. "Well...now that you mention it..." she said, and leaned in to whisper, "It really is...a very secret thing...that the Halsa..." She stumbled over the words, mangling their pronunciation. Shufi giggled.

"You are saying it wrong!" she exclaimed.

Isolde shushed her in a mock conspiratorial tone. "That...that person...tasked Father Tulok to do."

Shufi's eyes got big. "Really?"

Isolde nodded. "mmhmm"

"That must be really..." she searched for the word a moment and then loudly said, "Important!" Shufi said and then clapped her hands over her mouth. She lowered her voice. "The Halsa never asks Father Tulok to do anything. Everybody else gets called away, but Father Tulok always stays here. Do you think it is because he is special?"

Isolde listened to the child's words, pondering the information shared. "I...I think maybe it does." she nodded.

"I think so too," Shufi said confidently. "I think Father Tulok is the most special Father I have ever had and I know that he will take care of you on your mission. Especially since you are hamula now." she smiled at the woman.

"Hamula?" Isolde asked.

Shufi nodded emphatically. "Clasping of arms is for strangers, but embracing is for hamula. I saw you embracing, so that must mean that you are hamula!" she beamed, clearly thrilled with this idea.

Isolde nodded slowly, "I... suppose..."

"YES!" Shufi exclaimed and jumped up from the bed. "He is Father Tulok, so we can call you Mother Isolde!" Shufi smiled and bounded out of the room.

Isolde blinked, not quite certain of things any longer. In the back of her mind, Isolde was certain she heard someone chuckling.

Oh, sweet Wanderer's Soul, what have I done?

~~~

She was older than Tulok in relative years. The desert wear on her tan body and bleached blonde-brown hair told its own story along with the various scars. Rafa served as the local lead Reysis of all caravans heading in and out of Tarf-qua. She knew the trails and the people capable of making the journey. She sat in discussion with a few of the other merchants who were tracking their time before the next leg of their journey. Tarf-qua was not on a major route but offered a midpoint for many who traveled and needed a rest from a long push or from fighting off the desert's worst.

Politely approaching the table, Tulok waited until the last man spoke before interjecting, "Reysis, may have a moment of your time?" Rafa looked up and gave a stoic nod before motioning to the priest to sit down. "How is our guest doing?" she asked.

"She is healing well enough and will be leaving in the morning actually. With the blessing of His Radiance, I was able to aid her so that she is able to face her next challenge," Tulok replied. He pursed his lips together and then added, "However, her mission requires a bit of our assistance."

"Is that so?" the older woman asked. "If she has the coin, I could have her outfitted with a camel and enough
~~~

food & water to last her a month if she understands water discipline. It should get her back to Deneb-aal fine."

The big priest looked pensive for a moment and then spoke, "The Halsa has sent me word that I am to accompany her, though not to Deneb-aal. She and I are to make our way to the other side of the Iteru. I was hoping you could suggest a possible guide to lead us to at least Nahral. From there, we can make our way across and then on to her destination."

Rafa was quiet. It was said in games of chance – no one could ever figure if she was bluffing because her face was a stone wall. "Far be it from me to tell the Halsa anything. They are beholden to our Radiant Lord, may his Light shine upon all. You – you are beholden to their word because it is His word. I will be honest. I do not like it."

She continued, "I know you have done your own pilgrimage in the burning sands. There are Acolytes here that can take up your duties as you carry this out. However, a stranger from a strange land comes here with a mission from her god, it leaves me unsettled. Such might have been seen as a weakness for Setesh to have outsiders deal with issues within its land," she paused and leaned forward. "I can outfit you and her for the journey, and I can provide the name of a reliable Sun Guide. I will do all this if you can tell me how this will not make us look weak?"

The orc looked down but did not bow his head. Instead, he met the older woman's eyes. "Weakness is failing to understand that what we see of the world is but a single grain to His ever-watchful Eye. We know not the workings of the Gods, nor should we. We may question Their methods or bemoan Their intentions – but it is not always for us to know why something is happening. The Wandering Lord has given us one of His to be tested by the Everburning Lord of the Sands. Perhaps, in this you should realize that she was sent to us – we did not ask for her. She was sent here to be taught in the harshest places of what it means to serve and live for your faith. Weakness does not thrive here, and when she leaves for her cold lands, she will have been blessed to have had the weakness cut from her soul and be instilled with an appreciation of what it means to survive," he said with quiet finality.

Rafa gave the barest hint of a smile, "I will find you a Sun Guide to take you to Nahral; we will see you when His Eye moves on."

Tulok stood and bowed his head in thanks. Making his way to the temple's small archive, he looked around. There was no one there. He let go a deep breath and his shoulders slumped. He could feel it within him. A small fire that occasionally rose up within him. It was called the Gurkh. Every orc had it within him. The burning rage of battle and the need to explode. It was counterbalanced by the Ghal – The Scribe's gift of reason. When he met Rafa's eyes, he felt the Gurkh rise up and wanted to challenge the older woman. Then like a cool drink of water, the Ghal filled his head with words and inspiration. What seemed like a year of battle, settled in the look when he met Rafa's eyes. Reason wins because it needed to win the moment. He cared for Rafa and respected her as the Reysis. The Gurkh felt otherwise, though in the coming days Tulok felt deep within that he might need to rely on it to survive the desert. In the same vein, he hoped the Ghal would be there to lead him out of that rage – for Isolde's sake.

~~~

The scent of fresh-baked flatbreads and warm spiced meat filled the Temple feast hall. Adults gathered small children, while older children helped to arrange places for everyone to sit and brought out bowls for everyone assembled. Once a week, the inhabitants of the Temple of Tarf-
~~~

qua allowed themselves to indulge in the flesh of the livestock so carefully curated here. The rest of the week they supped on bone broth and stews made from organs and other parts of the animal, on lentils, eggs, grains, and nutmeats. Figs and dates that were brought in from neighboring villages were considered a sweet treat. Life in the desert was hard, and food resources were precious, but even here, there was joy in the gathering of family around a table.

Children were ordered, youngest to oldest at one set of tables. Some of the older children were tasked with caring for the very youngest, those who still needed assistance. Clothing was passed down from one child to the next, it was rare for a young child to be given a new suit of clothing, and far more likely that a larger suit would be cut down to fit several others. At the very end of the life of a suit of clothes, it would be cut into strips to be used as a trim along the hems of other garments. Long, loose shifts and baggy-style pants covered their bodies, both male and female alike. Some wore scarves, coiled atop their heads, the long ends of which could be pulled across the face. The *hatsha* served as both shelters from the Sun, and a filter for the fine dust of the sands. These were a luxury, and not everyone was allowed one. It was a badge of assignment, to those who worked with the Reysis, and served as foot messengers for the Temple. To those who gave such service, they were rewarded with enough fabric to create their own head covering.

The Lord of the Burning Sands was a demanding God. He demanded unyielding adherence to His laws and His ways. To go against these would risk not only one's own life, but potentially the lives of the rest of one's Hamula, village, or city. For as demanding as His Laws were, they were laws driven by necessity. The need for survival.

Members of the priesthood gathered solemnly at the

front of the Hall, waiting. Tulok joined his fellow brothers and sisters in faith, a towering mountain of muscle and might, clothed in the simple vestments of his devotion. The orc priest greeted each of his fellows, touching the fingertips of his right hand to his chest, above his heart, and inclining his head in a gesture of solemnity and solidarity. The gesture was returned in kind, in open acceptance of the humble duties each had vowed to undertake in the name of faith.

Tarf-qua Temple was one of the oldest established settlements in Setesh; though certainly not the most opulent, nor the largest. Its walls had been rebuilt several times over the course of many centuries since the first settlers had broken ground here and discovered the wellspring beneath the sands. Water meant life in the desert, and it meant trade and coin would follow. The wellspring was small, but its waters were clean, clear, and reliable. Tarf-qua's wellspring granted the village and the Temple a modicum of security in the area, but it had also been a subject of raids and skirmishes in the past. It had only been when the Halsa had blessed the ground as sacred and commenced with the construction of the Temple itself that the raiding had settled. Skirmishing over water among local tribes and Hamula was to be expected, but few would risk the ire of the All-Seeing Host of the Everburning Sun by shedding blood on His sacred lands.

As the last rays of The Radiant Lord's eternal sight disappeared from view, an older man tapped a large brass bell three times. The sound echoed clearly through the hall, bringing attention to the front and silencing voices. In unison, the priesthood intoned a prayer to the Heavens, calling for all to take up their duty of protection throughout the night, while the Lord of Heaven's gaze rested elsewhere upon the world.

For night is come
And shadows fall
Upon this place
Lord hear my call
Your grace is mine
Your might is known
Throughout this night
Your charge my own
Your servants stand
The pact is sealed
Until dawn shall break
We stand Your shield

Tulok bowed his head and closed his eyes as he sang the evening hymn. His voice sounded deep in his chest and rumbled throughout the hallowed halls. Even when guarded, his tones could be felt on the floor and rafters. It was a sonance that shook the soul. As the choir's prayer ended and the last of the notes slowly faded away, he opened his eyes and lifted his gaze once more.

At the back of the hall, stood the figure of Isolde duAvalonne. No longer dressed in the haphazard clothing which had been mended for her, she wore the traditional garb of the people of Setesh. Her leather cuisses had been restrapped and were now buckled over her trousers. Her metal greaves had been replaced by a pair of high, hard leather boots that covered her shins, loose-fitting pants, adorned with tiny embroidered suns bloused over their tops. One could almost see the leather leg armor through the caftan she wore, whose sides had been slit to allow for better range of motion. Her long brown hair had been washed and combed and pulled back into several braids that were coiled atop her head.

She met the big priest's eyes from her place at the back

of the hall, and placed her right fist over her heart and tapped it twice against her breast. She bowed her head.

The hall fell silent.

Chapter 6

Behdeti Kahr, the older man who had rung the bell earlier, carefully set it aside on a nearby table. He then turned and faced the gathered group and spread his arms wide. Hands, gnarled with age, slowly unfurled as he raised them toward the rafters. "Come and be welcome! Let us join together, and give thanks for that which Our Lord of the Blessed and Everwatchful Eye has brought unto us on this evening." The elder looked from person to person in the room. The light from the lamps and candles illuminated the area with a warm and inviting glow. His dark eyes finally fell on the countenance of the stranger in the back of the hall. His gaze felt heavy to the dark-haired woman as if he were silently measuring the weight of her soul. Isolde lifted her chin and straightened her shoulders, standing up straight and taking the full measure of her height. She continued to hold her right fist against her heart as she met the elder's gaze.

Tulok's eyes went from Isolde to Behdeti and he shifted as if to speak. The old man silenced him with a gesture.

"Who comes this night to our hall, to partake of the gifts of our Lord?" Behdeti asked in a heavily accented Trader's tongue, eyes still on Isolde.

The Avalonian Knight stood tall in the lamplight, ready

to answer the words of her Host. Guestrite and Hospitality were things she knew well. These were a mainstay of social decorum on the Island. To misstep in these matters of formality could mean that a Host could judge a visitor not to be a guest, but an intruder. More Wanderers had died in the misstepping of Hospitality than for any other reason known. There was a reason they were few now in number.

"I am Isolde duAvalonne," she announced. "Daughter of Niall, of the Council Whitebrook, bearer of the Grace of Kalanchoe, Flower of Lorraine, Keeper of the Light, and Witness of the Lord Wanderer of the World." She paused for a moment, as was customary.

Several of those gathered looked from one to another, speaking in hushed tones. Their voices fell silent at a glance from Behdeti.

"And why does the Lord Wanderer send his Witness to our Hall?" Behdeti asked formally.

Again, Isolde stood tall and regal in her repose and responded, "The Lord Wanderer would bear witness to all of Setesh, and seek the blessing of the Everwatchful on His daughter on this evening. That She may be welcome and give thanks for the gift of her life, so kindly bestowed upon her by the hands of His faith." her eyes moved to Tulok and she inclined her head in respect.

"And what thanks would you offer Our Lord for this gift?" the priest inquired.

"In as much as it does not conflict with my ordained oaths and orders, I offer my services to the people of Tarfqua for one year and one day, as is the custom of my people."

Again, hushed whispers washed across the gathering.

Tulok's eyebrows raised in both surprise and respect.

Behdeti Kahr regarded the young woman carefully once more. His dark eyes were like two pools of golden-hued shadow as they examined Isolde from across the room. Once more Isolde could feel the weight of judgment upon her. She stood firm and resolute in her ground. Finally, the old man nodded, as if satisfied with whatever it was that he saw.

"Our Lord hears your words and judges them to be true Ser Knight," he replied. A collectively held breath was released from the onlookers. Muscles held at the ready, relaxed. "We accept your offering, and welcome you to our Hearth and our Home." Behdeti inclined his head and held open his arms once more.

From across the room, Isolde pressed her fist to her heart, lowered her eyes, and inclined her head, bowing deeply.

"Be all honor and respect due unto you, be yours, and may my life be forfeit should I break with our accord or knowingly bring harm to you and yours," she replied formally.

The old man's face broke into a wide smile and he nodded, content with the exchange. "Come!" he said warmly and welcomed Isolde closer. The hall broke out into cheers, laughter, and merriment at that word.

Isolde relaxed noticeably, smiled broadly, and strode boldly across the room to clasp Behdeti's arm in thanks and welcome. "Thank you, kindly, for everything your people have done," she smiled.

Behdeti grasped Isolde's arm with his hand in response and held it there in greeting. "It is due to the kindness of Father Tulok, that you are with us today." he gestured to the orc. "Many of our people would have left you to the sands and the will of the gods." Behdeti looked over at Tulok, "His heart is too full of the Radiant Lord's mercy some days," he chuckled lightly. Tulok blushed and looked away. "Come, sit with us and share a meal before your journey begins," he gestured to a table and benches. His gesture included Tulok. "Rafa tells me that you are going to Nahral and will be crossing the Iteru?"

Isolde nodded and joined the older man, as he indicated. She waited until he sat and then took a position at a respectful distance, where he indicated. Tulok eased his massive figure down on a bench next to Isolde.

"Yes," she nodded and looked back at Tulok. "At least... those names .... sound. Correct?"

Behdeti nodded and then looked over at Tulok, "You took pilgrimage out toward Nahral, once, if I recall?"

Tulok nodded solemnly. "You are correct."

Behdeti hmed for a moment. "Do you expect that you will have issues with the residents of the Mahdina there?" he asked the orc.

Tulok frowned at the inquiry, a low rumble in his chest. "That was many years ago, Hemet," Tulok complained, using Behdeti's honorific title.

The elder turned his eyes on the figure of the orc priest, "And the rumble in your chest tells me that your Gurkh is not satisfied with the outcome, even so." he chided.

Tulok clenched his jaw, his meaty right fist bunching at his side for a moment. He took a deep breath and stretched his neck. He inclined his head respectfully.

Isolde wondered at the exchange, turning concerned eyes on the priest who had saved her life.

"Tulok?" she asked and quietly reached out to touch his knee.

He tensed at her actions and took a deep breath. She could see the muscles of his body writhe and constrict as he fought to constrain action with reason. "Please excuse me," he said in a controlled voice, then rose and left the room.

Isolde's eyes followed his departure.

"He's not a man," Behdeti commented after Tulok had departed.

The knight turned back to face her host. "Excuse me?" she blinked, uncertain of the comment's intent.

"Tulok. He's not a man," came the simple reply. "Your island is isolated from the mainlands, so I am certain these things must be new to you." Behdeti offered. He reached for a cup that had been specially crafted to suit his gnarled hand. "He is a servant of our Lord, and thus an equal in His eyes, but you must never mistake Tulok for being human. He is not, and he never will be."

Isolde shook her head and looked at the Elder; her eyes carried both curiosity and irritation in them. "I'm not certain why you are telling me this, Hemet Behdeti?"

"There are no secrets in a sea of tents, Ser Isolde," Behdeti replied as he lifted the cup to his lips. "Neither is there anything that goes on within these walls that does not also come to me." he looked out at the gathered peoples before them who had come to break bread and share the evening meal. "Hamula," he said quietly.

Isolde blushed furiously at the word. She was not certain if it were embarrassment or frustration at the assumption that irritated her. She set her jaw and turned to face the gathering, folding her hands before herself on the table's surface. She spoke without looking at Behdeti.

"It was a word, uttered by a child, in an attempt to seek clarification and definition of something she had witnessed and not understood fully." the Avalonian said coolly.

"And what was that, pray tell, that the child witnessed which would give her such an impression?" the old man asked, once more sipping from his cup and watching the gathering.

"An embrace," Isolde said simply.

Behdeti nodded and pursed his lips. "Born out of..." he trailed off.

Isolde's green eyes grew hard and cold at the implication of impropriety, she laced her fingers together tightly and continued to watch the Hall. "Born out of earnest thanks for the many things done for a stranger in a strange land. If I have erred in my assessment of protocols, Hemet, then I ask your forgiveness." the woman offered.

Behdeti turned his gaze upon Isolde once more and for the third time that evening, she could feel the weight of judgment upon her. Finally, Behdeti turned away from Isolde and looked back at the Hall. "Our Lord judges your words once more to be true," he replied.

Isolde did not move, nor register a response to his words.

"Father Tulok is a complicated creature, Ser Isolde," Behdeti spoke. "Your path and his have become entwined by a mandate of the Heavens, and by your own Oath. Take care that you do not misstep... Wanderer." The word was soft but carried a powerful intensity.

Without being bidden, words came to Isolde as she turned to the Hemet and replied,

"You have granted welcome and blessing to a Witness, Hemet Behdeti. Take care that you remember your own actions will be forever recorded in His eyes." reaching out, she turned her empty cup upside down and set it on the table before her empty plate, then rose. "I thank you for the Hospitality of your Hall and will be mindful of your words. Good evening," the dark-haired knight spoke, then turned and departed the Hall.

~~~

Stepping outside into the cool air, the orc was nowhere to be seen. While there were a few people out, none of them paid her any mind as she looked around for the way-
~~~

ward priest. The Temple proper only had one individual in it, a short man who almost looked like a dwarf – his stature and bulky build were similar to the dwarven people she had encountered before. Yet, he was also different. He was short and broad, as others of his ilk, but was without the massive beard they were known for. From the look of his face, he'd never had a beard before. Perhaps this was another quirk of desert life.

"Excuse me," she began, "I'm looking for Father Tulok, have you seen him?"

The shorter man regarded her for a moment and then said, "You must be the outsider from Avalon. I am Kada, one of the Acolytes that serves under Father Tulok. If he isn't in the Hall, you may want to try the Archive or the eastern dunes. He spends a great deal of time in both places." He paused, "Shouldn't you be in the hall enjoying the meal?"

Isolde looked down and gave a sort of half-smile, "There was a conversation and I ... lost my appetite."

The man nodded, paused and looked off to the side, and simply said, "ahh." The relaxed look of the expression said that there may have been something more. "Was it the Reysis or the Hemet that did it?" he asked.

Apparently, this was something that has happened before, she thought.

"The Hemet brought up something that happened to Father Tulok a long time ago... because we are heading for Nahral. Whatever happened there was a sticking point for Father Tulok in so much that he got up and left. I just wanted to make sure he was okay," she offered a small but kind smile.

Kada nodded and seemed to be chewing on something mentally. Satisfied, he motioned her over to one of the murals on the wall. The image was of a birdman with a long beak. He was holding something to write with along with what appeared to be a tablet. "What do you know of Orckind, Avalonian?" he asked. There was no emotion or inflection other than it being a simple question.

Isolde shrugged a little. Her knowledge was limited to stories and tales of other peoples. "I know that they were one of the races that made it from their world to this one. Though there were many types of orcs, like there are elves and dwarves," she said.

"Exactly, I am a Vidria, but still considered dwarven," he chuckled and stroked his bare chin, "Though there would be some dwarves that disagree." he gestured back to the mural. "Nevertheless, in the beginning, there were many orcs from the various worlds. Those orcs like... some that you may have seen... still bear the need for violence and rage. In some parts of Sanctum, they are warlords and marauders. In fact, when Tarf-qua first came into being – it was plagued by a group of marauders led by an orc named Kal-Met Thig. He was a cold and calculating bully who understood the need of when to take and when not to. He attacked departing caravans or raided the village after a caravan left. A few were killed in the beginning but it eventually became bruises and threats of violence that kept people in line."

Isolde listened and nodded and raised a questioning eyebrow, "What does this have to do with Father Tulok and the bird...person?" she asked, gesturing to the carving.

Kada smiled, "I'll get there. The interesting thing about Thig was the thing no one saw. For all of his bullying and beatings, he kept the trade routes free of other marauders and desert monsters. Those things he killed and exacted great violence upon. He technically kept them safe from the greater dangers in the desert. In a way, he was their protector who took his tithe when he needed to."

Isolde nodded in understanding. She was familiar with such tactics among some of the less scrupulous feudal lords of Avalon.

Motioning back to the mural, "Which then brings up back to the idea of Reason itself and The Scribe," Kada pointed at the mural. "The stories differ, but what is known is this. When the Orcs first arrived on Sanctum, they warred not only with the people here but with themselves. You see, to those Orcs – Strength and Might are the foundation for Leadership. They nearly wiped themselves out of existence. Then something happened. The Wise Scribe intervened. No one really knows why. Perhaps they were tired of watching the mayhem... perhaps they could not bear the idea of losing one of the handful of peoples that were saved from the Reaping."

Isolde nodded again, trying to follow along.

"The Scribe took matters into Their own hands and gave the Orcs the ability to think and reason so the blind rage of war was balanced by the ability to think and consider their actions."

Isolde's eyes widened. "ohhhhhh"

Kada smiled, satisfied with his brief lesson. "Now I'm sure there is more to that, but that is for our resident orc to tell you." He led her back toward the front entrance of the temple, "They are a people that need to find balance in themselves occasionally, even when instincts say otherwise. You may want to try the eastern dunes. He would have heard me talking about him if he was in the archive...and... probably stopped me or corrected me by now. Just head down the way and go left and head for the gate. From there just look up on the dune for the light. He'll be there."

She gave him a gracious smile, "Thank you Kada...er Acolyte Kada."

"It is just Kada, I am less an Acolyte and more of a teacher," he said.

She nodded her head, "Thank you Kada, it is appreciated." She turned to leave and then paused, "With Thig – what happened with him? I mean, Tarf-qua eventually learned what he was doing. What did they do?"

"Like what all scared, and hurt humans are want to do – they killed him," he said grimly. "One of Thig's first victims was Hemet's great grandfather, so you can say there is...history there."

"Oh," was the only thing she could say. She frowned a little, trying to take in everything she had been told. Nodding her head, she headed toward the eastern dunes.

Chapter 7

The Temple of Tarf-qua sat in the middle of the village. Surrounding the village itself were long sandstone pillars. Crafted by the magic of the Vidria, they marked the edge of safety around the village. At each of the four cardinal directions was a gate, but not one with wooden doors as the Isolde had seen in the past. Rather they were sandstone archways that were tall and wide enough for a few beasts of burden to enter. Outside of the gates, several yards away were a pair of braziers. At night with only the few stars in the sky, the braziers would serve as a beacon for those who were making their way across the blackness of the desert.

As Kada had mentioned, she saw a figure sitting between the two massive braziers. Looking at the footprints in the sand, she saw where his steps followed the trail up the dune. While she was not stealthy by any means, he said nothing as she approached him. She sat next to him quietly and looked out at the barren sea of blackness. There were sounds of the wind far off and the occasional cry and shriek of something in that darkness. "What is the Gurkh?" she asked, finally breaking the silence.

"Rage," he said with no hint of emotion, "It is Rage that each Orc possesses. Not like the battle-born rage of a berserker. No, Orcish Rage is a blind wanton need for destruction and violence." Tulok held his gaze on the dunes in the distance as he spoke, "You feel the pull to challenge any and all who you see as inferior... and intimidate or break them with your will... or fist." his eyes glanced at his hands and then back to the dunes and the skyline in the darkness.

"It is violence – pure violence," he said in a slightly bemused tone.

Isolde nodded, shifting next to the big priest. She pulled her knees up close and wrapped her arms around them, listening.

"To combat this...," Tulok paused, "No, not combat. To balance it. To balance it out, we have the Ghal. The Ghal is our way to think, to reason. To see more in this world...the beauty it has to offer. To write poetry and tell stories. To build homes, paint pictures... and not just sharpen a blade against a rock. The Ghal makes us more than that." He took a deep breath and released it slowly. "The Ghal made us more man than beast. However, sometimes I think it makes us more human than man tries to be," he added with a slight touch of bitterness.

Isolde said nothing but just stared off into the darkness. He was right, she thought. Sometimes the ugliest of things had been done in the name of humanity. Though no race was free from the cruelty of others and themselves. In this case, the orc was a victim of an age-old animosity that carried itself in the blood and memories of the descendants. The village probably experienced a quiet uproar when he first came into his seat of the temple's head.

She rested her chin on her knee, as she pulled her legs toward her body and hugged them with her arms. The Wanderer's eyes watched the orc who sat next to her, as he gazed outward toward the darkness of the desert. The light from the braziers gave his skin a warm hue, where it would otherwise be cooler in color, with hints of olive and brown. It was not so odd, she thought. The tone of his skin. There were many people at home whose skin tones varied; from the exceptionally pale of the townships of Whitebrooke and Lorraine to the olive-skinned peoples of Brede, the ruddy hues of Coria, or the ebony tones of the coastal villages of Salniae. There was even a rumor that one of the more isolated villages had a family whose skin was cornflower blue! She realized that Tulok kept his head shaved, though after meeting Kada – this did not seem to be a requirement of his faith. She had noted that many men kept their head hair in a similar fashion, though many also wore head coverings, to preserve them from the sun's blistering rays. She wondered at this, why Tulok chose to do so as well. The lower half of Tulok's face was bare, though, in light, she could see where he had taken care to ensure it was neat and clean. He would look different with a beard, especially with his broad jawline. The cultural style of many Seteshi men was to have a beard with no mustache. He would look older, maybe even more intimidating. Maybe that's why he is avoiding the beard growth she thought. In the right light, Father Tulok could be mistaken for a large human man. Perhaps someone from one of the Northern Reaches, tall in stature and broad of build save for one characteristic which he could not hide. A pair of tusks, two inches in length, jutted from his lower jaw and curved out of the parting line of his lips. The telltale symbol of his orcish heritage.

"Enjoying the view?" Tulok asked, his deep voice rumbling in his chest.

Isolde blinked and pulled herself from her observations. "Oh!" she exclaimed, shaking her head and sitting back up. "I apologize, I was just..."

"Witnessing?" he asked. His gaze remained turned toward the desert.

"I suppose I was... Yes," she admitted and looked away. "I apologize if any of my actions this past fortnight have placed you in a precarious position with the other members of your Faith... Tulok," she said his name carefully omitting the honorific of title in her address.

He spoke softly,

"Trials and tribulations – these I place before you
I give only what you need to overcome them
Ask when you cannot – do not ask when you can
To survive is to live, but live more than just to survive"

"When I was a child, there was a man that came to our village." He gestured to the north. "A week, maybe two north of here. There are very few settlements in that direction...many of them are Orcish – my people tend to keep to themselves. Yet, here was this lone man on a large beast with a massive hump. I had never seen such a thing. It was my first time seeing a camel. He said his name was Pamp and he was from the west. His Orcish was decent, but enough of the members of the village also understood the Trader's tongue enough that they were able to have a conversation," he said.

Shifting in the sand, he relaxed his shoulders, "Pamp said he was trying to map the land. Volman, our village's speaker laughed at the concept until Pamp showed him the maps he had drawn," turning to Isolde. "Now imagine this – you are the only human in a village full of Orcs. Massive beings who stand as tall as me. Even young children that could meet your gaze. They surrounded him and looked in awe as he showed his drawings. Then suddenly a few members of the village disappeared. They returned in a rush with various rolled-up bundles of animal skins. Another pair of villagers rolled a massive stone disc toward the tent reserved for village meetings. Bringing Pamp inside, the other villagers who fancied themselves as self-made explorers and observers displayed their own drawings. Some were crude, and others were elegant if not more so than Pamp's. It was an amazing sight to see."

Looking up in the darkened sky, "All that knowledge was shared. There was no fear. There was no judgment. There was just sharing of knowledge," he said, smiling at the memory.

"In return for sharing his knowledge, Volman gave him enough dry rations and water to continue to the next settlement with a mark of friendship to wear on his neck. Before he left, he took out a strange item from his pack. It was long and made from a material we had not seen. It was not bone or sandstone, but what he called ... spruce. It was rare because it was not made from the palms of the oasis – rather, he said it was made from the great trees of the west where they grow as tall as the dunes. It had long strings to which he pulled down and moved his fingers across. The tightened strings each made an amazing sound, especially considering most of the music that was created by my settlement was from drumming and singing. He started playing a song, and I remembered being lost in the words, *"To survive is to live, but live more than just to survive,"* he said quietly and let out a deep sigh.

"It was then I realized that I wanted to see the world," he said. "When I came of age, I promptly set out on my own journey, and almost died because I was young and stupid. Village life only prepares you halfway for desert life. If it were not for the Radiant Lord's intervention, and the kindness of Kault and Lalum – I would not have been found."

"Who are Kault and Lalum," she asked.

He smiled, "Teachers...wise and bickering teachers. For three years, I learned about the world with them and then returned home. After I shared everything I learned – I left again, because I heard the call of His Radiance. So, using the updated maps that Pamp had provided years before – I found a temple dedicated to The Radiant All-Seeing Lord, may His Light Shine on All. From there, I was initiated into his embrace as an Acolyte. One of the first tasks I was given was to accompany the original head of this temple to Nahral. I traveled from my Initiate temple of Obor-qua to Tarf-qua. I was told I was chosen because I knew how to make the trek in the unforgiving desert, but also because I spoke and understood enough Ophidian to be useful in Nahral." He looked over at Isolde and noted the confusion on her face, "Ophidian is the tongue spoken by the Sobekites who are the primary residents of Nahral," he paused, "Though I think they also wanted a large and fearsome looking thug to disway any sort of trouble," he said shaking his head. "But yes, while I could not speak it, I understood enough of the language to make trades and get by." He tapped his throat, "Human and Orcs lack the necessary muscles in the throat to speak Ophidian."

Isolde cocked her head to the side, "Wait, what? What do you mean?

"Oh," said the Orc, "I forgot, they aren't human, rather they are humanoid. They are a large, green reptilian people who are known for making deals," he added.

"Wait," Isolde said, "The Sobekites you mentioned earlier are lizard people?"

"Never, ever call them that," he said waving his finger and shaking his head. "They are a Reptilian race. Lizards are small non-sentient scavengers. They are pets who keep the pests at bay. Reptiles are considered massive and wise in the ways of desert life. They are the undisputed masters of that city and boast an amazing trade reputation. Through the gift of their god, the Smiling River Lord –

they can understand any and all languages. In the desert – they are known for providing anything you can ask for," he said.

"...but at a price," Isolde added. "They give you exactly what you want, though the price may not be what you want it to be," she said remembering the Orc's words from earlier. "So what happened on your pilgrimage?"

Tulok stretched his legs out in the sand and leaned forward, "Oooh, I misunderstood one of the tradesmen that accompanied us from Tarf-qua. I felt I needed to prove my worth and said I would handle the negotiations on his behalf because I understood enough of the culture and the spoken word." He sighed, "...sums, however, were not initially my strong suit. Nor were the names for certain amounts of goods. Things that I know now that I did not know then. I ended up promising a month's worth of foodstuff for their value in gold."

Isolde frowned. The people of her land did not bargain in such a way, "What was wrong with that?"

"We were not traveling with ...a month's worth...of supplies for the trade. I was relying on my Ophidian rather than the trade tongue because I was trying to show respect and hopefully win a bit more in trade. I am more fluent now than I was then...but not by much. Had I had any sense then, I would have used the shared trade tongue, but I was too concerned impressing the others."

Isolde's eyes widened a little. " Ohhhhhh".

Tulok nodded and continued his tale, "So the issue was that I had promised a great number of foodstuffs to be supplied to Sobekite traders in return for their fair share in gold."

Again, the knight's face showed confusion.

"The problem was that you cannot eat gold, Isolde. Like water, food discipline out here is what keeps this village running so no one starves," he paused and sighed.."The tradesmen – Jakub Kahr, was the brother of Hemet Behdeti Kahr," Tulok leaned his head back and stared at the darkened sky above them.

"So, after Father Denali had concluded his business with the Order of the River Lord, and learned of what happened – he laughed," he smiled a little at the memory "Father Denali was an old Vidria who always smiled. He understood, but also knew what had to be done. So, the burden of transporting the gold was placed upon my back. I carried it all the way back to Tarf-qua. Then, I stayed for a month hunting, cultivating, and butchering not only enough food for the village – but tradesmen of Nahral that were owed their due," he said quietly with a bit of regret. "Then I made the trek again and delivered it myself when another caravan left for Nahral. Needless to say, the tradesmen were happy as it was just business as usual. Father Denali ended up with part of the funds as a donation. It allowed him to employ some of his kinsmen, provide better border placements, and other improvements to Tarf-qua. I returned to Obor-qua. It was almost twenty years before I came back here. However, memories run long so my welcoming was...not as happy as I thought it would be. Hemet has never let me forget what happened," he ended.

"Twenty years?" she looked at him strangely, reassessing her initial thoughts of him, "If you don't mind me asking – how old are you?"

Tulok looked up and his mouth mumbled something quietly thinking, "I want to say that I think this is my fortieth year."

Her eyes widened, "You are FORTY years old?"

Tulok shrugged and smirked a little, "Well to be fair, I believe my people are longer lived than yours. If it helps... I think that makes me slightly older than you in life experience. Twenty-something – give or take a few years," he said.

Isolde blinked and shook her head. "Witnessed," she said and chuckled a little.

Tulok looked over at the young woman seated next to him on the dunes. She'd come to them beaten, broken, and close to death, a patchwork doll of rags and sand. Now, in the brazier's lights, he could see some of the nobility that she no doubt carried with her when she departed her cold homeland. Her hands were not smooth, they were the hands of someone who worked the land and a weapon. Her skin was pale for the deserts of Setesh, like the color of milk; a dangerous thing under the Everwatchful Eye of Heaven. He would have to ensure she had coverings or balm for her flesh on the morrow when they departed. Tiny spots decorated the areas of her skin that had seen sunlight. *Sunkissed* he remembered some of the women of the village said. The eyes of the people of the desert tended toward darker colors; Isolde's were a brilliant green. Their color reminded Tulok of the green peridot stones that sometimes traded. She was tall, and long, and gangly, like a young colt, still growing into its limbs; limbs covered in lean sinew and muscle honed for a hard life. Secrets hidden beneath both caftan and armor; knowledge that he possessed only from having been her healer.

"What does that mean?" he asked of Isolde.

"Hrmm?" the young woman replied.

"When you say that... to be a Witness. Since we are baring our souls on this night..."

"Is *that* what we are doing?!" Isolde laughed and relaxed a little. She stretched her legs out carefully. He could tell she was still favoring her knee and made a mental note of it.

She sighed deeply and turned her face skyward, leaning back into the sand and resting on her elbows. "I am the eyes of the Lord Wanderer, the Knight of the Quest, may His rest and ascension be well earned," Isolde replied.

"Yes, but...what does that MEAN?" the orc asked.

She leaned her head to the side and raised her eyebrow at him. "It means exactly that. What I see, He sees. What I learn, He learns,." she looked away and back at the sky, "There are reasons why my people are not always welcome in all areas of the world." She shrugged.

Tulok regarded the woman next to him, assessing her response. "Surely that cannot mean...EVERYTHING?" he prodded.

A gentle smile tugged at the corners of Isolde's mouth at his words. She shook her head. "No, it is not," she said quietly. "I am the light in the darkness," she spoke softly. "To those who have taken up His Call, we stand against the Darkness with the light of Hope... my sword and shield a bulwark against the agents of despair."

Tulok considered the woman's words carefully. "So... your God..."

"The Lord Wanderer." Isolde corrected the priest.

"The Lord Wanderer... tasked you with...seeing as much of the world as you can, bearing witness to ... everything possible...and... fighting against the elements of hopelessness and despair....in your...spare time?" he asked.

Isolde pondered the orc's words, her right foot tapping absently as she thought.

"Ya, that about sums it up, I guess," she nodded. She paused and then sat back up and shifted to direct her attention toward Tulok. "You know, I'm pretty sure Hemet is none-too-pleased with me right now," she started, changing the subject.

Tulok blinked and paused, trying to shift his train of thought to follow. "And why would that be?" The big man asked.

"Because she's gone and given the old buzzard what fore in the middle of the hall for mistreating the man that saved her life," an unfamiliar voice called from behind them both.

Chapter 8

Tulok shifted quickly moving to stand, Isolde rolled to the side, away from him to separate them as potential targets. Sand flew all around them.

Walking up the pathway was a short woman, dressed in the robes of the Temple. Her dark hair was pulled back by a scarf. She was half Isolde's height, but broad of the shoulder and hip. The knight wondered if this were another of the Vidria people. She appeared to be carrying a basket with her. She clucked at the pair as they moved to a position of readiness.

"Tsk, Tsk, coming all the way out here alone," the woman chided Tulok.

He looked down from his great height at the small woman. "Mother Ranpu...what..." he began.

"Shush you." she scolded the priest. She looked over at Isolde. "You've made quite the stir young lady," the Vidria woman commented. "Though that was not undeserved, still," she added.

Isolde stood and carefully brushed off her trousers. "My apologies." she offered.

Tulok scowled and looked back in the direction Ranpu had come. "How bad is it?" he asked.

Ranpu pondered her response for a moment, "I believe

Hemet said something about impertinent youth...and sending you both to bed with no supper."

Isolde gently bit her own tongue in an effort to not say anything. Tulok rubbed the back of his neck and shifted uncomfortably from one foot to the next. His eyes fell on the basket that Ranpu was carrying. "And THAT would be..." he inquired of the basket.

"Our guest's supper." she replied plainly and then glanced sideways up at Tulok, "With enough to share with you, should she be so inclined," she added, her words flavored with conspiratorial tones. "SOME of us, remember the Old Ways," she said to Isolde and inclined her head, offering the young woman the basket.

Isolde smiled and accepted the gift. "I owe you my thanks, Mother Ranpu."

"Psh." she waved it off. "You owe me nothing other than to enjoy your meal...even if it is with this great lout." she nodded at Tulok. Tulok raised his eyebrows and then folded his arms across his broad chest. "Oh, don't get all blustery with me, young man," she admonished. "Leaving on the morrow, and the two of you are off whispering in the shadows, like a pair of sneak thieves...when you should be eating supper, checking your gear, and resting."

Tulok pursed his lips together and nodded in agreement, forcing himself to stay silent.

Isolde stood next to him, both hands firmly grasping the handle of the basket, head bowed in silent rebuke. "Yes ma'am." She said with a nod.

"Good!" Ranpu nodded firmly and turned to walk back inside. "And stay in the light where we can see you both!" she continued. "Too damned many people already think you're addle-pated from the sun!" she waved in between the two of them, then stomped back down the dune.

Isolde looked up at Ranpu's words, a noticeably confused look on her pale features. “But...I..” she looked up at Tulok.

Tulok watched the tiny grumpy figure tromp back inside. He harrumphed a little. “I think that was meant for me,” he scowled a little, but just let out a sigh. “Remark aside – she was right; please excuse me. I should be prepping rather than out here brooding. We will be leaving about an hour before false dawn. I’ll send someone to wake you.” he paused. “Enjoy your meal,” Tulok added, walking off into the darkness of the dunes.

~~~

Travel in the desert was best completed before the heat of the day. Depending on the season, that could mean travel needed to happen before noon, or as early as a few hours after sunrise. In either case, travel during the full light of the day often meant certain death. Isolde tugged at the straps on her breastplate and shifted under its uncomfortable shape. It was new, and she had not had time to get used to it. It did not rub poorly, so there would not be raw patches of skin, but the weight was different and it affected her movements. She turned her eyes skyward to stare at the night sky. Legends told of a time when there had been more stars in the heavens. A time when sailors and caravans used them for navigation. A time when they were used to predict the seasons. A time when they held the stories of the world. They still told stories, but those stories were but a handful of what they once were.

Four bright lights twinkled in the firmament above. Four guides in the darkness. Four guardians against the chaos of the Reaping were all that was left now... Three were named for the fallen Champions of Our Lady of Justice, The Star Maiden – who stood as a bulwark against the tides of Chaos, and one was named for The Lifegiver. The last of the Divine who had given their life to preserve Sanc-
~~~

tum, The Lifegiver had once been known as Anuket, daughter of The Radiant Lord. The Faithful claimed that her Father now watched over all children in Her stead. The reptiloid desert people of Setesh took their name from Her. They had been Her last creation in a barren wasteland. It was said that when She fell, The Star Maiden wept diamond tears that birthed these four lights in the night sky, that mortals might not forever lose hope.

A cool breeze blew across the sands, and the hairs on the back of Isolde's neck rose. She shuddered slightly from the chill of the desert air. Something tugged at the back of Isolde's mind as she gazed skyward, something dancing on the edges of the Morpheum, the place of dreams. She shook it off and focused on the task at hand. Her hands inventoried her gear for the fifth time that morning, checking and double-checking everything she had against everything she had been given.

Travel in the dark was a dangerous prospect, especially for those not able to see in the darkness. To combat this challenge, the Seteshi had developed a system of tracking between settlements. All it took was a spyglass, a knowledge of which stars aligned where, and a team of runners, tasked with setting up small lighted beacons every kilometer or so. Sands shift, wind blows things over, beacons fall, these were chances that every caravan took. The Reysis learned the paths between the settlements. They learned the dunes, the shift and fall of the sand, the places where hidden sinkholes would claim a man's life, and the caches of water that would save them if caught unawares. The Reysis Rafa watched Isolde from across the way, her calloused hands knotted rope and counted lengths as she did so. Her demeanor had told the Wanderer that she did not trust her, nor appreciate her presence in her lands. Isolde looked in her direction and attempted to smile and nod at her in greeting. She sucked on a tooth, gathered her rope, and turned away from her.

Lovely. This will be lovely, she thought to herself. She reached for the talisman that hung around her neck; her fingers closing over its odd shape. She rubbed her thumb along one of its edges absently, gathering strength and sense of purpose from its simple reminder. A camel bellowed, breaking her from her thoughts. Its driver clucked at it, and made gestures that she did not understand. It bellowed in disagreement, but finally knelt and its tender began the process of harnessing and loading it with gear.

"It looks good on you," a woman's voice spoke. Turning to face the sound, Isolde saw the figure of Mother Ranpu walking up to meet her. "The armor," the Vidria woman commented, gesturing. "You made a good trade," she nodded, pleased with something unspoken.

"Oh...uh...thank you," Isolde replied absently. She looked down at herself, now clad in hardened leather, where she had been boasting polished steel upon her arrival. "I am glad it worked out for everyone," she offered a smile.

Ranpu scoffed at the tall woman. "The Island may not understand coin, but your people understand barter well enough!" she continued and walked up next to Isolde.

Isolde shrugged a little. "It didn't seem like too great a thing," Isolde began, "Ranfa needed metal for rivets for saddle tack and Limir needed metal to make tools for construction. Ranfra's wife makes boots and Limir's boy fashions leather for harnesses and armor. The metal would be harder for them to come by out here, than the leather pieces I needed..." she looked down at Mother Ranpu, "and somehow, I think Reynard would smile to know that my armor was back in the hands of people working the land... in whatever fashion."

Mother Ranpu listened to the strange woman and nodded. "You saved them well more than what you got in return..."

Isolde turned away and looked back over at the camels, a half-smile on her face, "If it offers their families some reprieve and allows them to prosper a little bit more..." she looked skyward again, "Then it was well worth the trade."

"You can leave that altruism here, sister." Rafa's sharp tenor commented. "You take that with you into Nahral and their people will serve you up for supper...if you are lucky."

"She's right," said a deep voice. Gone were the priestly robes of office save the lone sun medallion. Instead, he wore a set of flowing loose-fitting clothing made to capture the air and cool the body's perspiration. His bald head was covered with a matching headscarf, decorated with gold embroidery at the ends. This *hatsha* was designed to keep the sun from one's head while also providing a filter for the sand. He was properly outfitted for desert travel. The coloring of his clothing gave enough protection from the sun's brightest rays but also afforded him enough to blend in with the desert landscape. The only thing that stood out was a massive mace that looked like it was made of bone wrapped with hardened leather. A hit from it would probably cave her chest in.

Mother Ranpu walked over to the priest and boldly patted him, "It is good to see you travel again. Too much time in the temple can make you soft and the Radiant Lord does not need any more *soft priests*," She motioned the third member of their party.

Bengt Kalb was like the "middle child" when it came to the Acolytes of the temple. He was not as old and wise as Kada, nor was he seen as enthusiastic as Mata, the unseen woman who had been the one to assist in the undressing and redressing of Isolde's injuries. Isolde had later learned that Tulok had felt that the nature of a woman's body was best left in the hands of another woman where possible.

He had been introduced as Brother Bengt, though he seemed more concerned with the heat than niceties. He was sunkissed, but the perpetual sweat on his brow made him seem otherwise. Bengt had volunteered because he understood both Sobekite culture and their language far better than Tulok would openly admit. His introduction was simply a poor smile and a nod of the head.

The fourth member of the party reminded Isolde of the depictions of foreign warlords in stories. All members of the caravan seemed to pay deference to the tall man. Even Reysis Rafa bowed her head at the other man's approach. He had tattoos and scars on his face. His strong features and dark hair curled beneath his own hatsha. He was striking and by all accounts handsome.

"That is our Sun Guide?" Isolde asked the priest. Known only by his surname of Safar, he was the most fascinating man she had ever seen.

Tulok's gaze followed Isolde's. He chuckled quietly. "You may want to close your mouth when you stare at him," Tulok said as he patted her on the shoulder and began tugging on the camel's lead rope.

Isolde shook her head and stammered. "I was not staring, I was.... wait are we going now? Isn't there a ceremony or prayer we need to say," she asked as the camel tugged her forward to follow the next.

"Yes," Mother Ranpu called out, "Don't die. And bring back a story."

~~~

Camels were foul, disgusting creatures, and the Seteshi could keep them as far as Isolde was concerned. They were ill-mannered, smelly beasts that bellowed, spat, and bit. While many of these traits could also be assigned to horses,
~~~

at least a horse's gait was easy to manage. These creatures managed to annoy every sense that Isolde possessed. While she had been thankful for the brief riding lesson she'd had when she and Reynard had first arrived; her back end and tailbone were certainly not prepared for the hours-long trek of irregular, side swaying herky-jerky movements of these terrible land beasts.

She shifted in her saddle once more, trying to find some comfort and failing. She remembered not to try and ride it like a horse. Camels were not to be ridden astride. Instead, she looped her leg around the saddle horn and sat almost cross-legged, as she had been shown. Still, she felt as if she was either going to fall off backward or be pitched off forward half of the time.

The sun's rays were firmly behind them now as Radiant Lord's ever-watchful eye began his trek across the heavens once more. They had stopped for morning observances at daybreak. She had taken the opportunity to stretch and assess her personal situation as the rest of the Seteshi had faced the sun to offer solemn hymns and prayers to their God. She had taken a few steps away from the group to offer her own solemnities to her faith, and not detract from those who so very clearly outnumbered her.

The sands stretched out before them, miles upon endless miles of dusk, tawny and orange colored sand. She'd been fascinated by it all when she and Reynard had made port initially. Sands that rose and fell like sea waves. Sands that danced in the wind and under the vibration of foot traffic. Sands that even seemed to sing or sound like distant drums. She'd been thrilled with the newness of it. It was all something that very few of her people would ever see, and she was seeing it!

Now that fascination had ebbed away and the novelty of the dunes was more of an annoyance. It was an endless sea of rippled dirt – *Windside-slipside-windside-slipside.* She had no idea why anyone would want to live here.

Safar's lead camel pulled back and alongside hers. He kept his eyes on the shifting sands before them, and the skyline. "Tell me, Island," he began, addressing Isolde. His voice was deep and thick and flavored with his native accent. "Why do your people send you so far away from your home, to come out here with the people of the sand?" he asked.

Isolde sat up a little straighter in her saddle. Her tailbone complained. She ignored it.

"They did not send me away. I came here willingly," she answered.

Safar laughed a little, "No one comes to the sands willingly from your Island if they do not have trade goods to sell. Yet here you are – no goods to sell, trying to ride a camel, to the City that does not speak your tongue." He pulled his dark eyes off of the sands and looked her up and down. "Are you cursed then? Banished?" he lowered his voice, "Running from a husband?" he smirked at her, his white teeth gleamed brightly against his dark skin as he smiled.

Safar's previous appeal faded entirely with those words. The Knight Wanderer pursed her lips and straightened her shoulders and set her jaw. Clearing her throat, she turned away from the Sun Guide and fixated on the sands before her. "My husband is not yet dead a year, Sirrah, and we do not speak ill of the fallen from where I hail," she replied in a strained and formal tone.

The Sun Guide's eyebrows twitched slightly and he inclined his head. "My apologies, I did not know you were in your time of mourning." he tapped his fingers to his breast, "Let the Radiant Lord's grace shine upon him, and may he be judged worthy of eternity." Safar intoned.

Isolde bowed her head and closed her eyes and nodded. "Thank you," she replied.

They rode side by side, in silence for a little while, neither seeking to break the discomfort of awkward neutrality. Safar's gaze fixed on the horizon, his honey-brown eyes searching for anything that did not belong. He glanced back behind them at the train of traders and priests that accompanied their group. "I do not often see this many holy people outside the safety of the Temple walls, Island," Safar commented and looked back ahead. "Why are we really going to Nahral?" he asked.

Chapter 9

"I'm sure Father Tulok has given you all the information that you require," Isolde replied coolly to the Sun Guide who rode beside her.

"I cannot prepare us for the road ahead if I do not know all of the perils facing us," came the retort.

"I am not at liberty to discuss the details," she countered.

"The sands hold many secrets, Island. I know almost all of them," Safar replied, his eyes sliding over to Isolde and appraising her once more.

"Surely?" Isolde asked. Her green eyes glanced at Safar and then back. "You've aged well then," a slight smirk tugged at the corner of her lip.

Safar blinked at the carefully crafted insult, then his face broke into a broad smile, "Ah! I like you, Island!" he laughed out loud.

Isolde relaxed a little in her saddle and her face softened at the release of tension.

"We have started poorly. Allow me to rectify this." the dark man offered. "I am Reysis Safar, dancer of the sands, outrider of Litharge, and guide for your journey to the city of Nahral." he placed his hand over his heart and bowed his head.

Isolde shifted in her seat to look over at the man beside

her. His features were sharper than those of the Island-born, his skin darker. His face bore various tattoos on his chin and beneath his eyes. She had seen similar things on other people of Setesh. They held cultural meaning of some form. She assumed they were akin to the marking customs of the more barbarous people of the Northern Reaches.

"I am Isolde duAvalonne," she replied "Daughter of Niall, of the Council Whitebrook, bearer of the Grace of Kalanchoe, Flower of Lorraine, Keeper of the Light, and Witness of the Lord Wanderer of the World," she placed a clasped fist to her heart and nodded to him. "I would offer you my hand in greeting..." she began.

"But you are afraid that you will fall off of your mount?" Safar suppressed a smile.

"Is it that obvious?" Isolde whispered back.

"Only to someone who works with these beasts for as long as I." the guide replied.

Isolde pursed her lips, "You are lying to protect my dignity." she judged.

"Perhaps," Safar shrugged with the hint of a smile. His eyes caught something off in the distance. He furrowed his brow and reached down to pull a long tube of leather, metal, and glass from his saddle. He placed one end of it to his right eye and pointed the other in the direction ahead of them. Watching for a moment, he paused and gazed skyward and then off to either side of the caravan. He turned and called out to a younger man currently leading the caravan. The other responded back with a raised hand and turned his wrist in a circular motion.

"Something wrong?" Isolde asked.

Safar shook his head. "Our scout has located a position of safety where we will rest for the day. The sands must have shifted recently. We should have had another hour before finding refuge." he replied as he pondered something.

Though she couldn't see a hint of Safar's scout, "Is that bad?"

Safar looked back over at the woman, appraising her once more with his golden eyes.

"One is always happy to accept the gifts that the sands offer; for they do not offer them with any great frequency," he paused, "One is also wise to take caution when hidden things are revealed."

They locked eyes for a moment and Isolde could feel an unspoken aura of caution between them.

"Remain vigilant," Safar instructed and without further exchange, encouraged his mount to ride ahead.

Isolde watched the figure of the Sun Guide as he rode further apace, distancing himself from the rest of their small caravan. Something nagged at the back of her mind about the man. Something that spoke of secrets and ancient mysteries. Something that she had felt in the presence of only one or two persons before in her lifetime, which made it unique enough to bear interest and curiosity. Perhaps investigation. She wondered after the dark-skinned man as he rode away, pondering the possibilities of who he might actually be, that the Lord Wanderer's curiosity was piqued.

"Is it commonplace where you come from to stare after someone for that long?" Tulok's deep voice interrupted. "Safar is easy enough on your eyes that they will not suffer further injury..." a smirk played on the orc's lips as he rode aside Isolde.

"What? I... oh!" she glowered at the big priest. "Must there always be some manner of impropriety leveled on my actions by your people?!" she huffed. She reached for the end of her scarf and pulled it across the lower portion of her face. Only her eyes and the tiniest hint of her freckled nose showed.

"By my..." Tulok raised a curious eyebrow at the woman.

"Ah, you mean the general people of Setesh," he nodded, correcting himself. He noted Isolde's clear displeasure at the topic and it gave him pause. He regarded her carefully for a moment, then brought his mount closer to hers so they might speak more privately.

"Has something happened?" he asked with sincere concern. His eyes followed after Safar for a moment and then looked back at Isolde. "Do I need to..."

Isolde sighed heavily and looked over at Tulok. "I do not need you to defend my honor, Tulok," she countered, irritation filled in her voice.

"That was not what I..."

"Wasn't it?" She cut him off.

Tulok reached up and rubbed the back of his neck with a beefy hand and then rubbed his jaw absently. "You... may be right," he admitted, slightly embarrassed. "You are a knight of your own right. You are skilled with a blade, and you were chosen by the Lord Wanderer to embody His will upon this world." He placed his fingertips to his heart and inclined his respect. "You do not need a humble priest to defend you. My apologies."

Isolde regarded Tulok for a moment, her eyes falling to the giant mace strapped to his camel's saddle. She looked back up at him. "I don't doubt your ability to do so, Tulok..." she offered. "It's just..." she paused.

"Learning the ways of a strange land is sometimes confusing?" he offered gently.

She nodded and looked skyward for a moment and then back at Tulok. "Thank you for understanding," she replied, kindness and compassion in her voice and her eyes.

The giant of a priest leaned in and whispered in an overly furtive tone, "One would think that I might ...read... a lot... of books." he said through a suppressed grin. He winked at her.

"Och!" Isolde exclaimed as she blushed and flustered and reached over to punch him solidly in the arm. Tulok flinched a little at the impact, reaching over to rub his shoulder.

"Ow!" he exclaimed.

A sudden burst of conversation erupted from behind them as the other members of the caravan seemed to jump into a ready mode. Some reached for weapons, others reached for gear. All seemed certain that Tulok and Isolde were about to engage in battle. Tulok turned around in his saddle and waved them all down, speaking words in a language Isolde did not understand. Several heads nodded and shook with a few smiles as weapons were sheathed once more.

"What did you tell them?" Isolde asked.

"Hrm?" he asked "Oh that you called into question my matrilineal lineage for drinking the last of your spiced wine," he grinned and winked once more, and rode ahead to join Safar.

~~~

While horses can be ushered to gallop ahead, camels needed negotiating. The Orc began kneading the animal's neck – a training trick the village instilled on all their beasts of burden. While the camel's speed did not improve immediately, it gave a burst of speed to keep pace with the lead camel that Safar was riding. The man was staring at something hard in the distance. Following his gaze, Tulok waited for him to speak. It had been several moments before the Reysis sighed and looked at the orc. His face was a little dour and he quietly said,

"The dunes...do you see it?"

Tulok turned again and kept his eyes on the horizon. The desert was a sea of sand and while there is chaos, there are also patterns and stories that can be gleaned. At a young
~~~

age, desert children are taught how to read the dunes and how the sand can shift. Wind and travel can carve rolling dunes or massive peaks.

What one rarely saw was sandstone.

A series of flat structures jutted out from the distant dunes, like teeth. As they moved forward, the view became a little clearer. The natural flow of a dune had been violently broken by the creation of sandstone. While the Vidria had an affinity to shape the sand to their will – this was not with the same elegance. This erupted from the smooth slopes of the gentle sand like some violent claw reaching for the open air. Then it came into view.

A splash of dark red on the pale rocks. Safar swore quietly and the orc felt the anger rise slightly in him. From a distance, it looked like something living had been smashed to a pulp on the rocks. Yet there were no carrion eaters in the air or other scavengers doing their duty as the scent of blood could easily be carried on the air.

Both knew it for what it was – the Hand of the Changebringer, the Lord of Storms.

It was the Changebringer's rage that created the land around them when the people had come to Sanctum. Stories told of a time when the sands of Setesh were once verdant jungles until the Changebringer came. It was said that the anger and unparalleled rage at the loss of His home is what scorched the realm where He first stepped on the ground. The empty dunes stood as a testament to the power of the heavens, and the passion of the Gods.

While not a danger necessarily – the Hand paid worship to the turbulent god. Their appearance was far and few in numbers – but the devotion to their deity was beyond fanatic. They saw the desert storms as the divine hallmarks of their god's passing and the wake of their destruction as a blessing of change for the world. When the desert seemed too still, the Hand created make-shift altars to call down the winds and bring the 'Red Lord's' influence into the world once more. Most of Radiant Lord's devout leadership understood the reasoning for change in a static world. Without the storms, they would not create the cool weather of the night or help reveal things long thought lost.

For villagers and travelers like Tulok and Safar, these Hands of the Red Lord were crazed zealots who destroyed important landmarks along well-known routes in their obsession for change. From Vandals of Change to Fanatic Storm Chasers – the Changebringer's followers had been here which meant the road to Nahral would require caution.

"We'll continue onward to get some distance between us and them," Safar commented.

Tulok rested his hand on the hilt of his great mace "A good idea," he replied.

Safar looked back over his shoulder at the caravan slowly approaching. "Can she fight in the sand?" he asked of Isolde.

Tulok pursed his lips and nodded. "She can fight."

"Good."

~~~

The brutality of the desert heat faded as the sun disappeared beyond the horizon. The temperature continued to drop as the Radiant Lord's grace vanished farther and farther from the skyline and the darkened sky took up its place in the heavens above. As the first star – Braag rose, Safar had called the caravan to its halt for the evening rest. They would set camp here and pick up again in several hours' time when the light of the last star Cerys came fully into view. The group had moved in trained expertise to unpack the goods and gear, and set weights and ropes to tie down the woven tent. It was a long structure, pitched in several areas to grant some height. The sloping walls on one side
~~~

served as a windbreak. The tented area was then further divided into three sections, the main gathering area where talking and food would be shared a sleeping area for the men, and a smaller sleeping area for the women. In this case, Isolde occupied this area entirely on her own.

Gendered assignments were not foreign to Isolde; men and women of the Islands often occupied specific roles within her own community. There was a crossover between them, and duties were shared as well where skills were needed. One would never turn away a skilled tradesman or craftsman merely because they were a woman. Indeed, the political ruler of the Islands was always a woman. Currently, she was a young girl, one who had not even come into her own womanhood. Erissa, Oracle of The Stones, Bandrui of Fenian, Queen of Avalon was chosen by vision and signs from the Gods upon the death of the former Matriarch. Their religious leader was also female; an ancient elven woman of undetermined age. Bellicent was as terrifying as she was aloof. She had watched over the faith of the islands for more than 3 millennia. Few were still alive who remembered a time before Bellicent.

The Islands leaned toward matriarchal lineage and governance in many areas, but the separations of the sexes still existed. In her homeland, being afforded a place in the communal tent of her own would have been a symbol of honor. Here in Setesh, it was merely a gesture of a culturally observed divide.

She finished re-braiding her hair and coiled it back up, tucking it securely out of the way. Long hair, whipping in the wind, was a wonderfully poetic image; but also proved to be a terrible idea that often resulted in simply cutting the hair short rather than pulling the knots out. The fire crackled, its warm light offering solace against the chill of the darkness surrounding them. In the distance, priests and tradesmen checked over their gear and tended to their animals. Tomorrow should bring them to their initial destination. From there, they would negotiate passage across the wide river Iteru and plan their trek to the ruins of Ahsal. There they would discover whether there was any truth to the existence of a Cult of The Silent, and finally put to rest the last Quest of Reynard the Swift. Isolde closed her eyes and reached to grasp the token of her faith in silent prayer. As she did she felt the presence of someone who seated themself next to her. She finished her well wishes for her Knight, who had died on the shores of this strange land, then opened her eyes. The dark-clad figure of Reysis Safar sat next to her; his right hand held a long stick that he prodded the fire's embers with.

"You offer prayers for the peaceful rest of your husband, Island?" he asked gently. His golden-brown eyes watched the flames and did not turn to her.

Isolde shook her head. "No, for my Knight. Ser Reynard the Swift, may he be judged worthy to rejoin the cycle once more." she intoned reverently.

Safar pursed his lips and nodded. "Tulok tells me that you lost someone when you made landfall here." He looked skyward, scanning the expanse. "The Sands are often unkind to those who are not born of them." His eyes fell back to the figure of the pale-skinned woman seated next to him, "It is said that the Sands will have their payment in water or blood, even of the sand-blooded." His eyes watched her features, as one trying to gauge another or memorize a moment. "My sorrows for your loss," he offered. His words were sincere.

The Avalonian knight turned her face to look at the Sun Guide seated next to her. He was a man of unnatural grace. When he walked on the sand, it was as if he were part of their slip and fall. When he rode a camel, his movements were in perfect unison with the animal. A dark curl of long black hair had escaped his head covering, it found itself clinging to the coarse hair of his beard. Even this out-of-place image seemed like it belonged here. For a moment Isolde thought she saw something moving behind the golden flecks in his brown eyes. They watched each other for a moment, then she blinked and turned away.

"Thank you."

Safar nodded and turned his focus back to the fire.

Chapter 10

The younger man who had led the caravan earlier approached, waiting at a respectful distance for the Reysis to acknowledge him. Here the Reysis was King. To them was given all honor and respect. They would make all decisions for the caravan, and there would never be room for dissent or argument. For they were also responsible for every life that traveled with them. The loss of a single life would be remembered for an eternity on the lips of every caravan. It was more than pride; it was their calling just as surely as any priest or warrior. Safar frowned at the young man who spoke quickly in his native tongue, though all Isolde could do was follow his several hand gestures. Safar nodded, commenting quickly, and waived the boy on.

"Everything alright?" Isolde asked.

"It is nothing," Safar replied. He resumed his fire tending then added. "Nothing for you to be concerned with," he clarified.

Isolde nodded and looked skyward. She placed her hands on her knees and stretched her back and neck upward. The firelight bounced off of the shiny metal surface of the item around her neck.

"Your necklace..." Safar began, "I have not seen the like of it before. What is it?" he asked.

Isolde reached for the item and looked down at it. A small eight-sided box, crafted of metal and glass. Within it was suspended a tiny metal arrow. It wiggled and spun erratically. She smiled a bittersweet smile. "The symbol of my office," she replied. "It belonged to my Lord Knight. It would have come to me eventually..." she offered.

Safar nodded, "Ahhh, yes, I think I know of this now." he looked over at the tall woman. "But they do not work, no?" he asked.

"When it is important... they will," Isolde replied and then tucked the item away beneath the neckline of her caftan.

"How will you know when?" the handsome guide asked her in earnest.

Isolde turned and looked back at Safar and offered him a warm and genuine smile, her eyes sparkled like perfect peridots in the fire's light. For a moment, the chill of the desert vanished, and he was filled with a strange, but welcome warmth.

Safar's eyebrows rose slightly. He inclined his head politely.

Isolde whispered softly in the darkness "I just will."

"You are full of surprises, Island" Safar smiled appreciatively at her.

"Like your Desert?" Isolde asked, holding the man's eyes for a moment, before turning away.

"Perhaps." he chuckled a little.

The sound of heavy footfall drew the attention of the dark man. He looked in the direction of the sound and was met with the towering visage of Father Tulok. Safar raised his chin in silent greeting to the big priest. Tulok nodded simply in reply.

"I hope I am not interrupting?" Tulok's deep voice asked politely.

Safar watched Tulok and sat up straighter as if his frame might be taller or broader by doing so, "If I said yes, would it alter your actions?"

Tulok shook his head, "Probably not." he replied with a half-grin and sat, folding himself into a cross-legged position opposite the fire from Isolde.

Safar grunted and shook his head. He poked at the fire. "How are our friends?" he asked the orc.

"Still outside of range, but clearly patrolling the area and keeping an eye on us," Tulok responded.

Isolde furrowed her brow and looked between the two. "We have friends?" she asked warily.

Tulok nodded. "Storm Chasers... more than likely."

Isolde frowned and shifted her position slightly so she could see over Tulok's left shoulder into the darkness beyond. "And... those would be..."

"Followers of a mad God," Safar added sharply, a note of distaste on his tongue.

"Well THAT is simply charming." the island woman commented. "So, they are...unpredictable then?" she asked.

Tulok and Safar exchanged knowing glances. "In as much as we do not know their *current* motivations, yes," Tulok replied

Isolde looked back beyond the orc into the darkness, the light of the fire obscuring her view. She took a breath, held it, and then exhaled slowly, flexing the fingers of her right hand. "We expect issues then?"

"Always" both men replied.

"However, sometimes they are not the main issue," Safar added. He stared out into the darkness, "There are vermin called Sandtalons that follow in the wake of a Stormchaser. They can be an issue for the unprepared, though they are mostly an issue in the west. Here, we should be fine – but cautious."

The knight pursed her lips in thought and looked down at her right hand. She stood up and flexed her fingers, stretching them, and assessing their readiness. The priest's eyes followed her actions, watching her carefully.

"How is the knee?" Tulok asked her quietly.

Isolde rolled one shoulder and then the other, she scrunched her face up a little and squinted out into the darkness. "It will have to be enough, yes?"

"Isolde..." the big man began cautiously.

She shook her head.

Safar watched the exchange and finally looked to Tulok. "She is injured?" he asked with a note of concern.

"SHE," Isolde answered. "Is seated right here." She stood and looked down at the handsome Sun Guide, "...and if the Reysis has questions about HER... HE can ask HER directly." she said pointedly.

Tulok smiled gently at her reaction and shrugged at Safar, declining to answer.

The Reysis turned to look at her and then stood to face Isolde. Eye to eye he stared at the tall foreigner in the firelight. He looked her up and down as if assessing the health of one of his animals. "I need to know if you can handle yourself if danger comes to us, Island," he said directly.

Isolde met the eyes of Reysis Safar with unflinching confidence and unbowed assurance. "I think you will need to worry about the other members of your caravan, Reysis," she answered plainly.

Safar held a warning finger up to Isolde's face, then lowered it and poked directly at her collarbone. The finger met with the unexpected resistance of armor, hidden beneath her caftan. His eyebrows knitted together for a moment and his eyes slid back to Isolde's. Her eyes met his, a silent challenge coloring their green hue. "Find something out of place, Reysis?" the knight inquired in a tone of forced politeness.

Sensing the tension slowly building between the two, Tulok raised his hand and looked up at Safar, "If there is an issue," he turned his gaze to Isolde, "You will accept what I will offer you when the time is right."

Isolde narrowed her eyes and leaned her head in Tulok's direction, "What does that mean?"

"He brings the Radiant Lord's gifts Island," said Safar, "The Radiant Father is advising you to accept his help when the time comes as our lives may depend on it."

Before any rebuttal could be given, voices raised along the outskirts of the caravan's encampment. From beyond the security of the fire's light, someone was approaching. The wind picked up slightly as they approached. The robes and wraps that covered their body were tattered and frayed and whipped in the wind. The figure had their hands raised up in the air with their palms faced upwards and spread out showing they bore no weapon or ill will. The torches flickered as they approached and waited at the border of the encampment.

"It seems that we have a guest with manners," Safar said, "You should join me," he said to Tulok. Turning back to Isolde, "Come along Island, not many can say they have met one who speaks for the deserts." Safar turned and began to walk toward the distant torches with Tulok following. With the previous discussion either put on hold or ended, Isolde's mood shifted to a mixture of curiosity and quiet caution. She let out a small breath and followed behind the large priest.

The figure sat in the sand as their robes flicked in the wind – their arms raised with their palms facing the heavens. Safar strode forward with palms raised up in a similar fashion. Tulok was different in that he had his hands raised up but palms facing outward.

"Why are you doing that," Isolde asked.

"It is to show them that I am armed but I bring no ill. I am sure there is a similar gesture with your people. Given that you have your sword, I would recommend doing the same," the priest answered.

Nodding her head, she mimicked the orc and raised her hands up, and had her palms facing outward. As the three approached the torches, the figure made no move to stand. Isolde noted that they seemed very tall. While not as tall as the orc beside her, they were definitely taller than Isolde as she looked them over. Safar stopped just outside the torch placement and slowly lowered his hands down and two behind him followed suit, "Welcome Child of the Changebringer, Keeper of the Land, and Harvester of Storms – our business is only to rest before we move on. We do not wish any ill will to you or your Lord."

The figure's face was hidden in the wrappings and shadows. They replied in a gruff voice,

"The Red Changebringer sent a vision of evil on the wind. Something rotten has been lingering in His domain and now it has drifted further into the lands once again. He seeks to have His lands cleansed by any means necessary to prevent it from spreading any further." The figure turned its head towards Isolde and then pointed a finger, "Perhaps it is the wet foreign flesh that brings this evil with her." Turning their head toward Tulok, "Or perhaps The Radiant Lord has blinked and let the evil slip in despite His watchful gaze."

Isolde's mind raced to the box in her pack. There was a sense of guilt that rose up in her that she quickly shut down and hoped that it wasn't evident on her face. Before Isolde could speak, she heard a deep rumble come from

Tulok. His hands squeezed themselves into a fist. While the insinuation was insulting, Isolde could see the insult leaving its mark on the Priest. Yet, there was something else there as the rumble did not subside. Instead, Tulok moved a step forward past Safar and spoke in a harsh and guttural tongue.

"Is it The Changebringer's intention to spark us to fighting, Stormchaser or do you come with a purpose?" the Priest said in a defiant tone.

The stranger laughed and pulled down their hood. In the torchlight, their features were fully revealed. While longer and more rugged than any human, their face bore a definite feminine cast. Her hair was frazzled and knotted, and her face was gaunt, but the look in her red eyes was clear and defiant. A pair of small tusks jutted out from her bottom lip. Not only was the stranger a woman, but she was also an Orc. She replied, speaking in the same harsh guttural tongue.

"My purpose is clear Sun Child – there is a greater evil here in the land and the Changebringer has set his Hands into motion to remove that threat by any means necessary," she answered and with almost a smile.

"You have crawled into your rage so much that you cannot see that there is no evil here," Tulok retorted as he slapped his chest.

"Maybe you have forgotten your TRUE instincts…Reasoner," she added bitterly with a smile of disdain.

"I use my mind to live in peace, but do not think I am soft by any means. I can be something more terrible than you could imagine," Tulok said as his hands opened slowly and his arms slowly moved outward.

Safar and Isolde watched the exchange between the two Orcs. When Tulok spoke, something in him changed. Isolde and Safar both took a step back instinctively as they felt the violence surrounding the Priest. This was not the priest who blushed or was embarrassed that the Avalonian knew. No – this was something terrifying and at that moment, Isolde truly understood what the Gurhk was that each Orc harbored within themselves.

The Hand remained seated, but the smile on her face waived and with glinting red eyes, she met Tulok's gaze. The wind died down and there was silence on dune as both stared at each other for what seemed like an eternity. Slowly, the Child of the Changebringer lowered her gaze. The tension in the air died and the breeze picked up again, though softly.

She spoke quietly in the Trader's tongue, "There will be another storm coming soon. It will probably hit before you leave so I suggest you prepare. Know that there is evil here – while it may not be in your caravan, there is something in the land that requires cleansing. Our Lord has sent a storm to help ferret it out." She stood up and regarded them all, "There are rumors that it might be the work of the Silent One. We few have taken it upon ourselves to destroy them when they cross the land. Take care of the company you keep."

She looked at Isolde, and the knight could feel herself being weighed and measured. The Hand said nothing but nodded her head in satisfaction.

The menace that surrounded the priest had not completely faded away, but he replied, "Thank you for the warning..." he paused as he realized that they did not know her name.

"Koll," she said looking back to Tulok.

"Thank you, Koll, for the warning and the information. The Devout of The Radiant Lord seeks the same shared goal. Do you wish to share the hospitality of camp before the storm?"

Koll shook her head, "I have supped before I came here. One never knows when you will die and it is better to have eaten before you are something else's meal." She threw the hood of the robe over the top of her head and started to walk away, but paused. She looked back at Tulok, but with a different look in her eyes. She spoke in a softer tone in the same guttural language.

"You know...all that rage has to go somewhere. I can...show you how to get rid of some of that before the storm is upon us. I'll be over that dune if you choose to do so," she said before turning and walking back into the darkness, *"There aren't many attractive beings out here, though you would look better with a beard,"* she added before fading into view.

Whatever rage that was still in the Priest was soon forgotten. He stood there stunned, staring at Koll as she walked away. He turned and looked over at Safar who said nothing but gave Tulok a wide smile. Reaching over, Safar gave Tulok a light slap on the arm and laughed.

Isolde had seen many of Tulok's emotions play out on his face, but this was a mixture of embarrassment and surprise. "What did she say to you?" she asked the big priest.

Tulok ran his hand over the top of his head and coughed, but before he could say anything Safar interjected, "She said he would look more attractive if he had a beard... and then offered to help him grow one." Tulok said nothing and just turned and started walking back to camp as Safar smiled.

Isolde knitted her brow, "A beard? I mean she's right; a beard would look good on him but how would..." she paused and her eyes grew wide at the realization, "Oh...OHHHH...OH!" She looked back at the darkness but Koll had disappeared.

"Come on Island, we should probably give the Radiant

Father a moment to collect himself." Safar chuckled and tapped Isolde on the elbow.

"Actually...I think there is something we need to discuss – all of us," she said with a slightly guilty look on her face. "You asked about our purpose on the trip. I think we should tell you more before the storm hits.

Chapter 11

"You brought that forsaken object with you?!" Tulok spoke loudly at Isolde. It was not so much a yell, and certainly not a roar, but the giant priest was certainly displeased and there was no hiding it.

"What was I supposed to do with it?" Isolde countered. "I could not leave it back at the Temple. There was no telling how long we would be gone or when we would be back."

Tulok shook his head and flung his hands into the air in exasperation and paced the main area of the tent in frustration. Safar stood by the tent flap, his arms crossed, watching and listening to the exchange.

"Should I have dug a hole and buried it, and hoped no one else found it while we were gone?" she asked.

Tulok glanced at her and continued to pace, refusing to speak. His anger at the situation was palpable. Safar watched Tulok, assessing the level of rage that was currently being contained by the orc. He was struggling with controlled speech. The Reysis noted the observation and looked over at Isolde. The foreigner was clearly upset with the scenario. Her firm and sure countenance were flustered and unsteady. She was clearly faltering in her course of action.

Safar reached up and stroked his dark beard in thought. "What is this object?" the Reysis asked simply. Tulok waved at Isolde, indicating that she should explain, and he could not.

"The last duty I have to my Lord Knight." Isolde offered.

Safar urged her to continue, "Your flowery court phrases are appreciated; but I need you to speak plainly Island." Safar replied. "What are we dealing with?"

Tulok and Isolde exchanged glances.

Safar pursed his lips and spoke coolly, calmly and firmly, "I am responsible for the lives of every member of this caravan, and as The Healer is my witness, I will leave you both to the mercy of the sands, if you are keeping information from me...that...I...NEED." There was a power behind the Guide's words that would accept nothing more than compliance.

The Divine Powers that guarded and watched over the realms of Sanctuary were not always aloof and unknown characters of fiction or legend. Indeed, the Divine were very real; and many of them took a vested interest in the world and the peoples they had saved from the destruction of the Reaping. While They were forbidden from direct contact with the mortal realm; some were known to empower messengers to carry their favor to mortals who had caught their eye, or pleased Them in some fashion. The issue of this Divine Blessing often bore markings of their Otherworldly parentage. Perhaps it was unearthly beauty and grace, or even a terrifying visage that they had been blessed with. Perhaps it was inhuman strength, unshakable will, or even agelessness. Reynard the Swift's father had been such a one as this. His heroism had been legendary, and his courage unshakable. It left Isolde wondering about the power behind the Reysis's words.

"It ...it's a necklace...that has to be returned." Isolde stumbled over the words.

Tulok clenched his jaw. "It is a holy scarab." he managed.

Safar's eyebrows rose into his hairline. He looked directly at Isolde. "How did a holy scarab come into the possession of one of your people, Island?" he demanded.

Isolde looked between the two men. She took a breath, her shoulders slumped, she sighed deeply.

"I believe it was meant for the Magister of Deneb-aal. Reynard and I intercepted its delivery...by accident, from a Merchant who came to Brede, looking to deliver it to someone's next of kin, as the original purchaser was deceased. The merchant simply wanted to discharge his duty and be done. We agreed to make certain it made it to where it needed to go. That... trail...eventually brought us to Deneb-aal."

Safar inhaled sharply, it sounded like a hiss. "The Magister who was recently slain..."

Isolde nodded."The same."

Safar pursed his lips and thought some more, then continued. "Your knight, this is also where he died?" the dark man asked.

Isolde nodded. "Reynard sacrificed himself, to get me...and the necklace...to safety...so it could be properly dealt with," deep sorrow filled every word of Isolde's voice, as she dredged up the memory, still so new and fresh.

Safar raised the fingers of his right hand to his mouth and traced his lips in thought. He gestured to Tulok. "...and...the Radiant Father?"

Tulok glowered at Safar and then at Isolde, and continued his pacing. They could see the orc stretching his neck and shoulders as he walked. His hands clenched and unclenched at his sides.

Isolde's eyes fell on Tulok, they were filled with sorrow and apology, "There was a... Mazdan..." she said the word with a question in her voice.

"A Magi... spell crafter?" Safar offered.

Isolde nodded. "Yes. He told me that I should seek out the Temple of The Radiant Lord in Tarf-qua, and ask for their assistance, as this was a matter of importance to them."

"Why did you need a spell crafter? Why not ask another priest in Deneb-aal how to proceed or another merchant?" Safar asked, with genuine curiosity.

Isolde looked over at Tulok and then walked over to her side of the tent. She reached for her pack and untied its flap. Reaching deep inside, she slowly pulled out a small bundle, wrapped in what appeared to be white silk. The cloth was stained reddish-brown in some areas. The remnants of dried blood. The woman slowly untied the bundle, revealing a box, carved from dark wood. Etched along the edges and the top were various arcane symbols. Isolde was careful not to touch the box itself, and held it carefully, the scarf between the wood and her hand.

"Because I needed someone who could seal it and keep it safe," she said quietly.

As the box was displayed, Safar hissed once again and made a gesture. "The Silent! Put that away now!" he said quickly, striding toward Isolde. She moved to keep it out of the Guide's reach.

"No! You must not touch it!" she warned.

Safar stopped mid-stride as the realization came to him. Isolde moved to cover the box up once more and wrap it in its silken prison.

"That is what killed the Magister of Deneb-aal?" Safar asked.

Isolde nodded.

"Tell him how," Tulok growled.

Isolde balked at the change of tone from the big priest. She looked over at him with concern.

"Tulok?" she asked.

"Tell him!" the orc roared.

The faithful of the Lord Wanderer are gifted with unfailing Courage. They were charged with bringing inspiration and hope to the world. They know neither fear nor panic. Horror and alarm are foreign to them, such is the gift that His Divinity places upon their souls. Isolde duAvalonne paused at that moment, as the great creature who had been her boon companion seemed to revert to one of the barbarous monsters that roamed the coasts of her homeland. Reason left Tulok's eyes for the briefest of moments, and he was no longer the kind and gentle healer she had come to know.

She took a step back.

Safar moved swiftly to interpose himself between the gargantuan figure and the foreign knight. He spoke in the same strange tongue that the female orc had used earlier, and gestured with his body as was the way of the language.

Tulok snarled and gestured in response, slapping his chest and pointing at the bundle and then at the sky. Then he shoved past Safar and headed for the exit, pushing the dark man into Isolde with no more effort than one pushing a leaf on the water. Flinging the tent flap aside, he paused as the cool of the night air hit him fully. He lowered his head.

"I am... sorry," he said softly and strode out into the darkness, across the dunes.

Isolde watched Tulok storm away and moved as if to follow him. Safar reached out and grabbed her wrist, stopping her. "Reason has left him, Isolde." he used her proper name. "He needs time to purge his Rage. You cannot help him now."

Isolde continued to watch the doorway, part of her hoping that the big priest would step back inside, that he only needed to clear his head and catch a breath of fresh air. Then she looked back at Safar.

Safar gently released his grip on Isolde's arm, inclining his head in apology. "Tell me how the Magister died?" he asked her.

Isolde carefully took the bundle and tucked it safely back into the bottom of her pack. "I am not certain I know how to explain it." she replied, not looking at Safar.

"Try...please." the dark man asked.

"It was..." she began. "It was as if his body suddenly erupted into flame...but the flames did not burn him?" she offered. "They...seemed to desiccate him?" she said and looked back up to Safar. Safar's dark skin was pale. "And... empower...him?" she offered. "He was dead without being dead, and Reynard..." she took in a sharp shuddering breath. "Reynard stood as a bulwark against him...it...I was able to collect the...scarab...and shove it back into its box...but... Reynard...it...it was too late..." the knight swallowed a sob. Heated tears ran down her sand-stained face. She looked up at Safar.

The dark Guide's stern countenance faded for a moment, and he stepped in to offer the woman an embrace of support in a time of loss. It was accepted, and Isolde wrapped her arms around Safar and wept tears of grief for the first time since coming to this strange land. It was a moment of emotional need from both of them, born of the seriousness of the situation. After a moment, the sorrow had passed and Isolde nodded, stepping away. She reached for the end of her headscarf and wiped her face with it.

"I never meant to bring this upon your people." She said quietly.

"No." Safar corrected her. "You did not do this thing,

Island. Do not think that," he spoke clearly to her. "The assassin, who commissioned that item, brought this here...and now...we must repay them in kind."

Chapter 12

It is said that there is a silence that fills the ears right before a storm hits. This is because the Red Lord is drawing His breath and is about to release it upon the desert. The silence is often heavy and warm and leaves all waiting in anticipation.

When the light breeze died, everyone in the caravan felt it. It had been a few hours, but they were all prepared due to the earlier warning. A bright green banner had been tied securely to a pole in the middle of the camp. It bore no insignia but served as a visual reminder of one location and the direction of the wind. Outside each tent, a guide rope had been secured into the ground to allow travel between tents if it became necessary. The members of the caravan stood by their tent anchors watching both Safar and the lone banner. Both the Reysis and the banner were still as the wind they waited for. It was as if each were waiting for the other to flinch. Without the breeze – the heat from the sand rose up and caused brows and backs to sweat.

The banner flickered slightly and the tension rose up. Safar made no movement and no one moved. The wind's direction had not been defined and they all knew that they had to wait until the Reysis gave the signal. With the direction of the wind declared, they would spring into action and with the tent anchors and move accordingly. If they judged the wind wrong, the tents would be facing the wrong direction. This could cause their shelters to catch too much air to cause them to blow away or become shredded if the wind was powerful enough. Isolde's section of the tent was struck as walls became part of the reinforced shelter. Like the rest, she waited outside the tent with her hands on the anchor rope. There was no joking or laughter – just waiting. Like all of them, she was focused on Safar and the banner.

On the other side, Tulok stood with the beast handlers. Once the direction of the wind had been declared, the animals would need to be moved inside and with his added strength, he could help force a stubborn camel into a shelter for its own survival. He had not spoken to anyone and only nodded his head to acknowledgment to the other handlers as they took their places. After the incident earlier – the Orc had disappeared from everyone's view and no one wanted to ask any questions.

The breeze picked up the banner and slightly flowed from east to the west, but Safar waited. The breeze wavered and dropped.

Isolde hated waiting and she could feel the sweat running down her back and building upon her brow. She rubbed the rope in her gloved hands and shifted in place. She was not alone in this; stealing a glance, she could see the wait wearing on the others as they moved in place slowly so they could spring into action.

Suddenly the wind whipped from the west and blew down to the south. The banner snapped into a southern direction at the same time that Safar shouted a command and everyone sprung into action. The tents all shifted in tandem and others set to work pounding in new anchors. A few of the Vidria served in this capacity and they caused the sand to harden into place, anchoring the tent as securely as possible. Isolde marveled at the desert magic for a moment before she tied off the last secure portion and ducked inside. She was followed in by Arman, a Vidiran merchant who had helped secure the tents; the Acolyte Kalb who tried to look stoic but she could see the fear running in his eyes; and Safar who was the last person to enter the tents before the wind and dust became too much. Knocking the dust off his face and arms, he began securing the entrance flaps and then sat down with a deep sigh.

"The Stormchaser was upfront about all of this. Remind me to thank the Radiant Father later. She could have easily let us be caught unawares. If he had not established his place with her, she might not have been so gracious to give us the forewarning," Safar said gratefully.

"What do you mean by 'established his place'?" Isolde asked, "Like a wolf or a dog establishing dominance?"

"Yes and no, but I would not use that as an example around the Orcs," Safar said with a smile. "While it is a show of dominance – it is also a show of balance. Koll came to us rolling too close to her rage and I think that is what the Radiant Father sensed. Like calls on to like and it called to him to answer. However, his level of control was equally frightening." He looked over at Isolde, "The Radiant Father 'shamed' Koll into civility. The staring contest between the two was about control over their rage. The Radiant Father, despite what happened after, may have saved us."

"Did the *Storm Lover* say when this madness would cease," said a somewhat whiney voice in the back. It was Bengt Kalb and oddly, this was the first time Isolde heard him speak. She hadn't expected that tone and almost thought it was the Vidria rather than the man in the back.

Safar answered, "Unfortunately, the *Hand of the Changebringer* did not give us a timetable for her Lord's reckoning," he said with a harsh tone. Something in his voice said that Safar did not like this man, and everyone in the tent felt it. "Perhaps you would like to ask her yourself. I'm sure she is out there ready to take your questions concerning the matters of her Lord."

Offended, Bengt sat up, "I mean no disrespect – but we are being held up because there is a *chance* something *evil* is combing the desert? There are a lot of things out in the sands and not all of them are good! All I am saying is it seems a little too convenient for her to slow us down in the name of her *lord*. How do we know that this is not some sort of ruse to rob or take us captive?"

"You would have nothing to fear Acolyte – I am certain you will be quite safe from being taken as a captive," Safar said matter-of-factly. The dismissal of the comment was not lost on the Acolyte and he opened his mouth as if to say something else. Safar only raised his eyebrow and the other man forced himself into silence. The Reysis were kings of the road and what little wisdom the Acolyte possessed reminded him of that.

Arman cracked a small smile at Isolde but was careful to not face the Acolyte. While the Reysis had the ability to belittle a priest, a simple traveler could not. Instead, the Vidria merchant took out a small rock of sandstone and began working it in his hands. Isolde watched him play with the rock and started to shape it in his hands. Looking at the concentration of his eyes, she could see that this was delicate work instead of what he had done earlier. Before he just reached both his hands into the sand and it solidified into place. While amazing to watch – this was more fascinating as pieces took on an almost glass-like appearance instead of just hardened stone.

A scream of the wind came suddenly and hit the tent's side. It bowed deeply at the first hard gusts blew through the camp. Isolde had been through some of the worst rainstorms Avalon had to offer. Winds and rains that had devastated coastal villages. She remembered spending several months helping to rebuild a township that had all but collapsed entirely one season. This was different. The scream sounded like a wailing creature in pain. The sound boomed in her ears and cleaved into her spine. Safar sat by the entrance of the tent. He occasionally peered outside, to get an idea of how others were faring. Isolde stood and moved to the wall opposite the Reysis and sat. He looked over at the knight with a note of curiosity. Settling in, she met his honey brown eyes with her own and glanced briefly in the direction of both the merchant and the skinny Acolyte that were with them. She could feel the discomforting sense of unease on both of them. She looked back to the Reysis. Safar nodded almost imperceptibly. They were the shield against the storm for these others. Both serving as beacons in the darkness on this night. She took a deep breath and settled into a position of watchful waiting while the winds screamed around them.

~~~

The camels did not need much in the way of being persuaded into the larger tent. The creatures could smell the change of weather long before the caravan could. When the tent was erected, they simply waited to be led in. Tulok sat near the beast he had been riding, running his hands along its neck. The other herders were doing the same, though it was more for them to keep occupied than comforting the animals. Listening to the wind, Tulok let his mind wander to a time long before when he had gotten lost in a sandstorm. He was young and unprepared but wholly determined to make his way to somewhere new. If it were not for the kindness of two strangers, his story would have literally been lost to the sands. The camel next to him
~~~

stirred and raised its head up. Looking around, all the other camels had already followed suit. The rest of the herders all turned their gaze in the same direction that the camels were staring and listened. The wind screamed and the tent continued to move with each burst – but something sounded different. The howls of the wind were normally felt all around – but there was something more directional with it. Something large slammed into the side of the tent wall across from Tulok. The animals began to object and attempt to stand. Around him, camel herders grabbed their lead ropes and watched as something hit the wall again. The walls of the tent were made to take the punishment of a thousand grains of sand being flung at it with untold speeds. Whatever was being thrown was not heavy enough to breach the fabric. A third time something was flung at the wall – except this time it stayed. It was soon followed by rhythmic and frantic pounding. A person pounding on the tent wall! As realization slowly dawned, a long black object pierced the tent. It was red and black, and easily the length of an arm. The smell of blood and musk filled the tent and the camels began to pull at their reigns in a panic. The long talon-like object pulled itself out of the tent wall as those closest to it began pulling their animals to the other side.

Another puncture. Now they all could see the object for what it was – the barbed stinger of a giant scorpion. Looking at one of the herders, Tulok threw his lead rope at the man and unlooped the mace from his belt. Touching the medallion on his chest and murmuring a few words, the Priest summoned the power of his God. A bright light slowly began to surround the priest. The herders could feel the divinity of the Radiant Lord's presence echo through the room. Taking another step forward, Tulok pulled back with the mace and slammed it into the point of the tail. The chitin armor cracked under the blow, but the barbed weapon did not break. There was a chittering scream as the creature freed itself from the wall. The priest had hoped that the pain was enough to make it wary of striking here again. Dust and sand flowed through the holes, but no one moved as they waited to see if there would be any more strikes. The ground was hardened beneath the tent. It lessened the worry about the scorpion burrowing from underneath them. The creatures were not innately evil, so their presence there was not a surprise – but he needed to know more.

~~~

"Did that sound like someone screaming?" Bengt asked. Safar and Isolde looked over at him and frowned. "No, really – listen! I swore I heard someone screaming outside." He clutched at his holy symbol and began muttering prayers to his god.

Safar closed his eyes and focused on the sounds of the storm, trying to sort through them all. The howl of the wind, the flapping of the tents, the scraping sounds of sand as it whooshed across the fabric, the calls of the caravan in their own tents as they battled with ropes and anchors

The bellowing of camels.

The Sun Guide's eyes flew open. He reached for his flask and poured water over his scarf and pulled it across his face. He tossed the flask to Isolde.

"They need our help," Safar said quickly. "Water your scarf, it will help to filter the sand out. Water may not be falling from the sky, but you still cannot breathe the earth," he commented.

Isolde watched Safar's actions and followed his instructions. She wet her face scarf and tied it around her lower face. Safar shook his head and crossed to meet her. He pulled the cloth up and across her face once more, so that only the smallest slit of her flesh was visible. Just enough to
~~~

see. He tucked the cloth around her head expertly and nodded.

"Keep your head tucked and protect your eyes. The scarf will help with your breathing, but you are not a camel, and sand will get into your eyes and blind you if you are not careful," he instructed.

She nodded in understanding. Looking down, she did a quick inventory of her gear. Safar gestured under her nose. She looked up. "Eyes on me, Island, do you understand me?" the Guide asked. "The wind and the sand will disorient you. The sound will make you deaf. You keep your eyes on me. You step where I step, you move where I move." Isolde nodded once more. He reminded her of Reynard then, confident, firm, sure of himself and his surroundings. A teacher.

"Leave your shield, it will only get in the way and the wind will use it as a sail," he instructed once more. Again, she nodded.

"Wait, are you BOTH leaving to go out there?" the weasley figure of Bengt asked. Isolde could feel the panic on his tiny frame.

She turned to face the sallow-skinned priest and spoke. Her words were calm and sure. "I cannot fight what I cannot see Brother Bengt. Here there is only wind, and something seeking to cripple our caravan. Will you offer me the blessing of The Radiant Lord, so that I may protect you on this night?" The sallow-skinned priest paused at her words. Clarity of purpose returned to his eyes for a moment. He placed one hand over his heart and the other upon Isolde's head and intoned quietly.

He whose body is light
He whose soul is the sky
He who is Father of the World
Bless this child and show her the way.

Isolde bowed her head in thanks and stepped back to rejoin Safar. The Guide watched between the two, his eyes narrowing for a moment and focusing on Bengt. Then he nodded and touched Isolde's elbow. "Eyes on me," he repeated and flipped open the tent door.

Chapter 13

Wind and sand and sound assailed her senses the moment she stepped out. Unprepared for the force of the winds she staggered slightly, Safar reached out to grab her and steady her. He shouted against the howling of the wind that carried his voice away with it.

"With me!" he called.

She nodded and ducked her face to press into the headwind.

All around them, tent walls bent and bowed under the heavy hand of the Changebringer. Sand skittered across their billowing tops and slammed into their windward walls, threatening to cave them in. Barely visible light glowed from beneath loose edges as the tents flapped and railed and threatened to set themselves free in the winds. The light from the gaps in the tents bounced off of the swirling sand, illuminating the camp with an eerie glow and casting shadows that otherwise would not be seen.

Across the wailing of the wind and the howls of the sand, Isolde thought she heard another sound. Deeper, darker, out of place. Her eyes followed the booted feet of Safar who stepped ahead of her, bracing against the wind. He was leading them in the direction of the foreign sound. She tried to look up, to gauge position, understand distance, the merciless sands filled what little of her face showed, she blinked and ducked her head once more. The cloth at her face made breathing difficult, but it served as a filter for the fine dust that would have otherwise filled her lungs and ceased her breath altogether. She slowed her breathing. Shallow breaths, with the occasional deep breath. She plodded onward.

"There, Island, do you see them?!" Safar yelled, he reached back and tugged at her, turning to shelter against the wind as much as he could while pointing in the direction of the camel's tent.

Two enormous shadows played against the eerie cast of the lighted sand. One tall and broad, outlined in the shimmer of light, the other long and oddly shaped, larger than the size of a horse; its movements were quick and insectoid in nature.

"*Swammerdami...*" Safar swore under his breath at the sight.

"What is it!?" Isolde yelled in the wind.

"Emperor of the Sands!" Safar yelled back. "Scorpion, Island!"

Isolde shaded her eyes from the sands and looked toward the enemy and who it was fighting. There was only one other figure in the camp that could cast a figure of that enormity. She watched as the shadows seemed to dodge one another, a giant fencing match hidden by sand.

Tulok.

Isolde reached for her longsword and made it ready to unsheathe from its scabbard.

Safar yelled against the wind once more, "Watch the pincers first!" he called out as he moved to pull two wicked-looking long blades from his waist sash. "They are hard, like armor..." he reached out and hit her breastplate with the pommel of his blade. "And if it stings you, Island." he held her gaze, his eyes firm and intent on his message. "You will die."

They approached the pair, pushing through the wind and the sand, watching as the orc grappled with the poisoned tail. Tulok was positioned behind the great beast and was using his brute strength to hold on to the tail. His own weight and strength prevented the scorpion from using its deadliest of weapons. At the same time – it kept the priest from the combat. He had sacrificed his ability to engage the creature, to serve as a stanchion and hold it in place. Veins stood out on the bands of his muscled arms as he dug in deeper. Other members of the caravan had armed themselves with spears and swords and tried to attack the creature from the sides to no avail. Their weapons were useless against the creature's dense black armor.

"Aim for the eyes Island!" Safar shouted "If we can take one or two out, it may decide to leave. I will take the left, you go right. If it grabs your weapon – hold on to get close to it and then stab it in the eye with this," he said as he handed her a dagger. He grasped the hilts of his strange curved weapons and nodded at Isolde. Together they surged forward and each slammed the full force of their weapon in the pincers.

Throwing the creature off balance, the attempted surge only resulted in the creature spinning itself with the orc in tow. The creature pulled Tulok from his place in the sand and swung its tail, with the orc still attached, and slammed Tulok into the pair – knocking them to the ground. The orc roared in frustration and dug his feet into the ground. Hugging the tail, his arms wrapped tightly around one section of the deadly weapon. He reached for his medallion and began to pray.

The scorpion snapped its great pincher inches from Safar's stomach. The Guide shouted something that Isolde could not understand and he slammed his blade into the claw and broke through. It cracked open like an egg. The scorpion tried to pull back its pincher, but Safar held his blade tight and forced it to go deeper. The creature hissed and noise erupted from it that she had never heard before. It was akin to a scream. It was injured. In the moment of its pain, Isolde saw her chance and lunged forward. She stabbed into what she thought was its face. It was like a striking stone. She felt the strike reflect back into her injured arm. She yelled in both pain and frustration at the recoil.

"ONE EYE!" she heard Tulok shout, "IT ONLY HAS ONE MIDDLE EYE!"

Lord Wanderer help me, Isolde said to herself. She had to strike a one-eyed monster in the middle of the night during a sandstorm with barely any way to see.

You have more senses than your sight, a quiet voice inside her echoed. *You have one chance.*

Isolde closed her eyes and suddenly stood very still. Safar yelled at her to move. Tulok struggled to regain a hold on the creature. A pincer snapped near her cheek and snipped off a wavering bit of scarf over her face. She felt the change in the air around her, and around the creature. In her mind's eye she imagined one single black bulbous eye on the creature before her. Her fingers tightened on the hilt of her weapon. She reached back and lunged forward again. A warm presence, almost like a gentle hand, nudged her balance just a few inches over.

The creature screamed in pain.

The winds stopped.

Isolde's eyes flew open. Her sword was buried into the carapace of the creature, which was now flailing wildly in the sand. It began using its back legs to dig into the soft dirt and burrow backward, trying to get away. Realizing where the beast was headed, Tulok released his grip and flung himself away.

Isolde allowed herself to smile slightly and attempted to pull her weapon out of the creature as it scrambled away. It was stuck fast. She frowned and reached to place both hands on the hilt, attempting to dislodge the weapon, even as she was pulled along with the creature and into the sand.

"ISLAND LET IT GO NOW!" she heard Safar shout.

"NO, I CANNOT LOSE THIS!" Isolde shook her head and screamed back, trying to brace herself against the pull of the creature and free her weapon.

Tulok looked up from the sand and saw what was happening. Forcing himself up from his prone position, he moved to rush forward toward the knight. Before he could close the distance between them, Safar, moving faster than a human could normally, slammed his body into Isolde's. The force of impact freed the blade and flung the two away from the sand trap being created in the scorpion's exit. The two of them hit the ground and rolled. They came to a stop, Isolde sprawled on the desert floor, Safar atop her.

The dark man looked down at the knight and shook his head with both amusement and annoyance in his eyes and voice. "You are... stubborn sometimes...Island," the Sun Guide said as he smiled at her, taking deep breaths.

There was movement in the sand from behind them. Tulok shouted a warning but it was not soon enough. Safar's body stiffened suddenly and his back arched. His eyes grew wide with both surprise and pain. A stinger exploded from the center of his chest as the wounded scorpion found its mark, striking Safar from behind. Blood sprayed across Isolde and the sand. She screamed as Safar was yanked off of her by the creature and pulled back into the sand pit with the scorpion. Scrambling up, she leaped forward and grabbed Safar's hand. His fingers flinched, attempting to grasp hold of her. She felt herself being pulled into the earth with the sand closing around her. Sand fell atop her body, closing off the world above, filling her ears, her nose, her mouth. She struggled to hold onto Safar and to hold her breath. She felt something grab her legs and felt her body being stretched as the weight of the earth was refusing to let go of its Avalonian prize. Fingers stretched, grasped, slipped, and tried to grasp again. Tulok's tired body used the last of its reserves and pulled the knight from the earth; her hands empty.

"NOOOOOOOO!!!" Isolde screamed as she frantically tried to lunge forward into the sand, to recover Safar. The Orc's massive arms pulled her back and held her tight against him. She screamed and pounded at the sand with her fists.

The storm ended and the skies were once again clear.

~~~

Taking an assessment of the caravan took the rest of the night, and left them wanting for solid rest, as well as direction. Safar's absence was deeply felt, not only by Isolde and Tulok but by the rest of those traveling with them. He had been an almost legendary figure on these sands, and the thought of him being gone seemed surreal to many of them.

Gathered in reverent silence, the caravan paid respects to those whose lives had been lost the evening before. The Radiant Father gathered them to lift their hands and their hearts to the sky and ask that the heavens remember their fallen. In solemnity he placed his hand over his broad chest, covering his heart, and spoke faithful words, entreating the grim Lord of the Path to guide the souls of the recently deceased to their final rest.

"Let their lives be judged worthy, and may they not be left to wander the sands seeking peace." he intoned softly.
~~~

Isolde watched from a place of distance and respect at the simple ceremony. Losing companions on the road was never easy. Her father used to tell her that one could judge a person by the way they treated their dead. Lord Niall had been a man of faith, sworn as much to the mysteries as he had been to the town and the people. He...and they... were all gone now. She stretched and flexed her right hand; remembering the blisters from having dug so many graves. She closed her eyes and wrapped her hand around the totem of her faith and whispered a prayer for the dead, then left the caravan members to tend to their grief while she made ready her supplies.

~~~

Furtive glances and hushed tones followed Isolde as she took inventory of her gear and the goods she had been responsible for maintaining. Some made warding gestures as she passed by, others spat after her, still, others turned away entirely. It was clear they blamed her for the loss of Reysis Safar. The Knight Wanderer withstood their withering glares and continued her movements and actions, intent on purpose. Teeth clenched, shoulders set, the woman forced her body through the repetition of moving, stacking, sorting, and shifting.

Tulok's trained eye could tell that she was suffering. Not only was she enduring the physical pain of injuries that were still healing; but also the emotional turmoil of losing yet one more person in her life. He finished assessing the last camel; his eyes watching the foreign woman from a distance. The desert had taken so much from her since her arrival. It was a miracle that she was still sound of mind.

"...her fault, you know." he caught the last part of a sentence. Tulok's brow furrowed and he turned in the direction of the voice. Two men stood next to one of the camels, close together in quiet conversation.
~~~

"She brought something with her. That's what I heard..."

The big priest narrowed his eyes and stepped from behind the land beast. It lowered its head in complaint at being disturbed. Both men started and stepped back, averting their eyes and looking at the sand.

"Apologies, Radiant Father." one of them spoke.

"You know not of what you speak." Tulok cautioned in his deep voice.

The men exchanged glances. "Of course...as you say."

Tulok took a step in their direction, his imposing figure towering over them both. "Yes. As. I. Say." he punctuated. His tone would not accept the argument.

The men nodded and shifted uncomfortably in the sand. "Go and find Jamal, Safar's second. He needs to get our bearings after the storm, so we can plan our leg for today."

Neither man moved.

Tulok, tucked his chin and considered his words, then addressed them both once more.

"You can move... or you can BE moved. The choice is yours. I wrestled with an Emperor of the Sand less than three hours ago. You would not wish for me to apply that second option right now."

Both men quickly ducked their heads in respect and darted off to find the new Guide.

Tulok took a deep breath and centered himself once more. The irritations of the previous night still wore on his soul. His rage gnawed on the edges of his reason, seeking an avenue for an exit. He could not allow such to happen. Not here, not now. He glanced in Isolde's direction, watching her once more. She paused in her actions. She reached for her shoulder, shifting it and rolling it. Her face scrunched up almost imperceptibly. Tulok set his jaw and strode across the campground. Members of the caravan cleared a wide path for the big priest as he moved with determined intent.

Isolde turned her face in Tulok's direction as he approached. She held up her hand and tried to wave him off. Tulok held up a warning finger at the tall woman, then pointed at a bundle of bedrolls that had been stacked to be ready for loading. "Sit. Now," he ordered.

"I'm fine." she countered firmly.

"You are injured...still..." he replied in his deep tones, "...and a terrible liar."

Her eyes widened and then narrowed.

"I would prefer we not take our grief out on each other..." Tulok offered with a simple gesture.

Isolde clenched her jaw, swallowing words that begged to be free. Instead, she nodded simply and moved toward the pile of blankets and sat. Tulok reached for her arm, skilled hands and fingers gently prodding at joints and muscles, assessing the damage. He pressed at the joint of her shoulder, tracing muscle and ligament around the attachment points. She winced and hissed as she inhaled sharply. Tulok nodded and continued his assessment.

"You've torn it." he commented.

"Probably."

He pursed his lips and looked at the items around them. "..and continue to make it worse by working it without asking for help."

She grunted in reply.

Tulok pressed his index finger into a soft spot on her shoulder. She winced again. "His death is not your fault."

She did not reply, choosing instead to fix her eyes on the camels across the way.

"Do you hear me?" he asked her quietly.

She continued in her silence.

"Isolde..." Tulok prodded once more with his words and not his hands. His tone once again that of the gentle healer who had saved her life. Her eyes turned to look up at him. "It was not your fault. You did everything you could possibly have done..." he counseled.

"The sand will have its due..." Isolde whispered softly.

Tulok frowned, watching her. "Pardon?"

"Something Safar said..." she replied. "The Sand will have its due, in blood or water, even of the sand-blooded."

The healer worked the injured area gently as he spoke. His hands were warm and soothing. He nodded, "So it is said."

Isolde held the big man's eyes, "You saved my life a second time, Father."

Tulok shrugged and continued his ministrations, "My Lord would not have it be otherwise." He offered her a weary smile. "And we are not yet done, after all."

She chuckled a little at that. It was a bittersweet sound. "No, I suppose not."

He nodded and patted her gently on the shoulder, then moved to withdraw his hand. She reached up to grasp his hand with her own and just held it for a moment, looking up at him. She was road tired and soul-weary, alone in this world save for him and her God. Instinctively he touched her cheek with the back of his right hand and then tucked a loose strand of hair behind her left ear and then helped her to stand.

"Thank you." she offered quietly.

Tulok watched her and nodded and then looked to the sky. False dawn would be upon them soon. "Jamal should be able to get us to the city today," he commented. Pursing his lips in thought, he examined the surrounding area. Everything that had been recognizable just a few hours prior was gone. "We may have to press harder in the heat, to make it; but if Safar taught him well...and I have no reason to doubt that he would...he'll get us there shortly after nightfall." The orc's gaze lowered back onto the knight. "Will you be alright?" he asked.

"I can make the trek well enough." she nodded, stretching her arm and testing her knee.

Tulok tapped the center of his chest and replied, "I meant here." he said gently. "I can heal your body, but I have no salve to heal the sorrow in your soul..." he shrugged a little. "At least none that the Wanderer has not already gifted you with."

Isolde's eyes met Tulok's. They were filled with compassion and thanks. She reached out and placed her gloved right hand on his strong forearm and squeezed it. "In this...Your Radiance..." she used his title, "I think we will lean on each other for a little while if you will permit it...and if it will not be seen as a weakness in the eyes of your Lord?" she inquired hopefully.

Tulok looked down at Isolde's hand on his arm and then back to her face. He covered her hand with his own. "My Lord did not place us on this world to wander it alone, Ser Knight," he replied in kind.

They stood there a moment, two people sharing silent grief, and strength of purpose. The inclemency of the islands, and the savagery of the sands bound in destiny and design that neither could have ever envisioned.

Chapter 14

Jamal seemed young, even to Isolde, despite his tanned skin and distant eyes. It was the eyes that threw her. While they were not the strange eyes of Safar – this boy, no this Sun Guide's eyes had seen pain far too often for one his age. She looked around at the others and here and there she saw experience, pain, and pride – but Jamal's eyes stared beyond the sand. He was only a hair shorter than the knight, but she watched as he towered above everyone. Tulok and the new Sun Guide had walked over to the nearby dune and the orc lifted Jamal up in the air and then higher still. Tulok held him by the feet and stretched his arms out the full length. He was taller than a building at this point and she wondered what kind of vantage point was possible in this sea of sand.

Jamal retrieved a strange instrument – much akin to an ancient ship's sextant, but this was shaped differently and looked like it was made of bone and gold. He peered around the horizon as the priest slowly turned in a circle. On any other day, this would have been an amazing sight to see; yet no one was laughing. With the markers destroyed around them, Jamal was looking for distant anchor points to lead them in the right direction. They were less than a day's travel from Nahral, but if they choose the wrong direction, their lives would get much more difficult. The fight had not only taken the caravan's Sun Guide but one of the herders, a merchant, and his bodyguard. The scorpion had sliced off the leg of the herder and he eventually bled out, one of the first victims. The bodyguard had died from presumably standing in front of the merchant and died from the stinger's poisoned strike. The merchant was found against the beast tent as he was the last victim before Tulok grappled its murderous tail.

There was a light breeze in the air, but it wasn't enough to cool anyone off as the dawn was already approaching. They had lost rest and time so their only chance was a hard push to the city of Nahral before the brilliance of the Radiant Lord came down hard on them. Everyone stared at Jamal from afar; he was either their salvation or their doom and only The Radiant Lord knew.

Tulok lowered Jamal down and they looked southward, at least to what Isolde thought was south. The two hurried down from the dune and Jamal cried out, "Load up, the Eagle's Crest was untouched. We can make it there by midday and rest. From there we will make it to our destination by the time The Radiant Lord has moved on to the next land. We live to see another day!"

The tension broke at Jamal's proclamation, and while there were not any cheers – there was a definite positive feeling. Helping break down the sun tent that had been set up while the Priest and Sun Guide were on the dune, Isolde asked Arman, "So the Eagle's Crest was untouched? What is it?"

The Vidria gave a sly smile, "A testament to Vidria craftsmanship. There are those of us who do not agree with the Red Lord's need for change as some things must be rooted in place so that the future has a starting point to remember." The small man smiled up at Isolde, "Long ago, the first crafters who understood the power of the sand and earth wanted to create a monument to help travelers. There are three such structures, but I have only seen one. From a distance – it looks like crystal mountains breaking out of the sand. When you get closer – you see that they are the feathers of an outstretched wing. The crafters asked Him," motioning upward, "for guidance and an eagle circled them. Some say that this was the sign of another god who had died during the Reaping, and the crafters felt it was a fitting tribute. After it was erected – there was a violent sandstorm the likes of which no one has ever seen. Such fury would have broken down the stone. However," Arman pulled out the small stone from the night before, "our gift is built from the very sand that made up the Red Lord's fury. Instead of being destroyed – the first crafters made the monument larger with all the sand being thrown at them. The tallest feather is said to be four or five buildings high!" He laughed to himself as he and Isolde folded up the last of the fabric walls. "I'm sure the other two monuments have interesting stories about them – but the Eagle's Crest was the first to give the Vidria a place in the desert."

Isolde nodded, listening. She took the folded walls of the tent from the merchant and smiled at him. "Thank you for the lesson." the Witness inclined her head.

"My pleasure," Arman replied and turned to tend his own goods.

The caravan sprung into shared action and was soon underway. With the addition of unburdened camels, the trip to the Eagle's Crest would take less time. Admittedly the pace was a bit faster as Isolde spent the majority holding on to her seat. She still hadn't gotten used to riding camels. She almost imagined Safar smiling at her when he saw her trying to maintain her balance on it during the beginning of the trip. His advice did help her sore tailbone, but the memory stung because of how fresh it was. She had only known him for this trip – but his personality left its mark on her soul. Much like Reynard – the power of his charisma and character would be something she could never forget.

"You seem to be riding better," Tulok said.

She turned toward him, realizing she had been lost in the memories of two people. Reynard would have hit her backside with a stick of rattan for not paying attention while she was riding. Luckily the camel didn't follow her direction but the direction of the one in front of it. She turned to the priest who was keeping a partial eye on her as well as the path in front of them. Jamal was in the front as was customary of the leader, but she could tell from his glances that the orc wanted to help him. Doing so would have been wrong as this was what Jamal had trained for. This was the boy's moment to prove himself, and to help him now would be a disservice, so the priest only watched.

Rather than bring it to attention, Isolde answered, "A friend told me what I was doing wrong," she said with a kind of half-smile. She added, "Have you ever seen the Eagle's Crest?"

"Four times," he replied. "The first time was when I made my first trip to this city...and then three times after that going back and forth. I do not think I have made a trip to that place on pleasant terms save the first time. It is a magnificent sight to behold, so I hope your next trip to it is better than your first."

She nodded and remembered his story about the merchant and his own mistake, "Well they say the fifth time's the charm."

Tulok raised an eyebrow, "Do they now?"

She smiled at him and he quietly chuckled to himself, "I'm going to check on the rear and the rest of our travelers.

Jamal doesn't have a second, so I am going to lend him a hand."

"Did you ask him if you could?" Isolde asked.

His full attention was on her, "What do you mean if I asked him? I do not nee..."

Before he could finish, "As you told me, the Sun Guide's word is the law on the sands," interrupted Isolde.

"Then what does..." he stopped himself. He pursed his lips and looked down, shaking his head. "You are right, my apologies," Tulok said nothing more because he understood the point that Isolde was making. As much as he wanted the young Sun Guide to succeed, Jamal had to be treated as the Sun Guide with all respect that the position was due. "I will see where Jamal needs me." He ushered the camel forward and it sped up its pace.

Isolde smiled as he rode on.

"Reysis Jamal," Tulok called out as he rode up slowly, "May I approach?"

Jamal turned his head back to face the orc, "Father? Yes, of course, is everything okay?

"Things are fine, but I wanted to know where you needed me. As you do not have a second, I would like to volunteer myself to be your extra eyes where you see fit," the priest said.

Jamal looked at him curiously for a moment before turning his face back to the road. Tulok kept his camel at the same pace and did not usher it to proceed further. He could feel the eyes of those behind him watching. Jamal was leading them, but he had to show that he could lead them. They rode in silence for what seemed like an eternity in the orc's mind. Tulok hoped that The Scribe would inspire wisdom in the young man.

Jamal turned back to the orc, "You had mentioned earlier that you had been to the Eagle's Crest earlier. Take my place here – I want to see how we are running at this added pace. We may be able to go a bit faster but I want to check if our men can keep up. Oh, how is your friend? Is she able to handle the pace with her injuries?"

Thank you, Wise Scribe, he said to himself, "She is adapting well and if we speed up the pace, she will deal fine. Thank you for the honor of leading Reysis."

The two switched places and the new Sun Guide began his inspection of the caravan. As Jamal eventually passed Isolde and gave her a welcoming nod, the Avalonian returned it with a respectful bow of her head. Keeping her eyes on the road ahead, she watched the orc lead the train in front all the while listening to the conversation of the rest of the travelers around her. While she could not understand the language, she felt the confidence in their tone – Jamal would do Safar proud.

Chapter 15

The sand that stretched for endless miles in either direction slowly began to give way to broken areas of sandstone and calcified sediment, changing the landscape before them. Strange formations rose from the smooth surface of the desert-like malformed and listing mushroom towers. They stood as a testament to the ferocity of the wind and the voracious hunger of the Lords of the Sands. Here and there lone patches of green erupted from the colorless earth, hinting at the life that lay hidden somewhere far below. Camels stretched their long necks in attempts to grab at the tempting greens but were pulled back into line and clucked at in reproach. They lowed and groaned in displeasure, but continued along their plodding way.

Soft sand transitioned to a more solid surface as the sloping walls of the strange edifice that had been pulled from the earth by the shaping skills of the Vidria thousands of years past. Sandstone rose and fell, dipped and swooped in slopes and patterns that did not seem possible. Formations stretched like taffy and jagged rocks protruding from the sand like the claws of some long-dead beast lying in wait. Colors shifted from pale sand to warm, fiery oranges, rich with iron and oxidized for centuries. It was as if the heavens had laid out wide ribbons of layered earth, and then raised them to the sky, only to let them fall gently in place; then froze them in time before they could flatten once more.

The rippling sea of sand sloped and undulated, producing a radiant display of colors that abruptly disturbed the serene monotony of the dunes. The slopes climbed higher, like a vast tidal wave of sandstone; these camels then were truly ships of the sand. It was perhaps one of the most awe-inspiring sights that Isolde duAvalonne had ever witnessed in her short lifetime.

"You're gawking." Tulok chuckled from beside her, smiling at her amazement.

Isolde blinked and looked around and stared, and blinked again. "I... how...this... this is amazing," she whispered in awe.

Tulok nodded. "All done at the hands of the Vidria when they first came to Sanctum."

The Knight Wanderer continued to ogle the area. "But...why?"

Again, the gentle shrug of the massive shoulders. "Some say it was a test of their gifts here, others say they were tired of the sloping sands," he cast a side-eye at Isolde, "Some say it was done for the sole intent of irritating the mad god because they disagreed with His divine plan." a smile tugged at the corner of his mouth.

Isolde broke away from the sandstone monuments and looked over at Tulok, "What do YOU think?" she asked the priest.

Tulok looked up and around them, the heat of the sun was already beating on their backs. The sandstone mountains loomed in front of them; a promise of shade and shelter hid somewhere within their crevasses. "I think ... only the Vidria know the truth...and..." he paused to look back at the dwarven merchant who was traveling with them, "... and they will tell whatever story is needed at the time."

Isolde frowned and glanced backward. The Vidria merchant was cheerfully chatting away at several other members of the caravan, pointing out areas in the sand.

"I've heard four different origin tales of these formations. Each one from a different Vidria, during each of my passings. We may never know the truth of it all."

Jamal called the caravan to a halt at the base of a tall formation. Turning, he slid down off of his mount and began to examine the sand and the sandstone. He pulled his gloves off and placed his bare hands on the hot surface of the ground, and closed his eyes for a moment. Everything stood still, waiting. Isolde listened to the beat of her heart as it pounded in her chest, anxious to know what the results of the actions of the Reysis would yield. She looked over at Tulok hoping for guidance. He only shrugged in response.

"Speaking to the sand is not something my Lord teaches us." he offered quietly.

Jamal stood, brushing his hands off on his pants, and glanced skyward, tracing the horizon and then back to the undulating walls before him. He frowned and took several steps back, then adjusted his footing and titled his head to the side. Everyone held their breath.

Suddenly the Sun Guide's youthful face erupted into a broad smile and he reached to pull his gloves back on. He waved at the caravan behind him, and pulled his camel to a kneeling position, so he could mount it once more. The great beast did as it was bid and then rose awkwardly again.

"Iskandar's passage is clear!" he called back along with the caravan. "There have been no rains for a fortnight, and so there is no risk of flooding. We can take the passage through the Eagle's Crest, resting in the shade of Hakan's Mercy, and make it to the city by nightfall."

Tulok's gaze followed that of where Jamal had been looking. There, hidden against the weave of earth that raised to the heavens above them, was a passageway, perhaps six feet across, that ran the height of the mountain. Unless one knew where to look, its existence would remain hidden. Tulok mentioned that "fossil dunes" created canyons like Iskandar's Passage. Layers of sandstone and time created mazes of twists and turns or getting caught in unexpected flash floods, where the water had been held in place after a storm. Still were tales of creatures who lurked in the heights of such canyons, waiting for members of caravans to be separated from their groups; who took the opportunity to feast on the unwary. Tulok scowled and champed his teeth together in thought. He needed to trust the Sun Guide, but his book learning gave the big priest pause.

"Afraid you won't fit through the passage?" Jamal quipped as he approached Tulok, still grinning proudly.

Tulok harrumphed at the boy and sat up taller in his saddle. The orc was broad, but he was not beefy, though svelte was not a word that could be applied to him. "I am not so big as a camel, Reysis." he retorted.

"Then you will be fine." Jamal nodded.

Tulok rubbed along the edge of his jaw with a gloved hand and stared at the passageway in thought.

"Everyone dismount!" Jamal called out. "We go on foot from here! Single file! Lead your mounts. Stay well back from them, they WILL kick and they WILL bite!" he ordered as he left to ride up along the length of the caravan, ensuring everyone did as instructed.

Isolde turned and slid off of her mount with a more learned grace than previously. She patted the great beast's neck. It groaned at her in response. "Some issue?" she asked, looking up at Tulok.

"One hopes not." the priest replied and clucked at his camel to kneel so he could dismount.

Isolde looked back at the passage. "We have canyons like these at home," she commented. "We don't often venture into them."

Tulok nodded and checked the gear on his animal. It lay in the sand, quietly chewing its cud. "Probably for many of the same reasons, I surmise."

"Probably." she agreed. Then she reached out and patted Tulok firmly on the shoulder. "That is all right, Father." she began, a grin creeping onto her face and into her eyes. "I'll protect you," she smirked.

Tulok allowed himself to chuckle for a moment; the knight's smile and demeanor were infectious that way. He gazed up and into the canyon ahead of them. "You may need to," he commented. "I'll be hard-pressed to heft a weapon in this channel." He rubbed his chin in thought. "I may tie our mounts to follow each other and ask you to take the lead."

Isolde tilted her head in curiosity.

Tulok reached toward his camel and pulled a large staff from the packs, then stepped to stand directly behind Isolde. Despite her own height, the orc was still a head taller than the knight. He extended his massive arms, across her left shoulder, holding the staff as one might for striking. He shifted his grip, holding the staff with one hand, and then placed the other on her shoulder. "You can defend from the front in close quarters. I can offer distance, and ... by the Will of the Everwatchful... keep you alive to protect us both."

Isolde pondered the suggestion and set herself into a guard stance. Assessing the alignment of Tulok's reach, she adjusted her footing and bent her knees a little. It could work. She nodded and looked back at him. "I think we can make that work."

"Let's hope we don't need to," Tulok replied and pulled his staff back to a walking position.

Jamal strode back up to the pair from the rear of the caravan, leading his camel. He looked at both curiously. "Expecting problems?" he asked.

Tulok looked down at Isolde and then back to Jamal. "It may be the wiser course of action, Reysis." the big priest offered solemnly.

Jamal looked over the pair of holy warriors with an assessing eye, then sniffed once and nodded. "As you see fit then." he granted. "Should there be issues ahead of us, we will need your skills to be certain." he looked back along the trail of bodies and animals. "I've ordered our more ... delicate... travelers and goods to the middle of the train." he continued nodding with his head.

"We will be hard-pressed to reach anyone in the rear, should anything happen, so we will need persons in the rear as well who are capable. Do you agree?" Jamal asked.

Tulok turned his gaze back to see what he meant. The merchants were being led to the center of the line, and their hired hands and guards to the rear of the caravan. The priest could see Bengt being stationed with the merchants. It was assumed that the holy men were more than simple book learners. Many times, this was indeed the case, as the Ever-Watchful Eye was not one given to hermitages and libraries. Most followers of the faith had at least a basic understanding of arms and armor. Tulok nodded in agreement.

"If anything, Bengt can block the canyon with a camel...if nothing else..." the orc commented.

The young Reysis frowned for a moment considering.

"While I would prefer not to lose one of our pack animals in such a fashion, I can certainly understand the need for the sacrifice if it comes to it." he reluctantly agreed.

"Let us hope it does not come to that," Tulok stated, invoking the statement a second time.

Both Isolde and Jamal nodded in agreement; then the young Sun Guide turned and walked toward the entrance of the slot canyon. "We should have about two hours in the canyon until Hakan's Mercy. It will get hot, there will be no shade. Keep your heads covered." and then he began the slow and steady march.

The walls of Iskander's Passage were narrow and steep. One had to tilt their head at an odd angle to get a full view of how far above they reached. The twists and turns of the natural escarpment made assessment difficult, and if one starred up for too long – a form of motion sickness could take hold. Isolde kept her eyes on the trail ahead of her, having lost her sense of direction more than once from trying to stare at the heavens. It was confusing and laborious at the same time. The ribbon-like undulating stone only made the feeling of dizziness and confusion worse. She wondered how anyone could possibly live here.

Jamal led the group, followed by Isolde, Tulok, their camels, the merchants' group, the merchants' guards, and camel herders pulling their mounts at the tail of the train. Jamal had spaced them out thusly – should an attack of opportunity occur, this afforded the merchant caravan the benefit of both holy warriors and camels as padding, the best protection. Such protection also relied heavily on Jamal's sense of the weather. Should he be wrong about the last rainfall, or should rain come to them while they were in the canyon, then the merchants would be trapped between giant animals, trying not to drown. It was a calculated risk.

Some areas of the passage were narrower than others,

giving the group pause as they needed to coax the reluctant beasts onward. On more than one occasion, Isolde had heard Tulok take a deep cleansing breath as he forced his large frame, almost sideways through some of the narrower passages.

"You managing things, big guy?" Isolde asked over her shoulder.

"Hrmph" Tulok grunted in reply. "I was not built for tight spaces."

Isolde chuckled a little at that. "There is an entire clan of tribesmen in the Northern Reaches who could understand that sentiment," she commented. She caught herself trying to look around, and was once more caught up in vertigo. She focused on Jamal's figure ahead of her.

"Indeed?" the radiant priest spoke, his tone flavored with curiosity, "You mean to tell me there are men of my stature on your Island?"

Isolde shrugged a little, "My foster-sister's people are from there. She's told me many stories."

"You have a sister? Family?" Tulok prodded gently.

Again the shrug. "Ygraine. She's..." Tulok could tell she was counting. "She will be sixteen this Summer." There was a note of loneliness in her tone.

"You miss her." It was a statement and not a question.

"Sometimes," Isolde confessed. There was a pause. "Ygraine is...."

"A younger sister?" Tulok offered.

"I was going to say she's difficult." Isolde chuckled. "My father took her in several years back. She had nowhere else to go and had been separated from her people. We gave her a place to stay until we could contact them and arrange to have her returned." She reached up and rubbed the back of her neck. "It took some doing. Her people are nomadic...at best..."

"Ahhhh," Tulok nodded in understanding.

"Do you have family, Father?" she asked looking back.

Tulok's eyebrows bunched together, "It is...complicated. My parents died when I was younger. I honestly could not recall their faces. I was raised by those within the village. My parents fell victim to the desert's embrace...soft sand pulled my mother in and my father could not pull her out and in turn was pulled in, at least that is what my Eima told me. She said that they were hunters and while lying in wait, the sand just gave out and became a sinkhole." He spoke plainly.

Isolde listened to Tulok's words. Suddenly his insistence on pulling her from the sands made more sense. She nodded.

"I am told I resemble him... my father, but that is all. I had no siblings to speak of saving those of the village I grew up with. Even then – becoming a member of the priesthood distanced me further from them. I doubt anyone there would know me now." He looked down at the sand, "It feels like a lifetime ago, now that I think about it. I do not regret my choices and I cannot feel sorrow for the parents I did not know – but I think I would have liked the opportunity to have been someone's brother."

As the caravan proceeded forward, the walls of the canyon began to widen more and more. While the heat was still prevalent, the imagined pressure from the walls subsided and slowly became more hollowed out. A breeze picked up as if encouraged by the walls to flow throughout the passageway. Tulok reached back to place his hand on the back of the camel's neck, "You may want to brace and be ready to block them from advancing. They can smell it in the air."

Quizzically, Isolde sniffed the air and couldn't distinguish anything save the beast she was being accustomed to.

She looked back and saw that there was a shared disturbance with each animal. They knew something was there but was it dangerous?

"What are they being worked up about?" she asked.

"Water...Hakan's Mercy is down there," Tulok pointed to a naturally made archway.

Chapter 16

While not underground, Hakan's Mercy was an oasis that was partially sheltered by a sheer overhang and yet opened to a view of the dunes. What stood out was the striking splashes of green from several long trees native to the area. Isolde had seen these before when they made landfall. They were very different from the trees back on the wet island of Avalon. Tulok named them palm trees, and apparently, there were several different varieties. The bookish priest had gone on for some time about the various species of this specific flora. Their growth was not quick and they required a natural source of water. This did not make them an ideal source of building materials which was why they were replaced by stone, bone, and other found material. The palms were a sign of nearby water so their presence was always considered a good omen. Here – the palms and greenery surrounded a body of water; bigger than a pond but smaller than a lake – at least in the definitions that Isolde was accustomed to using. She wondered how many bodies of water like this one existed in these wastelands. The water glimmered in the sun's light, sparkling, pure, and inviting.

Leading the caravan forward, the shade, breeze, and the water was indeed mercy for any road-weary traveler. With the midday upon them, Jamal directed the caravan to position itself around the blue body of water. Each of the herdsmen led the camels to the water's edge to which the large beasts promptly lowered themselves to the ground and leaned their heads forward to drink. A few others began setting up a few tents to add to the shade with the backs against the carved wall.

Isolde released the reigns of her beast to one of the camel herders and began helping with the riggings of the tents. While she still felt a slight sense of apprehension from the other travelers, her knowledgeable handling of the tent rigging and working without being asked changed part of the demeanor to thankful nods and less baleful stares. She paused to stretch; tired, sore muscles complaining of use past their norm over the past day. She rolled her shoulder, testing it. Tulok was right, she'd probably done the muscles some small amount of injury between fighting the scorpion and trying to save Safar from the sand.

Safar.

Isolde's chest tightened suddenly and she swallowed down a well of grief born of exhaustion. How could someone she had known for less than a week cause so much pain at their loss? The Avalonian took a breath and closed her eyes, trying to center once more. Her calling was one of hope and courage, inspiration. It would do no one any good to see her giving in to the failings of her all too human heart.

"Does your God not allow His people to grieve?" a familiar voice asked. She turned toward the sound and was met with the concerned face of the Vidria merchant Arman. The stout, short man was gazing up at the tall woman, dark eyes colored with discomfort.

Isolde frowned a moment, faced with a question that she had never considered. The line between grief and despair was often fine and delicate; all too easy to tip from the grief of loss to the turmoil of hopeless despair. One had to dance that razor's edge with a careful step. Perhaps she was simply unsure of her own footing right now.

She offered Arman a gentle and tired smile. "It is permitted." she offered.

The dwarf nodded as his fingers absently toyed with a small rock in his hands. He looked down at this item and continued. "That is good to know. I had hoped that you did not follow some faith that left you devoid of emotion." his fingers continued their work. "There are many who shut that part of them away from the world to follow their cause. I am certain their lives are very adventurous..." he looked back up at her, "... and very empty."

Isolde's eyebrows knit together for a moment in confusion. " I am ...sure...they...are?" she offered.

Arman offered the young woman a sympathetic smile and reached his hand out to her. In his palm was a small token. She had seen these in the Temples and Tulok wore one. It was the single eye image within a stylized sun, "Please, a gift." Arman offered.

Isolde shook her head, "Thank you, I cannot."

"Please, for protecting us last night...and risking your life for a Sun Guide...a token of my appreciation." Arman insisted.

Isolde opened her mouth to protest once more, but the look on the merchant's face would not allow it. Reluctantly, she nodded her head and accepted the small item. It felt warm to the touch. She looked down at the small item to examine it. It seemed no longer to be a stone, but a carved piece of crystal or glass. On the backside of the amulet appeared to be a pair of crossed feathers delicately carved into the glass.

"What is this?" Isolde asked.

"The symbol of the Ever-Watchful eye, married to the eagle feathers, the symbol of Eagle's Rest... my people." Arman smiled.

"Thank you, Arman. This is..." she paused. "Thank you."

"Think nothing of it, dear girl. It is my pleasure." he nodded his head and held up his hands. "But you should rest. It has been a long day. Please excuse me." he murmured and departed.

The Avalonian stared at the small symbol in her hand and smiled and nodded. She tucked it away into her belt pouch and then ducked her head into the section of the tent that had been assigned to her. And slept.

~~~

Slick. Her hands were warm and slick. That was the first thing she noticed once the pounding in her head stopped. Her breath was ragged. There was a pain in her left side. She took a deep breath and regretted the action almost immediately. Sharp, stabbing pain radiated through her ribs and through her back. She cried out instinctively.

Wet. Her face was wet. She tasted salt and dirt and the copper taint that could only be blood. Was it hers? She feared more greatly that it was not. She gritted her teeth and forced herself to open her eyes, steeling herself for what she knew she would find.

Bodies littered the small grove, in whole and part, a haphazard scattering of human remains. Many of the bodies were bent at odd angles, having fallen, or been thrown in what appeared to have been a fray of some kind. Homespun cloth, leather boots and belts, linen, and felt caps. Normal, every-day people had been gathered here to celebrate today. They were not wealthy. They were not well-armed. They were merchants and farmers, craftsmen, and coopers. Among the bodies of these everymen, were the occasional body of the group of persons who had brought this carnage upon them. Black and red leather armor, slick with the
~~~

blood of innocents decorated the bodies of the men who had assaulted the village.

Her village.

Her people.

Her family.

Her eyes glanced down at her right hand, still gripping the now broken handle of a shovel. The other half of the tool was buried in the chest of one of the fallen; snapped off at the blade of the shovelhead. The sleeve of her kirtle was shredded and drenched in mud and blood. An hour ago, it had been unbleached linen, off white in color. White silk thread had adorned the hem in an intricate floral pattern, embroidered carefully and dutifully. Something to be retired to a cedar chest for a daughter to wear someday.

An hour ago.

She was on her knees in the grove, surrounded by the dead, covered in blood, mud, and gore. She blinked and carefully raised a shaky hand to wipe at her eyes and her face. She ached.

"Isolde!" a man's voice called out, breaking the silence of the dead.

Her hand gripped the shovel handle as she looked up to search for the source of the voice.

Light glinted off of the silvered armor of the figure that waded through the carnage to reach her. The crest on his breastplate was obscured by viscera. She knew him without seeing it though, by the broken compass that hung from his neck.

"Reynard..." she tried to call and could not find the wind in her lungs to carry the sound. She frowned and gripped the shovel handle tighter.

"God's teeth, girl, your bleeding out. Hold still!" the familiar voice ordered. Then there were warm hands on her side and the warmer feeling of divinity coursing through her broken body. She leaned into his armored figure, letting him take her weight as he healed her injuries.

His arm wrapped around her lithe figure and helped her to stand. She staggered. He steadied her.

She leaned her forehead against his breastplate. Her eyes closed. Her breathing eased. The pain lessened.

"They're all dead, Reynard..." she managed.

"I know." The deep voice soothed. His arm remained around her, protectively.

"I tried..." she tripped over the words.

"No. "Reynard chastised. His voice softened. "No, dear girl, this was not your responsibility. It was mine." He tucked his right index finger under her chin and lifted it to look deeply into her green eyes. "This was my duty, and I failed you, and I beg your forgiveness."

Gentle, soft, brown eyes met hers, brimming with tears. "I am so...so...sorry, Isolde."

There were no words. She merely nodded.

"Nathaniel?" Reynard asked carefully.

Her jaw clenched; she shook her head. Salt tears coursed down her cheeks, leaving clean trails in the mud.

Reynard nodded curtly then, and pulled Isolde to him, resting his chin on her head.

Alright then. Alright." He soothed, both to himself and to her. Her left hand reached for the leather of his cuirass and her fingers entwined there, clinging to him, her right hand still clutching the broken handle. Two survivors in a sea of death. They stood there for an unmeasured amount of time, remembering what it was to be alive. Finally, she felt him nod.

"Let's get you someplace safe, and I'll get to work on ... this..." he offered. They both knew he referred to the bodies of her fellow villagers.

She shook her head and pushed away. "No. They were my people. They are my responsibility. I can't leave them to you." She sniffed and wiped her face, smearing mud and blood and gore. She grabbed hold of her long mouse brown hair and quickly twisted it up and tied it at the base of her neck in a knot. She looked up at Reynard. "I'm the Alderman's daughter...and the Alderman is dead..." She laughed darkly. "...as are his electors... but I won't leave them here... like this."

A raven cawed in the distance, drawing their attention. Two sets of eyes alighted on the large blackbird, its feathers glistening in the mire. It pecked at the flesh of the deceased.

Isolde's hand clenched around the handle once more. "You'll not have him, Morrigan!" the young woman yelled. "Do you hear me?" she stepped toward the bird, holding the handle aloft like a sword. "Not now, not ever! You hell-spawned harlot, be gone!" she yelled and swung at the bird. It stretched its wings wide and with one effortless push lifted from the ground and into the air, clearing Isolde's swing easily. It cawed at her as it flew higher, its voice sounding like laughter.

~~~

She woke with a start. She was covered in sweat and sand, her heart beating against her ribs. Her face was soaked with tears. A painful pit occupied the center of her stomach. She turned to the side and wretched into the sand. Sitting up, she wiped her mouth with the back of her hand and remembered where she was...and wasn't.

"Isolde?" Tulok's deep voice asked from the other side of the tented wall. "You were crying out in your sleep. Are you well? May I enter?"

Suddenly flushed with embarrassment, Isolde reached to bury her vomit under the sand, covering its existence as best as she could. "Yes...yes..of course, Father." She answered.

Tulok pushed the heavy tent section aside, leaving it partially open for the sake of modesty. He ducked his head and stepped into the part of the tent which had been sectioned off for her. His red eyes looked down at the woman warrior, who was still seated on the woven sleeping mat.
~~~

The healer's eyes assessed her quickly. He gestured at an open section in the area. "May I?" he asked.

Isolde looked at where Tulok had gestured, it was not the befouled area of the sand. She nodded. "Yes, please."

Tulok eased his great bulk to the ground with measured skill and folded his legs into a seated position. He placed his hands on his knees and looked over at Isolde. "Nightmare?" he asked casually.

Isolde shook her head. "Memory." she offered.

Tulok nodded. "Ah." came the simple reply. He sat watching her for a moment. "A...time of...significant loss?" he asked carefully.

Isolde took a breath and pursed her lips. She looked at the ceiling of the tent, pondering her words. Her mouth felt coated. She reached and opened the leather drinking pouch, pouring water into her mouth. She swished it around for a moment, then held up her hand to Tulok, turned her head, and spat the fouled water into the corner of the sand where she had wretched earlier. Tulok watched on without evidenced concern. He waited for her reply.

"Before I became Reynard's squire, I was the betrothed of his best friend – Nathaniel Widukind," she spoke the name carefully and with tender regard as if it might break upon her tongue if uttered aloud. She paused for a moment and then continued. "There was an... attack..." she cleared her throat, "forces bearing heraldry I did not recognize..." she took another breath, and willed the bile back down that wished to rise once more. She drank from her water bottle.

Survivors?" Tulok asked softly.

Isolde shook her head. "None save myself and Reynard." she cleared her throat once more.

Tulok nodded, listening. He looked down at the sand in thought. "Your family?" he asked, not looking up.

"My entire village." came the flat response.

Tulok looked up at Isolde, surprised at the curt tone. “Nathaniel was your husband?” Tulok’s deep voice asked softly.

“Of no more than an hour...” Isolde replied bitterly and raised the bottle to her lips once more.

Tulok could tell she wished for it to be something stronger. His eyebrows raised in additional surprise at the revelation that this woman truly was alone in the middle of the Seteshi desert; with no people to return to once all was settled.

“I am terribly sorry for your loss.” Tulok offered, though the words seemed empty compared to the issue at hand.

Isolde nodded in acceptance, saying nothing.

He looked down at the ground and gave a loud, almost annoyed sigh. He looked up at her, “You know,” he started, “You are really making things difficult on me.”

Shocked, Isolde looked at him with wide eyes full of shock, “Wha..what do you...”

Quickly cutting her off with a wave of his hand, “Not only do you show up half-dead at my temple, tell me a story of the undead rising from the sands, carry around an unholy artifact, lead me back into a city that brought me shame,” he paused and looked at the ceiling, “Now you tell me as that your family and the man you loved are dead – I’m beginning to wonder if you have it in you to finish your knight’s mission at all. You are as sooner to collapse upon the floor and weep your life awa...”

Before he could finish his sentence, Isolde’s fist struck him clean across the jaw, anger filled her eyes as she stood, staring down and facing the callous words of the priest.

“Do NOT think for one minute I am less than anything Ser Reynard saw me as!” she said with words filled with defiance. For that brief moment, a light glow surrounded the young woman as she stood tall.

Tulok rubbed his jaw in a half-smile, "I'm counting on it."

Isolde's eyes narrowed and widened again, "You...You," she lowered her voice, "are such an asshole... I know what you are doing!"

"Yes," the orc said, "I am hoping it worked because I know pain. I have heard a lot of pain here in the ever-burning sands. I needed you to give your pain a voice – a story. Like I told you back in the infirmary – I can fix your body – but I cannot fix the pain inside of you. Pain like that needs to be let out or else it will fester and rot the soul."

He flexed his jaw back and forth, a bit of redness began to show at his chin, He slowly pushed himself up to stand. "Unlike you, I have the advantage because all my pain and anger come out in rage. I can do something with that. I can use it as I did against that scorpion. However," he paused looking down and slightly ashamed, "there is not always a giant scorpion to fight and I lose myself too much into it. You...," he looked down at her, "You have the ability to do even greater things than simply scream at the sand. I'm sorry you were not allowed your time to grieve. Had I known this – I would have waited longer at the temple for you to work this out before immediately leaving. So know this," he slowly reached out for her hand.

Isolde regarded him carefully before offering out her own hand.

Tulok's large fingers took her wrist and laid the flat of his hand upon his chest just below where the sun medallion sat.

"When this is over, I will offer you all the chances you need to grieve. To wail, to scream, to cry, to hate, to reconcile what you have in you – all of it. It needs to be aired so You," he pointed toward her, "Can be made whole again...or at least as reasonable as you will allow," he added with a small smile.

Isolde's eyes glistened for a moment as if tears were about to fall. Instead, she leaned into his chest and let the tears quietly shed. She shook her head – balled up her fist and lightly hit him twice on his upper chest, "Gods...," she said and slightly laughed. "The clergy at home offered their condolences and prayers, but you sun people are just harsh aren't you?"

She felt the rumble of his chuckle in his chest, "It goes with the territory" he said, and hugged her. A few more tears flowed freely as pressure subsided in her chest. She took a few deep breaths and nodded her head, "Do they teach you how to take a punch as part of your priestly duties."

The priest patted her on the back, "Only when necessary," he let her go and she wiped her face with part of her sleeve, "Though there was a Gnome woman who somehow managed to grab my ear when she was no taller than my shin....but that is a story for another time."

She flexed her hand a bit and smiled at him, "You're like hitting a side of beef sometimes."

Tulok laughed, "Well this beef needs you to get ready, Jamal saw another caravan headed this way. They will be here within the hour so our time here is done," he headed out – paused and looked back at her, "...if it comes up – you were startled and saw a baby scorpion on my face and swatted it with a tent pole, right?"

Trying desperately to suppress a smile, "It looked HUGE – like the size of my fist! The Radiant Father already forgave me, but I feel so bad about it!" she said with almost practice concern.

He wagged a finger at her and then left.

For a moment, the world felt quiet. She took a deep

breath and sat back down on the rug that served as her bed and laughed quietly.

Chapter 17

The caravan they passed was a mixture of color, people, and languages. There were many customary hand signs and nods as well as someone Tulok referred to as a priest to The Grim.

"He is the god that Judges Souls when they pass from this world to the next."

The priest was a woman with long black hair and very almond-shaped eyes clad in grays and gold. Isolde had seen Elves before, they were common enough at home. She did not think she would see one in the desert as the barren wastes seemed odd for their people. Tulok conversed with the priest for a few moments before moving on. Though while the conversation seemed pleasant, the orc rode with a slightly sour look on his face.

"What did she say?" Isolde said cutting to the point.

Tulok sighed, "Let us just say that while we work together – the Radiant Lord of the Sky Above will always find an... *interesting* conversation with the Grim Lord Below."

The Avalonian laughed and shook her head, "I can imagine that discussion on theology goes far and wide between your two groups."

"Indeed," he said a bit sullenly. "We have two hours to

the Eagle's Crest, and then two hours as the Radiant Lord's Merciful Eye moves on from Setesh to the rest of the world. My counterpart advised Jamal and me that the way is clear from the direction they have just traveled." Tulok pondered something for a moment, then "I let her know where and how to find Safar's body, so she and hers could perform their duty."

Isolde was quiet for a moment, at that. She chewed on her bottom lip and nodded. "I'm sure that is for the best."

They continued on in silence.

The ride toward the Eagle's Crest was more invigorating as she could see the glass spires ahead of them. Pointing them out to Isolde, Tulok began giving a rather flat overview of the structure up ahead. Only partially listening, she gazed in wonder at the intricate crystal spires that rose from the desert floor. Arman's earlier description was only an inkling of what the structure really was. Seven feathers, crafted from the sands of the Seteshi desert rose toward the heavens. They were a milky green in color, not as dark as peridot, but more clear than aventurine. The Vidria Crystals gathered the light from the sun and seemed to almost glow. Fractures within the sculpted forms and spires refracted the light, leaving dozens of multicolored rainbows on the sand. Each feather was named after the Gods revered in Setesh with the seventh feather dedicated to those that were lost in the Reaping. As they got close, she could see the care and details of each of the outstretched wing tips – all reaching toward the sky. In the setting sun, they gave off an amazing combination of orange, red, and yellows that seemed to 'hum' with warmth.

The caravan came to a halt as all members of the caravan sat or stood silent and in quiet reverence of the monument. Isolde later learned that one could whisper out prayers and wishes and that the wind would carry them out to the Great Radiance Above. While she did not do so, she saw her friend mouth something quietly as he touched his chest. He explained the ritual afterward, but refrained from telling her what he said, "All wishes and prayers are personal Ser Knight, allow a priest that."

She rolled her eyes with a bit of jest, "Fine....keep your secrets."

When the caravan moved past the structure, they found themselves looking downward. Like a crack in the earth – there was a wide black line that broke up the monotony of the land. This was the Iteru and it cut Setesh in two. It was a massive sight – a river that was wider than any lake and seemed as endless as any ocean she had seen. On both sides of the river, she could see corresponding glows and tiny lights moving in the sands around it.

"Is that Nahral?" she asked as she squinted her eyes.

Tulok gazed at the city for a long moment before speaking, "On both sides of the Great Iteru, Nahral brings wealth, joy, and prosperity to all that enters into her doors."

She looked over at the orc, "Are You going to be okay?"

Tulok signed, "I shall manage."

~~~

The light slowly moved across the horizon, and the caravan made their way down from the dunes to trails below. The final stretch did not become a race to the city – rather it became louder and busier. Nahral was aglow in the distance and could be seen with lines of lights going to and fro. The mixture of sounds broke the repetitive nature of the caravan as the air was filled with conversation, laughter, and the occasional tune of music. Isolde watched as a myriad of various peoples were coming from the south and the north. Some looked road-weary and tired while others possessed a vibrant and exciting demeanor. Jamal led the caravan behind another that was already following a well-worn
~~~

path, and in turn, another caravan followed behind theirs. There were occasional calls and cheers to those leaving and to those going as well as varied words of advice of who had the best bargains and who best to avoid.

At one-point, Tulok leaned over and said, “You get what you pay for, keep that in mind.”

Isolde simply tapped her nose in acknowledgment.

As the caravan neared the city gates, imagery of the Smiling Lord became more and more prevalent. Statues of a tall figure with an elongated face that more a smile of pointed teeth decorated the exterior columns of the city. Along the outer walls, images and various scripts gave color to the sandstone structures. After a while, she understood that the message was the same but in different languages. They all had a stylized version of the Smiling God with the following accompaniment;

The Smiling God welcomes you to Sanctum.

Here, the people rejoice in The River Lord’s mercy and bounty!

Behold the Iteru river, the lifeblood of the deserts! The River Lord would not stand to see such desolation, and in His wisdom and might, He called forth the flowing waters of His dominion to carve a path of life and bounty through the endless sands. The Riverlord’s grace is unending. See His smiling visage in all the rivers of Sanctum; an endless network of connected, flowing waters of life, trade, and prosperity. Rest well knowing The River’s mercy reaches all lands.

She looked over at Tulok who bore a slightly bemused expression, “I think they have added a few more languages since I was last here. Who knows – you might be the reason they added the Avalonian mural next week.”

“AVALONIAN YOU SAY?” called a voice from one of the shabby roadside market stands.

Members of the caravan turned their attention to the few road peddlers who stood outside the city proper. A man with sun-bleached and dusty clothing addressed them. His eyes and teeth were bright and friendly. "I have a blackened pearl from the deepest waters of a lost island near the Great Kingdom of Ava..."

Before he could finish, the ring of a gold coin filled the air and the small object flew into the basket that the road peddler had to the side. "Oh, Mighty Radiant Lord – let this charity provide a path to Light this humble merchant's way toward Your Merciful Grace."

The road peddler paused; his eyes went wide as he saw that the orc had provided the gold coin. He stood in shock for a moment and then hurriedly touched his chest and his head and went on his way.

"What did you do that for?" Isolde asked.

"Those that sell wares outside the gates of the city have broken the laws or contracts within the city. They are banned from setting foot inside until they make things right. Many times it is something financial so they sell various trinkets and wares out here. However, buying from one can guarantee a swarm of them will descend upon you with various stories of ancient treasures from your homeland."

Isolde nodded as she listened.

As they slowly rode forward, "However, me offering them some coin as an act of charity from the Merciful Radiant Lord – May He Guide our journey through the Smiling Lord's domain – is a simple way to prevent this. The road peddlers will swarm a traveler – they will not beg the Lord of the Sky's charity, but will gladly accept it."

"...but that man could have been starving or had a family," Isolde started.

"Yes, he could have. That is very true. He could have also been a man who swindled his brother's wealth in order to take his brother's wife or some other horrible situation. Either way, you cannot allow yourself to be drawn into the story that is being weaved," Tulok motioned at the upcoming city, "You will hear all kinds that will pull on your heartstrings. Stories of dying mothers, starving children, lost relatives, ancient secrets...all of them are hooks to grab your attention. I know you have markets on your island that are probably just as similar – but here, a story is what sells one's wares. If you see something that you like, ask about the cost. If you wish to know its origin – ask how it was made, what it is made from, and the name of the craftsman. Listen to the answers, but pay attention to what is actually said."

Isolde frowned at the explanation. The island had no such people living on the outskirts of society. The villages worked to take care of each other. No one was ever left to starve.

Tulok reached into his pocket and produced another gold coin. It was worn and not as shiny as the one he tossed to the road peddler, "This coin is part of a cache unearthed in the ruins of Canopus. There are only a dozen more like it in the world that bear this mark. Some say that specific coins actually create a map based on the indents here and here," he motioned.

"With this map – a pathway to the mythic city of Eydafu will open up in the sands to reveal the final resting place of the First Ones."

Isolde looked at him with a bit of skepticism and then finally said, "Really?"

Tulok shrugged. "Stories sell. This single coin cost me a month's worth of endowment money from the temple. As a follower of an Acolyte, I was given a small stipend to cover any costs that I see fit for the temple. It is also understood that this stipend can also be spent toward bettering yourself so that you may, in turn, better the temple." He sighed, "...and like an idealistic traveler – I bought it thinking I could make a name for the temple to provide lost knowledge. Well – the coin was part of a cache of coins. That was true. The story of Eydafu was a legend that got passed around on occasions because with enough of these coins you could in theory form a map." He shook his head and placed the coin back in its pouch, "I later learned from a merchant inside the walls that the man that sold it to me had lost all of his money funding an expedition based on the legend of Eydafu. He had based his findings on a map he was sold by a road peddler outside of the city. So, to recoup the money, the merchant continued to sell the legend. Needless to say, the level of my embarrassment knew no bounds. Father Denali said nothing afterward once it was explained to me that I had fallen for a story."

"I thought you said that you don't get cheated in the city," Isolde asked?

"That is correct, but I was outside the city and law is a bit...gray here. Again – they will not cheat you, but the value of the object you purchase is what you will believe it is worth. Even in the city – a story sells it," he said with a tone of caution.

Up ahead, a green reptilian creature was conversing with Jamal at the head of the caravan. The individual did not bear the feeling of desert wear – rather his deep green scales reflected slightly in the growing torchlight. He was speaking and marking in a large book as well as looking down the line of the caravan. For a moment, Isolde felt the creature's pale-yellow eyes on her, and then it blinked slowly as it moved further down the line. Above the city's main gate was an archway. She pointed up at the archway and gestured to Tulok. He looked up and read aloud,

In The Oasis City, none thirst, none hunger, none fear. For

here, all Understand that only together do we Survive through the might and mercy of The River Lord.

Chapter 18

The smiling God called the River Lord, was himself a crocodile. To be clear, The Smiling God, like many of the Divine entities worshipped in Setesh possessed both animal and human features, the exception being the Radiant Lord who was depicted as the sun. The statues, carvings, and paintings of the River Lord always portrayed Him as a massive human figure with the head and tail of a giant crocodile, whose mouth always seemed to bear the slightest smile aimed at the onlooker. One supposed it was meant to bring a sense of cheer to an otherwise terrible creature; to make him appear more inviting, and less likely to drag you beneath the surface of the Iteru. Isolde regarded each image warily, as she was not certain that she believed the sentiment of safety. Crocodiles were fearsome beasts, not to be tarried with, that would just as soon drag an entire Ox into the water, as bathe in the sun. Her village had lost more than one animal, and life, to one of these creatures in her time on the island. Open water was never taken for granted; there was almost always something lurking beneath a glassy surface. She cast her green eyes about, searching the buildings and the people of the City; wondering if the same held true here. Tulok's story had made her cautious from the onset; and though she was very eager to see all that the City had to offer... as was the charge of a Witness for the Lord Wanderer. She was also careful not to let her curiosity get the better of her.

Where water had been a priceless commodity on the sands behind them, here the water of the Iteru flowed freely. Taking their inspiration from their sovereign deity, the designers of Nahral had crafted both walkways and waterways as a means of travel here. Canals led from various parts of the City to others, traversed by flat bottom boats and elaborate barges. Here and there, stone steps were carved down from the main road to narrow alleys that ran along the edges of the canal. Boatmen on their watercraft floated here, waiting for travelers, and travelers walked from these locations up to the main thoroughfare and the throngs of the City proper. The buildings here were crafted from sandstone and mud brick, taken from the silt of the Iteru, or shaped by the hands of the Vidria.

From their windows and on their walls, buildings displayed colorful banners or other fabrics woven in patterns that Isolde had not seen before. Lanterns painted in vibrant hues hung from ropes above them, lighting the walkways. Their light and color created a warm and cheerful environment. Merchant stalls lined some streets with peddlers hawking their wares to any interested in a sale. Handcrafted metal drinkware, and eating utensils, brightly colored woven caftans and scarfs, rugs, incense burners, jewelry, and foodstuffs all within an easy arm's reach to any passing traveler. The bazaars and merchant's rows of Avalon were well worth noting, but they were nothing like this. Isolde caught herself marveling at the vast array of merchandise more than once, and had to refocus on following Tulok's massive frame through the crowd.

The light of the day gracefully faded slowly as the sun began to vanish. Merchants slowly began to pull doors and shutters closed, to lower awnings and prepare for the evening ahead. A few shops remained open, despite the failing light of approaching twilight. One of these was a shop filled with light itself. Sitting on its stone-carved steps and along its edges, windows, and eves were dozens of lanterns. Metal lanterns, blackened with soot and tooled with intricate designs. Metal lanterns with colorful glass panes. Lanterns decorated with multi-hued stones that cast designs and shadows all around. Lanterns with mirrors. Lanterns with Mosaics. Round lanterns. Square lanterns. Lanterns that sat on the ground and lanterns that hung from the ceiling on delicately crafted metal chains. Isolde never knew there were so many ways to display light. She stood on the steps of the merchant's shop in awe.

A man's voice broke her trance. She looked around and then down at the Vidria merchant who was looking up at her expectantly. She shook her head. "Oh! I'm terribly sorry, I... I don't understand..." she apologized.

The dwarf's eyebrows rose slightly and he nodded. "Ahh, you are not from the desert then. I can tell by your accent," he said to her in the shared tongue.

Isolde smiled brightly at him then. "No, I'm afraid not." she turned her eyes up to the lanterns once more. "Are these your work? They are amazing." she offered.

He shook his head. "Oh no. A craftsman crafts, a merchant sells. They are not the same here."

Isolde furrowed her brow in confusion at the concept. "Oh...I ...see?" she mused.

The small man regarded her for a moment as if assessing her. He caught a glimpse of the broken compass that hung from around her neck and looked back up at her with a look of surprise. He pointed at the object. "You have come a very long way?" he asked.

Isolde looked down to where he was pointing, and

placed her right hand over the item, then tucked it away once more. She nodded. "I have."

The merchant nodded again. "Come, come then. Let me show you the lights that only the sand of Setesh can create..." he smiled and gestured for her to follow him.

Tulok's heavy hand landed on Isolde's shoulder. She winced. "Argh!"

"I thought I'd lost you..." the big orc said from behind her. He looked down over her at the merchant and up at his wares.

The merchant frowned a little. "No harm. She was interested in the lights." he offered a smile.

Tulok looked over the shop and back down at the Vidria. He hummed at him.

"They are just lanterns, Tulok!" Isolde complained.

"No no...not JUST lanterns, young miss.." the merchant objected. He gestured back at his wares. "These are lights which can carry you to another world if you allow them to."

Tulok scowled at the merchant.

"In..a..manner of speaking." the merchant clarified. He lifted one of the lanterns made of mosaic tiles, "Under the right light, and against the water, this one creates rainbows in the darkest of night, that you may travel... in your mind's eye...to the mystic shores of... Avalon? "He asked, looking at Isolde. She smiled and nodded at him, he smiled in return and continued. He gestured to one of the metal lanterns with carved patterns on its edges and sides. "This one, if placed in the center of a tent, creates a marvelous sunburst on the ceiling, inviting The Radiant Lord Himself to join you..."

Tulok removed his hand from Isolde's shoulder and stepped slightly to her side, so the merchant could see the symbol of his faith proudly displayed.

The merchant balked a little and continued,

"...which...you...clearly do not need because He is already with you in the figure of His Radiance..."

"Mmmm" Tulok folded his arms across his massive chest.

Isolde looked up at him and then back to the merchant. "I am terribly sorry; the Father needs to make certain we arrive somewhere on time. May I call on you tomorrow to discuss your wares?" she asked politely.

The merchant seemed shocked at the request and was not entirely certain how to respond.

"I...well...yes...of course..." he stammered.

"Excellent! Very good to meet you then!" Isolde smiled and held out her hand.

The merchant's eyes locked on the offered handshake and reached out to grab Isolde's hand with his own. Too quick, the proffered prize was pulled from his grasp by the priest. Tulok's fingers wrapped themselves around Isolde's wrist and pulled her away.

"If there is time, we will come by tomorrow, Shopkeep." he replied curtly and turning Isolde around, gave her a gentle "nudge" down the walk.

Isolde glowered and waited until they were out of ear's reach of the shopkeeper, then, "What the hell was that all about?" she demanded in a hushed but harsh tone.

"I promised you that I would be frugal with your coin." came the reply. "We still have lodging, food, and information to pay for before we even cross the Iteru. A lantern...while...excellently crafted they may be... is not something we can likely afford at present, Isolde," he explained.

Isolde sighed in resignation. Tulok was right. The matter of coin and trade were so very different here than they were at home. It was certainly possible that she could have ended up bartering away the hair on her head and not even known it. She scowled and nodded. "When we are done, might we see if there is enough coin for one? I would like to have something...not surrounded with death...to remind me of this trip," she asked.

Tulok nodded and patted the knight gently on the shoulder. "A reasonable request," he agreed. Looking up at the various signs on the street corners, Tulok gestured down the way.

"The Temple is this way. We will check in with them there, and then see about lodging for the evening."

~~~

The village of Tarf-qua was originally founded around a simple but valuable oasis. As more travelers came upon it, the makings of the village began to take root. Later, with the establishment of the Temple of The Radiant Lord – the village grew more. The temple itself is usually the first thing travelers see as it stood two stories tall and was constructed large enough to house the village of 70 souls or so. By village standards, Tarf-qua's temple was nothing to scoff at, and it was comparable if not better than some of the official towns within Setesh. Tulok had seen the grand temple in the capital of Ophir and had heard stories that while not grand, Litharge also housed a decent-sized temple dedicated to the Sun God.

In a word, the Temple of The Radiant Lord within Nahral was, 'Modest' which was what Tulok said as they arrived at the front of the temple. The two-story temple was slightly bigger than most of the merchant buildings, but still proudly adorned with the markings to the almighty Sun God. What struck the priest oddly was the attachment of an inn to the side of the building with an elegant-looking sign that read "Mercy's Shade". The lights were on inside and the sounds of talking and laughter drifted out to the streets. On the other side of the Temple appeared to be
~~~

a cafe of sorts with a simple sign "Light's Warmth". Like the others, their shades had been pulled down to show they had closed. The last time Tulok had visited here, the ground on either side was vacant for what he thought was a sign of respect. Perhaps the land had not been sold yet.

He sighed and looked up at the temple again, "Modest indeed."

Looking around the area, Isolde noted that there was not one empty space for a building in the area. She looked up at the orc whose face seemed a mix of apprehension and embarrassment,

"Well, at least the lodging is close to the temple as well as a place to get a meal. Plus I think the temple is sort of sponsoring them." Her voice of optimism broke the apprehension of the big priest. Isolde pointed toward a few key markings on each of the respective businesses.

The eye within the stylized sun was prominently displayed over the thresholds, the doors, and even sculpted in the glass of the windows. While it did not fix the situation, he nodded his head and began moving toward the doors of the temple.

Morning services would not begin for several hours yet, but the temple seemed to be a flurry of activity. Two robed Acolytes were placing travel packs near the front doors when the orc walked in. One was a male Vidria and the other a Human female. Both looked at Tulok and Isolde wide-eyed and called toward the back, "Radiant Father he is here!" They immediately took a knee before Tulok and spoke simultaneously, "Oh Radiant Father who stands as the Radiant Lord's Cherished voice among his Devout, bless us this day for we travel under his Merciless Watch."

Tulok looked down at them in surprise, then to Isolde. He shrugged and turned his attention back to the two, holding his hands out over their heads, "As the Radiant

Lord continues His journey across the skies, may His Blessing guide his Faithful on their journey to the lands beyond. Let them know peril and perseverance as there is no obstacle too great for his Faithful to overcome." A glow flowed from the Orc to the two Acolytes as they raised their arms and heads up to the air. Both then stood up and took the priest's hands in thanks. Each then went over to Isolde and took her hands in thanks as well for bearing witness. Picking up their packs, they walked out the doors of the temple.

"What just happened?" Isolde asked.

"I think...I think they were heading on pilgrimage and needed a Blessing?" he said with the confusion returning to his face.

"Two things," she said, "One, why were we not given a blessing like that when we left Tarf-qua, and two – they said *You* were here as if they were expecting you. Were you expected here?"

"Well – to bless a caravan that I was in would be considered self-serving. Since I was riding in it, having a priest is normally considered a blessing enough," Tulok said as he scanned the room, "However, you are right – they said..."

"Oh! You came too early Radiant Father! Well of course you did!" said a slender-looking priest from the back of the hall. They were dressed much like Tulok signifying them as the Head Priest of the temple. Coming closer to the pair, they pulled back their hood revealing Elven features. He reached out and took Tulok's hand with both of his, "I assume you are going to perform the morning rituals so everything has been laid out in preparation. We usually get a handful of followers at dawn so I'm sure you will want to take the time to acquaint yourself with the trappings here. It should be similar to your previous temple, and I'm sure they will have more than enough room next door."

Tulok started to raise a finger in question, but the other priest waved his hand,

"I know – but do not worry about it. I already had my bags taken care of so your laymen," motioning to Isolde, "would be free to greet those that came in." He looked around the temple and smiled back to the pair, "She is a modest temple but she serves The Radiant Lord well and those that visit her." He patted the orc on the shoulder and walked out the doors.

"Um...what...what was that?" Isolde asked.

Confusion still marked Tulok's face as he looked around, "I think...I just became the head of this temple?"

There was a knock on the frame of the door; a female Vidria stood in the doorway. "I take it you must be the new Father. I'm Dain, I run Mercy's Shade next door. I apologize for the tardiness as I always try to welcome the new priest, but we had an issue with a patron who overstayed his welcome. Had to give him the boot for being a good-for-nothing mooch. I can provide you the same deal with lodging as the previous priests who had overseen the temple."

"Previous priests?" Tulok asked with a confused tone and an emphasis on the multiple priests that had been in this position.

"Oh...I want to say we had almost a half dozen in the past year," she said looking up as if to recount the previous faces, "You're number five, your Radiance."

"Five!" Tulok said a bit startled, "I'm sorry Dain, but I think there has been a bit of confusion." Tulok began to recount their travel from Tarf-qua to the city – quietly omitting the losses they had suffered, and what had happened when they had walked into the temple.

"So Father Kem just patted you on the shoulder and said goodbye!" Dain said with a bemused look on her face, "I'm sorry your Radiance, I don't mean to make light of your situation – but you have to admit that is funny." She shook her head, "Davo and Merta got your blessing, left and then Father Kem after that..." she continued to smile. "Well, I believe that means that this temple's actual replacement is delayed if they were expecting them today. I can have lodging set up for you and your caravan's people while you wait for the new priest. I know that it is the temple's policy to always have their Radiance on hand. Hopefully, it will only be a short wait."

"That would be deeply appreciated." Tulok nodded and bowed his head in respect.

Dain waived it off, "It is just good business, Your Radiance."

Tulok chuckled a little, remembering where he was, and in what City. "Of course, it is."

Chapter 19

Mercy's Shade was more along the lines of an inn that Isolde was used to. There was a large common room where customers gathered to relax, share each other's company along with tales of the day's worries, woes, and wiles. Mercy's Shade also offered a simple, if filling, selection of foodstuffs for the evening meal. A hot pottage stew with a chunk of fresh bread, a small plate of various pickled vegetables, or fresh fish from the Iteru were available for those residing at the Inn. Dain was very clear to everyone who crossed her threshold, that this was an INN, not a Tavern, and not a public kitchen. If they wanted more than what she had to offer, they would need to go see her brother at "Light's Warmth" or find sustenance elsewhere.

After the last several days of traveling, coupled with the several long weeks of rehabilitation, the ability to rest and relax was one that Isolde savored dearly. As she settled down into what turned out to be a very comfortable chair; she was reminded of the many times she and her father had hosted visitors in their home in Whitebrook. Alderman Niall and his family had enjoyed the largest home in the village; as befitting a person of his family's standing. While they had no servants, they did employ two families to help with the running of the small estate. Visiting tradesmen, merchants, and travelers all paid a visit to the Alderman's home. Many times, her father would give them lodging for their time in town. It was customary and considered a great honor. Isolde remembered riding out from the manor house in the evenings to let the merchants and bakers know that someone was visiting, and to be ready to show off their best wares when she brought them through on tour the following morning. It was all part of the routine.

A twinge of sorrow tugged at her heart for a moment at the recollection of things now lost. The raiders had been very thorough in their destruction of Whitebrook. Not only had the attendees of her wedding all been slain, but most of the buildings and shops in town had been looted. Many had been burned. The charred remains of her family's house were all that was left standing. Isolde had been silently thankful that her mother had not lived to see any of it. Lady Whitebrook had died of fever the previous Spring and been spared the horrors of the following year.

You are Lady Whitebrook now, Isolde thought to herself. She shook her head. No, she was Ser Isolde duAvalonne. Isolde Whitebrook died with the rest of her villagers, alongside her father. There was no Council Whitebrook any longer, and so no claim to lands or title could be hers, duAvalonne was the name given to bastards and children without families or land. They belonged to the whole of Avalon, and to no one, it was appropriate. She'd argued for weeks with Reynard after the first time she introduced herself with that surname. He felt it was an insult to her father, her people, and to Nathaniel.

"I can't very well take Nathaniel's name, Reynard!" she'd shouted at him one night.

"You were betrothed for YEARS, the words had been said, no one will know!" he countered.

"-I- will know."

It had not been one of their better moments in their relationship.

She leaned her head back and stared at the ceiling, tuning out the noise and bustle around her and just -existed- for a moment. Had it already been a year? She'd told Safar that she was still in her time of mourning. Without knowing the specific date, it was hard to know the truth; but it was roughly that long ago that her world had decided to take a monumental shit on itself. Only a year, and yet it seemed so long ago.

They'd grown up together – she, Reynard, and Nathaniel. Nathaniel Widukind. His family had been one of the worthiest houses in the region. Their name, their lineage, their history, their ties to the land were all of equal or even greater value than her own; and Lady Widukind was Lady Whitebrook's best friend. So, it made perfectly good sense that they would match their children for a union. It was a political match, a strong one that would have raised both houses in the eyes of the Courts and increased the *leug* of both families; but Isolde was fond of Nathaniel in a way that she knew he did not share with her. Reynard always used to tell her *not to worry, Nathaniel would come around eventually, just give him time.*

"I would have given you a lifetime..." she said softly.

"May I join you?" a voice broke her distraction.

Isolde blinked and sat up suddenly, looking around. A square, squat, beardless man stood across from her, gesturing to one of the empty chairs next to her. Arman. Isolde smiled at the merchant and nodded.

"Of course!"

"Thank you.," he replied and pulled up a seat. "Father Tulok sent word to Jamal where you would be staying, should any of us need lodging for the evening. The Sun

Guide was kind enough to share that information with those of us continuing our journey across the Iteru."

Isolde sat forward, her fingers laced between her knees, her full attention on the Vidria.

"You are going to the other side of the river as well?" she asked.

Arman nodded and brushed off a section of his tunic. "Indeed. I have family on the East bank, as well as business associates there."

"Then I am glad to have another familiar face to share this journey with!" the young woman smiled brightly.

"You have business on the East Bank as well?" Arman queried.

"There, and beyond." Isolde sighed, clearly not looking forward to more weeks of sand in her boots.

"What in the name of the River Lord could draw your attention *beyond* the other side of the City?" Arman asked with wonder.

A commotion at the front door halted Isolde's reply, as the figure of Brother Bengt all but collapsed through the entrance.

"Water, food, a bed without sand mites..." the skinny priest whined as he entered. "Please, for the love of our Lord, tell me you have a room?"

Isolde rolled her eyes skyward. For all that she missed Whitebrook, she hoped she was better behaved than Bengt.

Dain dusted off her hands and trotted over to meet the sallow man at the door. She looked him up and down. "Yes, of course, we have a room for the faithful who have come to serve at the Temple...and others."

"Oh, thank you, good woman. Your words are a balm upon my weary soul. Surely the grace and mercy of our Everwatchful Lord shall bless you for your kindness."

"Kindness gets a blessing. Coin gets you a room." Dain replied curtly.

"But surely..." he protested.

Isolde pushed herself up out of her chair with a groan and stomped over to the priest.

"Brother Bengt!" she smiled and opened her arms wide. To those watching, the smile did not reach her eyes.

Bengt almost recoiled at the sight of the knight. "Ser...Ser Isolde...I...hello." he stammered.

"I'm sure Father Tulok will be very glad to see you!" Isolde said with a loud and exaggerated tone.

"What? I... Tulok..." Bengt began looking around.

Isolde nodded, taking the priest's elbow. "Mmmm-hmmm" she nodded and started to usher the man to the door. "He's right next door...at the Temple...of your Lord...getting ready for dawn prayer..." she looked back over to Dain, "He hasn't had his supper yet either..."

Dain nodded and smiled and headed to fetch supper for His Radiance.

"But...neither have I...." he continued.

"Well, I am certain that our Host will provide enough for the both of you..."

"I certainly shall." Dain continued with a smile as she disappeared behind a pair of doors.

"Excellent!" Isolde smiled. "I was going to wander over there and offer to help him myself, but now that you are here...it wouldn't look good for a layperson to be assisting with such things when a member of the faith is...right...here." She commented pointedly.

Suddenly all eyes in the Inn were turned on Bengt. Waiting for his reply.

The skinny, sallow priest narrowed his dark eyes and glared at Isolde. There was no easy way around this situation. "You are a hateful woman," he whispered.

"Tulok controls the purse. You want the Temple to pay for a room? Go help him." she countered coolly.

Dain returned and shoved two bundles at Bengt, filled with warm, fresh food. "There you go, I'll send a couple of bottles over shortly. So nice to see the Temple in such good hands," she smiled and ushered him out the door. Wiping her hands on her apron, she looked up at Isolde with a renewed interest.

"You don't care for that boy much, do you?" she asked.

Isolde looked toward the door and shrugged a little. "I don't care for his thinking that his suffering on the road here was worse than anyone else's; nor for the thought of him shirking his duties and leaving Tulok to take care of what was just left behind, she replied.

Dain pursed her lips and nodded. "A fair point." She sized up the woman for a moment. "So, what can I do for YOU then, since the Father's already paid in advance for your rooms for the next 3 days."

Isolde looked down at the stout woman, and her features softened greatly. "Honestly? I'd be happy with a horse trough, or whatever substitutes for it here, and enough water to get the road off of my body and my clothes." She looked down at her gear, covered in sweat and sand, scorpion entrails, and blood.

Dain chuckled deeply. "I think we can do better than that. There's a washbasin in your room, I'll send up your supper and hot water. Leave your clothes by the door, I'll have them scrubbed."

Isolde bowed her head deeply at the dwarf. "My thanks."

"It is just good business... Ser Isolde."

~~~

Morning services went off without an issue. Less than a dozen people showed up for the service, and yet each one followed in step with the orc's chants. No one questioned
~~~

the change of person or the nature of the Radiant Father at the dais. Everyone sang the praises to the Radiant Lord and took part in the Rising Rituals as they thanked their god for his gift of light and fire as well as to bring health to the sick and courage to those lost to despair.

Afterward, each of the devout lined up and waited, in turn, to stand within the circle of light created by the skylight above. The skylight has been carved in such a way that it captured the light as the sun traveled the skies. While in the circle of light, Tulok gave the blessings of The Radiant Lord to each that stood there. Isolde watched from the rear of the room and noticed that as soon as they stepped into the light, they began to sweat as if they had been outside in the sun for an hour. As they stepped out of the circle, each one left with a sense of confidence and assurance. The first was an older man who nodded to Isolde and handed her a small pouch that jingled. She tried to shoot a look at Tulok but he was still providing blessings. She accepted the small pouch and looked as the next person was coming, but with a small basket of eggs. At the end of the services, there were several pouches of coins, the aforementioned eggs whose quantity had grown to about two dozen, a few stylish medallions all bearing the stylized sun insignia, and few colorful headscarves. Most of the items she carried in a large basket that was placed by the door, undoubtedly for moments such as this.

She looked at Tulok after the last member left their gift in the basket, "I am not sure if this is part of a ritual or what, but they just kept giving me things!"

He looked at the basket she was holding and ran his hands over his head, "Well...in some temples, it is a courtesy to leave a small donation so that the priest can have things fixed or purchased. Though," he picked up the coin pouches and opened it up. It had several gold pieces which caused him to raise an eyebrow, "I think donation here is taken to another level."

Isolde nodded in understanding. "People often bring gifts and exchange goods at home. We take care of our holy places and people because they take care of us." She helped carry the basket to a table in the back of the Temple where Bengt was stationed. He had an open book, a pot of ink, and a quill pen at the ready. Tulok exchanged glances with the younger man.

"Record it all, and we will set it to its proper place as needed."

Bengt nodded; this seemed a task that he was familiar with. He cast Isolde a sour glance as she deposited the basket.

Tulok folded his arms across his massive chest and glowered down at Bengt. "Do you have some issue with a visitor in the House of our Lord, Brother?" he asked pointedly.

Bengt shook his head and looked back at the table. "Not at all... Father," he said the word with some hesitation.

"Good," the orc nodded curtly.

"Do they do the same thing in Tarf-qua?" Isolde asked curiously. She finally had a moment to truly look at the trappings of the interior of the temple. Tulok and the exiting priest had both called it modest, but in her mind, all she could think of was 'ostentatious'. There were golden fixtures and colorful murals much like Tarf-qua – but larger and grander for such a small space. It was clean and orderly like Tarf-qua, but everything seemed 'new' rather than 'well-kept'.

"In a way," Tulok said, looking around as well, "Since people visit every day, the craftsmen offer their time to fix anything that may need repair or add to the coffer if they know that something must be purchased from a merchant...but this..." he shook his head, "...is different."

The door opened behind them and in walked a Gnomish woman bearing similar, but smaller vestments of Sun God. Behind her were two Acolytes – both elves clad in desert gear.

“Father Kem I presume,” she said as she looked up at the priest.

Tulok knelt down on his knee and gave a respectful nod, “Not...exactly.” The Gnomish woman gave him a look of confusion and the orc began retelling their story once again.

Chapter 20

The Radiant Mother, Selwyse Mindyne, was less than amused that Father Kem had all but abandoned his post without following proper protocol. While she could certainly forgive not checking a name, there was a world of difference between a male orc and a female gnome coming to relieve him of his post. Without missing a beat, she drafted both of her elven acolytes, Tulok, Bengt, and Isolde into taking inventory of the entire Temple to see what other corners may have been cut during his haphazard governance. She was nothing if not thorough. Isolde happily slipped out once or twice over the last two days to speak with Dain and her brother Durnaeg to make arrangements for meals and apartments for their rest. Selwyse had been in the process of railing against the sloppy work that she was being tasked with taking over, and Tulok simply knelt on one knee, listening, nodding, and apologizing while looking ever so much like the child being yelled at for something his brother had done.

"Thank you very much, Durnaeg," Isolde smiled and folded the cloth covering over the large basket of foodstuffs meant for the priests of the Temple next door to *Light's Warmth.* Where his sister kept the Inn and simple provisions for those staying at her establishment, her brother operated a venue with more variety. The small cafe-style tavern boasted several outdoor tables and chairs, and a few benches. The tables were low and fashioned from carved wood with ornate metal tops. They seemed impractical to Isolde but were certainly lovely. The dining area was shaded from the heat of the sun by a colorful awning woven from multicolored silk. Its colors drew attention to the establishment from a distance. It was a place of welcome invitation. Freshly baked bread, sweet desserts, candied fruits, savory meats and hand pies, spiced wine, and rich, thick beer made from local grain and spiced with pomegranates and coriander that Durnaeg prided himself on were all available. Isolde had tried to talk him out of the recipe, but he had politely declined...twice.

"It is for the Temple, I'll be sure to put it on their tab, dear lady." the stout man smiled as he wiped his hands with a rag. He was a round-faced man, with the clean-shaven countenance of the Vidria desert people. His hands were broad and strong, and clearly accustomed to hard work, his skin tan and weathered by from years of exposure to sun and sand.

The voice of the Radiant Mother could be heard from where they stood. Isolde winced a little, Durnaeg chuckled. "She's quite the fireball, isn't she?" he laughed as he listened to her going on about some other failing of Father Kem that she had just discovered.

Isolde nodded, "She is at that. I feel sorry for the boys..." she shook her head.

"Ah, now, they'll be fine." Durnaeg consoled, "The Sun Lord's people like to be tested, don't forget. The easy road is never one they will choose. She's just reminding them of it." he winked at her.

She laughed. "A fair point, a fair point indeed."

"If you don't mind my asking," Durnaeg began. He

stepped up on a riser behind the bar counter of the cafe which allowed him to meet the gaze of more patrons.

"Yes?" Isolde replied politely.

"You aren't from here. You didn't come upriver on a barge. You don't *look* like any of the people of the area. You're trying really hard to fit in..." he gestured at Isolde's clothing and armor. "You aren't one of theirs...." he hitched a thumb in the direction of the Temple. "What in the name of the River Lord are you doing in Nahral?" he asked.

"That obvious?" Isolde asked and blushed a little.

"We don't see many Islanders in Setesh, let alone this far South. You all stand out a fair bit." Durnaeg replied. He poured her a glass of dark brown liquid and pushed it over to her.

"You gonna tell me how you made this?" Isolde asked for the third time. She wrapped her long fingers around the glass and pulled it to her.

"Nope. Family secret and my sister would hang us both if'n I did!" he smiled and rested his hands on the edge of the bar.

"I believe she would at that." Isolde nodded and lifted the glass in thanks and toast, then drank deeply from its contents. She set the glass down, licked her lips, and then wiped her mouth with the back of her hand. "I never would have thought it possible to make something that good without hops." She replied, savoring the taste.

Durnaeg nodded appreciatively, "You Islanders kill half your palette by adding bitters to your beer. Never understood the appeal." he wiped the bar absently. "Is that why you are here, looking to acquire a better recipe for your kegs?" he smiled.

Isolde shook her head. "No. I wish it were that easy...or pleasant."

"Ahhhh...." the Vidria barkeep nodded.

"Finishing an errand for a dead friend." she offered.

Durnaeg frowned a little at that. "In the middle of the Seteshi desert? He was either a very dear friend, or you have a life debt to settle."

Isolde pondered the contents of her glass for a moment, then lifted it and finished its contents. "Maybe a little of both," she murmured.

He nodded in understanding. "Well, we are happy to give you some respite on your journey, then. Do make certain the Radiant Mother gets her supper." he nodded at the package on the counter.

Isolde touched her brow in thanks and reached for the bundle. "I will do just that. You have a pleasant rest of your day, master Durnaeg. I expect I will see you again tomorrow."

"And you as well, Ser Knight."

Isolde grabbed the heavily laden basket in one hand, and gathered two bottles that had been placed with it with the other, then headed back to the Temple, steeling herself for the harsh words of the Radiant Mother once more. The tiny woman's voice carried out the open doors of the Temple. Passersby turned their heads to look in the direction of the Temple with curious eyes. Isolde smiled and waved at them with her bottle-laden hand as she took the steps up to the doorway.

"Pleasant day to you!" she called down brightly from the top step. The natives of the City shook their heads and continued along their way.

"Mistress Isolde!" The gnomish woman's voice snapped from behind her.

Isolde winced, like a child being scolded by a parent. "Oh boy..." she whispered under her breath and slowly turned to face the Radiant Mother of the Nahral Temple of Ra.

She looked down at the smaller woman and smiled brightly. "Yes, Your Radiance?" she asked politely.

Mother Selwyse was less than half the size of Isolde, but what the gnome lacked in height she seemed to make up with spite. Her flame-red hair was braided and pulled back into a severe knot on the top of her head. As was the case with most of her people, her features were sharp and bore an appearance that made them look almost chiseled. Her long-pointed ears extended past the edges of her skull and were adorned with golden rings and cuffs. Her eyes, like Isolde's, were a brilliant emerald green. She wore robes the color of the sand, edged in finely embroidered designs of gold silk. Her parchment-like skin was weathered from the desert. Determining the age of the gnomish peoples was always a challenge as they seemed to appear ageless for most of their lives, then suddenly one day they seemed to become wizened advisors. Isolde had never met one that appeared to be in their middle years of age. She often wondered if they were all hidden away from general view somewhere, engaged in some strange secret construction activities. Selwyse's demeanor and carriage lent Isolde to believe that she was a woman of many years experience, who had seen more than one city in her assignments.

At home, this would have earned her a heavy measure of respect and worth; as one was judged by one's actions and lineage more than one's personal belongings.

"Brother Bengt tells me that you are in possession of an item of some ... interest." the Radiant Mother began.

Isolde's eyes slid over to the figure of Bengt at the back of the Temple. Bengt smiled sweetly back at her.

"Eyes here, young lady," Selwyse demanded.

"Yes, Ma'am" Isolde bowed her head in deference.

"Well? Have out with it." the gnome continued.

Isolde frowned a little, thinking.

Selwyse began to tap her foot impatiently.

"By all the Gods, girl, this is not that hard a question."

Isolde pursed her lips and set the basket and the bottles down next to Mother Selwyse. She took a knee so that she could meet the eyes of the revered figure.

"Your Radiance," the Wandering Knight began, "I am... indeed...in possession of an item of some interest. It was entrusted to myself and my Lord ...may he rest in power...that we bear it to its final destination on your shores." Isolde spoke in clear, even, tones as she explained the duty she had been assigned. "It is believed that the item is possibly the target of a familial curse and must be set to rest, so the souls of the departed may be..."

"May be properly weighed, measured, and judged." Tulok's voice echoed from somewhere within the Temple.

Isolde looked up searching for the figure of the priest.

Selwyse scowled to hear Tulok respond. "You and I have had this discussion, Father Tulok. If there is an item of power within this City, that affects our flock, and calls for the duty of our Lord..."

"Then you will be pleased to know that it will not be here for much longer," Tulok replied, stepping from the shadows and into the light. He looked tired. The big Orc's jaw was set and his countenance firm. He folded his big arms across his chest and looked down at the tiny woman. It was an intentional position and posture of power.

Isolde looked between the orc and the gnome, pursed her lips, and very slowly pushed herself up from her kneeling position. There was clearly an argument between the two. She took a step back and down one step.

"It is not my intention to bring strife to your doorstep." She offered, holding up her hands.

"It is the charge of the Everwatchful to give out punishment and justice to those who would seek to avoid the peaceful rest of the ever after." Selwyse began. "Your charge..."

Tulok cut Selwyse off. "Is mine and not yours." He said flatly. "Neither is it mine to take from SER Isolde." he used Isolde's honorific pointedly, "...any more than it would be for the most Holy Lord of the Setting Sun to deny a duty assigned to a Knight of the Questing Lord."

Isolde turned curious eyes to Tulok.

Tulok did not look at Isolde but maintained his gaze on the smaller figure of the Radiant Mother.

"Correct me, if I have misstepped, Mother Selwyse." He commented. "Please," he then gestured over to Isolde. "Would you start a war of faith by attempting to deny a Wandering Knight their sworn Quest? Would you invoke the wrath of HER Lord upon this House?"

Selwyse scowled and gritted her teeth.

Do...PLEASE...tell me that you would wish that upon this Temple and this City?" Tulok asked.

Realization of what was at stake finally dawned upon Isolde. She frowned a little and shook her head. "I cannot set aside my charge, Your Radiance," she stated. "I understand that this is a matter of importance, but Father Tulok *has* been charged with assisting me in this endeavor...and... everything it entails."

"Child..." the gnome began.

Isolde shook her head. "No, Your Radiance."

"Excuse me?" Selwyse said in an offended tone.

Isolde squared her shoulders. Rather than take a knee, she took another step back and down one step to bring the two women to eye level, both standing, facing one another. "I am Ser Isolde duAvalonne, sworn knight and holy Witness of the revered Lord Wanderer. I am a woman, married, and widowed, who has buried both Father and Mother. I am no child. I grant you all the honor and respect that is due to one such as yourself is owed, but you must do the same for me."

There was silence between the members of the diverse faiths as they each took the measure of the other. Tulok slid his gaze over to Isolde and nodded almost imperceptibly to her. Isolde stood her ground, her hands down, at her sides, palms facing out, expectant. Selwyse looked the younger woman up and down, then turned on her heel and walked back into the Temple.

"Bengt, fetch the supper for the FAITHFUL." she commanded and disappeared within.

Tulok pursed his lips and rolled his eyes toward the sky in irritation. Isolde could see him clench his jaw. He inclined his head and reached to touch the fingertips of his right hand to his forehead. "Let the Radiant Lord's Grace bring Light to you and yours, Mother." he managed in a forced tone as Bengt slithered into view, and reached to gather the items from Durnaeg. He smiled an oily smile at Tulok and then Isolde.

"Pleasant day to you both," he offered insincerely.

There was a low rumble in Tulok's chest. He glowered down at the smaller priest. "You bring dissent to the House of our Radiant Lord," he warned Bengt.

"And you side with the duties of a foreigner's god over your own," Bengt quipped back. "I am not the one who needs to evaluate their actions...Father." He lifted the basket and the bottles. "May His Mercy cleanse you of your failings and through test and trial may you find favor in His eyes," he intoned and wandered back into the Temple, leaving Tulok standing on the stairs.

Isolde inhaled deeply and stretched her neck from one side to the other. She closed her eyes and pursed her lips. "I...am... sorry...Tulok." she offered in a quiet and sincere tone. "I do not wish for you to fall from grace with your people over this..."

"Don't." the big priest replied.

She looked up at Tulok. He was looking down at her from the topmost step, towering above her. She frowned in confusion.

He shook his head and stepped down from the doorway to the bottom step: one step lower than Isolde, but eye-level. "His Grace and His Mercy brought you to my hands, and with these hands, I saved a life that would have otherwise been claimed by the sands. The Light Bringers themselves assigned this task to me...not to Selwyse...not to the Temple...to me." he looked directly into her brilliant green eyes. "The easy path is not His, nor shall it ever be mine." he extended his hand to Isolde. "Just as this is your Quest, too is this my Test. Let us each prove the other worthy."

Isolde's eyes gleamed with warmth, pride, and respect. She reached out and clasped his arm with her hand, in the fashion of her people. "Honor and reverence to you and your Lord." she smiled warmly and sincerely.

"Let His Grace bring Light and Wisdom to you and yours," he replied, grasping her arm with his outstretched hand.

"Food now?" Isolde smiled.

Tulok nodded, relaxing. "And wine...lots of wine."

The pair released their grip on one another, turned, and headed down toward the market to look for a meal.

Chapter 21

Rooms at Mercy's Inn were more opulent than Isolde anticipated them being. It had been some time since she had slept in soft sheets, with a goose-down pillow. Tulok had sighed and shrugged as he examined the rooms they had been given. Apparently, since the Mercy catered to the faithful of the Temple, they had also adopted many of the standards of decor often associated with the same. The walls were without cracks and boasted fresh paint. These were adorned with elegant multicolored tapestries and scarves. Everything had a hint of gold to it, from the fine line of gold edging along the windowsill, to the tiny gold patterns embroidered on the coverlet. Isolde shucked her boots off and tossed them into a corner with a heavy "thud", then unbuckled her cuirass and slid out of it with expert skill, dropping it to the floor.

She sighed and groaned with relief as she did so, then sniffed. Ugh, she stunk. Shedding her sand-colored kaftan, she tossed it into a chair. Over the back of the chair was an outer robe with decorative woven patterns in blues and tans. She stood in her underpinning shirt and trousers and stretched, free of the confines of foreign garments for a moment. It was all so new. She smiled softly for a moment and turned her head to the ceiling, arms outstretched.

"All for you, My Lord." she intoned. "Let my eyes be your eyes, my memories become yours, let me find joy in my duty to You." She took a deep breath and held it, and settled into the silence for a moment.

There was no true place of worship for Him here; Isolde had inquired from Dain her first night here. No scribe to take her testimony. No Well of Memory for her to tell her stories to. There was a small shrine, with tiny notes posted to it, and colorful ribbons tied to it. She'd torn a strip of cloth from the hem of her tunic, whispered memories to it, and tied it to the shrine. It was the best that she could do.

Her right shoulder ached. Opening her eyes, she lowered her arms and stretched her neck a little. Durnaeg's brew was certainly relaxing. She shook the tension out and walked to the washbasin on a stand in the opposite corner. It was deep and made from hammered copper, polished to an almost fiery sheen. Isolde poured clean water into the basin, dropped a cloth of woven cotton into the liquid, and then slowly began to wipe the day's road soil from her weary frame. Tomorrow they would depart this City and its odd trappings, venture to the East Bank, and from there...farther into the desert to search for the Ruins. Clean water became soiled with sweat and dirt. It was not as cleansing as a proper bath would have been, but she had not seen one of those since they had left the islands. She missed the cool damp of moss and the pattern of rain falling on a rooftop. The wet smell of grass, and the sweet smell of hay. She missed the land. Bracing her hands on the edge of the washstand, she lowered her head. Was this why Reynard had tried to talk her out of this path? Because the blood of Avalon flowed so deeply in her veins because those of her lineage was so tied to the islands?

"We all have a calling", she said to the empty room. Was it a statement of reassurance? Perhaps.

A heavy knock sounded at the door. Isolde raised her head and tossed the rag into the water. It splashed over the edge of the basin and onto the washstand. "Just a moment." She called to whoever was on the other side. She reached for the ornately woven robe and threw it over her athletic frame, buttoning it at the waist to hold it closed. Striding across the room, she flipped the brass latch open and pulled the door open.

A familiar massive figure, clad in holy vestments and armor filled the doorway. Tulok stood before her, head bowed politely. A pair of what appeared to be scroll cases peeked out from under his arm. At his feet was a basket filled with food and two bottles. Isolde eyed the orc priest and his collection of items. She cocked her right eyebrow and looked up at him. Tulok noted Isolde's manner of dress and cleared his throat uncomfortably.

"My apologies, I forget that others do not remain awake as long into the night as I do. Is it too late?" he asked politely.

"One supposes that it all depends on what you need?" Isolde replied curiously.

"Ah. Yes." The Radiant Father replied. He jostled the scroll cases out from under his arm. "I have secured the information we need for our next leg of the journey. We should discuss where we are headed tomorrow." He looked over her shoulder to see the disarray of her room. "I can, of course, have this conversation in the morning, if that would be easier?" he offered.

Isolde shrugged and stepped back from the threshold, gesturing for Tulok to enter. "Not at all. Please." she smiled.

Tulok nodded in thanks, ducked his head, grabbed the basket, and stepped into the room. Isolde closed the door behind him as he did so. The big orc looked around the room, searching for a clean surface to place things on. Isolde watched his eyes.

"Ah! Hang on," she replied and quickly moved to shuffle various items off of the lone small table in the room. She dropped them unceremoniously onto her bed. "Table is clear. Go ahead."

Tulok nodded and carefully deposited his goods onto the table. With one massive hand, he very carefully, and meticulously swept aside any remnants of items left behind.

Isolde watched him, folding her arms across her chest. "You...ah... Gonna fold my clothes when you are done there?" she asked mirthfully.

"If given my druthers...yes...or at least show you how to hang them properly..." he commented.

"Yes, mother," Isolde joked.

Tulok grunted in response. Once he was content with the cleanliness of the table, he popped open one of the scroll cases and unrolled what appeared to be a map. Four small stones slid out of the case as well. He placed them on the edges of the map and then stepped back. Rubbing his jaw, he gestured at the drawing. "This is what I was able to uncover from the Temple archives this afternoon."

Isolde furrowed her brows and stepped up next to him and looked down at the map. A wide, blue line wove its way down the long edge of the drawing. Small drawings of various shapes and sizes flanked each side at different places. They appeared to be representative of cities and villages.

"The Iteru?" Isolde asked.

Tulok nodded. "Indeed." He pointed at a small section on the western edge. "We are here." he drew his finger across the river to the eastern shore. "Tomorrow we take a barge across the Iteru to the East Bank. We shelter there for a day while I negotiate for a Sun Guide to take us..." he placed his finger toward the middle of the map. "Here". The area of the map was empty, save for a drawing of two small feathers. "The Ruins of Ahsal."

Isolde hrmmed and reached for a chair. She dragged it over to the table, turned it around, and straddled it, leaning on the back with folded arms. "Not a lot between here and there," she commented.

Tulok shook his head. "No. There isn't," he replied softly.

Isolde scratched at her nose absently as she considered the map. "How far out is it from the nearest settlement?"

"Four days North from Kas-qua." he placed his finger on another section of the map with small green marks and a blue dot. "Which is another four days East from Mukt-aal," he moved his finger once more to a larger green area that seemed encircled by hills or mountains, "which is six days north of East Bank."

Isolde whistled low. "A fortnight north and east from the East Bank, into the middle of the desert..."

Tulok nodded. "That is what I have been able to decipher from the tomes in the Temple library here, yes."

"No faster way?"

"To a set of ruins that should not still exist? No," he replied.

Isolde leaned back and looked up at him. "Should not still exist?"

The orc pursed his lips in thought, then ran his tongue absently over his right tusk, pondering his reply. His eyes looked to the window of Isolde's room without comment, strode over to it and pulled the shutters closed, then walked to the door and flipped the latch to lock it.

Isolde raised her eyebrows at such actions. She looked around the room. "You want me to check under the bed?" she asked jokingly.

"Yes. Please." came the reply.

Isolde blinked. She nodded and slowly pushed herself up from the chair, then padded over to the bed and dropped quickly to the floor to peer underneath. She was met with darkness and an absence of dust.

"Nothing here but freshly oiled wood," she commented from her position on the floor. She rolled over onto her back and looked up at Tulok who towered over her. "So?" She asked, then sat up. Tulok offered her his hand, she took it and he quickly pulled her up to stand.

"I will say this as clearly as I need to." his deep voice sounded. "There are NO, heretical Cults in Setesh." his eyes met Isolde's. They were hard and cold. "None."

Isolde's eyebrows knit together. "I... alright?"

"NONE," Tulok repeated firmly. Then his voice lowered drastically, "but if there were...whatever is left of them...MIGHT be in Ahsal..." he whispered.

Isolde's face was filled with confusion.

He sighed. "The Everwatchful Lord bears no challengers to His Throne or His Name. All are destroyed by His righteous fury." the priest continued. "None are left behind to take root and poison this world."

Isolde pondered the words offered. "So...ohhh...." she nodded. "So, there...used...to be an issue in Ahsal..."

"Ages ago," Tulok added.

Isolde nodded, "A very long time ago...so long as to have been forgotten?" she asked in a leading tone. The orc nodded. "And someone kicked over a rock..."

"And found a nest of scorpions." was the answer.

Isolde sank down onto the side of her bed and chewed on the edge of her upper lip. "Oh boy." She folded her hands between her knees in thought. "And now there is a Witness involved..." She looked up carefully at Tulok.

He nodded. "To whom is given the charge of recording the truth for posterity..."

Isolde wet her lips. "Are we.... Do we have a problem... Father?" she asked quietly.

Tulok regarded the young woman sitting before him, whose life he had rescued from the thirst of the sands. "You can tell no one of this, Isolde," he replied flatly.

Isolde exhaled a held breath and sat back. "I am not certain I can promise that Tulok," she replied. "I mean, that is what I DO..." she objected.

The priest rubbed the back of his neck with a beefy hand. "I know...believe me...I do." he fretted. "Just...keep it to yourself and.... you know... Him?" Tulok glanced skyward.

Isolde considered the words, then pushed herself up off the bed and stepped over to the basket. She pulled both bottles out and shoved one at Tulok. "Open it." she said firmly.

Tulok blinked in confusion but did as he was bid. "I am not certain I understand? What does..."

She wagged her finger at him and pulled the cork out of her own stoppered bottle. "A secret for a secret." the Knight said. "As is the custom of my land, you bid me keep a truth to my heart, safe from the ears of man. This I will do, but you must carry one of mine as well. Should either of us break our vow, the other is free to share the truth of the other." She held up her bottle. "Say yes."

Tulok's eyes widened in understanding. He nodded. "Yes. I agree," he replied.

Isolde nodded. "Good. Ask me something."

The orc blinked and regarded the tall woman standing before him. The Knight Wanderer. The Holy Witness of The Landless Lord. The foreigner, from a land that few had ever left, and fewer had ever seen. How many years had

Tulok poured over tomes of ancient history in the Temple, searching for information on obscure topics and legends? There was precious little about Avalon, only rumor and conjecture about its people and their origins. The words were out of his mouth before he even considered their weight.

"Is it true that all the people of Avalon are made of magic and the Morpheum?" Tulok regretted the words immediately.

Color drained from Isolde's face at the utterance of the words. She cleared her throat.

"A secret for a secret," she whispered and nodded.

Tulok's eyes widened a little as he watched her face blanche and her shoulder sink, "Isolde, I apologize..."

She waved him off. "The question has been asked. Let it be answered, and kept in your heart."

Tulok nodded.

The woman took a breath and rubbed the back of her neck. "Once upon a time..." she began. "The realm of Avalon and her people resided elsewhere...as did all the people of Sanctum." She closed her bright green eyes, invoking memories told around fires and at hearths and in the halls of her homeland. History. Ancient and sacred. "When the mad God of Time and the Undoing waged His war on the Heavens and the Realms of the Peoples, seeking their destruction to feed his own insatiable desire for power...the Lords of Sanctum came here, and brought with them their people...or as many as they could..." she took a breath. This was all common legend, spoken across the whole of the lands.

"Many perished in the Crossing. Peoples, traditions, faiths... Gods..." she said softly. "They are all merely wisps of memories on a loom of an ancient tapestry somewhere now." she continued. Her bright green eyes opened and she looked at the ceiling. "Save for one land. Avalon." She lowered her eyes from the ceiling and turned them to Tulok. "When the Reaping came to us, our Ladies did not simply whisk the people from the land and bring them to safety, as so many other Ascendants had. They invoked magics ancient even to them and wove the blood of every Avalonian into the land itself, and brought the ...entirety...of Avalon to Sanctum." She winced a little at saying it here. "Everything that made us who we were was carried here...at the expense of the Ascendency of many of Them. I am the land, and the land is me. We flourish, and it flourishes. Should we perish, leaving something unfinished that prevents us from being returned to the cycle..." she trailed off a moment, leaving it unspoken.

Tulok nodded in sudden understanding, "Your late Knight's quest..."

Isolde nodded. "Reynard's spirit cannot be returned to the cycle until this is complete, and Avalon suffers for his absence," she said softly. She looked up at Tulok then, "Avalon's power and its magic flow in every one of us who are descended from the first families...the survivors of The Crossing. It calls to us when we are away, and it opens its arms to us in dreams, so that we can always find our way home."

He nodded slowly. "And the Lord Wanderer bids you Witness the world for Him..."

"To help recall that which was lost, that it may never be lost again."

Tulok pondered the information and lifted his eyes to meet Isolde's. He nodded and raised his bottle. "A secret for a secret."

"So, let it be done," she replied, and they both drank deeply.

There was an uncomfortable silence between the two

for several moments, as the depth of their sworn Oath to the other slowly sank in. Isolde drank deeply from her bottle once more.

Tulok swirled the contents of his bottle in contemplation.

"I forgot you were a scholar..." the woman replied, and stepped across the room to sit on her bed once more. "Clergy usually want to know about the significance of our Groves or the holy Matriarch." She bent forward, resting on her knees, and looked up at him. "The ties to magic and dreams... aren't ...really...known...to many." She chewed on her lip and looked away. "Many of the People don't understand it in any great detail. I only have a very basic understanding myself; truth be told."

Tulok nodded, not looking at her. "Is that why..." he paused for a moment considering, then continued. "Is that why there are so few of your people who leave the Islands?"

Isolde shrugged a little and drank from her bottle. "I can't speak for the actions and motivations of others directly..."

Tulok nodded in response, "And if it were widely known that the gifts attributed to many of your people were tied to the health of the land, and vice versa..."

"Aspiring Conquerors would begin to lure my people away, and to their deaths, to ensure they never returned...our magic would falter...we would fall...and so we just really don't talk too much about that little detail..." The Knight spoke darkly. She looked to Tulok and sat up. "Just as I am certain your Light Bringers would be swift to silence any tongue that dared speak of ... Heretical Cults in the Deep Desert that threatened the Heavens, and the Supremacy of the Everburning Throne."

Isolde watched as the priest bristled at the words. She

chuckled a little and raised her bottle to him, "As evidenced." she commented.

Tulok took a deep breath and blew it out, then stretched his great height. His shoulders and back snapped and popped as his muscles rippled across his broad frame. He looked over at Isolde. "You walk in dreams then? Like the legends say?" he asked her.

She snorted loudly and shook her head. "You got one secret out of me already tonight, Father. Try not to be greedy."

"Fair statement." He inclined his head and tipped his own bottle back.

Isolde leaned back on the bed, resting on her elbows, and regarded the big priest. "Not exactly how I expected any of this to go, I have to confess."

"Trapped in a foreign land until you set your knight's soul to rest, and oath-bound to an orc?" Tulok asked her. There was a hint of mirth in his tone.

"Pretty sure that counts as a ... new and unique experience... for the memory well." Isolde chuckled.

"Great, I have been immortalized..." Tulok replied and drank once more.

"Not unless I stop by the shrine before we leave." She corrected him with a half-smile.

"Well, I guess we need to make that stop tomorrow then." he smiled at her.

They laughed a little, the tension finally breaking. Isolde sighed and shook her head. "Are we gonna be ok then, Tulok?" she asked.

Tulok shrugged and leaned his hip back onto the table, it creaked and groaned under his weight. "That all depends on what the Sands have in store for us, I mean..."

"No." Isolde stopped him. "That's not what I meant. The Quest will be what the quest is fated to be, and we will see the other side one way or another, in that I have faith...are WE" she gestured between the two of them. "Going to be ok ...after all of these...revelations?"

Tulok took a deep breath and set his bottle down behind him, careful not to place it on the map. "My Dear Lady Isolde..." he started. She held up a warning finger at the use of the term. He continued, "Holy Witness and Wandering Knight of the Landless God." Tulok lifted his right hand and placed it over his chest, across his heart. "I have battled the sands and death itself to keep you in this world, you have slain emperors in the desert, and risked that same life in my defense, and in the defense of people, you barely knew. In spite of the vast differences between our faiths, our peoples, and our cultures – you have been nothing short of accepting, tolerant, and welcoming... traits that are not easily come by in the sands of Setesh. It has been my honor to be your traveling companion, and I continue to see it as so." He stepped over to her and offered her his hand. She took it and he pulled her up. She was a tall woman, though not so tall as to be able to meet his eyes directly. Tulok stepped back slightly, to not be quite so imposing a figure. He placed his right hand on her left shoulder. "Oaths do not bind us to one another out of force, but rather out of need....and trust. You would honor me further if you would allow me to call you... friend."

Isolde duAvalonne bright eyes glittered in the light from the lamps that lit the room. She smiled warmly at the big priest and nodded.

"Witnessed."

Chapter 22

The next day was mostly uneventful, save for morning and afternoon rituals that Tulok and Bengt attended. From an outside observation – one could only perceive a stern and unified front when it came to faith. Even Radiant Mother Selwyse's attitude seemed equally reverent of the two. Isolde overheard a few of the devout discuss the service at *The Light's Warmth* as being very solemn and more dignified than the previous priest had been. She wondered what sort of a man the former Radiant Father had been to have earned such a poor reputation here, then she remembered that Tulok had mentioned that Ra's faithful did not often remain in the River Lord's domain for long. She chuckled a little as she swirled the contents of her mug. *If they only knew* she thought to herself with a bit of a half-smile.

As if on cue, the figure of Bengt appeared at the front of her table – sweat already staining his brow, "Ser Knight," he said with as much measured formality as he could muster.

Isolde blinked and looked up at the skinny priest.

She inclined her head. "Brother Bengt, a pleasant day to you. How goes the afternoon services?" she said with a pleasant smile that Acolyte couldn't tell if it was genuine or feigned.

"The praise that we offer in the name of The Almighty Radiant Lord is neither good nor bad, it is All and Just. As it is when He passes over us, gracing us with the light," he replied with a certain dignity to his voice but Isolde could see the smugness in his eyes. He knew where he was, and he knew his audience.

The other devout in the cafe all raised their hands and heads upward and softly spoke, "Grace us with your Light our Radiant Lord."

Bengt had caught Isolde alone, and in a room of others of the faith – His faith. Isolde quickly assessed the room. If this was the time for things to go south – Bengt had the perfect opportunity to do so. Isolde realized her options were limited, so a touch of hospitality, swallowed pride, and humility was in order. She was in THEIR house after all. The knight smiled and bowed her head, touching her compass, in reverent respect. Bengt raised his hands as if to say something more when Isolde reached forward. Bengt paused and flinched at the sudden contact. He cracked open his eyes only to see her lifting up a cup to him with a smile,

"Would you care to join me, Brother Bengt?" She offered with a note of friendly invitation.

For a moment, his face was frozen in a pained smile as he tried to discern the meaning of her question. Everyone was watching them. He could feel the energy and attention in the room shift.

Before he could answer, Isolde's face filled with shock, "I'm sorry Brother, I hope I didn't make any offense by offering you a drink after service – is it okay to do so? I do not wish to offend you or your culture. I mean, is it okay if I offer you a seat even?" She smiled and withdrew her offered cup, a slight flush of embarrassment on her freckled cheeks.

The small man's mouth twisted even more with confusion. It was the look of someone trapped in their own snare, looking for an escape.

There were a few quiet murmurs of '*...she is respectful, unlike other foreigners I've seen...*' and '*...a culture that respects other faiths is remarkable...*' Bengt nodded quickly and then quietly lowered himself to sit across from her. He poured himself a cup of the spiced herbal tea that was being served. The moment of what could have been passed and he looked unsettled. It was not polite to gloat, but part of Isolde wanted to enjoy this moment.

He took a small sip of the spiced drink and made a sour face, but still raised his cup back to her, "Your gift is appreciated." His smile was unsteady, but he continued to drink the contents down.

Isolde watched him for a moment as he drank down the beverage. She offered him a genuine smile. "There, we have shared a drink together at the table," she nodded happily.

Bengt frowned, suddenly concerned that he had been trapped in some strange foreigner's tradition. Isolde held up her hands, asking for patience.

"We are going to be traveling together for some little while yet, Brother." she began. "I would...like to make amends for any misgivings... and begin anew if you would permit?" she asked sincerely.

Bengt continued frowning and staring into the bottom of his cup, as he contemplated Isolde's words. He downed the contents and met her eyes across the table. "It bears considering." With the cup empty, he set it down and started "The Radiant Father has asked that you accompany me down to the docks so as I may procure a barge across the Iteru. He gave me a price point for passage, and has asked that you act as my escort to ensure no unsavory types get the wrong ideas."

Isolde nodded, "What about the Radiant Father? Where..." she looked around hopefully for the big orc.

Their conversation was interrupted by members of the devout walking by the table and offering small gestures of thanks to the Acolyte as they left the cafe. Bengt relished the attention with a smile that made Isolde think of the River Lord. Maybe he was in the wrong faith. She leaned back in her chair and allowed the sallow priest his moment.

Once the faithful had departed, the room was mostly empty except for the cafe's Vidria owner who was picking up the bowls and cups. Bengt leaned forward, "His Radiance is seeing to the needs of *HER* Radiance and the Temple's." he began. "He will be spending the next few hours hanging up new trappings since She feels that the current ones are too worn and shabby." Bengt's dislike of the Gnome was evident and possibly greater than the disdain he felt for Tulok.

Isolde's eyebrows rose in surprise. "Too shabby?!" she exclaimed. "They look like they've been hanging less than a month!".

Bengt shrugged. "It is Her duty now; she will do as She deems needed." Bengt leaned back a little. "Father Tulok advised that the plan is to leave when the Radiant Lord's Eye is fading so the water's reflection will not be so direct... but unfortunately will be hungrier," he said with a bit of apprehension.

Isolde cocked her head to the side, "What do you mean?"

Bengt looked around the room empty again, "The River Lord's children inhabit the banks of the Iteru."

Isolde shook her head, still not understanding.

Still seeing her confusion, he sighed and then whispered, "Crocodiles – they keep themselves mostly under the water during the day and start to emerge when the worst of the day's heat has passed. The River Lord's devout cast offerings into the water at sundown. We will be coming out when it is feeding time."

"Why would Tulok want us to go during their feeding time?" she asked with a bit of suspicion.

Bengt shrugged, "I have no idea. I like it less than you do. I have no desire to be here. I would rather be back home in Tarf-qua, but we all have our duties to perform." the statement was perhaps the single most earnest thing Isolde had heard him say in the time she had known him.

"We have limited funds and movement across the River at that time of day is the cheapest fare for three travelers with no... appreciable... cargo. I can make sure that we only pay for what we want and not anything more."

Isolde remembered Tulok's last experience here and his failed negotiations. He had asked Bengt to handle this, so he would not have to. Isolde looked over at Bengt for a moment, Bengt shrugged, neither confirming nor denying the unspoken question in her green eyes.

"Whatever you do," he started but with a strange sense of conviction in his words, "do not make or accept polite promises to anyone ... anywhere ... as we get closer to the docks. The power and lure of the River Lord is stronger there. His people will be looking for those who do not understand their ways...and you stand out."

Isolde opened her mouth as if to object and then thought better of it. She nodded reluctantly.

"We will be taking both cart and barge transports to the Dock Master. There, we will check in with them... as well as give the EXACT weight of yourself AND your possessions. Once the totals are calculated, he will give us a writ of passage and the names of active barges. We will go to the names listed and see who can take us. Once we have that secured, I will send a message to the temple. We will wait for Tu…" he paused and relaxed his shoulders, "We will wait for the Radiant Father to come, and then we will leave across the river."

Isolde nodded in agreement, for as shallow as Bengt was – he was also aware of their situation and environment. His warnings weren't so much for her, but also to protect himself. If she was acting as his bodyguard – making her aware was not only necessary, but it ensured his own survival. That was something she knew she could count on when it came to the small man.

"When do we leave?"

~~~

It was not a simple cart ride from the cafe to the docks, rather it was a mixture of cart and barge transfers from one portion of the city to the other as the pair went deeper and deeper inside the city, toward the river itself. The city was enormous and it would have been very easy to become lost in the endless twists and turns of the vast metropolis. Travel in the pulled carts was certainly more enjoyable than travel by barge, Isolde thought. It wasn't because of the difference of comfort, rather it was the unsettling feeling of knowing that the dark shapes in the water were crocodiles relaxing in cool water below. It was something Bengt made a point of bringing to her attention when they got in the first boat. He had meant it to spook her, but her polite smile deflated any would-be satisfaction from her fear.

While she maintained a strong, and polite face, she always felt a pair of reptilian eyes peering at her from the water's surface. The Lord Wanderer's knights were not given to fear, but alert caution was certainly warranted.

Each time a mode of transportation changed for another, Bengt argued and directed all the drivers and ferrymen in a mix of Seteshi and the trade tongue. His words were clipped, and his countenance firm. He was clearly
~~~

skilled in this aspect of his duties. For every agreement made, the jingle in the purse of coins became smaller and smaller. The last ferryman dropped them off in front of a bustling tavern that boasted a large patio with several patrons enjoying a midday's drink. They were one more ride away from the dock itself – which according to Bengt was going to be the most expensive of the rides.

Bengt looked in the purse and was counting its contents as he mumbled to himself. He walked toward the small shaded throughway created between the tavern and another building. Isolde followed behind him feeling happy that she was no longer in confined quarters with him.

"Excuse me," said an elf who peeled himself off the shaded wall, "Is there a temple to the Sun God near here?" he asked smoothly.

Bengt looked up from his purse with a look of disdain, "The nearest one is near the front gate; why would The Radiant Lord intrude upon the River Lord's domain?"

Isolde looked at the elf as he slowly approached. His posture was relaxed and graceful. His figure was tall, lean, and lithe. His eyes were focused and sharp. His clothes were clean and the colors muted. She hadn't noticed him until he spoke up.

Nor the three others behind you

Tiny hairs rose on the back of Isolde's neck. Instinctively, she spun on the ball of her foot and placed one hand on the hilt of her sword and the other holding its sheath. She took a position of defense between Bengt and whatever was approaching from behind. Another elf and two humans approached them; wicked-looking knives drawn. Their curved blades were meant for bloodletting. Isolde had seen the handiwork of such blades before and knew of their simple power to make stitches and hand pressure on wounds useless. She took a deep breath and set her stance at the ready.

Bengt's panicked voice sounded from behind her, "You...you DARE threaten a Priest of the Radiant Lord?!"

Out of her peripheral, Isolde saw the other elf draw his own blade as well.

"Like you said Father," he stated in a smooth voice. He smiled a wicked smile. "... your Sun God is too far away to hear us in the shade... and the River demands tribute" He lunged forward toward the pair.

Time seemed to slow down. Isolde drew her longsword from its sheath and swung it in a wide arc in front of her. Behind her, she could hear Bengt speaking in a panicked voice before he threw his hand forward and a ball of holy fire flew at the first attacker as he called down the power of his God. The elven attacker howled in pain.

Isolde pulled her swing up short. The passageway between the buildings which was normally roomy enough for travelers was not conducive to a four on two fight. She would have to be careful. She pulled the hilt toward her hip, pointing the tip of the blade at the assailant, and turned her body so her shoulders were no longer square, narrowing the target.

The sudden appearance of the blade gave the assailants pause. They adjusted themselves with the narrow space. Isolde readied herself to either block an incoming blow or lunge forward to stab, keenly aware of the room she had to work with.

The leader growled in pain as the radiant fire burned his chest, singing flesh and clothing, "Take her down you idiots!"

Bengt spoke in a hurried voice, " The Radiant Lord sees your wickedness and turns His eyes from you that you are no longer blessed in His Sight!" He fumbled with his sacred symbols, calling the favor of heaven down once more. There was a flash of light from behind Isolde no one expected.

The three attackers staggered for a moment and then rushed forward, blinded by the momentary flash. One took the lead while the pair followed behind, blocking any attempt to escape should the lead's attack fail. Isolde braced herself, wishing for her shield. She would have to block the blow and redirect it with the hilt... if she were lucky.

The injured elf yelled something at Bengt in a language Isolde did not understand and rushed forward. His wicked-looking blade came down in a clean arc, seeking the soft flesh of the sallow-skinned priest, who stepped to the side. The knife came down hard into the wall – much to the attacker and Bengt's surprise. Bengt's eyes opened wide and then he gave a sickening smile.

Isolde's first attacker swung. She brought her weapon up to block, and caught the blade on her bracer, as she twisted the length of the blade sideways. The second took advantage of the opening and brought his knife down toward her chest. She closed her eyes and braced for the impact and the pain. There was no deflecting it. There was an audible clunk and slide as the knife's blade met Seteshi hardened leather armor. She staggered, bracing one foot behind her to stop the stumble. Her tunic shredded; the Knight Wanderer righted herself quickly. Her assailant swore. She leaned away, hips twisting, left leg taking her weight as she bent her right knee. The third attacker never had a chance to bring his blade up as Isolde kicked him squarely in the chest sending him flying back out of the entrance of the passageway toward the outer walkway.

Bengt called to his God once more

"The Sun is my Justice and His Light is my shield" as the lead elf drew a second blade and attempted to ram the dagger into the acolyte's stomach. The blade was stopped short as the yellowish glow that surrounded the small man prevented the blade from piercing his body.

Bengt bent forward slightly, as he instinctively pulled his stomach away from the blade that sought his demise. Isolde felt the blade of the first attacker hit her right shoulder blade, meeting the 'clink' of Avalonian steel that was affixed to her leather cuirass.

"*Thank you, Reynard...*" she whispered, thankful for what remained of her knight's armor.

The second attacker held back his blade. Meeting Isolde's eyes, he twisted his blade to the side, wrapping his fingers around the hilt tightly, and punched her square in the face. There was a sick crunching sound. The blow rocked Isolde for a second. She staggered and shook her head, tasting blood. The courage of The Lord Wanderer overpowered pain and outshone fear, it was His blessing on his faithful. Isolde looked up at her attacker and smiled as blood began to leak from her nose. "

If you insist..." she smiled through bloody lips, a horrific sight. He balked. She rushed forward, pulled her head back, and slammed her forehead into the man's face – blinding him in blood and pain. He crumpled to the ground.

Putting his hand in the elf's face, Bengt spoke with conviction, "The Radiant Lord Purifies All" and another ball of holy fire slammed into the elf's face at point-blank range. He screamed in agony and fear.

The scream caught Isolde's attention for a brief moment but it was enough. The first attacker brought his blade across her left bicep. Once more blood flowed. Grunting in pain, Isolde shifted again. Blood flowed down her arm and covered her hands, making them slick. She shook off a memory that tried to force itself to the forefront and raised her blade above her head, opening herself wide to attack. Her attacker moved to step close. Close enough to bring him into range. Instead of slashing – Isolde brought the heavy metal pommel down on the exposed crown of the man's head.

There was an audible pop. He fell to his knees with a long groan as dark red blood escaped from his scalp and flowed freely down his head and face. He wobbled for a moment, then fell over.

The world was without sound as the rush of the fight narrowed her vision along with the pain and the faraway sound of voices. None of their assailants were standing as they groaned on the ground. She looked over as to see Bengt standing over the lead elf, yelling and pointing at him. She leaned back against the wall to catch her breath when she heard something towards the passageway entrance. Grasping her blade, she readied for another attack. A tall lizard-like creature clad in a red tunic bearing a stylized golden image of the crocodile god came toward her. His hands were exposed and turned toward her. Her mind's fog remembered that gesture.

She relaxed her grip on her weapon.

The Sobekite was gesturing toward her and saying something. She understood none of it. Isolde shook her head and looked at him again.

"...are bleeding. Please either put the sword in the sheath or on the ground," the Sobekite said in a calm and almost assuring voice. They took careful steps toward her.

She nodded and placed the longsword back into the leather and hooked the strap in place. Blood from her arm had dripped down the hilt and guard and covered the blade and scabbard. She would have to clean them both later. Sound returned as the rush faded. She shook her head to clear it.

There was a Sobekite on the other end of the passageway flanked by a human – all wearing the same red tunic of the Sobekite that Bengt was speaking to. In front of her was the one that asked her to put up the sword. Close by, an elven man in the same styled tunic began to gather the blades from the ground.

Bengt's shrill voice was full of fire and conviction as he went on and on about thugs attacking a member of the revered clergy. Isolde's attention was drawn immediately to the sickly sallow priest and his heated words. She had heard this tone before in courts and markets. It was the tone of landed gentry being affronted by something and demanding that the city guard take this seriously. She knew where his words would be going next, and they would not be helpful to their situation. She steadied herself and stepped to Bengt and quickly interceded,

"BROTHER Bengt," she started loud enough to silence Bengt from causing more issues, "and I were attacked by these four men."

The uniformed guards all turned their attention from Bengt to Isolde. She raised a soiled hand to wipe at the blood still seeping from her nose. It smeared her pale face. She held her nostrils shut with one hand, to staunch the bleeding and winced.

"My name is Isolde duAvalonne, Holy Witness to the Wandering Lord." She began through her pinched nasal tones "... and I was asked to protect this man while he traveled to the Dock Master. I did only what was needed to defend ourselves and did my best not to bring any lasting harm to any of them – despite their intentions to do worse."

The Sobekite nodded and looked around," I think you may have taken a bad hit to the head Ser Knight," they commented, using her honorific respectfully, "...There are only three men here."

Isolde slowly dropped her hand from her nose and looked around, counting bodies. One of the elves was missing.

"I kicked him in the chest to get him away from us.... and sent him reeling back...", a horrible feeling welled up in Isolde's stomach as the blood faded from her face. She put a hand over her mouth as she looked up at the scaled creature, "I...I only meant to kick the wind out of him, not to..." Her eyes looked past the reptilian creature. Not six feet past the alleyway, the road gave way to the water's edge and the river below. Isolde could not finish the sentence as imagery flooded her mind of the elf being eaten alive by beasts with calm-looking eyes.

The Sobekite looked at Isolde for a moment as if weighing something internally. His reptilian face was hard to read as she looked up, unable to say anything. Seemingly satisfied, he nodded his head, and then walked toward the end of the waterway and looked down. No one said anything for a few moments. The only sounds were the groans of pain from the attackers as shackles were being locked onto their wrists.

The guard turned back with an odd smile, "As they say, none go hungry."

Despite how horrifying the words were, somehow, she couldn't believe how reassuring it sounded.

Chapter 23

It had been ruled self-defense by Constable Yalmig, the one with the 'calming' presence. As such, the small pouches of coin that each of the assailants had on them were given to Bengt in reparation. Isolde felt it more akin to a small bribe just to keep the holy man quiet. Yalmig did not seem to have a problem doing so, and she got the feeling it was not the first time that reparations were paid for silence. The amount was more than enough to pay for the last barge ride to the Dock Master and cover any other '*necessary*' expenses that they might come across Bengt added. Isolde rolled her eyes and stared at the floor of the barge.

Given the cramped quarters of the fight, she was glad Tulok wasn't there, though he would have made better company otherwise. Thin and irritable as he was, Bengt was the best person to have had there. Admittedly she was liking the acolyte a little bit more, especially after seeing how useful he was in a fight. However, each time he complained or made some comment about the world around him, it brought him right back down to the same category of a pair of used shoes. Sometimes comfortable, often with holes, and always with a bad smell.

Isolde had experienced the Avalonian docks growing up – what she saw took that concept to an entirely different level. While she could not pronounce the actual name, the Trader's tongue called it the River's Mouth. It was a sprawling dock that seemed to run up and down both ends of the bank and even on the other side of the wide Iteru. Boats and barges of all sizes were kept tethered to the banks and many more sailing and rowing down the Iteru's dark blue road. There was an assortment of cargo being hoisted to and from the boats – all heading to destinations unknown. There were pack animals being loaded as well as creatures she had never seen before roamed free: birds with colorful feathers and dangerously curved talons and beaks; a large cat-like creature whose eyes seemed to glow and follow the crowd below. If a creature needed to be purchased or shipped – this would be the starting point.

Exiting the barge, they were directed to a waiting line that led to a large building. The wait in line was not long as everyone had schedules to maintain. When they entered the Dock Master's office, they were greeted by a Gnome who began firing off questions at Bengt in the trade tongue. For once, the acolyte seemed to recognize that opinions and observations were not necessary and kept everything matter of fact. After the questions, they were directed to another room filled with scales to which Isolde was directed to stand upon.

The gnome fired off more questions to Bengt to which he looked over to Isolde, "Will that be all of your gear for the trip?"

She thought for a moment and shook her head, "Bedding and food but I'm not sure how to account for that."

Bengt looked in the air as if calculating and then spoke to the gnome. Satisfied, the gnome directed them to another larger room where several other groups of people were waiting.

The stay in the waiting room was longer than the line

outside, but at least was shaded and the air was kept cool, if humid.

"How did we do?" Isolde asked as she looked around.

"Well," Bengt said with an odd smile, counting the coins in the purse, "Even with armor, you're not as heavy as you look."

It took a bit of will to prevent the wandering knight from smacking the small man over the head. Instead, she coolly replied, "Well I'm happy to have saved you a coin or two."

The acolyte looked up and then the realization of what he said dawned on him – his face flushed red and he began to sputter and eventually put the purse away. For the rest of the time, he sat quietly looking down at his lap. Another Gnome appeared from a doorway and called out.

"Ahem...he means us," Bengt said quietly and stood up. Isolde said nothing but smiled at the Gnome and followed him toward the door, leaving the Acolyte behind.

Down another hallway, they were led into a large office that bore three desks. Gold and alabaster graced the walls as well as carved jadeite stone. It reminded Isolde more of temples or places of worship rather than a dock master's office. The largest of the desks was on a dais and sat above the other two. It was currently vacant, but one of the smaller desks had a Sobekite sitting at attention while looking over various papers and scrolls. Their eyes blinked calmly as the pair approached, and a friendly smile graced her scaled lips.

"According to the paperwork," the assistant began with a soft tone to their voice, "You are looking for a barge across the River Lord's Gift to the Eastern Banks. The passengers include two honored members of the Sun God's Clergy – an Orc and a human, weighing approximately 164 tals, and a Knight Wanderer from the far east islands at 68 tals even. Very interesting to say the least."

The statement hung in the air, but nothing more was said. Isolde expected more questions, but instead, the assistant produced a document with her signature and handed it to the Gnome who in turn handed it to Bengt. "Pleasant journey to all and may the River Lord provide a fruitful bounty wherever your travels take you."

Before Isolde could utter thanks, the Gnome was ushering them out of the room as another person was being let into the office.

Friendly, but also efficient in their work as Isolde thought as they made their way back out.

Once outside, the Gnome pointed to an area of the dock that looked like a tavern of sorts, but with a large blackboard posted outside of it. Making their way down, she looked at Bengt, "You said that it would be dangerous to speak here. It didn't seem that bad."

Bengt finally felt that he could speak, "That was the easy part. The administration is run to the letter so that all who come here cannot say they were treated unfairly. It is the Barge captains that will be part where we have to come to some accord. Our total weight exceeds the passenger barges so we have to deal with a combination of cargo and passengers. They are less comfortable and more cramped."

"I thought you said we did well?" she asked.

"You and I did well...our...third passenger...limited our options," he said as politely as possible so as not to raise any possible insult.

"Ah," was all that Isolde could say.

"Please do not take this the wrong way," Bengt started which immediately put Isolde on guard, "When we enter into negotiations with the captains – do not say anything. Just look unreadable, no smiles or curt looks. They are very...fickle. We may have a writ for passage, but we still have to bargain with them."

"I believe I can do so," she replied with no humor in her voice. Her face had begun to darken as the bruise began to form and the dried blood on her face with the busted lip bore its own intimidation.

"That's excellent! Just...like...like that..." Bengt remarked and then felt the weight of her gaze and knew that his earlier remark had not been forgotten.

"Uh...let's...let's go."

~~~

The large blackboard outside listed the names of the barges themselves, their respective captains, current weight capacity, and time of departure. There were only three barges available at the time listed and one was already full.

"*The Cat's Eye* under Captain Heyal, and *'Nomes All* under Captain Tage," Bengt read from the board. "If we are lucky – they will hate each other."

Isolde raised an eyebrow and then understood the meaning. Rivalries in a bidding environment were considered a traveler's boon as one rival always tries to under-sell the other. It would simply be a matter of letting personalities take their toll.

The River's Delight served as both a tavern for local barge captains as well as an impromptu office. Like all taverns, it had its fair share of conversation, laughter, and heated arguments.

As they were about to enter, a sour-looking Vidria forced the doors open, "Outta my waa...," he stopped short of Isolde.

Bengt had not been an obstacle, but the look from the Avalonian gave him pause.

"Um, excuse me uh miss," and sidestepped as she strode forward with Bengt behind her.
~~~

As she entered the tavern, she realized it was more like a large covered terrace than a building. The back section of the tavern gave everyone a full view of the Iteru as well as the various traffic going to and from along its banks. She stood there and a slight flare of homesickness rose up with the view, though it was hard to pin down where it had come from.

Her memories were displaced as Bengt greeted the bartender with his shrill but polite voice,

"Hello bartender, can you please point out which of these fine people are Captains Heyal & Tage." His voice came off louder than it should have been.

Isolde could feel every eye in the room drawn to the presence of the small man. The bartender was an elven woman whose back was turned from the bar as she filled a pair of tankards. Her shoulders were tattooed with a stylized scorpion. It was similar to the images that Isolde had seen around the city. It was another deity in the desert she was unaware of. She made a mental note to herself to ask Tulok about it.

The elven woman's hair had been pulled back into several tight braids with various bits of metal accessories. Her muscles bunched at the sound of Bengt's voice and she spoke as she slowly turned around, "Well if you have two eyes you can..."

Her look was tired and gave the impression that this was the straw that was going to break the camel's back. However, that was stopped short when she saw Bengt's sweaty smiling face and medallion of The Radiant Lord around his neck, "...priest...ahem...Father, your Radiance – my apologies. I thought you were someone else."

Instead of throwing his usual set-upon countenance, Bengt replied in a gracious tone,

"No matter and no apologies necessary. You are a person of importance so your time and patience are valuable. If you would be so kind, can you please point out Captains Heyal and Tage."

Isolde willed herself to continue looking at the river. The amount of politeness coming out of Bengt was a little more than she could stomach. She watched as the bartender motioned to a lone individual that sat near the corner of the room looking out at the river.

"Captain Tage is the one with a white stripe in his beard. Captain Heyal, just walked out of the bar a few minutes ago in a bit of...huff," she said.

"Ah, we...uh...ran into him at the door. Will he be coming back?" the small man asked.

The elven woman smiled at the priest, "He was having trouble with his barge, so I'm not sure when he will be back." The words were polite, but Isolde could see that there was much more there – yet all of which was lost on Bengt.

Following her instructions, the pair headed toward a quiet corner of the room. A gnome sat on the barstool, looking out over the river and sketching scenery before him. The art was meticulous to say the very least as there were very few marks that showed correction and each line was deliberate in its stroke. The detail in the image was enough to catch even Bengt's dull mind. The more they stared at the picture, the more they almost saw motion in the water and the drifting of the boats and barges in the distance.

The artist cleared his throat, "While not saying anything is appreciated – it is unsettling to have two people stare at you with their mouths open."

Turning around to face the pair, the Gnome regarded them both with a stern look that was reminiscent of a teacher looking at his students. He paused for a moment seeing Isolde's bruised and bloodied nose. She smiled. He continued. "I suppose you are looking for passage across the Iteru?" His face was deeply tan and the beard he sported was a pale blonde with a single stark white stripe down the center. It was a curious sight, but one that gave his face more character in the afternoon shade.

Bengt nodded his head quickly, "Yes – we...we are, good captain, we uh, have our writ from the harbormaster for three passengers, only traveling bags."

"Three? I see," he said and held his hand out.

Bengt narrowed his eyes and was about to speak when Isolde pulled the slip of paper out of his hand and handed it to Captain Tage. The Gnome shook his head slightly and then nodded his head to Isolde in a quiet thanks. He looked over the documents and coughed slightly.

"232 tals?! How big are your bags Father?"

"Quite normal I assure you, good captain. It is our third passenger. I am but a humble Acolyte in service to the Radiant Lord. The Father is of the Orcish people. The bags are standard, it is just the allotment for his Radiance that we find ourselves coming to you."

The Gnome reached into a front pocket of his vest and pulled out a pipe. Lighting it up, he took a puff and began tapping his fingers on the counter, as if putting weights and items together.

"I will have to move some things around to counterbalance the weight as well as provide an area for the three of you to occupy. Before you, all I had was strictly dry goods, so this will cut my lunchtime to make adjustments. Bearing those labor and time costs to myself and my crew, it will be twenty...each."

Bengt's smile froze and flipped on itself as he heard the price, "Sixty? For three people during the roughest time of the day? The standard fare is 5 for a single person to cross and you want four times as much? For sixty we can buy our own skiff and row ourselves!"

"Then might I suggest Arvat's further down the way. I'm sure he can get you outfitted with a lovely child's raft that will fit your financial sensibilities just fine, *good brother*" Tage said and began to turn around.

The blood in Bengt's face rose to angry red, "Well! I will..." before he could finish, Isolde placed a firm hand on Bengt's shoulder and stepped forward.

"Sir – if it is a matter of labor, I would be willing to lend a hand to help lighten your crew's workload." she offered.

Tage paused and looked back at the young woman with the same schoolteacher scrutiny. Then he looked back at the small acolyte who was fighting with his own dignity.

"This is called a reasonable conversation – you should take notes – Brother." He turned his attention back to Isolde, "We are to ship off in 4 hours. Each hour worked, I'll knock off two coins from each passenger. You haul your own gear and bring your own drink. What say you?"

While the concept of money was foreign, sums were not unknown to the young woman as well the ability to barter. She rubbed the bottom of her chin and looked around the room.

"What about three coins from each passenger, and I will get a small keg to bring aboard for the crew to enjoy as well as provide some insight on Avalonian ship knots?" she countered.

"Islander, eh?" Tage said with a bit of realization of what kind of woman he was dealing with, He puffed on his pipe in thought. "Two and a half and never mind the keg. I don't need those knuckleheads sloppy – on or off the barge."

"I would consider it a kindness if you had someone bring our bags aboard. I stopped a mugging earlier and I would not want anyone else to strain themselves," she said as she faced Tage, but let her eyes slowly drift to the side where Bengt was standing. Tage smiled and rolled his eyes, "Fine – two coins and a half for each hour worked, trade-in Avalonian knots and a *courtesy* bag handling," he said as he held out his hand.

Isolde grasped his outstretched hand, "Deal and Witnessed," she said.

Tage nodded his head and released the shake, "Well come on then – time's a-wastin." He hopped off the barstool and headed toward the door, "Leta, am I good for the day?"

The bartender nodded her head, "Better than Heyal," she said with a smirk. Tage laughed and headed out with Isolde in tow. Isolde paused and turned around to realize Bengt was still standing there, his mouth wide open and face full of shock.

"Oh Brother Bengt, please let the Radiant Father know to meet us at the barge in four hours. Please ask him to bring enough to drink for the trip. You will be fine here, yes?"

Bengt's head moved slightly in acknowledgment though his understanding of the situation was still catching up with his facial expression.

As the two were heading out the door, the acolyte heard Tage ask, "Now tell me why is a lady like you getting mugged in a city like this?"

Isolde laughed, "Getting mugged was easier than fighting the giant scorpion two days ago."

"Wait – what?" was all that could be heard from Tage as the tavern door closed behind them.

Chapter 24

Traveling the desert was different than navigating a City. This was doubly true for someone the size of Father Tulok. There were few options for a person of his size to traverse the distance from the Temple to the harbor. It was a hike, to be certain; but it saved him a hefty purse of coin, not to mention avoiding multiple uncomfortable discussions with canal bargemen about his weight, his size, and whether he could swim should the boat capsize because of him.

Free from the demands of the Radiant Mother Selwyse, Tulok was once more able to clear his mind and focus on the task at hand. The Radiant Mother had drained both his reserves of patience as well as gifts of the Radiant Lord. The truly divine blessings of The Radiant Lord of the Skies were not something called upon all the time. Calling upon the divine faith when others are in danger was one thing – but the Radiant Mother had him perform these acts of faith in order to endorse the validity of the temple on its parishioners to demonstrate that The Radiant Lord was alive and well within the River Lord's city. While a risky move – it was her temple now and so she would reap any consequences of her choices.

However, Tulok saw it for what it was – presumed

humility. Sending the large priest out after having him expend the reserves of his divinity would ensure that he could not rely on their god's strength for the beginning of the trip. He was aware of what she was doing and said nothing. Tulok's day-to-day in Tarf-qua was all about doing things the hard way. He only invoked his Lord's Blessings when necessary, so rather than call her out on it – he let her have the tiny victory.

The walk did him some good as well. Relearning the streets and layout of the City, remembering which areas needed to be avoided when on foot, and encountering a few new locations along his path were all part of Tulok's afternoon. He had been able to hire a small cart to carry their personal gear to the port. With the ornate symbol of the Temple prominently displayed on the various items, few would be willing to attempt to steal or otherwise hijack the transport. He sent a note along with the bags, to advise Bengt and Isolde that he would be arriving separately and on foot.

Tulok gazed skyward at the colors on the horizon. Sunset would be in about two hours. He frowned a little at the idea of being on the water when sunset observations should be occurring. The presence of the river predators seemed more of a small inconvenience compared to being denied the ability to perform the Dusk Litany. He hoped that Bengt had remembered this when making arrangements. They could, of course, renew their pledge once they made landfall on the East Bank, but there was an order to things that the orc took comfort in, in maintaining the schedule of prayer.

He smelled the water long before he saw it. While there was an ever-present scent of river water throughout the City, the smell of the Iteru was a unique aroma that was both heavy in the air and damp upon the lungs. Setesh lived and died by its access to water. The Iteru was the lifeline for the whole of the Realm of Setesh. Its waters provided food, in the form of fishing, silt for planting, and life-giving liquid for all plants and animals. It was a source of travel and trade. The Children of the River Lord knew well the importance and value of this land and its marriage to the waters. This was why they had chosen to build not just on one side of the Iteru, but to extend the breadth of Nahral to both banks. Further down and up the river respectively, the cities of Ophir and Litharge sat on opposite banks. The Capital and the Necropolis each stood on their own sides of the Iteru; one at the delta, and the other farther and deeper into the desert. They were the largest cities on either bank... Here; however, the City of the River Lord stretched wide across both banks, claiming each for themselves, making it arguably larger than either. One could stand along the river of the Iteru at any point in Nahral and see the distant other side. On a calm day, when the Sun God's light graced the smooth surface of the water just right, the river looked like a polished mirror, and each side could be a reflection or a desert mirage copying the line of the other.

Tulok never had occasion to travel to the East Bank of the Iteru and visit the other side of the City. When he had been here last, all of his business had been conducted on the West Bank. Seeing the other side of the Iteru, and indeed, everything beyond would be new for him. He reached down absently to pat at the scroll case that contained the map to Ahsal. It was his only possession that would help them reach their destination. Tulok had spent several hours reviewing the map and cross-referencing its markings against other notes in the various tomes within the Temple. Part of him wished they had time to visit the great Library in Litharge before undertaking this journey.

He was certain that all of the information he needed; not only on Ahsal but on the scarab that Isolde carried, would be in one of their books there. While the sands had forged Tulok into an orc who could carry his own weight in a skirmish; in his heart, he was a Scholar who would have been more than happy to spend his life reading books, scrolls, and recording history.

The press of shops began to break away and lend itself to warehouses, suppliers, and dockside taverns, inns, and bars. The workers and sailors who made this area of the City their home, slid suspicious eyes over in Tulok's direction; their countenances only changing when they noted the symbol of faith the orc prominently displayed. Then careful and respectful nods were offered as they continued about their business. He had made arrangements with Bengt to meet him at the Dock Master's Office before sending Isolde off with the greasy acolyte earlier that morning. It was a central enough location to ensure they would be able to find one another. He had also advised Bengt to look for their goods to arrive there before he did.

Tulok frowned as he approached the familiar building that housed the Dock Master's Office. The cart he had hired, and their goods, were sitting outside the doors to the receiving bay. A young boy sat atop the bags, tossing a ball against a stack of barrels and catching it as it rebounded back to him. Tulok approached and politely cleared his throat.

"Good day," the big orc nodded.

The young boy – Tulok guessed him to be about seven, with desert tanned skin and dark thick hair, looked up at the orc in the priest's robes. Tulok was not a typical sight in many cities; here in Nahral, he must have been just another regular oddity that traveled the River's Gift.

"Hello!" the boy smiled and waved. "You are the Orc

Priest of The Radiant Lord that is gonna pay me for watching his bags until he gets here?" the boy asked.

Tulok blinked, unprepared for the comment. "I...um...I suppose I am..."

"Good!" the boy hopped up off of the bags. "The courier stuck around for almost an hour, and then a skinny priest came by and asked if he could wait until you got here. Courier had to go; so I offered to wait." He smiled up at the big priest.

"How very resourceful of you," Tulok replied carefully.

"I know, right?" the boy beamed.

"And where might this...skinny priest... be at present?" Tulok asked, looking around.

"Oh, he is over at *River's Delight*." the boy pointed over to the dockside tavern.

"Of course, he is..." Tulok grumbled. He looked at the boy. "There was a woman, in armor, with him. Is she there too?"

The boy shook his head. "Oh no, Father. No woman with the priest in the bar. She left with Cap'n Tage and is helping him and his boys over on the '*Nomes All*." he nodded again. "Oh...she is a mess, Father. Looks like she's been in a fight."

Tulok tensed. "Excuse me?" he said in a guarded tone.

"The woman. Got a sword and armor, funny accent, pale, like those little grubs you find under rocks sometimes. Looks like she got a busted nose. Her face is all red and bruised up. I mean, I don't think she's the kind of woman to just let a fella hit her, so I figure she must have given as good as she got, ya know?" The boy bounced his ball.

There was a slight rumble in Tulok's chest. "Thank you." he managed to say.

"Sure thing. Umm... you gonna pay me now?" he asked.

Tulok took a deep breath. "I shall, but I would like you

to stay with the bags for a few moments longer if you might? I need to find my fellow. *River's Delight*, you said?" Tulok's tone was even and cool.

"No problem, and yup, right over there." he pointed at the shop where Bengt supposedly sat, drinking, and waiting for Tulok to arrive.

"And the '*Nomes All?*" Tulok asked

"She's moored in the last berth at the end of the dock. See you in a little bit, Father!" the boy smiled and hopped back up onto bags.

Tulok turned in the direction of the *River's Delight* and strode with intent down the dock.

~~~

Bengt stared into the half-empty tankard – it was his third. The ale was good but the water was more expensive than the drink in front of him, so he chose a different way to keep himself hydrated. He smiled to himself for his own sense of frugality.

Leta, the Bartender provided no conversation, and only spoke to the small man when he needed a refill. The other occupants of the tavern kept among themselves and the feeling of loneliness surrounded him. Staring into his cup, he began to lament this whole trip. A merchant a few months back had mentioned Nahral had a habit of cycling through priests. Volunteering for this awful trip was his chance of getting out of Tulok's massive shadow and running a temple as it should be. He had longed to get out from the Temple of Tarf-qua. There was no way that Tulok would be removed. The younger people liked him; he had helped raise half of them. He was liked and trusted – well mostly trusted. Some of the elders still did not trust the orc and they had good reason.

"Orcs are dangerous and fickle creatures," he said quietly to himself.
~~~

Bengt suddenly felt a large hand on his back, grabbing his robes, and lifting him into the air. He felt himself slowly being turned around and saw two red eyes staring at him

"They are FICKLE because they are more EMPATHETIC. They are ruled by their...EMOTIONS...more than most creatures here on Sanctum. The TENDENCY for violent RAGE ONLY happens if it is not met by REASON. Solid, unfaltering REASON." The rumble in his chest was deep and the words were said with a practiced motion to ensure that each was clearly understood.

For a moment Leta felt she should say something, and then she noticed the medallion of The Radiant Lord and the orc's manner of dress. Far be it for her to interfere in matters of faith, but it was her bar.

"Would your Radiance care to quench his thirst?"

Tulok held Bengt aloft for another moment, the intensity of his glare almost gave off searing heat that prevented the smaller man from meeting his gaze. Bengt had heard about Tulok's eyes when the orcish rage was behind them. It took every bit of will within the little man to not wet himself.

Without a word, the orc released his grip and dropped Bengt to the floor like a bag of potatoes. Turning toward the bar, he leaned forward with his arms crossed and holding on to his biceps. Leta could see the fight for restraint in the massive hands as his fingers dug into the skin. Tulok looked forward at the four large casks.

"Something...dark, please."

Leta gave a calm nod and pulled out a larger tankard and began to fill it. Placing in front of the orc, "Anything else I can help you with your Radiance?" she asked.

"Yes," he said and took a drink from the tankard, "The lady that was with *my acolyte*," he said as he directed the words to Bengt on the floor. "I was told that she looked a little...rough when she came in. Would you be able to give me a better description?"

"Oh yeah, she was ripe busted a bit, but nothing too bad. From the looks of it, she took a shot or two to the face and had some wound on her arm. She had quite a bit of dried blood on her face when she came in. She might not have realized how bad off she looked. However, she seemed to be in fine shape. She walked fine, and I understand she is paying for her way with Captain Tage by doing some cargo lifting. She looked like a woman who knew what she was about," Leta said in a matter-of-fact tone. "According to what I heard as they were leaving – she and your acolyte were mugged."

Tulok took another drink and his eyes closed. He took a deep breath and his shoulders relaxed a bit. He felt a bit of the anger inside turn on himself as it was he who had told Bengt that Isolde would be his escort. She did her job exactly as was expected of her. If they were in fact mugged in broad daylight – a clergy member for that matter, that was an issue.

He took another drink, "Thank you Miss...?"

"Leta, just Leta your Radiance. Will your acolyte be needing anything more?" she asked with a slight smile.

Tulok looked down at Bengt who had not moved since he hit the floor. The big priest reached down toward the small man who immediately put his hands up as he closed his eyes.

Bengt felt a tug at his belt and opened his eyes. With careful fingers, Tulok opened the coin purse and stared at its contents. The Orc's gaze returned back to the small man – it was a mixed look of both disdain and disgust.

Turning his attention back to Leta, "No, I think he is good for the moment," and took another long drink.

Chapter 25

The rhythm of the song helped the movements aboard the ship among those topsides as the cargo was loaded, and the ground tackle checked and double-checked. The crew of the *'Nomes All* seemed in good spirits, despite the heat and sun overhead. Perhaps it was due to their general nature, but was probably more due to the presence of the ragamuffin woman warrior who was hefting crates and shoving boxes around that would have taken the rest of them hours of extra time to address.

Armor pulled off and set aside, sleeves rolled up to the elbows, undershirt loosely tucked into her belt, her hair pulled back from her face, wisps of long dark curls teasing at her temples, Isolde smiled and sang along with them all as they worked. While no trained singer, her voice was not unpleasant and her upper register added a nice counterbalance to the deeper tones of sailors. Covered in sweat, river water, and beer, the Avalonian matched move for move, and beat for beat as she followed the instruction of the Quartermaster in handling the goods and storing them where needed.

"You watch the balance on that shipment of grain!" he yelled at them. "You put it where I tell you to put it and not an inch further, or we'll all end up feeding the River Lord tonight!" Kelvor Pepperboom shouted from atop another box at the other end of the ship.

He, like the rest of the crew, was of the gnomish people. His older countenance was displayed vividly in his silver hair and beard, while his tan skin showed time from the sun. His eyes were a brilliant blue that glittered with exuberance. A cursory glance would make one believe that his right arm was decorated with ritual scarification. Closer examination revealed that Pepperboom's entire right arm below the elbow had been replaced by a cleverly crafted substitute made from wood and metal. It moved like an arm made of flesh and blood would move. Intricate carvings decorated the whole of the prosthetic, denoting various places and people of importance. He folded his arms across his narrow chest and observed the actions of the foreigner. The hint of a smile tugged at his lips to see her carrying her own weight without so much as a wince or complaint. He'd had her wash the blood from her face before starting in on the work, as he did not want onlookers to think he or his crew had caused her harm. Despite the quick clean-up, she still sported a deep bruise across the bridge of her nose, and the beginnings of a matched set of black eyes were slowly making an appearance. Kelvor recognized the wound from his own days brawling in back rooms. The girl had clearly taken a punch to the face, and a solid one at that. The reddish mark on her forehead implied that she'd also headbutted her assailant. Whoever this woman was that had paid for berth across the River, she was not someone to be meddled with.

Isolde continued her singing, hefting and shoving at the direction of the others, deeply involved in the work, and oblivious to anything else. She missed entirely the heavy booted steps on the dock or the heads that turned to look past her. It was only when the song stopped entirely, that she blinked, a confused look on her pale and sweaty face. Noting that the attention was directed behind her, she slowly stood up straight and turned around.

The massive figure of Father Tulok stood at the gangplank, looking onward. At his side, the smaller shape of Brother Bengt was negotiating with a young boy about the delivery of several bags. Isolde smiled seeing Tulok and waved. Tulok however did not smile. The orc's eyebrows rose high in shock and surprise to see the injuries on the young woman. He moved to take a step forward and then stopped himself.

"Permission to come aboard?!" he called out.

"What are ya that asks to board the '*Nomes All*?" Kelvor called back. He knew to expect a member of the orcish people for this crossing; he just did not expect him to be quite so...big.

"Father Tulok, and Brother Bengt, in service to the Devout of the Lord of the Skies, Bringer of Light, Radiant Lord of the Everburning Sands. We have paid for passage on your fine ship."

Kelvor looked the big priest up and down from his distance and nodded. "Welcome aboard, Your Radiance."

"My thanks." Tulok nodded in thanks and stepped onto the ship. The deck creaked beneath his weight and the whole ship sank significantly on one side.

"Oy!" Kelvor yelled. "You stay amidships until we get everything balanced, Your Radiance."

Tulok blushed slightly and nodded, moving to the spot that Kelvor indicated. "Of course." behind him Bengt wrestled with some of the bags until a couple of the deckhands bustled over to help him.

"Isolde..." Tulok spoke to the woman, "I heard... are you, all right?" the healer asked.

It was clear that he wanted to step to her and examine

her injuries. Not wishing to earn another scolding from Kelvor, Isolde obliged the orc's curiosity by meeting him where he stood. She looked up at him, her green eyes glittering, despite the obvious mess that she currently was.

"Good Lord in the firmament, woman..." Tulok shook his head as he reached to touch her face and gently examine it. She winced a little as he poked at the bridge of her nose. "What did you get hit with?" he asked, bending forward to examine her more closely. She scowled and pulled away from his fussing.

"A fist, almost the size of yours," she replied.

Tulok's eyebrows raised in shock.

"Almost." She clarified and winked. She winced a little and thought better of it.

"Who were they?"

She shook her head. "No idea. They did not seem interested in stealing what we had, or they would have tried to nick Bengt's purse and run. They came at us with knives and intention."

Tulok pondered her response. "We will have to take precautions going forward then."

"I think I did pretty good for myself, thank you." she objected.

Tulok pursed his lips and hrmmed, "This time." he reached out and tapped the broken bridge of her nose. She hissed in pain and slapped his hand away. "Next time, it may not just be your good looks that get broken," he continued.

She harrumphed at him, "I was never winning any beauty contests, Tulok. Now I have character!" she grinned. Her right eye was still slowly swelling up from the bruising.

Tulok frowned. "I have a poultice for your eye. Take a seat and let me fix it."

Isolde looked over at the Quartermaster. "Have I earned my keep, Master Kelvor?" she called out.

Pepperboom turned bright eyes on the Avalonian Knight and nodded with approval. "You have, Ser Knight. I release you from your obligation. Let your Healer tend to your wounds."

Isolde touched her forehead in thanks and turned back to Tulok who was already reaching into his pack to pull out a variety of small bags and pouches. She watched the priest begin his ministrations, her eyes following his hands as he opened, measured, mixed, and mashed.

Across the din of the ship, Bengt's whining voice drew her attention away from the healer. Turning her eyes in the Acolyte's direction, she noted that he was standing near the railing, a look of horror on his already sallow face. Isolde furrowed her brow.

"Be right back," she said to Tulok, patting him on the arm and walking across the deck. She looked out in the direction that seemed to draw Bengt's attention.

"Everything all right?" she asked as she approached.

Bengt jumped, and started, surprised and not expecting Isolde's presence. He uttered some exclamation that she did not recognize and then blushed furiously and apologized. "I am terribly sorry, I did not know you were there." he stumbled over himself.

"Understood," Isolde replied and offered the skinny man a small smile. "So what has your attention?" she asked and nodded out toward the water.

"Um... downriver..." Bengt motioned and looked in that direction, then looked away again.

Several species of animals made the River Iteru their home. A variety of fish and waterfowl, some small and varied families of terrapin, half a dozen breeds of snakes, and both crocodilian species; alligator and crocodile. The river flowed from one end of Setesh to the other, cutting its way through the barren desert with its life-giving essence. This far inland, the river was fresh water and the animals present here were those who resided in those waters. Isolde's eyes followed the direction of Bengt's indication. At the water's edge, some hundred feet away from the '*Nomes All* a great commotion was taking place. Splashes and flumes of water erupted from a frothing, writhing mass of reptilian bodies. The setting sun colored the whole of the water a blood-red; but Isolde wondered if that only hid the truth of the undulating mass. She scowled and held her right hand up to shade her eyes in hopes of getting a better look.

"What is that?" she asked.

"Sacrifice to the River Lord, Lady Knight." Captain Tage answered brusquely. "Have you secured our cargo, Mr. Pepperboom?"

"Aye Captain, we are secure."

"Weigh Anchor! Cast Off!" Tage called out.

In trained unison, the crew of '*Nomes All* each took their positions, releasing the plank and returning it to the pier, freeing ropes that held the ship in dock, and six of them hauled the heavy anchor aboard.

The gnomish Captain tromped over to where Isolde and Bengt stood, watching the frenzy downriver. He peered in the direction and nodded satisfactorily. "Good. That should buy us enough time to get at least halfway across before they are done."

Isolde looked down at Tage. "The crocodiles...you are...feeding them?" she asked.

Tage harrumphed a little. "Feeding the River, my dear. If we feed the River now, then maybe she will smile on us and let our crossing be without incident," he replied in a tone that one might use when instructing a child. "River is full of freshies here, can't see 'em all. We risk running over some of them in the crossing...and some of them don't take kindly to that." He nodded downriver. "Give 'em something to draw them away from where we are, clears the route, lessens the chances of having the ship attacked by some bull who decides the ship is a threat."

"All clear, Captain!" Pepperboom called.

"Mister Botgrime, you are on Lookout, take the position!" Tage called.

"Aye Captain!" a younger gnomish lad replied and scampered toward the bow of the ship. He pulled a telescoping spyglass from his belt and began to search the waterline and the far coastline.

Isolde listened to Tage and nodded. "Drawing the predators away from the clearing, so the sheep can pass..." she said quietly. "No... that makes sense." She looked back at the frenzied feast downriver. "What do you use?" she asked in honest curiosity.

Tage looked up at the tall woman with an appreciative nod, "Normally we just carry dry goods, so I'll pay for boar to be dumped for 'em. But this time..." he looked at Isolde and then to Bengt and over to Tulok. "This time we have precious cargo, so I added a water buffalo to the menu to help us get across." he tipped his hat to Isolde.

Isolde smiled through her bruises and touched her heart and her forehead in thanks. "My thanks, Captain."

"Let's hope your Landless Lord can buy us some extra time from the Smiling God, Lady Knight," he commented, tapped the brim of his hat, and then turned to walk over to join Pepperboom.

Isolde folded her arms across her chest and looked out on the river, having forgotten that Bengt's panic had drawn her attention here, to begin with. "So..." the skinny man interrupted her musing.

She looked over at him. "Sooo... what?" she asked.

"So, you are not concerned about all of... that?" Bengt gestured toward the frothing waters.

Isolde shook her head. "Nope. Solid thinking on the Captain's part." she nodded.

Bengt frowned, "I would have thought..." he began. Isolde cocked her head to the side a little, regarding Bengt.

"Would have thought what, Brother?" she asked. "That a foreign woman could not possibly stomach the idea of animals ripping each other to shreds not a hundred feet away from us?" she asked plainly.

"Well, I mean..."

Isolde sighed and lowered her arms, then placed her right hand gently on Bengt's shoulder. "I have stood in a field filled with the bodies of dozens, having just watched them murder one another and be slain. I have carried those same bodies and set them to rest, to ensure the safe passage of their souls, regardless of whether they were friend or foe. A few dozen reptiles tearing into their supper? I think I will be fine...but thank you for your concern." She offered a gentle smile.

Bengt frowned a little, confused at the woman standing before him. "You are an odd woman, Isolde," he replied.

Isolde smiled brightly at that and patted Bengt on the shoulder. "You are not the first to say so, nor will you be the last." She winked at him.

Bengt scowled a little uncomfortably.

"Now, if you would excuse me, I can feel Tulok's disapproving glare boring through the back of my skull. I need to let the mother hen tend my injuries before it gets worse." She nodded her head, turned, and walked away.

Chapter 26

The orc priest maintained his position in the center of the ship, surrounded by several crates and bundles. He had been reminded that he needed to remain where he was unless he wanted to tip the entire barge over. This did little to improve his mood, as he watched his charge from a distance. She was injured... again, and while it was while performing the duties to which she had been assigned, Tulok could not help but blame himself a little for her newly broken nose. She had walked away from him as he was preparing a poultice for her swollen eye and the bruising on her face. When he looked up from his pack, she had been watching the river in the distance. He followed her gaze to the river's edge and watched the writhing frenzy of crocodiles feeding. He remembered watching similar sacrifices when he was here last. It was not unusual for Captains to pay to Feed the River as a blessing for their crossing. It was both a practice of logic and reverence. Tulok nodded in appreciation of the Captain's actions as he recognized what was happening; all the while wishing that the Avalonian would not stand quite so close to the edge of the railing. Too many were lost to the River every year for misjudging its danger, and Isolde seemed to possess no sense of self-preservation whatsoever.

Tulok had heard it said that the Landless Lord blessed his people with wills of iron, and removed from their fated looms the threads of fear. Tulok had never met one of His people, and now that he had – he wondered if their lack in numbers was somehow due to the lack of caution that fear provided. He sighed deeply at the realization that Isolde would always charge blindly into the world, and if she were to survive it, she would need someone to patch her back up in the end. He turned his head toward the sky and his eyes toward the sun as it approached the setting horizon, seeking the warmth and guidance of His Radiant Lord.

"If this be Your will, my Lord..." the priest said quietly.

"Hi, there!" Isolde smiled and stepped up to Tulok. He blinked and looked at the woman. The bruising on her face was spreading. He frowned.

"By the grace and mercy of our Lord woman, are you incapable of staying put together for more than a week at a time?" he scowled and reached for her face.

She stood her ground and tilted her chin down toward him, allowing his examination this time.

"I am not certain that I have ever tried," she replied as Tulok gingerly tested skin, muscle, cartilage, and bone.

Tulok frowned. "Your nose is broken, and I think your left cheekbone may be cracked. The eyes seem fine, with no threat of loss of sight. Thank the heavens for small miracles." he muttered and very carefully began to apply a salve to her busted lip and across one cheek.

"Augh, that smells awful," Isolde complained.

"It smells better than the poultice, I assure you," Tulok commented and directed her to take a seat on the gathered boxes in front of him. He handed her a cloth wrap. "Close your eye and press that across it and hold it on that side of your face for about an hour. It will take the swelling down and speed the healing." As he handed her the poultice he reached up and placed his thumb and forefinger on either side of the bridge of her nose and tweaked it quickly. There was a nauseating snap, followed by choice words from Isolde, as she raised her left hand to ward him off.

"Warn a girl!" she complained to him.

Several of the crew chuckled at the exchange and went back to their duties.

"Would you have let me fix it if I had?" Tulok asked, wiping his hands on a clean cloth and then tucking it into his belt pouch.

"Probably not," Isolde replied.

"Mmmm" Tulok nodded, "Hence why I did not ask."

Isolde held the poultice to her eye and plopped down on a crate, glaring at the big man.

"If it is your intention to throw yourself headlong into the world, then you must allow me to perform the duties to which I have been assigned as well." He stated and folded his massive arms across his broad chest. "Or have you forgotten that you are still my patient?"

Isolde grumped, "Are you always so insufferable?"

"Not always, sometimes I sleep."

They stood there staring at one another, the warrior and the priest, both stubborn and firm in their beliefs.

"Confessor off the starboard bow!" the voice of Kelji Botgrime called loudly, breaking the moment. The crew suddenly jumped into a variety of actions, taking positions to secure both the ship and the cargo.

Tage and Pepperboom exchanged quick looks and parted company; Pepperboom returned to the crew at the stern of the ship, while Tage marched toward the bow.

"Find your partners, men. Teams on either side. I want eyes on that water!" he called out as he reached for the glass from Botgrime.

"Where did you see him, son?" Tage asked in a guarded voice.

Botgrime pointed out past the bow of the ship to the right, toward the center of the river. Tage raised the glass to his eye and peered through it." Son of a motherless bilge rat..." he swore quietly. "What in the name of the Nepidae are you doing here, Old Man?"

Isolde and Tulok exchanged glances. He offered her a hand and helped her to stand, without a word. She nodded in thanks.

"Problem, Captain?" She called over to Tage.

"Well, I suppose that all depends on the Old Man of the River out there," Tage replied, his eyes still affixed to the glass.

Several of the crew exchanged worried glances.

"What are we dealing with?" Tulok asked.

"Salt croc." Tage replied.

"I thought this section of the river was freshwater?" Isolde asked.

"Salts don't give a shit, girl. Freshies are the only ones that have to watch their water. Salts come and go as they please." Tage answered. "Confessor's been the king of the Iteru for as long as anyone can remember. Some people think the Smiling God likes to wear him once in a while and go for a swim. Blessing in disguise...." Tage continued, as he watched the creature.

"So, seeing him is considered a good thing?" She asked.

"Not unless you want to lose your ship to the River Lord," Tage swore again. He handed the glass to Botgrime. "You keep your eye affixed to that glass, and that glass affixed to that scaly bastard. He disappears 'neath the water, I need to know immediately."

Botgrime nodded quickly and resumed his position.

"Helmsman Cogrivet, we need to adjust our course!

Twenty-five degrees to the Port, let's give the Old Man a wide berth and hope he doesn't feel His territory is threatened."

With those words, a team of the crew joined the Helmsman at the stern of the barge and helped to shift the huge wooden tiller arm attached to the rudder. "Brace for the turn!"

"Brace for the turn!" the crew called out in unison.

Tulok reached to grab hold of the stack of crates, Isolde followed suit.

"Turning!" Cogrivet called and he and his team began to push the tiller arm as the ship began to pivot in the newly chosen direction. Around the edges of the ship, the crew braced for the turn and grabbed hold of railings for security.

Isolde and Tulok braced their legs as the ship swung right. Being at the center of mass for the vehicle, the shift was barely noticeable for them. One moment they were pointed in one direction, the next, another section of the horizon line came into view. The transition was smooth and skilled.

"Man overboard!" was the call that sent panicked chills up the spine of every sailor and passenger aboard any boat that ever sailed. When those words were shouted across the deck of *'Nomes All* Isolde could feel the collective crew suck in a breath in unison. Eyes darted back and forth; headcounts being taken. Partners being accounted for.

Tage growled loudly across the deck. "Who's missing! Where's the rope? Eyes on the water now!"

A chorus of voices began to call back as crewmen sounded off, over it, all Pepperboom's voice yelled back. "The priest, Captain. He went over the rail! Starboard Stern!"

The color drained from Tulok's face at those words. His

eyes darted to where Bengt had been standing last. The skinny priest was gone, in his place were several members of the gnomish crew, frantically looking over the side. Tulok took three strides in that direction. The ship began to list and tip due to his great weight. Tage yelled at him to stop.

"Stay amidships, Father!" Tage instructed.

"That's my Acolyte!" Tulok protested.

"And my passenger! You stay where you are, or the ship will flip!"

Tulok turned concerned and panicked eyes in the direction of the water, helpless to do anything.

"I got it," Isolde said calmly. She placed her hand on Tulok's arm.

He looked down at her. "You cannot..." he shook his head.

She was already pulling off her boots. "Can you swim?"

He shook his head. "No."

"I can." the reply came.

"But... the river..." Tulok blinked, suddenly aware that he could well lose both Bengt and Isolde in short order.

"Raised on an island, Father. Water is second nature to us." she continued and tossed her boots aside. She shucked anything of significant weight and stood before him only in her pants and shirt, her broken compass relic around her neck. "Have faith." She nodded at him and padded quickly toward the rail. Looking over the edge, she could barely see where Bengt's flailing form was in the dark water. She looked skyward. The sun was setting. She would lose whatever light there was if she didn't act now.

"Give me the rope!" she called to one of the crew.

"You can't..." Pepperboom cautioned.

"Give me the damned rope, Master Pepperboom, and let me save my man," Isolde said firmly and held out her hand. There were times when the chosen of the Heavens commanded a personality that would brook no argument. Pepperboom met the green eyes of the Witness of the Landless Lord and for a moment felt the security and confidence that inspired her. He nodded silently and handed her one end of the heavy hemp rope. She nodded in thanks and wrapped it around her right wrist.

"Father of Dreams, lead me in the Darkness." she whispered softly and added, "Apologies, Lord of the River, you cannot have this man today." She took a breath and dove over the edge. The waters parted for her with barely a splash.

The waters surrounding Avalon were always cold and crisp. The waters of the Iteru were heavy and warm, the consistency of birthing fluid, and laden with rich minerals and silt. They were not clear. As Isolde surfaced to regain her bearings, she searched the water for Bengt.

Following the calls of the crew and the splashing of the water, she was able to pinpoint where the priest was flailing and trying to stay above the surface of the water. Isolde kicked her strong legs out and began to close the distance between them.

"Confessor's submerged!" came the call from the bow of the ship.

Tage began swearing, loudly. "Eyes on the water, every pair. Now!"

Teams of two split to either side of the ship, keeping the weight balanced as they searched the waterline. Tulok craned his neck, in an attempt to see. Even with his great height, his vision was limited. He reached for the medallion that hung around his neck, closed his eyes, and began to pray.

"Lord of the Skies and Everburning Sands – we ask for the protection of," he began – trying to will himself still in order for The Radiant Lord to hear his pleas. Forcing the sounds and the yells out of his mind – he continued to reach beyond himself, but there was nothing there. There was nothing to draw on. Then the thought hit him deep in the chest, Mother Selwyse's "lesson" of humility! He had nothing to draw from. The ever-merciful Radiant Lord only gave enough for his followers to draw on – no more and no less. His rage mixed with his shock and his horror. Looking out towards the fading sun, all he could do was simply pray. His words were simple, "Please...my Lord, please..."

Pepperboom leaned over the rail. "Hurry, girl you are about to have company!" he shouted.

"I am the Light in the Darkness..." Isolde began to recite her vows in her head, as every stroke brought her closer to Bengt. She could see the look on his panicked face now. It was the look of a man staring death in the eyes, who still had weight in his heart that would prevent him from returning to the Cycle. Someone who feared the end and what waited in the beyond.

"Help! Help me!" he called out.

"I'm coming, Bengt!" she replied.

"Help!" he called out once more. Water filled his mouth. He coughed and flailed.

"Where's the Old Man?!" Tage yelled on the ship.

One by one, everyone called back that they did not have eyes on him.

Hands reached for hands, flailing, grabbing, grasping, clinging. Sudden weight dragging them both down. She kicked up and pulled their heads above water. "Stop flailing, you'll drown us both!" She scolded.

"Help!" Bengt yelled again.

"I've got you, Bengt." Isolde tried to soothe. She offered

him her arm, while she used her powerful legs to tread water briefly. "Take the rope."

Bengt shook his head. "I can't, I'll drown."

"I've got you, "she said again. "Take the rope, they'll pull you in," She continued to kick, slowly dragging them both back toward the ship.

"She's got him!" Pepperboom called. The group at the edge of the railing grabbed hold of the rope and began to pull, drawing them closer.

Tulok opened his eyes and looked toward the railing his eyes filled with hope.

"Confessor!" came the call from the stern of the ship. There was a sudden and loud crashing sound. The entire ship rocked and rolled.

"Get them out of the water!" Tage yelled.

Bodies shifted; balancing weight as more came to help pull the rope. Once more Tulok stepped in that direction, once more he was told to remain where he was.

"Give me the other end of the rope!" the orc roared.

Quickly, hand over hand, the shipside end of the rope was passed back to the huge orc. He wrapped it around his wrist and forearm...and pulled.

Isolde and Bengt were jerked quickly toward the side of the ship. A rope ladder hung from the rail. The crew reached toward them. The water roiled near them and a flash of a scaled white tail breached the water and slammed against the side of the boat. He was underneath them. Bengt began to panic once more. He let go of both the rope and Isolde and climbed over her to reach the ladder, clinging to it.

The weight shifted suddenly on the rope in Tulok's hands, he staggered backward regaining his balance.

"Isolde!" the orc roared.

The ship shifted, tipping in his direction. "Father! Stay where you are, or you will kill us all!" Tage yelled.

Bengt felt the ship rise out of the water, lifting him away from the horrors of the River Lord's domain. He scrambled further up the ladder as he watched the end of the rope that Isolde once held fly past him. Hands grasped hold of his tunic and heaved him over the railing and back onto the deck. Below, Isolde kicked toward the ship, watching the water, and reaching for the ladder.

"Come on, girl!" Pepperboom called. Several crew members reached for her, their arms were far too short to cross the distance.

The water roiled next to Isolde; she felt the pressure change as the liquid wooshed past her. A heavily scaled body brushed against her, sending her turning away from the ship. She blinked and attempted to regain her bearings. She was without either arms or armor in a predator's environment. The safety of the ship was too far away to reach immediately. She'd seen what happened to people who had fallen prey to the alligators along the rivers of home.

The tail of this creature was easily as long as any of the largest alligators she'd ever seen. If it decided it wanted her dead, there would be nothing to stop it. One crushing bite and she would be in twain. Once more she felt the water change around her. This time the giant creature swam past her, between her and the ship, keeping her from her destination. As its massive tail passed her, she was struck with its heavy weight, sending her farther away. Almost with intent.

She heard Tulok's roaring voice from the ship's deck above her. The crew began to scramble to gather the rope and ready to cast it at her again. The water roiled once more. In the distance, the sun's rays kissed the edge of the horizon as the Lord of the Sky closed His eyes on this vision of the day and turned His gaze elsewhere. The Holy Witness reached for the compass that hung around her neck, the symbol of her faith. She kicked at the water, staying above it as she watched for the great beast.

"Scaled Prince of the River, Smiling Lord of the Iteru..." she began. "I Witness your Holy Vessel, Share with me your will." the sacred warrior spoke in reverent tones.

Witnessed

The great beast called Confessor slammed into the figure of the woman in the water, sending her even farther from the ship and separating her from her companions. Isolde shook her head, trying to regain her bearings. Water filled her mouth. She pushed forward and up, gasping for air. Suddenly she felt a giant clawed hand wrap itself around her forearm and drag her beneath the surface of the waves and into the darkness.

Chapter 27

His red eyes continued to stare at the water in disbelief – his mouth open in a soundless cry. The flip of the wide, white, tail was all that he saw before she and the reptile were gone. The water gave no murmur or flash of movement – just the tranquil wave of the river's current.

All of the eyes turned and stared at the orc in a mixture of anticipation and fear.

There was no Gurkh, there was no Ghal...there was only Grief.

Grief so loud that the very wail gave those ships and creatures around pause. Those on *'Nomes All* winced in pain as the weight of sorrow felt heavier than the orc's own massive frame.

Every muscle in his body wanted to move, to thrash, to do SOMETHING. Yet – the other lives around him. Other innocents around him – all of them would be in danger if he moved from his seat. Instead, his fingers dug into his thighs – gripping them until his knuckles were pale.

The crew said nothing and quietly pulled up the rope as a few simple light spells were cast quietly at the bow and stern of the barge.

"Father I..." Bengt began, but his words were stopped cold as the orc looked at him. This was not a look of violence or menace from earlier. This was something else that the small man could not fathom but yet understood.

Loss.

The look was its own force that surrounded the massive creature – yet, it made him smaller. His shoulders slumped, soon followed by his forehead resting on a crate in front of him. There were no tears that fell from his eyes – only hoarse breathing.

All of this took place in less than a few minutes, but to everyone aboard – it felt like hours had gone by. The crew who had taken many forgettable and nameless passengers marked the moment as a loss of one of their own in a way they could not explain. Perhaps it was the fact that she knew the way of the water and did not give them grief for their sailor humor or attitudes. In those brief hours – she had made an appreciable place among the crew. The only evidence that she had been there in the first place was the bag that sat next to the priest, her armor, the bloodied outer clothing, and her boots.

From the bow of the ship, Captain Tage stood with his back turned, his hands behind him, and looking towards the lights on the eastern bank. There was silence save for the water that slapped against the side of the ship.

Pepperboom broke the silence with a slow deep voice. The lapping water kept a rhythmic beat to his words.

Cast me down the river blue
Know me soul's meant for you
Cast me down the river blue
Yello' eyes be a kindness too
Cast me down the river blue
Know our words always true
Cast me down the river blue
Cast me down...
Cast me down...

Cast me down...

...

...to you...

One by one, each of the crew repeated the somber verses as they went about their work. Neither Tulok nor Bengt said anything and simply listened as the Gnomes sang their river dirge. Their voices began to mesh together with the world around him. Time – like the darkness of the night, seemed to go on forever until he no longer felt the shifting of the boat.

The sound from the world around him came roaring back. Tulok realized that there were sounds, scents, and lights all around him. The crew in their kindness worked around him, and by the time he realized that he and the boat were unloaded – a few hours had already passed.

Somehow, he was onshore holding his things as well as Isolde's. He blinked, and then he was somewhere else sitting down. His things were beside him and Isolde's bag sat in his lap. Again, he did not recall moving. He just was there. Bengt was talking to him but there really was not any sound until now. They were sitting at a table in what looked like a tavern. A mixture of people was all around him. Before him was a single candle giving them light and a bowl in front of the acolyte.

"...kindness, I think," Bengt said looking down at his bowl.

The smell of a meaty stew wafted into the orc's nostrils. The normal comfort of food churned his stomach and his face grew pale. He pushed the bowl to the side and turned his face away from it.

Typically, Bengt would have opened his mouth to relay some judgmental indignity – but the small man said nothing. He cleared his throat a bit.

"I mean to say, it was a kindness that the captain did not

allow us to pay." The acolyte's fingers were knotted together as he spoke. He did not look at the Orc and only kept his focus on his hands. "I know you were planning on going further east with...her."

The priest could not tell if it was sorrow, shame, or fear that prevented Bengt from saying Isolde's name. In his mind, he was relieved that he chose not to say it. The rage in his stomach had begun to thaw as his sense of self began to take hold. The priest narrowed his eyes at the acolyte.

"What of it?" The words were cold and the chill of them made Bengt wince. The light from the candle offered a harsh countenance of his Orcish features and his red eyes look like something from a nightmare.

"I.. I, uh...can, if you would like, um... assist you. You know for the rest of the way. To where, uh...you were going," he stuttered out.

Tulok's head tilted to the side slightly as he regarded the offer. Closing his eyes, the orc ran a hand over his scalp. He loathed the man sitting across from him. He was a sniveling excuse for a human being and he wanted nothing more than to pick him up and toss his body into the river to trade for Isolde's. It was a horrible, dark, and selfish thought. The Gurkh within seemed to smile and relish at the concept of vengeful violence.

He really wanted to do it.

He shifted in his seat and his foot touched cold metal. He looked down beneath the table and there was the shining piece of metal attached to the back shoulder of Isolde's leather armor. It was dented, presumably from the attackers earlier – though that seemed forever ago. The Avalonian script and design were elegant and it showed some sort of beast rearing up on its hind legs.

She was always breaking – but never stopped working. Her armor was much the same.

He closed his eyes and took a deep breath. He let it out slowly and he could feel the swell within quiet down.

"We were going to Ahsal..." Tulok said quietly.

Bengt raised an eyebrow, and then slowly looked around the room. The tavern was loud and busy for the evening and the crowd seemed to do its best to avoid the gaze of the Sun Lord's Chosen. While often viewed as sanctimonious – the Devout were also about justice and enforcing the Sun God's will. No one wanted any trouble from the pair – especially when one of them was an Orc who appeared to lack emotion or any kindness.

Reaching down into his robes, the Orc produced a scrap of parchment and a black piece of writing chalk. In carefully drawn symbols only known to the clergy of The Radiant Lord – Tulok wrote out the following – much to Bengt's surprise and horror.

Cult of the Silent One – enforce His Will or report if too numerous

Bengt looked up at him and then back down at what was written. He said a small prayer to himself as Tulok rolled up the small paper and held it to the table's candle. The flame easily took and the Orc held it as it blackened to ash. He set it down on the small saucer beneath the candle and watched it burn to nothing. Reaching over, he tapped his fingers into the ashes and mixed them into the melted wax.

"Isolde..." his eyes closed and his upper lip twitched, "She and I were going to explore the area as it may have been directly related to the events that brought her to us. While she will not be able to finish what was started, I will ensure that it was not done in vain." He leaned forward, to the Acolyte, "Do you understand that it has all been about duty now?"

Bengt's face ran flush and his forehead began to glisten.

He wiped the top of his head with his sleeve but said nothing.

"I am going to see this through to the end because I am duty-bound to do so. You can walk away now and forget what you have seen, but know what I do is our Lord's Will. Make your choice so I can figure out what I must do from here," Tulok said in a quiet but firm tone.

The acolyte leaned forward, his nose resting atop his knotted fingers. He nodded his head slightly, "This is His Will...I will go and make travel accommodations. A Sun Guide to the next settlement, our own traveling beasts...food, water...when..." He looked up at Tulok, "When do we want to leave?"

"Tonight," he said simply.

"Tonight?" Bengt replied with a bit of shock but shook it off. If there were caravans leaving, they would be doing so for the next few hours. There was not any time to waste. He stood up and left a coin on the table for the untouched meal. "I'll be back shortly."

"Bengt – as I am bound, now – so are you," Tulok said.

There was a moment of silence as the two faithful of The Radiant Lord stared at each other.

Bengt nodded his head, "Yes, I am," and turned to head out.

Tulok pulled the warm bowl of stew close to him and used the spoon to move its contents around. Softly to himself, he said one word out of earshot of all there.

"...witnessed..."

Chapter 28

Air filled her lungs suddenly. She gasped and choked and coughed, kicking and reaching. She opened her eyes, expecting them to be filled with silt and water. She was met with the twilight of the desert. Her clothes were wet, but she wasn't cold. She carefully rolled over and pushed herself up. There was a fire. A large body of water was beyond the fire's light, the sand sloping down into its cool depths. Large trees surrounded the edges of the life-giving oasis. The bonfire blazed quietly with the occasional crackle. Her bare feet dug into the sand. It felt warm. Turning her eyes skyward, she noted the color of the heavens, purplish-blue with the barest hint of orange on the horizon, as if daybreak was coming – but not quite there yet. It was a lingering twilight that caused her to look up in the night sky. In it were hundreds...no, thousands of tiny lights. It was as if the blanket of the night were full of holes...no... stars...the sky was filled with stars.

But...how?

She didn't notice Him next to her. He was just there as if He had always been there. She did not jump at His presence as they both seemed to marvel at the sky above.

"I'm told they were a memory of the world," He said softly. His voice was deep and rich and had a similar rumbling timber to...to someone she knew. The name escaped her for the moment.

The stranger spoke again – His voice still comforting, reassuring even, "Are you hungry Avalonian? – Food will be ready soon."

She turned and looked to where He stood, but He wasn't there anymore. He was on the other side of the fire – stoking it to the point where she could feel the warmth on her face.

She blinked, shaking her head to clear it. Now she focused on Him. He was tall, taller than most men, almost as tall as...someone. She grasped for a name, but could not place it. Light-colored robes lay gently across his shoulders, open to the waist. His bare chest was pale – even in the fire's light. Pale even against the tan of his robes, almost without color. His broad nose and full lips called out his desert-born heritage, but his skin was not the sun-kissed tan or ebony of the Seteshi people. It was the white color of the sun-bleached sand. His hair was a mixture of whites and yellow, completely unkempt – but yet fitting.

He looked up at her and smiled. His smile was inviting – his eyes were a deep yellow.

"We have much to talk about," He said.

She should know Him. Somehow. She blinked again and once more looked around, taking in her surroundings. She was still wearing the simple shirt and pants she had been wearing when she entered the water. Why had she gone into the River? A man. She was saving someone? Her right hand reached up to touch her face and her head. Her nose was sore, as was her right cheek. Did she get hit and fall overboard. No... there had been a fight.

The albino watched her muse through her memories, smiling and nodding.

"Still remembering, yes?" He reached toward the fire

and pulled a pot away from the fire. Had there been a pot there before? He poured two cups of dark liquid from the pot, set it back on the fire, and walked over to her. He offered her one.

"Tea?" he asked, smiling.

She nodded. "Yes, thank you." she accepted the cup from his hand. It should have been scalding hot, it was just warm enough to be perfect. She inclined her head in thanks. The Man nodded and smiled.

"None go without in my Kingdom." His deep voice spoke as He watched her sitting before Him.

Isolde furrowed her brow a moment as the tea touched her lips and she drank from the cup, accepting the Hospitality that was offered. She recognized those words. The drink was dark and soothing, but also bitter on the back end. As her mouth was filled with the drink, memories washed over her fuddled mind.

A river. A ship. A priest. A scarab. Her eyes opened wide as her hand spasmed, the liquid in the cup splashing over the edge and onto the sand.

"Confessor!" she whispered. A pulse of fear's adrenaline teased at her but failed to take hold.

The Man smiled and shrugged His shoulders slowly. "Perhaps. I have been called this in the past." The light from the fire danced across His too-white skin, revealing a pattern of tiny scales that glistened and then disappeared. He appraised her from across the fire. "Interesting."

Isolde looked around the Oasis once more, clarity slowly returning to her mind. "Where...where are we?" she asked carefully. "I remember... the water."

"Mmmm" the Man nodded, pursing His lips together. He lifted His own cup to His full, pink lips and sipped the contents carefully. "Yes. The lifeblood of Setesh." He murmured. "You denied the River a gift, do you remember?" He asked, smiling behind His cup.

Isolde furrowed her brow in thought once more. She reached for her cup. It was empty. She held onto the empty vessel in the darkness. Then her eyes widened once more and she whispered, "Apologies, Lord of the River, you cannot have this man today..." she looked up at the albino, realization coming to her. She set her cup aside, sat up straight, and bowed her head in reverence, "My deepest apologies for what I have done, I could not let him die."

"Why not?" The question was flat.

She fought the urge to look up at the creature by the fire and kept her head bowed. "I...we...we need him."

"For what?" Again, the question carried no emotion.

"To help us reach our destination." She answered.

"Which is?" the deep-voiced albino asked.

Isolde paused and did not answer the question posed. It was not an easy answer, and the information could well be tied to the Oath she had already sworn. She could not betray Tulok or the Temple.

Suddenly the Man was squatting before her, His body between her and the fire, His face inches from her head.

"Threads of Fate are wrapped around your soul, Islander." He whispered in a deep husky voice. "The magic of your people. I can SEE it." He inhaled deeply, taking in her scent. "I smell the water of your people in your blood, even now." He inhaled once more and His smile faltered for a moment. "Ahhh...yes...there it is...the magic binds you to one who serves my brother..." He chuckled darkly and hovered near her still. "I am surprised. Both the Lord of Heaven and your Wandering Lord are jealous creatures. How they must bicker over this..."

He stood abruptly and walked away.

Isolde sat quietly, listening to the fire crackle, the wind

blow across the sand, and the water ripple in the distance.

"What could possibly interest the Everburning Throne and that Landless Lout..." the albino mused, tapping His lips with the fingers of His left hand in thought.

Isolde bristled at the insult to her Lord. She stretched her neck and clenched her fists onto her knees.

The albino watched from a distance, the smile returning to His face.

"You don't like that, do you, little one?" He asked through His broad smile. She heard the soft padding of feet on the sand and felt His presence near her once more. "It bothers you, so far from home, the only Voice and only Eyes He has here, in this distant land...to hear His name besmirched?" The Man's voice was close to her ear now. She could feel His breath on her skin. He smelled of the sweet earthy scent of rich, life-giving water. She felt Him inhale deeply once more, along the length of her neck.

"You. Owe. The River. Little Girl." His voice almost purred. He hovered there again, His lips almost tasting her flesh.

She could feel the life-giving energy on His body. She shivered unconsciously. He pulled away and stood.

"It would be considered an honor in Setesh for me to come to you, and your blood would make a rich and unique combination here...but you have already sullied your soul with another, " He spoke bitterly, "...and the River seeks no war with the Court of your Lord.

"Yet. You. Must. Pay." His words were careful and precise. His yellow eyes stared at her from across the fire, filled with an ancient hunger.

Isolde listened to the words of the creature called The Confessor, and she knew He was right. She had denied the River a sacrifice, and a sacrifice it was owed.

"Take my blood," the young woman said softly.

The Confessor harrumphed at her, “If I wanted you dead, girl, I would have eaten you already.” He folded His arms across His chest and watched her. His eyes glittered in the darkness.

“No.” Isolde lifted her head; her green eyes met the eyes of the creature called Confessor. “You said it yourself. You can smell the water of my people in my blood.” She continued.

The albino narrowed His eyes. “Go on…”

“Take my blood, and the water therein, tied to the lands of my home. Mix it with your own. There are no shrines to the River Lord on the Islands. Do this, and there…may…be.” Isolde offered.

The albino continued to stare suspiciously at Isolde from His place across the fire.

“The River Lord hails not from the Court of my Lord, and so He cannot build houses in His name there.”

The albino hissed. He sounded like a giant crocodile.

Isolde held out her hand.” Blood to Blood, I offer you a foothold, small though it may be.”

The albino stared at her hand.

“I will not build it for you. You will have to find those to do it for you. It is a lock that you have been denied a key to. I offer the key, nothing more, and then we are even.”

A strong white hand found its place into hers. It was warm and inviting. Yellow eyes met hers, unflinching, a mouth filled with far too many teeth smiled broadly down at her.

“Done and Done” He hissed.

There was a sudden burning pain in the palm of her hand. He held her there, as the pain continued to slowly creep up her right arm. Blood began to drip from their clasped hands and pool into the sand. The pain continued up her arm, past her elbow and into her shoulder. She moaned and winced and began to writhe. The Confessor smiled, as the blood slowly disappeared into the sand, leaving no trace in its place. He released Isolde. She collapsed forward, left hand holding her up, as she cradled her right arm across her chest.

The Confessor chuckled deeply and moved to take a step back, then stopped and blinked. He shook His head a little and stared at the hand that had once held Isolde's. A small port-wine stain colored His palm. He snarled at the paladin, "What have you done to me?" He demanded.

Isolde lifted her head weakly to stare at the creature. "The only way... you can have a key... is...to be bound...to the land...as I am..." she breathed and offered the ancient creature a smile. "As it prospers, so shall you...and if it dies..."

The creature roared in anger at the woman and the sky. Then there was darkness once more.

Chapter 29

It had been two days since Tasmina left the eastern side of Nahral. The trip was no different from others with the exception of two private passengers. They were looking to travel to the Mukt-aal and had already purchased a trio of mounts. She shot a look behind her at the unlikely pair following along the path. Father Tulok and Acolyte Bengt presented themselves as knowledgeable travelers and understood the rules of the caravan. They were members of Sun God's clergy so she spoke with the required amount of respect. They had come prepared for the journey, but the Sun Guide could feel the weight each of them bore.

At first glance – she questioned the travel ability of the smaller of the pair. Normally she would have stuck the man in the middle of the caravan to be less of a hassle to those around him. Yet something in his eyes was feeling a quiet sense of confidence.

The orc on the other hand seemed hardened. While the Orcish people were known to be hardy and abrasive – this one was all and yet none of these things. Something had happened between the both of them – and neither chose to share it. They did not conspire and in some ways, they only tolerated one another's company during the trip. The Radiant Father provided the Radiant Lord's Blessings at dawn, noon, and dusk, as well as shouldered the work as needed. The Brother provided support as best as he could.

On the third day of the trip, the Sun Guide watched as the Brother began to struggle with their pack mount. The orc came over with an unhappy disposition, and the two exchanged words in quiet, but sharp tones. At one point, it looked like the orc was going to lay hands on the smaller man – but instead, finished securing the load that the Brother had started. Tasmina half expected to see the smaller man gloat or act smug. Instead, he took the leads of the other mounts and pulled them to their places in the caravan. Curiosity was starting to gnaw on her.

There was a story – possibly a tragic one, but it was hard to tell how.

The sun had already withdrawn itself for the evening and camp was set up in the last of the rocky sandstone foothills that had become few and far between. They were two days out from their final destination, and the trip had been blissfully quiet.

While the rocky foothills were safer than the open dunes of the west, they still presented their own challenges. Through their Lord's Grace perhaps – but until their mounts were unloaded, this trip was far from over. Members of the caravan sat around a few of the fires, each preparing an evening meal. The Sun Guide found the clergy speaking to an elven trader. They had been going over a newly drawn map. "I would have never guessed you were a student of cartography, your Radiance," Tasmina said as she sat across from them. She reached over and stoked the fire a bit, "Anything I can help with?"

Tulok looked up mid-sentence, "How many...Oh! Good evening Honored Gui..."

"Please Father," she shook her head, "Titles waste

breath and moisture out here when a name will do. Treat it with respect is all I ask."

With a satisfied nod, "Very well – good evening Tasmina. Not so much as a hobby – rather looking for confirmation on the way to Kas-qua."

The Sun Guide raised an eyebrow, "That...that is a bit of a trip. So, it isn't just Mukt-aal?"

"Less than a trip, and more of a pilgrimage," Bengt interjected with an odd smile.

While the orc did not outwardly say anything, his frozen expression gave up more information than he realized.

Cautiously, she continued to probe, "Really? I've always understood that when one undergoes a pilgrimage – it is solely in the company of others within the faith. It is how The Radiant Lord tests your faith and endurance?"

Bengt raised a finger, but Tulok cut him off, "Less of a holy pilgrimage Tasmina – and more of a personal one. When we left the Eastern Bank – did you hear about the accident on the Iteru?"

"Yes," she said thinking back, "A traveler fell overboard and was killed by the River Lord's children."

Tulok nodded his head, "Her name was Isolde duAvalonne, she was a Knight of the Wandering God. She was a stranger in this land who was on a quest. I intend to help finish what my friend could not." He hadn't said her name out loud in four days and he still felt numb.

Reading the unspoken emotions in his red eyes, the Sun Guide gave him a quiet nod,

"My condolences for your loss, your Radiance. I know the pain of losing friends – and she must have been a valued soul to bring you out this far." Whoever this person was to the pair she could see that the loss weighed more on the orc and the other man.

"My recommendation is when you get to Mukt-aal – talk to one of the local merchants there instead of a Sun Guide. The trek is easier this time of year. Many of the traders between the two areas know it well enough that the trip can be manageable with proper precautions," she said a bit pointedly. "A majority of Sun Guides make their coin going north to the capital, so you have better luck finding a local source of help," she added.

Giving that same odd smile, Bengt replied "With any luck, we might be able to see the capital when we are done."

The Radiant Father gave a sort of assuring nod. The Sun Guide saw it for what it was and gave him a warm smile in return before she rose up. "Then I would recommend resting for a bit after you've eaten. We have two more days left. Also – Mukt-aal can be an interesting place. Last port before another long journey, so it can get a bit...colorful, but I think you will do fine there."

With that, she turned from the group and walked toward the supply tents. Wherever they were headed after Kas-qua, the unspoken intention said they did not intend to make it back. They did not look like ones to take their own lives, but they did not expect to survive the end of their journey. Far be it for her to interfere with a traveler's decision – much less the dealings of the clergy, but she felt the orc's sense of sadness. She rolled up her sleeve a little and rubbed the skin of her right forearm. An intricate tattoo covered her flesh in the figure of a black scorpion. She looked down at her arm and gently touched it.

"May they find the grace to see themselves through their journey." Rolling down her sleeve, she continued her prep for the next leg of the journey.

~~~

Darkness wrapped itself around her like a warm and welcome blanket on a winter morning. It was comforting,
~~~

safe, and familiar. A soft thump-thump-thump sounded from somewhere outside the darkness. The sweet scent of lavender and fresh-cut hay drifted across the darkness, rousing her from what was surely sleep's sweet embrace. Her eyelids fluttered. Gentle daylight breaking through the darkness. Soft sheets and a plump feather-down mattress wrapped her in familiar comfort. She yawned and stretched and opened her eyes slowly. Warm, red, embroidered velvet curtains hung around the dark wood-carved four-poster bed. This was familiar. She knew this place. She was safe here.

Sitting up in the bed, she tossed the coverlet and sheets aside and threw her legs over the side of the bed. She was in a linen dressing gown. Fine silk embroidery adorned the edges of the sleeves. She stared at it for a moment, feeling like she should recognize the pattern. She blinked and looked away to cast her gaze around the room. A wash-basin, pitcher, washrag, and fresh flowers sat opposite the bed. A small writing desk and chair. A carved oak armoire. At the foot of the bed sat a heavy cedar chest, pillows, and blankets folded and placed neatly on the top. A pair of ornate slippers sat perched by the armoire.

Boots. It should be boots. She thought to herself. Then the thought seemed remarkably silly. *Why would she have boots in her bedroom?*

She opened the armoire and instinctively reached for the blue and white overdress that hung there. Beside it was several other dresses of blues and greens. On the other side of the rack were a pair of men's trousers and shirt. Beneath those a pair of men's boots. She frowned and ran her right hand over the shirt in curiosity. These were too big to be hers.

Of course, this is why she thought there should be boots here. At least he put them away this time.

He who?

She paused and thought and blinked and shook it off, pulling the kirtle on and lacing it quickly. She stopped at the washbasin to quickly brush her hair and wind it up onto her head. She poured water into the basin and splashed her face, and stared at herself in the mirror.

Green eyes stared back at her out of a perfect porcelain face, with full pouting lips. She reached up to carefully touch the bridge of her nose and her cheeks, not certain why.

That is not your face. This is not your home.

She shook her head and splashed more water on her face, trying to shake the feelings and thoughts off.

"Isolde!" a man's voice called from the other side of the door. Her heart fluttered and her stomach knotted, a warm flush coming to her cheeks.

"Oh... oh my..." she blinked and reached for the small, mouth-brush to scrub her teeth and chew a spring of mint.

"Isolde!" the voice called again, this time just on the other side. Someone knocked gently. The latch wiggled and the door pushed open.

A man in his early twenties poked his head inside the room. He was tall, his shoulders and chest broad, dark close-cropped hair sat atop his head. Steel-blue eyes smiled at her from a square-jawed classical countenance.

"There you are, you sleepyhead," he smiled and stepped in. He peered over his shoulder quickly and then pulled the door closed behind him. "We have a few minutes before the Alderman comes looking for his daughter..." he whispered and stepped to her, pulling her into his strong arms.

Isolde's eyes fluttered and her knees went weak for a moment. The man caught her in his embrace. "Nice to know I still have that effect on you..." he smiled again and bent his head in to place a deep kiss on her pink lips.

Isolde's hands reached for him, fingers curling into the fabric of his shirt, pulling him close and clinging to him. He was warm, and strong, and... here.

No. No. No. No! the voice in the back of her head screamed at her.

He broke from their impassioned kiss to look deeply into her eyes. "Good morning...wife," he whispered in a deep and husky voice.

She blushed demurely and looked away. "You are terrible." she giggled.

The man smiled and leaned in to nuzzle against her neck briefly and then pulled her to a standing position once more. "So, you keep telling me." He kissed the tip of her nose and stepped back.

She blushed again and reached up to fix her hair which had come undone in their embrace. "You said..." she paused. "You said my father was looking for me?" she asked.

Your father is dead.

She frowned and blinked and rubbed the bridge of her nose. There was pain. She winced a little.

"Are you alright love? Another headache?" the man asked, his voice filled with concern.

She nodded. "It would seem so."

He nodded and moved to place his arms around her in support. "The healer said you might have them off and on for a little bit after your accident."

"My... accident?" she asked, looking up at him confused.

"Ah." he nodded. "Memory issues too, this morning?" he smiled gently and leaned in to place his warm lips to her forehead. He smelled sweet and musky. "They will fade in time," he murmured against her flesh.

She nodded and leaned into his embrace. "You take such good care of me..."

Stop it.

"And I always will," he replied, then looked down at her. "Now, if you think you can... your father is waiting downstairs with the notary for you to sign those papers..."

"Papers?" she asked.

He sighed. "It will be fine. I told him that you might not remember and we might have to do this another day..."

"No... I... I am sure I will be fine." she insisted.

The man smiled, "That's my girl." he nodded and threaded his fingers into hers. "Now let us find your shoes and we can get this taken care of."

She nodded and walked over to where the slippers were perched. She slid them onto her feet. They were a perfect fit. She felt his hand in hers, gently tugging her toward the door.

"Come on, now." he encouraged her.

She nodded and followed him out the door.

The house was filled with the bustle of family and friends as if it were a time of celebration. The warm smell of fresh bread and roasting meat permeated the air. Laughter and joy washed over her as she walked hand in hand down the stairs next to the tall smiling man.

"There are our newlyweds!" her father's voice greeted them at the foot of the stairwell. Isolde's stomach knotted and there was a sudden pain in her chest. Her face blanched. She felt nauseous. She reached to steady herself against a wall.

He's dead. They are all dead. None of this is real.

"Whoa, whoa there..." the man at her side reached to hold her up.

Isolde shook her head and reached for the man at her side.

"I told you she needed more time," her father scolded the man.

"And I told you that you needed to have more faith in your daughter's resolve to see this through," the man countered.

The two men stood staring at one another for a moment. Isolde shushed at them both.

"Please, I will be fine. I just need to sit down."

"Of course," the man agreed and ushered her to a table. Standing opposite her was another man in robes that she both did and did not recognize. The robes were white, trimmed in gold. He was a big man, tall and broad, with swarthy dark skin and amber eyes. He smiled gently down at her. There was a familiarity in that smile. Something about him made her feel comforted and safe.

"Interesting." the man who seemed to be her husband commented quietly.

She turned her eyes up to see him. "What is?" she asked.

The man smiled down at her and placed his hand on her shoulder gently. "Nothing, my love. Just musing on how well you are doing." he squeezed her shoulder gently. "I am very proud of you."

The squeeze of his hand on her right shoulder made her wince slightly. He pulled away.

"I am so sorry, I forgot," he apologized quickly.

"If you need more time, Isolde." her father began.

Daughter. He always called you Daughter. He never used your birth name.

She frowned and shook her head. "No. No, it's fine, I am fine." she looked up at the men gathered around her. She sat up straight and smoothed her dress and offered them all a pleasant smile.

"What is it you needed me to sign?"

Her husband nodded to the white-robed man, who produced a parchment from his belt and unfurled it on the table. He placed several map weights along the edges of the parchment. It seemed to be a map of some kind. She frowned and stared at it. It was familiar.

"You just need to sign at the bottom, dear." the man smiled and indicated where there was a line at the bottom of the parchment for a signature.

Isolde stared at the drawings. She knew this place. It was her mother's estate. This was hers.

Her birthright.

"Why..." she looked up at the man in white. "Why am I doing this?" she asked.

Her father looked at the man who was her husband. "He saved your life. You owe a life debt. Remember?"

She nodded absently. "Of course,...the accident..."

"Yes."

"and... this will settle the debt?" she asked.

The man in white nodded quietly. "It will," he replied. His voice was a deep, familiar rumble.

She nodded and reached for the quill, neatly poised next to the inkwell at the edge of the table. As she pulled the quill across the map, her fingers brushed against the compass rose drawn onto the border there. She paused and stared at it, her fingers gently tracing its elegant and familiar lines.

"Where is my necklace?" she asked, staring at the compass.

"Your necklace?" the man asked.

Isolde nodded. "Yes. The necklace Reynard gave me." she turned her green eyes up to the man who was her husband. "You remember Reynard, don't you? Your best friend...husband?" She asked.

Panic flooded across the blue eyes of the tall handsome man. "Not this," he whispered.

"Not what?" Isolde asked, staring at the man.

"Please, just sign the paper," he pleaded.

She turned her eyes back to the map, staring at it. Shadows began to dance at the corners of her vision as the scene around them began to shift.

"Isolde, please." he pleaded once more. "You can have all of this, the life you wanted...WE wanted..."

She furrowed her brow. "You never wanted any of this." she shook her head. Pushing her chair back, she stood slowly, bracing herself on the edge of the table for support.

"I... I want it now." the man protested. "Please. Isolde." he reached out and placed his hand on hers. "Please don't let them send me back. It is so cold there..." he pleaded.

Isolde faltered for a moment at those words and looked up at the man who looked so much like Nathaniel. It would be so easy. She had already walked away from it all, what harm could there be in simply formalizing it, in exchange for all of this? A second chance. A second life.

"Please, Isolde... I love you." Nathaniel begged.

Pain welled up and washed over Isolde duAvalonne at those words. She pulled her hand away from his and stood straight and tall. She turned cool green eyes on the visage of the man she would have loved forever if he had ever once said those words.

"No, you don't. You love Reynard." She said flatly.

The visage wavered before her, panic flooding his face. He turned to look at Isolde's father.

"Please...no.."

"None of this is real..." she whispered quietly, then her eyes looked up at the man in white. "I will find you, Tulok."

The figure of Isolde's father growled in anger, his face flushing scarlet with anger.

"ENOUGH!" he roared.

And the Darkness washed over her once more.

Chapter 30

As the sunset on the final day, the caravan viewed the jutting edifice of the Mukt-aal. Discovered farther back than any one being could remember – the large oasis was carefully nurtured by all those that came into possession of it. In the early days of Sanctum, there were stories that Humans, Vidria, Elves, and Orcs warred over this spot in order to claim its resources for their own people. Yet as time and hardship went on – it no longer became about the individual, rather it became about the group. The original warring parties and their ancestors soon laid a communal claim to the land that would become Mukt-aal as each was burdened with its upkeep. For if one failed – all would fail.

As years went by – it soon became the last juncture for those traveling to the north, onward to the grand city of Ophir, the Capital of Setesh. As one went further east – there was very little in the way of vegetation. The heat of the Sun Lord's Grace faded away with the chill of the eastern sea. What did not grow by the sun's warm heat, died by the sea's cold chill. This far out east – Mukt-aal was the last stop for any sense of civilization.

"Should we look for the temple?" Bengt asked as he looked around. There was a healthy mixture of Elves, Humans, Gnomes, and Orcs who all traversed the area. As he watched the crowds of travelers, shopkeeps, and laborers – the orcs seemed to outnumber the working population two to one.

"There seems to be a lot of your people here," he added.

Like Bengt, Tulok had surmised the same. The difference in their observations was that the priest noticed the small sigils adorning various signs and buildings. Of the three or four that were carved into each of the buildings – one, in particular, stood out. It was akin to a half-moon with a slicing wing through it.

There were several stories when it came to Orcish pictographs. Much like the priestly language used by the clergy of The Radiant Lord- it was said that the original Orcish language seemed to be only images rather than lettered words. Regardless, this particular image drew a mixed feeling in Tulok's chest – home.

"Uh...are...are you alright Father?" Bengt asked cautiously. Since leaving the river, Tulok had been essentially devoid of emotions. The smiles and reassuring nods were all tools that clergy used to inspire faith and hope in others. For the priest, however, it was to mask the pain within that riddled his thoughts with self-doubt. The only driving force was to finish the job that he and Isolde had started.

After a pause, Tulok answered, "Yes Brother, I am as well as I need to be," he said – the mask of priestly stoicism took hold once again. "The set of symbols on this sign – they are clan symbols of my people. This one," he pointed to the half-moon, "is the one for my clan. Though," he began to look around at all the buildings. "I am not sure if it signified past, current or established leadership. I did not realize they migrated this far east...much less on this side of the Iteru."

"Do you still have a family?" the small man asked.

"Technically yes – but all within a village are family, so

growing up it was hard to say who was and was not a blood relative. Though it really did not matter. It is neither here nor there, but you are right – we should check in."

Dismounting, they led their mounts to a livery stable that was near the front entrance gate. The stable could easily support up to 50 or more pack animals, mounts, and other exotic creatures that needed to be kept under lock and key. A young elvish woman seemed to be the one in charge and gave a respectful nod to both men as they came up.

"How may I serve the speakers of The Radiant Lord? Care for the day or longer?" she asked.

"A day – possibly two if you please," said Bengt with an ingratiating smile. Normally Tulok would feel his eyes roll in his skull, but he stopped himself. The Brother was trying to be helpful.

"Easily done your Radiances, water and feed are counted within the price," she answered with a smile. Adding on, she asked, "Do you require further storage of your traveling goods as well?" as she motioned to the third camel.

"Ah...yes, please. Also – could you point us in the direction of the nearest house of worship?"

Completely silent during the exchange, Tulok felt his chest tighten slightly. It felt like he was being watched. Turning his head to look behind him, he watched the crowd – but no faces or eyes stood out in the sea of busy, happy, and tired faces. The feeling faded – but did not seem to go away.

~~~

The temple was smaller than the one in Tarf-qua. It stood at the northern part of the outpost near some of the housing for those that made Mukt-aal their home. Unlike Tarf-qua, this building was not just home to The Radiant
~~~

Lord – but to all others within Setesh's pantheon. A large circular room that bore an alcove to the six desert gods who had survived The Reaping. Each shared the one building – though Radiant Lord's presence was just slightly bigger than the others. The Radiant Father of the Oasis was a middle-aged human man with small patches of gray mixed in with his light beard. He gave a tired smile to the pair as they entered.

"Welcome brothers I am Yassin, Priest of the Dawn of the First Order to the Lord of the Skies, Bringer of Light, and Radiant Lord of the Ever Burning Sands. I bid you welcome to Temple of Shared Strength."

In turn, both priests touched their medallions and bowed their heads. Tulok spoke first, "I am Tulok, Priest of the Dawn, in service to the Lord of the Skies, Bringer of Light, and Radiant Lord of the Ever-Burning Sands."

"And I am Bengt Kalb, Acolyte, and Devout of the Radiant Lord," the smaller man added, "We thank you for the warm welcome Father."

"Certainly brothers, certainly. Let me guess – you are making your way to the Grand Capital?" Yassin asked.

Tulok paused and considered his words, "We were wondering what you could tell us about the road to Kas-qua?" Tulok asked.

"Kas-qua? Sounds like you are in the mood for an adventure," Yassin said with a bit of a laugh. "Please have a seat. I will have Sister Vayela and Brother Khet bring some refreshments. All of us have made that trip a few times during the year, so we would be more than happy to share our experiences." He turned away from the pair, and then paused and held up a finger, "Remember – always keep your weapons sharp – lest something sharpens its teeth on you." He chuckled to himself as he walked off to one of the side rooms. Both Bengt and Tulok lightly shared in his laugh and then looked at each other.

"He was joking, wasn't he?" Bengt asked hesitantly.

~~~

"Sun Vipers..." was the only thing Bengt could say after they left the Temple. "I...I was not very fond of snakes to begin with but...Sun Vipers..."

The conversation with the members of the temple had been enlightening to say the very least. The path to the Kas-qua was less sand and dune and more sandstone, hard-packed dunes, and drier air – if such could be imagined. While giant scorpions were few and far between in the eastern areas, Sun Vipers were known to have nested within the rocky alcoves of the sandstone outcrops. An unsuspecting traveler would be caught unawares as the creature struck from the natural holes in the weathered stone. There were also stories of bi-pedal jackal-like creatures who attacked in packs – but these were not the children of the Grim Lord of the Below. These fallen creatures were said to be something unholy altogether that even The Grim himself turned his back on long ago.

To further warn or add to Bengt's apprehension, Sister Vayela said that while it was not completely confirmed, travelers who died in the wastes came back to terrorize the living. The restless dead were not unheard of in the world. These creatures however craved not flesh, but the very moisture from your body. These seemed even more horrifying in the description. The story made Tulok's skin crawl. It would be a four-day journey best experienced in the company of others.

As they departed the Temple of Shared Strength, they both agreed that the most immediate concern was food, a drink, and rest. Staying an extra day to source out other possible travelers going to the Kas-qua was going to be nec-
~~~

essary if they were to make it further along. Father Yassin had been kind enough to provide a writ for the pair to stay in Gulvan's Shade – an inn whose owner provided a discount on lodging for any of the traveling clergies.

Gulvan was an older-looking orc whose strength and hairline had faded with time – but not so much that he could not still throw out anyone who became unruly. Tulok surmised that Yassin pointed them to this particular inn so the big priest could find accommodations more suited to his dimensions, rather than trying to fit into a bed-sized for a human. Bengt took a seat at an empty table within the large hearth room, while Tulok made his way to the bar top.

"Welcome your Radiance – I hope that your travels will be swift and your peace will be restful under my shade," the older orc said with a practice cadence to his voice.

"Thank you, and May the Light of The Radiant Lord continue to shine favorably upon your house," Tulok said while giving a nod of respect to his elder.

"I am Gulvan, and you are welcomed in this house. How long will you be resting with us?" the older orc inquired.

"We intend to leave tomorrow night for the Kas-qua, so a single room for the both of us if possible," Tulok replied as he motioned toward Bengt at the nearby table.

"I believe I can make that accommodation your Radiance. In the meantime – please relax in the common room with your brethren. An evening meal is being prepared – included with the cost of your room of course," the innkeeper added with a bit of a smile.

Tulok gave a small smile. It had been a while, but he accepted the joke in kind. Where the followers of the River Lord exacted a cost for everything, the priesthood of The Radiant Lord was financially known for both their wealth and their frugality. Polar opposites in many regards – but understanding the balance of the world's riches was one of the many lessons taught to devout. Gulvan had probably dealt with both sides of the coin from those coming from Ophir and was prepared to accommodate the culture of his guests.

"That will be fine *honored elder*," Tulok said – adding the honorific in the Orcish tongue.

Gulvan bowed his head, "*And The Radiant Lord honors my House.*"

"*Honored elder – I've seen the mark of Lan-Not. How did they come by here, and are there any still here?*" Tulok asked as he pointed at the cluster of sigils near the bar.

"*They do – are you blood?*" the old Orc replied with a curious eye.

"*As quiet as the night's air moves,*" Tulok replied solemnly. This had been a common saying among those within his village growing up. It felt like forever since he had uttered those words.

Gulvan nodded his head once, "*There are those of that clan that have made their way here from the far west. Years ago when my hands would rend the stone – a group of travelers made their way here. The Mukt-aal was struggling to find its place as many were uncertain of the future and its resources for survival. Sensing an opportunity, they took control of weaker leadership and forged a new way for all of us. While there is prosperity – their methods sometimes can...*"

Before he could finish, clomping footfalls stopped at the door of the inn which opened to reveal a Gnome. She surveyed the room with a turn of her head, and then stepped aside and held the door open for the orc that followed her in.

A look of disdain colored the orc's as if there was a smell within the inn that offended his nose. A pair of scars crisscrossed his features – the intersection fell right over the bridge of his nose. They were the largest and most prominent feature on his face. His deep red eyes looked directly at Tulok. It took a moment, but then Tulok recognized the features and sighed inwardly.

"Well look what the raptors rejected," the orc said with a smug look.

"Hello Cathurg, it has been a long time," Tulok replied.

"Oh, my apologies – your *Radiance*. Title is due when it is *earned*, is it not?" Cathurg said as he gave a slight bow toward Tulok.

He then looked at the common room and his upper lip twitched.

"*Gulvan – ask the jackal bait to remove his sweating body from my table. I do not need its stink to foul your inn too much. I wish to sit and talk with my cousin,*" he said to the older orc. While his words were terse, the tone of his orcish was cordial and polite.

Before Gulvan could reply, "*That jackal bait is my Acolyte, and like me – earned his place within the house of our Lord,*" Tulok replied with similar, but terse politeness.

Cathurg raised an eyebrow, "I see. Very well then, *Your Radiance*," he spoke the title again with emphasis, "I shall endeavor to be a better host to the clergy of The Radiant Lord. Please – introduce me to your Acolyte. I'm sure he is an... entertaining fellow."

The Gnome had already made her way to the table that Bengt sat at. She pulled out the chair for Cathurg who said nothing, but only waved her away. Bengt stood up immediately and bowed his head forward in greeting to Cathurg.

The orc gave the small man a smile, "*At least this one has manners,*" he said in orcish.

Bengt said nothing, his eyes sliding over to Tulok. Tulok knew Bengt could understand him. The art of language was Bengt's hobby – though Tulok wondered if the man only learned other languages to call out others who spoke disparagingly at him.

"This is Acolyte Bengt Kalb of the Temple of Tarf-qua. Brother Bengt – this is Cathurg, a cousin of mine from where I grew up in the north..." Tulok said.

"Actually, it is Raab Cathurg of the Mukt-aal, Your Radiance." Cathurg corrected. "Like I said – title is due when it is earned," he said. He turned his attention to Bengt, "So you have come all the way from Tarf-qua? That is a considerable journey indeed – full of exploration and wonder, eh? I am sure you were exposed to many new and exciting things." While polite, the Raab's manner of speaking was more akin to an adult and a dimwitted child. Clapping his hands together, "You know what – let us consider this your formal *family* welcome to the Mukt-aal."

He stood up from his chair with open arms, an overwhelming sense of smugness filled his voice as he spoke, "In fact, I will ensure that your stay here will be a memorable one." He reached into his pocket and pulled out a small coin purse.

"You – take this to Gulvan to cover the room and board for these two," Cathurg said to the Gnome as he jingled the bag in the air.

Silently, she rushed over and reached for the coin purse. The orc held it just out of her reach and smiled.

"You know – if you grew an inch more, this would be much easier," and dropped the coin purse. Expressionless, she snatched it from the air and then gave a respectful bow before hurrying toward Gulvan.

Cathurg laughed, "Just a little fun with the help, gotta keep them on their toes somehow." He slapped at the table as he continued to laugh as his own joke.

Bengt gave a smile with appreciable laughter, but Tulok

read it in his eyes. Neither one of them cared for this being. It was going to be a very long day.

Chapter 31

Gulvan's cook – whomever they were, had amazing control over their stews – from which there were three to choose. Despite being set apart by price, each bowl was worth the money a hungry traveler paid. It should have been a quiet and delicious meal for both priests, yet its aromas could not counter the sensation of disgust each felt for the orc sitting across from them.

Cathurg was not obnoxious or slovenly by any means. His manner of dress was clean and very well kept. His robes bore golden embroidery of endless dunes drifting in a pattern on a sea of cool linen. Even the few pieces of jewelry he wore were simple displays of wealth with nothing too garish. His tone was polite, even jovial, but also bore an unmistakable edge when the conversation was directed at Tulok. During dinner – Cathurg talked about life before he came to Mukt-aal, and how the previous Raab was a poor leader. Tulok took a casual glance around the room as they ate. The majority of the guests in the common room were Orcs – but still a mixture of races that represented Setesh. None of them looked up or in their direction. There were some that did their best to blend into the background and the natural shadows in the room. Their conversation was either non-existent or too silent to hear. No one wanted to be noticed by any means. While none showed it, Tulok could see it flavor their posture and movements. If fear was a color to paint the soul with – it was Cathurg who held the brush.

"A sad and sorry individual, if I ever did see," Cathurg said with almost a smile. "This Gnomish Raab had allowed himself to be beholden to the *Mya-tal* Clan. He was paying them a monthly tax to ensure the peace of the oasis. Again – even for a Gnome he was more than a disappointment. It is hard to discern one from the other, eh Tulok?" he chuckled as he jabbed the priest with his elbow.

Bengt took a small glance at the orc's attendant – she showed no emotion at the slight. Either she had selective hearing, or she had gone numb to her employer's comments. The stew in front of him lost all of its appeal.

The jab wasn't painful, but Cathurg quickly put up his hands in a position of contrition that was just outside of mocking. "My apologies your Radiance – I do not want to seem like I am being overly familiar. I mean it has been what – almost two decades since you left our humble beginnings in Kol-qua. But it seems I have gotten off the path."

Suddenly, Cathurg snapped his fingers and the Gnome was at his side once again, "Advise the ol…the honored elder that we need the table cleaned, and something stronger to wet the tongue."

Turning back to his audience, "As I said – the little Raab lacked the necessary strength of character to do anything about the situation. So, I took it upon myself to correct the situation. I took a few of our kinsmen as well as a handful of people here who had iron in their blood. Good people mind you. A few very remarkable humans, and some elves. The *Mya-tal* made no secret of where their camp was. Arrogance was their first mistake. I mean if you are going to be bandits in the desert – do not let those who you terrorize find you. It was an idiot's mistake."

A younger Orc came up to the table and began to remove the bowls and cups as Gulvan walked up with a tray of fresh cups and two pitchers. Placing the vessels in front of everyone, he poured a thick, and spicy-smelling liquid into each cup. With the other pitcher, he topped off the cups with what looked like water.

"Per the Raab's request – something with a bit more bite. I call this Veiled Wine. It is brewed from the red pepper flowers that grow near the edge of the oasis. Our cook uses the dried version to add flavor to his stews. I tried using it as a tea but found its effects...a bit heavy shall we say."

Cathurg tapped his finger on the table in a small sign of impatience that was not lost on the older Orc.

"So, through a recipe of my own making – it provides something stronger than ale...but regrettable if too much is taken at once. The key is letting the water seep into the mixture after a minute, and you will find it enjoyable – at least I am told. Please, enjoy."

Cathurg sighed and rolled the cup on its base to swirl its contents. He motioned to Tulok and both he and Bengt did the same. All three took a test sip of its contents. Its flavor was a potent mixture that punched deep into the tongue with a bevy of spiced honey, herbs, and fire.

Tulok exhaled and tried to cool his mouth down as the fire crept down his throat. Bengt's face went flush as he began to cough, and motioned to the younger orc for water.

Cathurg looked thoughtfully at his cup and took a deeper drink, "It takes a bit to get used to. Now – where was I? Oh, the bandits. Yes, now mind you – we were not assassins who struck in the middle of the night. The purpose of the visit was to make a point. However, some of the citizens here were...a bit... excited... at the chance to get their hands red after a few years of poor leadership. Throwing away your money tends to embitter people. So, the plan was to hit their camp as the sun had set. Now let me tell you, your Lord's Eye was so fierce that day that he killed two of the citizens before we ever made our move."

"Wait," Tulok said, "Where was the camp? How far away was it from here?"

"Oh, about four or five hours depending on how you traveled. We left here just after the high point of the day. I had warned them all that in order to complete the task at hand – risks needed to be taken. They all knew what they were getting into. I never promised to protect them – only to help them in our common cause," the Raab said coolly.

"How many died in the attack?" the Tulok asked.

"Eight came with us, and two came back. The humans – always surviving, even when the odds are against you, eh Brother," said Cathurg to Bengt.

Bengt gave his best ingratiating smile, "Sometimes, Honorable Raab, sometimes."

"Now my brother's son lost his hand in the scuffle – not his good hand, thank the heavens," and motioned to Tulok's medallion, "and your Lord of course. We were successful in our mission."

"So you killed all the *Mya-tal*? How many of them were there?" Tulok asked though a sense of fear sat in his stomach.

"Oh, no cousin. I am not a bloodthirsty monster. I would never wipe out an entire clan," he took another deep drink from his cup, "No, but a lesson needed to be taught. You see, the bandits were camped an hour outside the oasis. Leaving during the daytime helped us slip past them undetected because any being with common sense would not travel at that hour. It gave us the advantage that we needed to make it to the *Mya-tal* village. The leader of the bandits was named Shular, and his mate and sons were in that village," Cathurg said.

"You...you attacked a village?" Tulok in growing shock.

"Technically – my kinsmen and I were only there to abduct Shular's mate and his two sons. The citizens of Mukt-aal had grit and fire in their bellies. They attacked the front of the village by setting fire to a few of the homes and causing chaos. Again – they were overzealous, but I could respect that. Though I do not know how they managed to kill any of the villagers. I mean – they were Orcs after all. We are not ones just to roll over for someone's spear, right?" he said with a chuckle.

"What did you do afterward?" Bengt asked.

"As I said, a lesson had to be taught. We tied them to pillars of stone that I had the Vidria create, and made sure they would face the morning sun. I sent a messenger to Shular's camp late into the evening. You could imagine the look of horror and anger that was on his face as he saw his mate and his Legacy tied on those pillars. I think that is what hit him more, "Cathurg said as he leaned back into his chair looking thoughtfully at his cup.

"Of course, his Gurkh could be felt for miles. A rage like that could have never been quenched with words, I'm sure. No, he rushed down the dune like a mad idiot – he never saw me in the shadows of the rocks. As he passed me, I slashed the back of his legs bringing him low to the ground. He screamed in both pain and anger. He was lost to it...completely lost to it. Removing his head was more of an act of mercy at that point. There would be no coming back from that kind of rage. However," Cathurg raised a palm up, "the lesson was made. Their leader was dead, and their homestead attacked. Mukt-aal was no longer a place for them to terrorize. In their wisdom, the remaining leadership named me Raab, and we have been doing very well ever since."

The Gnome appeared at his side and held a small stack of envelopes to him, "Oh, I had almost forgotten. If you will excuse me your Radiances, administrative duties calls. We'll talk later, I am sure," he said as he rose from the table.

"Honorable Raab, what of the *Mya-tal* now? Do Shular's sons resent you or have they made peace with this place," Bengt asked.

"Oh no Brother," he said as he shook his head, "There is no resentment at all. After I killed Shular, I wanted the bandits, the *Mya-tal*, and everyone here to know that peace is paid with blood. I simply killed the rest of his family."

With that, he turned from the table and walked out with the Gnome shadowing him.

Bengt blinked as his mind took a moment to process what had been said.

Tulok stared at the door, his jaw set tight. He had no words.

~~~

Dinner was still not sitting well and Tulok's stomach continued to churn. Perhaps under different circumstances – the food and wine would have been fine. The encounter with his cousin threw everything off. Shock and disbelief were unwanted tastes in his mouth and no amount of ale or wine could drown it out. To that point – the priest realized that he needed to keep his wits about him going forward. Cathurg was a bully who used to use his fist to make his point – but this...this was something entirely different. His level of practicality on the matter of establishing peace and leadership only begged the question of what else had he done?

"That's another thing," Bengt added, "He was not angry
~~~

like you – no offense, but for an Orc he was less with the growls...but that calm...," he shook his head, "That calm is terrifying."

Tulok raised an eyebrow and shot the smaller man a warning look, but then just shook his head.

"He made his choice – he tempered his Reason. When The Scribe gave us the gift of Reason – we still maintained our Rage, but now we had an opportunity to be something more. All the cunning and guile mixed with strength and will – it can make an Orc a champion for his people...his God...or in Cathurg's case – a tyrant."

Tulok shook his head and stared at the floor.

"...in a way...that makes him...better than me."

Bengt stopped pacing and stared at the figure across the room from him. Against his better instinct, he picked up a washbowl and threw its contents across the room. The shock of the lukewarm water caused Tulok to snap his head up with rising anger. Before he could utter a word.

Bengt snapped at him, "How is that monster better than anyone except other monsters?!"

The question made the Orc's eye twitch, "That monster made a choice to master his primal self. He is not in a constant struggle for control."

"Then why are you?" Bengt fired back.

"I..." the anger slowly ebbed away, and a sense of shame-filled him, "I... most Orcs who choose Ghal – the Reason, do so as an active decision. They spend months, even years channeling the rage to contain it – temper it. When they have mastered it – they have accepted the balance into themselves. They still get angry – but they do not tap into that Rage unless they absolutely have to." He turned his head toward the window. He couldn't look at the man across from him.

"After my pilgrimage – I left for the temple to join the

priesthood. I was excited to have found my purpose – to learn and experience the Ever-Burning Lord in all His glory that the need for control...the lessons," he shook his head. "I threw myself into learning – the very essence of Reason because I did not want anyone to fear me. The problem is you push yourself too much in one direction – you lose yourself to the other. You either become too much a feral beast...or... you lose that vital spark of creativity, your drive and purpose, and just accept whatever is brought to you – even your death."

He sighed deeply, "When I realized what was happening, I tried to bring back that fire within me, and it came back...just now it was harder to control. So now – I'm still trying to master a basic concept children understand better than I do. That boy helping Gulvan has more mastery of the path than I do. So yes – when I say that Cathurg is better than me, I honestly mean he is better than me."

His gaze fell to the floor once again, and the room filled itself with momentary silence.

"Have you ever considered His Unblinking Eye saw this in you, yet he still chose you?" Bengt asked, "His wisdom is infinite and perhaps this struggle is a long lesson intended for you. Orcs are long-lived, Father. This is a task intended for you. Do we not tell our people that *The Ever Burning Lord sees your struggles, but in order to persevere...*"

"*...you must feed kindling to the fire within your soul. When your spirit is ablaze, know that I am with you and there is nothing that can stand in your way,*" Tulok said, completing the verse.

There was silence again.

Tulok looked over at Bengt, and straightened himself up, "Why are you being nice to me at this point?"

Bengt looked at the floor for a moment, "If you are going to sit here and wallow – you would not be doing your job. I would be failing at mine in not aiding the Radiant

Father of my temple. So if anything – this is what I am supposed to do."

The Radiant Father regarded the Acolyte across from him for a long moment – each meeting each other's gaze.

Tulok stood up and ran his hand over his head, "You also know what Cathurg thinks of you, and given the story from earlier, you know he would have no problem killing you."

"There is that too – yes," the small man nodded, "but safety in numbers – right Father?" Bengt asked with half a smile and a slight shrug.

Tulok just shook his head and laughed to himself, "I like us being civil."

Bengt nodded his head and then turned his head outside. Looking back at Tulok, "The light is fading – we probably should go to the temple."

Chapter 32

Sunset oblations were slightly different from those in Tarf-qua – but each temple added a unique flavor to how Radiant Lord's unblinking eye moved on to the other parts of the world. While it differed from temple to temple, the Sunset oblation seemed curiously more important to all those within the Temple of Shared Strength. Father Yassin was thankful for the two extra bodies as the temple was packed. According to Brother Khet, there was a line out the door. The prediction had been for a long and cloudless day which meant that Sky Lord's Eye would be unrelenting to all those who would travel. The opportunity to accept a blessing before you traveled was not lost on anyone.

Half an hour after the last parishioner accepted their blessing – the five members of the clergy were finally able to sit down.

"I have not seen that many caravans come through at once since last year. There must be something interesting happening in Ophir," said Yassin.

"They could be going up to Port Kraken – there were some faces that seemed a bit more pale than usual," said Khet with a slight smile.

"Where is Port Kraken?" asked Bengt.

"North of the capital – it is a seaport that is a few

months' travel up the coast. They trade goods between this continent and Avalon," said Yassin.

Tulok said nothing, and Bengt simply nodded his head. The words had an unintended sting to them, but rather than say anything – Tulok simply stood and stretched out his shoulder,

"I think – I should get something to eat after all of that."

Yassin smiled, "That is a wonderful idea! Let us treat you tonight as our thanks for your aid. I will not accept 'no' for an answer!"

Tulok nodded his head in acceptance, "Brother Bengt and I will secure a table at Gulvan's."

"Excellent – maybe we can sample that Veiled Wine he makes?" Yassin asked excitedly. "Have you tried it? I heard it is quite interesting!"

Tulok and Bengt looked at each other.

"It is," both said in unison.

~~~

There was a warm breeze in the air that cooled the sweat on the body. The breeze was another sign that tomorrow was going to be unforgiving. Regardless, the streets were busy with activity as both shopkeepers and food places began their nightly trade. Bengt caught several looks from the various Orcs plying their business. Each gave a respectful nod toward the smaller man, but each kept a soft eye on the Radiant Father.

"Is there a reason why you are catching their eyes?" Bengt said quietly as they walked toward the inn.

"I'm not sure. We saw some of them earlier when we first came in," Tulok said.

"It feels like they are waiting on something. Are Orcish priests supposed to do anything in particular for their people?" Bengt asked.
~~~

"Well the first thing is to not be a weakling or serve those who are weaker than you," said Cathurg.

Tulok and Bengt turned to see the Raab pull himself out of a chair on the porch of one of the establishments.

The large area was filled with a sea of red eyes – all of them quietly staring at the trio.

"*Blooded Citizens of the Mukt-aal,*" Cathurg said aloud in Orcish, "*Clan Sik-iln, Clan Mya-tal, Clan Sha-brd, and Clan Lan-Not – a moment of your time. Tonight, we have a guest in our midst – Tulok Blood of Lan-Not ti Kol-qua. Also known as Father Tulok for the Radiant Lord.*"

All eyes were on Tulok – a sea of curiosity and apprehension. Cathurg spread his arms wide, drawing the focus and attention of the crowd to himself, and away from the priest.

"*Tonight, I come to you NOT as your Raab, but as one of your own blood. Tonight, I stand here to accuse this one in our midst of not only being unworthy of the blood in his veins but see him pay for a coward's action long ago,*" Cathurg said loudly. He began walking in a wide circle – speaking to the audience as one would a showman displaying a wild animal.

"*This pitiful excuse that stands before you, this...Tulok,*" he said with almost a smile to the priest in the middle. "*Even now, his very nature is to demand your respect for his god. He needs you to look at that shining medallion on his chest and acknowledge his station above yours. All of these things would be worth noting if it were not for shame that helped him gain these things. You see – he abandoned Kol-qua. You all know the Rite of Marn...*" Cathurg looked around the assembled group. Many of the orcs folded their arms across their broad chests and nodded solemnly as the Raab spoke.

Bengt cast his gaze toward Tulok, but the priest was silent.

Tulok's head was unbowed, his eyes and jaw set. His face was expressionless except for the sounds coming from his hands. Looking down, Bengt could see orc's fists balled up – the knuckles were a pale tan. Tulok's arms were a bulge of veins and strain. The acolyte knew that his priest was using every ounce of his will to remain silent.

"*The Rite of Marn is a quest that we each have taken and survived. However, this one...*" he motioned to Tulok, "*...this one was on Marn for three years. Yes, you heard me right THREE YEARS! Unbelievable!*" Cathurg gestured again. Looks of shock and disdain began to color the faces of the assembled. "*What could one of the blood be doing for three years while his village awaited his return?*" Cathurg turned to Tulok, "*Would you like to tell them?*"

Tulok said nothing, but stared blankly, his breathing slow and even.

Cathurg smiled, "*Lizards...he was acting as a servant to the DAMN LIZARDS.*" Cathurg shouted to the crowd. "*The arrogant Anuket and the greedy Sobekites. He was their personal servant, learning at their feet the so-called 'ways of the world' like a dog learning tricks for treats. He was not surviving the wastes of Setesh alone. He was not fighting to live to make his name known to his tribe. NO... He did NONE OF THIS!*"

There were murmurs in the crowd as many began to regard Tulok with a more scrutinous eye. Bengt saw the looks shift from apprehension to disgust as they stared at the priest in the center of the verbal storm. Yet – Tulok said nothing, though Bengt could see him slowly squeezing and relaxing his fists. The muscles in Tulok's forearms bunched and relaxed.

"*Then this one before you came back three years later to his home.*" Cathurg gestured once again. "*My Home...OUR HOME like some triumphant conqueror. He did not return with food. He did not return with wealth to trade. No... he came back with maps. Which I am certain were appreciated – when we chil-*

dren." he stated snidely. "*No... he came back with nothing to speak of in his three years of leisure play and servitude.*"

Cathurg turned his eyes to Tulok and lowered his arms. He lowered his voice and shook his head. "*He tells his tale with NOT an OUNCE OF SHAME to our elders. He brings them stories for their entertainment which obviously caused them to look the other way at his uselessness,*" Cathurg pleaded to the crowd, slapping one hand into his palm to emphasize each syllable.

He paused and made his way to a female Orc who had her arms folded across her chest as she stared at the priest. Leaning close to her, he whispered loud enough for others to hear, his eyes drifting toward Tulok, "*I have heard that priests are not allowed to take wives. Do you suppose that he knew his shame would eventually be caught by others? Perhaps...perhaps he ran into the priesthood because he knew no one would take him for a mate? What do you think?*"

The female Orc looked at Tulok, leaned forward, and spit on the ground.

There were no friends here.

Cathurg smiled and leaned away, standing up once more, "*So I come here – as a member of the blood, not pass judgment on a priest,*" he paused, "*Far be it from me to say anything against the Mighty Sun God.*" He looked to the sky for a moment and then lowered his eyes to fall on Tulok.

"*No – what I do here today is render judgment for the blood of my clan – no... for the blood of all of you, the people. I am here to pass judgment on one of our kind. A failure in the eyes of our blood.*" Cathurg raised his massive arm and pointed an accusatory finger at the priest.

"*Tulok Lan-Not ti Kol-qua – you are a coward in our eyes...*" Cathurg's red eyes glimmered in the fading light with mania and rage. "*...no in THE EYES OF EVERY ORC IN SANCTUM. We all can feel the imbalance in you. Your presence is a* *black mark upon the strength and cunning of our kind."* His voice rose in timbre and urgency, the passion in his blood was almost palpable... *"You have lacked the basic gifts that make an Orc in the eyes of the Scribe."* Cathurg took a step toward Tulok. *"Where were you when Kol-qua denied the Howlers?"* Another step. The Raab's massive fists balled at his side. *"Where were you when its children had thirst with no well in sight because the Mad Sand God buried them all? WHERE WERE YOU TULOK?!"*

At that moment Cathurg rushed forward and struck his fist low and fast into Tulok's stomach. The air escaped Tulok's lungs as he doubled over around Cathurg's fist.

"YOU WERE BUSY LEARNING STORIES OF THE DEAD AND FORGOTTEN RATHER THAN THE NEEDS OF YOUR OWN PEOPLE! WHILE WE WERE DIGGING NEW WELLS AND GRAVES, YOU PLAYED HOUSE MAID!" Cathurg's other fist came down on the back of Tulok's head.

A painful sound issued from Tulok's lips.

"YOU SELFISH MISERABLE COWARD!" Cathurg pulled his arm away from Tulok's stomach. He reached for the side of Tulok's head *"THAT IS WHAT YOU ARE! A COWARD IN THE EYES OF YOUR BLOOD AND I PASS THIS JUDGEMENT UPON YOU AS BY THE RIGHTS OF THE RITUAL OF MARN!!"* Cathurg brought his knee up into Tulok's face. Blood splattered onto the ground.

With each accusation – Cathurg struck the priest from all sides – the groin, the abdomen, the face, and the head. Each blow casting judgment of both blood and pain.

Tulok fell to his knees – blood spat on the ground with each cough and breath, but he did not raise his hand in defense.

Bengt made a single motion, but Cathurg's look was filled with death and horror. The Acolyte could only raise his hand limply and shake his head. He shook his head slowly as if to say 'no – stop' – but Cathurg heard nothing as he continued to pummel the fallen priest.

Tulok continued to accept the punishment meted out by the Raab – cuts and abrasions welling up on his flesh, as his blood poured out onto the sand. A mighty blow to the back of Tulok's head knocked him forward. He caught himself on his hands, panting and spitting mouthfuls of blood and bile.

After what seemed like an eternity, Cathurg raised an exhausted fist high as Tulok's hands were firmly planted on the ground. The Raab had readied a killing blow – every orc could feel the power in his fist as he raised it up to the faded horizon. With a motion as fast as lightning, Cathurg brought his massive fist down upon the disgraced priest.

Tulok's body shuddered from the impact, yet – he did not fall.

Cathurg snarled and reached back again, he lashed out with all the rage and might that the Gurkh allowed him and pushed his fist into the back of Tulok's head...

Tulok did not falter.

Bengt's eyes widened as he watched the giant priest quickly reach and pull Cathurg's curled fist off the back of his head. Rising to his feet, Tulok twisted the wrist and elbow of the surprised Raab – stretching him beyond his height and forcing him to stand on his toes. Tuloks face bled freely. His massive muscles rippled with pent-up emotion. His jaw clenched. His lips pulled back from his normally peaceful countenance into a snarl.

The first blow hit Cathurg square in the face that should have sent him reeling, but Tulok's grip on his twisted arm only put painful pressure on the Raab's shoulder. Cathurg cried out in pain. Without hesitation, Tulok punched again, and again into Cathurg's face. The Raab's body flailed with each blow, unable to defend or escape. A roar followed each and every hit, and the sound of the roar was echoed by the smacking sound of flesh on flesh.

Tulok did not stop.

What became two blows soon turned into several, past the point of counting. His roars and cries of pain echoed as one as he continued to punch Cathurg in the face. The unrelenting rage in his eyes was horrifying and filled with anger unseen. Years of anger held in careful check erupted to the surface. They were mixed with the unfathomable grief commanding his mind.

Cathurg tried to pull away, but the white-knuckled grip on his arm would not let him go. The priest's fist continued to pound away. Blood poured down the pulp that was once Cathurg's face.

Then with a slip of his hand, Tulok dropped the Raab to the ground. He crumpled like a broken doll. Tulok reached for his mace and raised it high. It was a weapon he seldomly used, and despised wielding. Rage and Reason were both gone from his eyes as he began to bring in down on the Raab's head...

"FATHER STOP!!!!"

The mace faltered mere inches away from the Raab's already battered form.

Tulok turned his attention to the small man to his right. Bengt – for the first time in his life was truly scared with tears streaming from his eyes.

"...Please...Father...it is done..." was all the little man could say.

Reason pulsed back slowly into Tulok's brain as he looked at the man, and then back to Cathurg.

The Raab was broken, bruised, and bloodied.

The weight of the mace felt heavier in his hand.

He stepped away from the Raab on the ground with the same swiftness of one who stepped on something hot.

He looked around to the crowd, "I.... I...." he started but could not find the words as the fuel of rage still rushed in his veins. His heart pounded in his head. All around the looks of disgust had turned to horror as they looked at the bloodied fist and mace of the priest.

"Cathurg is right," Tulok said softly. The area was so full of silence it felt like a heavy weight on all of their shoulders. "I was gone for three years...the Anuket and Sobekites...they taught me the value of choice...of life. I saw a hard...life...and easy life. I had a choice. I choose the hard life."

He let the mace drop to the ground as the adrenaline of battle began to fade from his body.

"I choose the life that requires me to serve others. Not just my clan – but those that believed in my God," Tulok looked up at the crowd. Blinking away the blood he addressed those gathered.

"We are a savage people of reason and I found my solace in my ability to lead those who were lost. I came back to Kol-qua and gave my elders the story of my travels. I did not bring treasure. I did not bring glory. I brought back words. Words of knowledge like The Scribe gave us understanding."

The horrified crowd began to slowly stir. The Scribe – regardless of religion, was still considered revered among all of the Orcish people. Some nodded quietly.

"I took those lessons – those words... and gave them to the elders. I provided knowledge of new wells...new outposts and new dangers to avoid. I learned much in my travels with the children of The Star Maiden and The River Lord. My survival was dependent on my hands and my head. I worked every day for three years – not for them, but WITH them. This is Setesh – the realm of burning lands. Working with them to survive and learn was the price I paid for my life." Tulok closed his eyes and shook his head remembering.

"Cathurg was right. I died.... I died in the sand and the mercy of two strangers gave me life."

Tulok's eyes opened and he forced himself to stand over Cathurg. Bruises and blood covered his broken face. His legs trembled with exhaustion and strain. The sea of orcish eyes regarded the priest carefully. Tulok's eyes fell on the female orc that Cathurg had spoken to earlier.

"I accepted a chance at living not because I was weak. The Radiant Lord laid challenges before me and I died...but in His mercy I was reborn. I failed and I persevered." Tulok spoke. The female orc nodded in satisfaction and lowered her arms. Tulok turned to address the whole of the crowd.

"I AM STANDING HERE NOW BECAUSE I REFUSED TO DIE!" he yelled at the crowd. "I AM NOT A COWARD AS THIS ONE WILL HAVE YOU BELIEVE! I WAS TRIED AND TESTED BY A GOD AND FOUND WORTHY OF LIFE!"

He kicked Cathurg's body over onto his back and stared down at him.

Leaning forward he roared at the fallen Raab,

"A GOD FOUND ME WORTHY TO SERVE HIM!"

Standing tall, Tulok looked at the crowd around him. What was once only orcs had been filled with many of the denizens of the Mukt-aal. All of them stared at the orc and at the fallen Raab. There was a sense of admiration in their eyes as their eyes looked upon the Priest of the Radiant Lord.

Reason had finally caught up with Tulok as he looked around the crowd. His eyes finally came to land on Father Yassin and his fellow followers of the faith. Yassin stood there with his acolytes – the look of shock on his face did not betray any emotions.

The sense of shame crept up inside Tulok's chest.

He walked towards the Radiant Father, "I am..."

Before he could finish, Yassin held up a casual hand to silence Tulok "You are right Father...it was an excellent night for exercise. The warm night air is wonderful for encouraging the spirit! I will see you at Gulvan's – try not to be too long...". Yassin smiled and walked around the crowd with his two acolytes in tow.

Tulok looked to Bengt, a sense of confusion filled his face.

Bengt shrugged, "I think Radiant Father Yassin will be buying you the first round?"

Chapter 33

There was not enough ale in Gulvan's to lessen the pain in Tulok's face. Despite the offers from Yassin and Bengt, the orc wore his bruises like a mark of penance. While there was no cheering or revelry at Gulvan's – there was a sense of ease in the air. Cathurg had been beaten down by one of the blood. The Rite of Marn had been invoked and every orc in the Mukt-aal knew that Cathurg had lost. While his claim on leadership of the outpost remained, the leadership (*or tyranny*) he held over the orc people was gone. The Raab no longer possessed the majority of physical power or respect within the outpost. Even those that were considered his subordinates were enjoying themselves within Gulvan's inn.

The older orc said nothing to the priest of the Radiant Lord as he brought them all tankards without saying anything. All he did was place a hand on Tulok's shoulder.

"I have steak that could fit over your eye...if you have the coin, Father..."

Bengt silently interjected with a nod and the passing of several coins into the innkeeper's hand. Gulvan simply nodded and later returned with what could have been a day's supper and respectfully laid it on the bruised face of the priest. The meat along with Gulvan's spiced tea wore away the pain, though there was still a sense of shame on Tulok's shoulder.

This was not lost on Gulvan as he looked at Tulok. With the second round, Gulvan leaned forward and said quietly in Tulok's ear, "Victories are meant to be celebrated – smile you damn idiot or I'll give you something to smile about!"

The shock of the words brought Tulok out of his somber stupor. He looked over to Gulvan and simply nodded. When the other Orc had left, Yassin leaned over and asked, "What did he say?"

Tulok gave a half-smile, "He said – be an Orc."

~~~

Darkness. Chill, crisp and cold, that bored into the depths of the soul. The chill reached deep into her very bones, there was no escaping it. Her eyes sought to focus on the emptiness that surrounded her. To make out shapes, forms, anything. She could feel her hands and feet.

She was aware of her body and herself. There was an absence of sound, of smell, and of sight. The only sensation was the chill of an unearthly cold.

Reaching her hands out, she took a tentative step forward. It felt like walking in heavy mud, like the very air was pushing back against her, and sucking at her feet, to hold her in place. She took a breath and pulled her foot free and stepped forward once more. It was a hard push and the effort was draining. Another step.

Taking a breath, she spoke softly in the Darkness,

I am the light in the darkness,

She pulled her foot free and stepped forward once more.

so shall I breathe life into embers,

She tucked her head and braced her shoulder, as one who would walk upwind in a storm, pushing against the chill and the cold that surrounded her.

and kindle that light,
~~~

Her left hand reached for the broken compass that hung around her neck. She wrapped her fingers around it tightly. It felt warm to the touch.

for unto me is given this charge –

Her body began to draw warmth from the compass, her passage became less arduous.

let Hope never falter in my presence

In the distance, a tiny bead of light appeared. It was a red-gold beacon in the absence of color that surrounded her. She nodded and directed her path in that direction.

so long as I draw breath

The darkness gave way, like pushing through the overgrowth of a thicket and entering an open clearing. Isolde stumbled forward slightly and staggered, regaining her balance. Her eyes slowly adjusted to the change in lighting. She blinked and focused on what was before her.

An older woman, dressed in simple robes, sat by a small fire. The robes were a pale yellow, the color washed from the fabric from years of use. At her waist hung a ring with several keys. Her black hair was streaked with white and flowed loose across her shoulders and down her back. Across the fire was an iron spit, and hanging suspended from the spit was a brass cauldron, perhaps large enough to hold two tankards of liquid. The woman turned striking blue eyes toward Isolde at her approach. She offered the woman a gentle smile, as she gestured for Isolde to join her.

"Welcome child. Please," she spoke. Though the woman's voice was soft, it carried with it a sense of power and dignity.

Isolde stepped forward, toward the light and the warmth of the fire.

"Thank you." she inclined her head politely.

"You have come a long way." the woman in yellow offered.

Isolde nodded. "I suppose so..."

The woman looked off into the distance. The horizon presented what appeared to be the shore of a river or lake. Several boats were tethered there. A dozen people waited on the banks.

"You are looking to cross the river then?" she asked Isolde.

Isolde's eyes followed to where the woman gestured. There was something familiar about the line of the river and the boats lined up there. She looked away and back to the fire. Her eyes focused on the cauldron that was suspended over the fire. There was a symbol engraved on one side. Isolde stared at it. The fire's smoke partially obscured the design, but it appeared to be a wagon wheel, or some other round, wheel-like symbol. Isolde tried to peer into the cauldron to view its contents. She could see nothing. A noxious aroma rose from the cauldron.

"I... suppose I am?" Isolde commented.

The woman nodded and watched Isolde. "You are too heavily burdened to cross," she said simply.

Isolde looked down at herself. She was wearing only her shirt and pants. Her compass hung from around her neck. She frowned and looked back at the woman. "But...I... have nothing, and have left everything else behind already..."

The woman smiled once more. It was the warm and comforting smile of a mother or a grandmother, a teacher, an advisor. She shook her head. "Unburden your soul, my Child." she spoke gently.

Isolde's eyes widened slightly. Of course. She looked around, trying to get a better visual of her surroundings. Three paths seemed to lead to this location. The woman's fire was set in the center, where they all came to meet. In the distance, three ships waited to carry people to the other shore. They stayed well away from the water's edge. Isolde squinted, trying to see the far side. There were hints of blues and greens, yellows, and whites. Light against the darkness. Something inside told her that the far bank was warm and welcoming, filled with rest and remembrance. She remembered the stories of the Faith growing up. The Summerlands was a place of rest, remembrance, and eventually – rebirth. These must be the banks where the Cycle ended and the new journey would begin.

She frowned.

Was she dead then?

The woman at the fire turned warm and welcoming eyes on Isolde. "Cast aside that which weighs you down. Accept its lesson, and move forward." she held an open hand out over the mouth of the cauldron.

"Give the Darkness its due, Child of Light."

Isolde stared at the woman and the cauldron. She remembered standing by the fire on a mid-harvest eve every year. She remembered whispering a pain, a sorrow, a loss into a cauldron and asking that the daughters of darkness carry that miasma to their Lady, to tend it and remove its weight from her heart. It was a time of cleansing and rebirth, of forgiveness and acceptance.

"A burdened soul can never move forward." the woman spoke. Her voice continued to be both warm and welcoming.

Isolde turned her eyes to the shoreline.

"I carry the unfinished burden of another." she looked at the woman. "If I give it to you, can you lift the burden from his soul... and allow him to move on?"

The woman's eyes softened, and she nodded. "This I can do." She gestured to the cauldron over the fire.

Isolde nodded and knelt by the fire. She bowed her head in reverence ingrained in ancient ways. "May my words open the gates of truth, as surely as the wisdom of your keys.

Take then this weight upon my soul, the burden of another, that which binds his feet to a world no longer his own." The fire crackled a little louder, burned a little warmer. "Let his duty be done, let him journey to the Summerlands."

In the distance, one of the figures wandering the bank seemed to pause. It looked back in her direction. For a moment, she felt the presence of her Lord, her Knight, her friend. A salt tear drifted down her cheek as she looked toward the shoreline.

"In death let him be released from his Oaths, as I release him from His Oaths to me."

Isolde.

The name danced on an unfelt breeze, caressing her ears with their notes. "I release my sorrow; I release my anger. Take my uncertainty and regret." her eyes focused on the figure in the distance, "And forgive me my jealousy. It was never yours to carry."

The fire glowed blue-green and rose in height. Its heat burned white-hot. Isolde could feel it on her skin. In the distance, the figure turned and began to board one of the ships on the riverbank. Isolde lowered her head, a great weight lifted from both her mind and her heart.

"May She find your sacrifice worthy" the woman intoned and nodded her head simply. "May you accept the keys She offers you and may your weakness make you strong."

The fire subsided and returned to its previous height and warmth. Isolde raised her eyes to look at the woman once more.

"Unburden your soul, and cross over, child." the woman spoke gently and gestured once more to the cauldron. "Let your time of battles be over, and let the Cycle renew once more."

Isolde turned her eyes to the shoreline and the boats

that waited there. The figure that was Reynard stood quietly looking back at her. Silent and unmoving. In the distance, the warm dancing lights of the Summerlands glowed invitingly from the other shore. If she closed her eyes, she believed she could hear children laughing and the songs of the ancients drifting on an unfelt breeze.

"My love for Nathaniel..." Isolde whispered.

The fire crackled in response.

Yes.

"My desire to have been a better daughter..." she continued.

The fire's heat rose a little.

Yes.

"My need to find my own place outside my family name..." Isolde's eyes fixated on the boat and the shoreline.

Yes.

The fire rose and began to shift its hues from oranges to blues. It was warm. The warmth seemed to fill all of her being as if it were burning away parts of her. It was painless, and cleansing. She sighed at the relief that it brought.

Something burned at the center of her chest. Instinctively she reached up and wrapped her fingers around the small broken compass that Reynard had entrusted her with. It was hot to the touch and singed her fingers. She frowned and looked down at it. A small glowing golden thread wrapped itself around the compass and around her hand, the thread fell to the ground and seemed to trail off into the distance.

"Clip the thread. Unburden your soul." the woman spoke softly. She reached out to offer Isolde a pair of sewing shears. Isolde took them into her hand and stared at them and the golden thread. She looked up at the boats and the glowing shoreline in the distance. She closed her eyes and wrapped her hand around the shears.

You would honor me further if you would allow me to call you...Friend a deep voice echoed in her head.

Suddenly her thoughts were awash with sights and sounds, memories and feelings. A warm laugh, caring hands binding her wounds, a patient smile, frustration, anger at a situation neither of them could control, shared grief, shared calling, an eternity of difference, and yet...

Tulok.

Isolde opened her eyes and looked down at the shears in her hand, then up at the woman who sat quietly watching her.

"Unburden your soul and move on." she said once more.

Isolde shook her head and let the shears fall to the ground. She pushed herself up to stand and looked off into the distance once more. The figure on the boat nodded once and turned away. The ship pushed off from the bank. Isolde turned to look at the woman clad in yellow.

"I cannot. My Quest is not yet finished." Isolde replied.

The woman nodded. "Go then in peace, Child of Light. We will meet again."

Darkness washed over Isolde once more, like a warm and welcome blanket.

Chapter 34

Fire flew from Bengt's hand and scored a hit across the back of the creature, burning into its fur. It howled in pain for a moment but was cut short as the body of another creature was thrown into it. Tulok roared – not in rage, but in a form of challenge. Their leader attempted to take the Orc from behind, but with a sidestep, Tulok slipped out of the creature's claws. With a twist of his body, Tulok swung the mace deep into the creature's chest – lifting it off the ground and flailing through the air.

"Yassin never said there were Sandtalons this far east!"

"Then maybe we should go back and tell him to update his map!" Bengt shouted back as he swung his staff at the clawed hand swiping at him.

Sandtalons were one of the mysteries of the desert. The Grim's faithful hunted them down with prejudice though it was unclear as to why. The creatures did not resemble the Grim Lord's favored jackals and were more like spotted dogs with deformed faces. In the west, they were known for raiding caravans just before The Radiant Lord rose up to greet the land again. Packs of four or five would be directed by a leader. If you were lucky, killing the leader would cause them to run away. However, if there was dissension in the pack – they would just keep attacking until one showed leadership. In the past, there were attempts to communicate with them, but each was met by fierce violence. Even those who possessed magics or artifacts that allowed them to peer into their mind only found it devoid of sentience with only a vibrant sense of savagery coupled with instinct. How and why they were created was anyone's guess. While there were many theories and rumors, their origin seemed to be a mix of curses to failed magical experiments.

None of which mattered as the pack had descended on Tulok and Bengt on the second day of their travels. The Sun God's light had only begun to change the sky from inky blackness to a dark slash of navy. With only the most minor of spells to rely on – both priests were forced to rely on tactics and strength.

Tulok had hoped by yelling loud enough, it would either elicit a challenge or scare off the threat. He had hoped for the latter but was rewarded with the former. The largest of the pack rushed him. The horrid-looking creature brought in both claws and dug them into the Orc's sides. The force of the impact had initially thrown Tulok off his feet, but the Sandtalon did not expect Tulok to continue to roll with its claws still in him. Painful as it was, Tulok reared back and roared again – smashing both fists down on the creature's already scarred face. There was an audible crunch as he felt something warm pool up.

The priest stood up, removing the clawed hands from his side. The four sets of blackened eyes stared at him for a brief moment and they surged forward.

"Shit..." was all the large priest could say as the new leader jumped towards him.

This was not how they imagined spending their morning.

~~~
~~~

"I'm sorry, but that just seems like a questionable use of His Divine gifts!" Tulok argued back.

"The thing is dead now, isn't it?" Bengt said flatly, "Sun Vipers are immune to everything non-magical and reversing the gift....in order to harm it ... seemed logical!"

The man-sized creature lay dead and halfway out of its sandstone burrow. Waves of heat emanate from its body, even after death. Its scales were a mix of golds, oranges, and yellows near its face but the rest of it took on a dry and mottled brown. It was perfect camouflage to have while waiting for its prey. The creature had taken up residence in the ruins of a small house – at least that was what both priests surmised it to be. It had been the only structure for miles. It was two days away from both the nearest sources of water and it was too ruined to provide any answers or origin. It was a perfect shelter for a few hours and provided the foundation for their shade.

"If it was forbidden, do you not think there would be consequences already. Our Lord is known for his quickness to right a wrong especially when it comes to his gifts."

Tulok just stared at Bengt who simply returned his gaze. Both turned their heads toward the setting sun and waited. If The Radiant Lord was going to do something to either of them – now would be the moment. Both men took to their knees and began the prayers to the setting sun. As the last of the light faded – both opened their eyes and stared at one another. They held their breath.

Nothing happened.

Tulok gave a deep sigh, "Fine...you were right. If the Lord of the Ever-Burning Skies saw fit to allow you the use of His gifts in that fashion – so be it. However, I will never condone its use on people. Creatures trying to kill us is one thing... Sentient beings," he shook his head, "We are supposed to be healers to aid the people."

Bengt sat silently for a moment, "You know...there are..." he looked at the horizon. It was already pitch black and the only light was heat still coming off the Sun Viper that resembled the embers of a campfire.

Confident that the sun's light was no longer there, and their Lord no longer watched them directly, he began again, "There are stories that there are some of the priesthood that are more...martial than they are healers."

"You're confusing those with Devout..." Tulok began.

"No, these are not His champions," Bengt lowered his head and quietly spoke, "The champions are seen by the people. They are open and visible. They wield His justice and vengeance with equal hands. However, there are stories of priests who do what is necessary for all of Setesh and the priesthood – no matter what."

Tulok smirked, "You honestly believe that the Aswa..."

"DO NOT SAY IT ALOUD!" Bengt chastised him with a slight tone of fear and panic.

Whether Tulok believed it or not, it did not matter. Bengt certainly did. Despite the injuries and fighting the last couple of days – they had not quarreled with each other. It was nice. Somehow, through all of this – both seemed more tolerant of each other's place in the world.

Tulok raised his hands and grimaced slightly as his sides were still healing, "Alright – I will not say the name aloud. However, those are just stories brother. I have heard them as well, but I have yet to see the value of such a concept. Why would there be a need for such a group? If there was anything that could threaten or challenge the..."

Tulok stopped and looked at Isolde's bag. The box that started all of this was still nestled inside along with her possessions.

He stared at the bag for a long moment, and then back at Bengt.

Bengt slowly nodded his head but said nothing.

The world felt a bit heavier on Tulok's shoulders suddenly.

"...tell me what you've heard," the Orc asked, "Please...I want to know everything."

Bengt shook his head, "Father, I only know what I've overheard and even then – some are probably misinterpretations or subject to another's perception. In all cases – the stories share a few similarities...."

Bengt continued to speak about various stories of villages being attacked in the wake of a terrible evil that had suddenly disappeared without a trace. Other stories of nomad bandits being swallowed up by the sands that were thought to be solid earth. Each story shared the background character of a lone priest providing aid in the aftermath. Someone who just faded into the background and was soon forgotten. Whether it was one or a group – the stories all shared similar ties.

It was an unsettling feeling that sat in Tulok's chest. This all could just be nonsense and just the fantasy stories of young acolytes and laymen with aspirations of heroism.

Yet – for something as unsettling as a cult vying for power, a Champion should have been brought in. It was a nagging thought that consumed him since they left the River Lord's city. Why would they send him? He was no one.

He was just a priest...wasn't he?

~~~

Bengt laughed.

Tulok shook his head, "That's not what I meant!" The Orc leaned his back against one of the palm trees and sighed in exasperation. There were several around the two large springs that the oasis got its nickname from. The
~~~

priest was embarrassed and was thankful that the firelight hid the flush in his face.

They had crossed into Kas-qua or Twin Springs several hours earlier. While not a village, the outpost played home to a few sandstone structures – but that was all there really was. The area served to host a few Anuket, a pair of Orcs, and a handful of humans. Only a few of them made the springs their home, due to their distance from everything else. Many traveled to Mukt-aal or to other villages further east and west. Very few called it home, but all took part to ensure the integrity of the springs and protected it from danger. They saw the two priests as a sign of good luck as both were called upon to purify the water and offer Ra's blessing.

As the day came to a close, the priests set up their sleeping tent near one of the structures that provided rest for their mounts. They talked about the journey up to this point, when Tulok had brought up Cathurg and Kol-qua.

"I think what got me most was when they all looked at me." He began "I could have made any other choice that day. I could have left the village on a different day. I could have gone another direction. It would not have mattered to Cathurg. If it was not something of value he could fit into his hand – it was not worth it. Then he threw everything into that question!" He shook his head, "That woman spit on the ground when he brought up finding a mate. I hated him but I was so mortified."

"Think of it this way, I am sure you could have done better than her Father. Not that I know Orcish aesthetics, or your own...erm... preferences, but she didn't seem your type," Bengt tried to add with an encouraging tone.

Tulok shrugged, "The Stormchaser's offer ... was... appealing..."

"Wait – Stormchaser? The one you all spoke with was

an Orc? A female Orc? Why am I always left out of the interesting events in this?!"

Tulok raised his hands, "It was Safar's call..." and he began to relay the story to Bengt – including the Stormchaser's farewell offer.

Bengt could only laugh. For as sullen as the man was at times, his laugh was actually jovial – despite it being aimed at Tulok.

"Please Father, I of all people do not need an explanation. Our Lord of the Above does not prohibit relationships among his faithful," he paused and continued to laugh,

"Though he might wonder at your choices."

Tulok's face was red and he just rolled his eyes.

"That is the last time I tell you something personal Brother Bengt!" said the Orc in a half-hearted protest.

"Father – you were the one who brought it up! If the Stormchaser had invited you to share her tent, who am I to judge? Besides – call it what you will. It was probably a missed opportunity to discuss...faith," he tried to stifle a giggle and could only smile.

The Orc could only shake his head and lean back against the tree. He stared up at the night and the three stars in the heavens above. He looked back at Bengt and finally chuckled,

"Discussion of faith...really?"

Laughing had seemed like a foreign concept up until now. At that moment – both priests were thankful for it.

Chapter 35

There was neither pain nor pleasure, heat nor cold. She was not hungry or thirsty. When consciousness returned to her once more, she knew she was not in the physical realm. Things felt familiar and yet different in a way that few places could. Tulok had asked her once if she could travel dreams as her people could in legend. There were truth and fiction both to that question, which was why she had chosen not to answer it, to begin with, and deflected the answer entirely.

Her statements to the River Lord and Tulok about being bound to the lands of Avalon were not exactly as truthful as they could have been. She felt bad about not being truthful with Tulok. He deserved better of her. It was just hard to explain to those, not from the island.

She opened her eyes and felt...nothing. It was not a specific sensation, so much as a lack of sensation that told her where she was. With an effort that could change. *Lucid Dreaming*. The ability of the sleeper to mold and modify their own personal dreamscape. It was a little bit like that, except her body was not asleep somewhere and she was not dreaming. She was awake and her entire self was somewhere in the realm of dreams.

This was the tie that all Avalonians shared. A unique

bond with the place of dreams. Some said it was because none of them were fully human and that all those who came to Sanctum were able to do so because there was a little of the Morpheum in their blood. Some said it was because they were all descendants of ancient fairy-kin. Isolde had no idea what the truth of the matter was. All she knew was that every child born of Avalon had a tie to the realm of dreams that allowed them to walk the Morpheum just as surely as one did the realm of the physical. Some ancient stories said that her people were burned as witches or demons in the time before the War. That humans not of Avalon looked on her people with suspicion, hatred and fear. There was some truth to those stories even here in Sanctum. Those blessed with the ability to warp the weft and weave of magic were often shunned and the cause for concern in cities beyond the island nations. Their Matriarch was always chosen through gifts of magic and omens that were tied to these links and abilities. Trying to explain to an outsider that your people were governed by a child because that child's soul had traversed the Summerlands and been returned to the lands to take Her rightful place, just as the Matriarch before Her had was not something easily explained or accepted.

She was sitting on a hill overlooking a lake. There was a meadow across the other side of the lake. Tall trees followed along its edge. They looked like oak trees. White barked ash peeked through here and there. She looked around to try and get an idea of where this place was supposed to be. On the northern edge of the lake stood a small cabin built of wood and lime and brick. It was simple but appeared sturdy. She could make out a bench and a chair on the porch. A plume of smoke rose from the chimney. If she thought about it, she could smell the aroma of wood smoke burning in the air.

Sound.

The gentle sound of water lapping at the banks of the lake and the occasional splash from fish in the water. Wind in the trees. It was light and soft, like a gentle sigh. She could smell and feel the damp on her skin.

Her fingers felt the soft tickle of grass under them. She stretched her hands and felt the cool of the damp earth beneath her. The sky above her was a light blue, the sun was somewhere in the distance. Fluffy white clouds decorated the skyline.

"You are awake. Good." a man's voice said from somewhere behind and to the side of her.

It seemed familiar, like a voice she had known her entire life. She did not feel the need to prepare herself for a fight. Instead, she lolled her head in the direction of the voice to see who it was.

His silver-gray beard was neatly trimmed and matched the neat cut of hair on his head. He looked her over as he walked up from the edge of the lake. Clad in faded dark pants with a linen shirt, his sleeves were rolled and pushed up to the elbows like someone who worked the land. The collar of his shirt was open and revealed a brilliant blue tattooed torc that embraced his collarbone and disappeared around his neck. He carried a long pole with a string on one end as he approached.

She frowned and sat up, trying to place the face and the voice. The torc tattoo nagged at the back of her memory. He waved her off.

"You do not need to get up, I need to sit for a few." He said and walked up to where she sat on the hill. "May I?" He asked and gestured at the space next to her.

Isolde nodded. "Go ahead."

The older man nodded and eased Himself down. Isolde watched Him with interest. For His age, He seemed well kept. His shoulders were not broad but were cut to give the impression of strength. His jaw was strong, His teeth straight, His eyes were the steel gray of a summer storm. He was rugged. A man who had seen more than His fair share of the world. He seemed like someone who would be more comfortable in armor than sitting on the bank of a lake with a fishing pole.

"I...know...you." Isolde offered.

"Well, I should hope so." the man nodded and chuckled. He gestured at the compass that hung around her neck. "Though this is not really me, and we are not really here."

Isolde's eyes widened in shock. "My Lord!" she stammered and moved to stand.

"Stop it, girl. Sit down and relax," the Wanderer spoke. His voice was deep and commanding. Isolde felt compelled to do as she was bid.

"Yes, Sir." she nodded and sat like a scolded child.

He looked over at her and shook His head. "Oh stop, there is no trouble." He offered and turned His gaze to look out at the lake. "You know where we are?"

Isolde nodded. "The Morpheum?"

He nodded and looked up and around. "Far cry from home..." He murmured. "You brought me all the way to Nahral. Could not have been easy to get this far. Or to warp all of this..." He gestured to the scene around them. "Harder to warp the farther you are from home... but you knew that, hmmm?" He slid his eyes over to Isolde.

She nodded.

The Wanderer pursed His lips and watched Her. "That's why you didn't just walk to where you needed to go from here?" He asked her. There was the hint of curiosity in His voice, coupled with the tone of one who was seeking a response for an action.

"I... I was not certain that I could get there from here..." Isolde shrugged.

He pursed His lips and nodded. "Probably not. Probably a good choice." He reached up and scratched at His beard. "Probably would have ended up in the middle of a sandstorm and shredded by the winds..." He mused.

Isolde turned curious eyes on the figure seated next to her.

"You...should not ...be here..." she said cautiously.

"Hrm?" He asked and looked back over to her. "Oh. You mean the balance and the whole...Gods non-interference thing?" The Wanderer asked.

Isolde nodded. "Well, yes," Isolde commented. It was well known that while the Lords of Sanctum had a vested and often active interest in the mortals of the realm, they were held in check by an ancient agreement. When the realm of Sanctum was created and its people brought to the safety of its shores after the Reaping that had ravaged the known worlds, rules had to be set into place. Without rules, the world would have fallen into chaos, disorder, and destruction. Everything the Lords of Sanctum had managed to preserve would have been lost. And so it had been agreed upon that every eternal would have its match, its equal, its balance in the warp and weft of power. Should one step outside the rules of engagement and interfere directly with the realm mortal, their counterpart would be given the same right. This check and balance helped to ensure that the more headstrong powers did not operate blindly. Knowing their counterpart would be given the chance to perform some ... miracle...of equal weight and the worth was often enough to give even the foolhardiest pause. This did not stop the celestial powers from being involved in the workings of their creations; they were simply rarely involved...directly.

The Wanderer shrugged. "Sometimes I find loopholes. This is one." He pulled His knees up and wrapped His arms around them and looked out onto the water. "You have done well, Isolde."

Isolde blushed deeply and bowed her head. "Thank you... sir."

"Do you like this place?" He asked

Isolde frowned and looked around. "This place...in the dreamscape?" she asked, confused.

He laughed out loud. "No, oh... no... I meant ... here..." He gestured out to the area.

Isolde looked out at the lake and the meadow and the trees. It was simple, soothing, familiar. "It is lovely." she nodded.

The Wanderer nodded. "Then it is yours." He said.

"Excuse me?" Isolde stammered.

"This is the Well of Memory outside of Brede. It needs a Keeper. It is yours." He offered.

Isolde furrowed her brow and shifted her position to look over at the entity seated next to her. "But ... I have not completed my Quest. There is still much I need to do..." she protested.

The Wanderer turned to look at Isolde. "You took up your Knight's Quest when he fell in battle. It was noble and worthy." He spoke plainly. "You have tried to die three times on this Quest. A Quest that was never yours." He lifted his arm and gestured off back behind her. "You just released his soul at the Crossroads, and he has been granted peace." His gray eyes met hers. They were kind and filled with the light of compassion and the strength that was hope.

"You are done, child. You do not need to do this anymore. Come home."

Isolde looked deeply into the eyes of The Wanderer.

Her stomach knotted, and there was a pain in her chest. She longed for the ability to return home and hang up her sword. To whisper her story to the well of memory and live out the rest of her life on the shores of the islands. To go home.

"I want that..." she whispered. Her eyes glistened with unshed tears.

"Here now, none of that." The Wanderer comforted and reached to place weathered, calloused hands on her face. His thumbs brushed her tears away. "Come home." He said once more, gently holding her face in His hands.

Isolde reached up and placed her hands over His and closed her eyes. Thoughts and desires battled inside her. She was set upon this path by the actions of others. Those who had taken everything from her. Choices made in anger and in haste. Now she was being given a chance to have a place once more. A name, a purpose. A life of her own.

I already have that.

She swallowed hard and opened her eyes. The Wanderer was still there, still staring gently into her face. Still waiting.

A bittersweet smile tugged at The Wanderer's lips. He nodded, knowing her heart without ever needing to hear the words. He leaned in and pressed His lips to her forehead. "As you wish." He murmured softly. Leaning His forehead on hers for a moment He touched her cheek and whispered "I will always honor your choices, my child."

"Thank you." Isolde managed to say through a broken voice.

His hands released her face and the Wanderer moved to push Himself up. He reached for the item that had been a fishing pole. It shimmered and wavered and slowly changed shape into a long sword. Light reflected off of the lake and up onto His figure. Isolde thought she saw the outline of ancient and well-beaten armor around His body.

"I am proud of you, girl." The Wanderer nodded.

Isolde smiled and bowed her head in reverence.

"Please excuse me now. I need to have words with a dragon about trying to beget a child upon my Witness." The Wanderer's eyes hardened and His countenance became grim. "Sleep now, Isolde duAvalonne, you will remember none of this when you wake."

Darkness consumed her once more.

Chapter 36

The map ceased to be helpful four hours outside of Kas-qua. A general direction and an estimated number of days of travel were the best they had been able to obtain as far as directions were considered. Kas-qua was the farthest settlement in this direction that any of the travelers or caravans remembered anything about. Beyond here was simply barren wasteland until one reached the far coastline. No Sun Guide was willing to travel with them on their journey, and Tulok had not been terribly forthcoming with the details of exactly why two members of the clergy were headed into the endless sands. No amount of money, factual or promised, could secure assistance.

Tulok sighed as he buried one of the canvas tent corners in the sand, using its weight to hold it in place. They had traveled from sunset until almost mid-evening. They were tired. Their mounts were tired, and there was only hope that kept them pointed in the direction of their destination. Bengt held the map up, gauging direction based on the position of the three stars overhead. He oriented himself and then placed several dark-colored rocks in the sand, pointed in the direction he believed they needed to go.

"If the books you referred to back at Nahral are accurate, "the skinny acolyte commented, "Then Ahsal is another day, perhaps two, in that direction." He pointed off in the distance as he carefully folded the map and tucked it away.

Tulok nodded. "That is what all the translations indicated," he answered as he continued to secure the tent for the evening.

Bengt rubbed his chin in thought. "There have been no recorded Cults of The Silent, in at least a century. Are you certain that is what we are looking at?" he asked and made his way over to the tent. Ducking his head, he stepped inside and began to carefully move things around, straining to lift packs and bundles.

"Let me." Tulok offered, stepping in and moving the items for Bengt. He used the weight of the packs and bundles to help secure sides and ropes in the loose sand. Bengt nodded in thanks. "Perhaps?" he offered sullenly.

Bengt's eyebrows raised a little. "I hope you did not drag us both out here to the end of the world on a ... perhaps... Tulok."

Tulok scowled and continued working. "The Magistrate's words indicated their involvement...and the scarab..." his voice trailed off as his eyes landed on the bundle that carried Isolde's belongings.

Bengt pursed his lips and shook his head.

"And the Devoted agreed that it was a potential worth investigating," Tulok added

"And if it is...what is suspected?" Bengt trailed off.

Tulok considered his reply and the situation. He reached back to rub his neck as he contemplated it all. They were not well equipped. He had planned to have additional people with him at this stage of the investigation. Safar to guide them. Isolde's sword for backup.

Isolde.

There was a pained tightness in Tulok's chest at the

thought of the Avalonian Knight. It had been several days since her loss, but the wound was still fresh, and deep. He straightened his shoulders.

"Then we hope that His Eye and His Will are with us, and guides the feet of our camels more swiftly than theirs..." he answered the smaller man.

Bengt took a deep breath and blew it out slowly. He nodded, the severity of the situation finally settling in on him. "All right." he nodded.

Tulok looked over to Bengt, sizing him, and his answer up.

Bengt shrugged slightly. "His ways are hard but fair."

Tulok nodded in agreement. "Indeed."

Both men were silent for a while, as they finished setting up camp. When they were done, Bengt took a seat on one of the bundles and looked up at Tulok's massive frame. "I had expected more resistance from the local fauna this far out...based on the stories."

Tulok looked out across the sands, watching them dance in the wind. "I would be careful with that, Brother...the last thing we need is more of the Emperor's Children to take an interest in us."

Bengt shuddered a little at the thought.

"But you are right. We should have seen something out here by now." Tulok agreed.

"There was the Sun Viper skeleton..." Bengt offered.

Tulok pursed his lips and hrmmed, "But it was largely intact. So, what killed the Sun Viper?"

Bengt chewed on the edge of his thin mustache in thought. "Another Sun Viper?" he asked.

Tulok shook his head and took a seat. "No, no sign of another one in the area. And the kill was fresh. Something killed it and left it there."

"What would do that?" Bengt inquired.

"That is indeed the question..." Tulok replied.

"I never apologized..." Bengt offered quietly.

"For?" Tulok sat with his hands between his knees, opposite the little man.

"Isolde," he said the name carefully.

Tulok bristled and took a deep breath, sitting up and stretching his neck.

"I know you were close, and... I..."

Tulok stood abruptly. "Stop. Leave it," he spoke firmly.

Bengt took a breath. "Radiant Father, I cannot." the small man replied.

Tulok set his jaw and turned irritated eyes on his Acolyte.

Bengt thought for a moment and held up his hand, begging patience from the big priest. "We are leagues from civilization, Father. This could well be the last time either of us has a chance to unburden our heart before the Lord of the Crossroads carries us to final rest and our souls are weighed and judged. Will you deny me this?" he asked in earnest.

Tulok looked as though he was going to stop Bengt's words, but as he listened he realized the often-annoying little man was right. Despite everything, they were still men of faith, and that faith was leading them potentially to their deaths. It was the least that Tulok could offer Bengt, to listen to his words and offer him solace.

Tulok swallowed pain within his heart and nodded, turning to look down at Bengt once more. "I will hear your words, Child of the Sun, that you may leave nothing undone should the jackals attend you on the morrow," he intoned reverently.

"Thank you, Your Radiance."

The orc nodded and stepped over to Bengt, then reached out to place his massive hands upon Bengt's head.

"*God of life*
Prince of Everlastingness,
Sovereign of all Gods
Creator of Eternity
Maker of the Heavens
Though your eye be turned
from us at this moment,
may your ear hear the words of this man,
your servant,
and may he find mercy under
your Everwatchful gaze.
Let his Ka find balance
and be seated without cessation."

Bengt remained before Tulok, with his head bowed, as he accepted the words of the Radiant Father that were meant to ease his soul across the bridge of the afterlife should it come to him. These would typically be words uttered by a priest of the Crossroads, the Grim Lord of Below; but there were no priests of the God of the Dead to offer His words to at this juncture.

"I am sorry for the death of the Avalonian knight." Bengt began. "Her life is on my hands. I could have done more. I should have been more careful. I should have paid attention to the instructions that were given to me. Instead, I was too fixated on the sacrifice to the River Lord to heed the warnings I was given."

Tulok held his hands in place and listened to Bengt's words. His jaw tightened slightly.

"I did not think that she would jump into the river to save me..." Bengt continued. "And I did not think to see the ship again." Bengt's voice was shaky as he continued. "When... when she reached for aid...I... did...nothing."

Tulok's fingers tightened around Bengt's head for the space of a heartbeat as he felt the rage well up within him.

His pulse beat in his ears. The muscles of his shoulders tensed. He could feel the human's fragile bones beneath his massive hands. It would be so easy to give in to his rage and end Bengt's life. Tulok closed his eyes and forced himself to relax his hands.

"I beg forgiveness for my cowardice and arrogance, that cost a brave...and innocent...woman her life," Bengt's tired and achy voice wept in the darkness.

Tulok's lip curled as he looked down at his Acolyte, taking in the weight of his confession. Assuming that Bengt was responsible was different than knowing it. Anger, grief, and rage surged up inside of Tulok. He yanked his hands away from Bengt's head and stepped back, a low rumble in his chest.

"I'm sorry..." Bengt wept.

Tulok took another step back, and shook his head, struggling with the red wave that clashed against the stoic shore of his mind. He staggered, losing his balance, and went down on one knee. Bowing his head Tulok dug his hands deep into the sands, willing his anger out of his body and into the earth; praying that it would find purchase there and not elsewhere.

There was a far-off sound of gurgling. It was almost like a drowning man's voice pleading as he fell below the surface. Tulok closed his eyes and shook his head. The sound continued. Tulok opened his eyes and turned around. Two dark-robed figures stood next to Bengt. One held the Acolyte's head back. The other stood to the opposite side a wicked-looking blade in their hand. The blade glistened and something dripped from its edge. A dark river of wet coursed from the gaping wound in Bengt's throat. He collapsed to the ground, lifeless.

Tulok roared and moved to stand, red rage consuming him.

"Take him down." the figure holding the blade ordered and stepped into the shadows of the dunes.

A heavy canvas tarp was thrown over the giant figure of the orc priest. Ropes were brought to bear upon his weight to bind him. Grabbing a section on the tarp, Tulok tried to wrench the tether away from one of the hooded figures but was only rewarded with pain. Suddenly pain ran over his arms, his back, and his face. Small barbs were woven into the fabric – the more he tried to tear it away from his body, the more they latched in and pulled at his flesh. Soon there were more figures throwing a rope around him, and someone chanting. He turned to the voice and saw a shorter figure among the hooded strangers. The faint torchlight illuminated the chanter's face,

"Arman?!" Tulok spoke through the struggle.

The shock of the familiar face was soon met with darkness. Arcane magic and ancient words had coalesced into a black cloud that rendered the orc unconscious.

Once the priest had succumbed to the magic, the figures quickly acted as hunters might with a great beast in the wilderness, they stripped him of all his clothing and vestments.

"Leave nothing," said a feminine voice, "he will be properly shaded for the time being." Stripped of everything, Tulok was bound in rope, stripped of his senses, and his pride. Nothing more than an animal trophy. He was rolled back into the painful netting as several of the hooded figures began to ready themselves for the task to come.

"I found it Nebiyre," Arman said as he walked out of the tent. In his hands was a small ornately carved box.

"Excellent." The woman who had slain Bengt replied. She held out her hand and was given the box. She examined the box carefully as she moved it around in her hands. Her right forefinger traced the bindings that had been placed there, "Interesting." There was a howl of exhausted pain that turned her attention to a now writhing, howling mass that was Tulok's bound figure. She smiled. It was not a pleasant thing.

"Do not hurt our guest too much." Nebiyre cautioned the dozen robed figures that encircled Tulok. "But do make certain his hands are secured. No... godly invocations from this one..." she warned the others. She watched Tulok's bound form from a distance. "Bring him." she directed,

"What shall we do with their gear?" one of the figures asked.

"Keep the mounts, burn the rest. Let the carrion feeders deal with the body." Nebiyre replied and turned to walk over the rise of the dune.

Chapter 37

Something was crawling up her calf. She twitched and shook her leg. The sensation stopped, then returned once more. Instinctively she reached down to brush whatever it was away. She felt slight resistance and then it was gone. Her body ached. Her face felt dry and she was covered in sand.

"Now, now, you don't belong in there – we've had this discussion," a voice spoke.

Isolde slowly opened her eyes. She was in what appeared to be a small home of some kind. A large figure wearing sand-colored robes stood at the doorway. On its outstretched hand was a large black scorpion. The figure knelt down and placed long fingers into the sand outside the threshold. The scorpion crawled down and away. The figure was not human. Long fingers ended in wicked-looking talons and the hands were covered in delicate scales. Sobekite? Anuket? Isolde could not remember the difference between the reptile people of the desert. She blinked and tried to focus; her head was swimming.

The figure turned back at the sound of Isolde's movement.

"Oh, my goodness, you are awake!" they exclaimed and headed back in Isolde's direction. The figure held their hands up, palms out, the gesture of peace, Isolde reminded herself.

"Slowly now." the sand-colored reptile cautioned and reached out to offer Isolde a steady hand. "We found you face down by the Springs, my dear. Do you know how you got there?" they asked.

Isolde shook her head. "No...I..." she reached to balance herself and realized she had been resting on a cot. The frame of the cot was built for someone much larger than she was. She looked up at the figure, realizing how much larger than she was the figure happened to be.

"Thank you," she offered.

"Yes, well, it looked like you had been through quite the ordeal already. We could not just leave you there." The creature blinked and turned its head to the side. Its slightly scaled lips turned upward, hinting at a smile.

Isolde nodded. "I... we were in Nahral... there was ... an accident...on the river..." she blinked and rubbed the back of her head. There was a large bump there. She winced.

The creature nodded. "That would make sense based on what Lalum said," they nodded.

"Lalum?" Isolde asked.

The creature nodded. "You'll meet them, they just went for supper and should be back soon," they regarded Isolde, the membranes on their black eyes blinked. "Oh, forgive me, I am such a terrible host sometimes!" they exclaimed. "I am Kault. You are not from here, I can tell." Kault attempted a smile and offered their hand to Isolde. Isolde accepted it carefully. Kault's skin was not rough, as she had expected, but more like the flesh of a serpent, at least on their hands. They were the soft color of the gentle sands, browns, and tans, with a cream undertone. The lizard people she had seen in Nahral were darker colored.

Not lizards, reptiles, but not lizards. she almost heard Tulok's voice chastise her in her mind.

"It is good to meet you, Kault. I am Isolde duAvalonne, Witness to..."

"Augh! She's one of the Wandering Lout's people!" a deep voice called from the doorway. Another creature, like Kault, entered the room. They were darker colored and wore robes of greens and brown the color of river silt. Their eyes were tinted reddish amber. They looked over at Isolde and harrumphed.

"Lalum, how rude!" Kault chastised.

Lalum frowned and deposited a basket on the table. It contained a variety of foodstuffs. "What? I need to be nice to every stranger that crosses our threshold, even if their people like to hunt ours?" Lalum folded their arms across their chest and stared at Isolde.

"Oh, I cannot believe that to be the case, Lalum!" Kault exclaimed and looked back at Isolde. "You don't do you?" Kault asked.

"Do what?" Isolde asked, confused.

"Hunt Sobekite and Anuket?" Kault asked simply.

Isolde furrowed her brow, "Uh...no...not at all...I...we..." she shook her head and looked over at Lalum, "I am terribly sorry if your people have been hunted by humans, but until I came to Setesh, I had only ever heard stories of your people. We do not have..." she paused for a moment and looked at Lalum, "Sobekite and.." she looked at Kault, "Anuket?" she questioned for affirmation, "on the island."

"Of course not!" Lalum protested. "You hunted them all to extinction there and none would dare go back!"

"Lalum that is a lie and you know it!" Kault hissed at Lalum. They looked back at Isolde. "Don't believe them, dear. Our people were born of Setesh by the will of the gods themselves." Kault turned irritated eyes back to Lalum, "Not for any other reason."

Something nagged in the back of Isolde's head. A combination of names and people that seemed familiar. Like she should know these two entities somehow.

Lalum continued to stare at Isolde. Their unblinking eyes reminded Isolde of the Confessor. She shifted uncomfortably. Lalum harrumphed at Isolde once more.

"We shall see," they commented.

Isolde looked away from Lalum and back to Kault. "Thank you for your generosity. I really do not know how I got here... or honestly...where...here...is." She blushed a little.

"Oh you poor dear." Kault comforted.

Across the room, Lalum rolled their eyes. "You would take in every homeless waif along the Iteru if I let you..." they commented gruffly.

Kault ignored Lalum's comments. "Now then, you mentioned being in Nahral, and there was an accident on the river? Who was with you? Maybe we can help you find them?"

Isolde turned hopeful eyes to Kault. "Oh, that would be so helpful if you could!" she exclaimed. "They have to think that I am dead ...and... oh... I really hope Tulok does not blame Bengt..."

Kault and Lalum exchanged glances. Kault looked back at Isolde. "Tulok?" they asked.

Isolde nodded. "Father Tulok, priest of the Radiant Lord, out of Tarf-qua, do you know him?" she inquired hopefully.

"Well that all depends. The Tulok we know was an Orc..." Kault began.

Isolde nodded emphatically, "Yes! That would be him! Seven feet tall, three feet wide, wicked temper, but sweet smile, great with a mace, but would prefer to be in a Library reading books?"

Lalum nodded and dropped their arms. "That is indeed Tulok." They turned to the basket and began to unpack it.

"You know him then?!" Isolde asked of them both, realization finally coming to her. "Wait! He told me about you two! When he was younger and, on his pilgrimage,"

Kault looked over at Lalum, "Oh! He remembers us, Lal, how nice is that?"

"Lovely," Lalum commented and continued to unpack.

"He and Bengt were headed to Mukt-aal, then to Kasqua before going to Ahsal."

Lalum stopped moving and looked over at Isolde. "He was going where?"

Isolde paused and chewed a little on her bottom lip. "Um... Ahsal... we... had to... check something out at...the ruins... there."

Kault and Lalum exchanged concerned glances. Kault walked over to Lalum and placed their hand on the other's arm. "Lal, we have to."

Lalum shook their head. "I can't. Normally I would, but I can't."

"Why not?" Kault demanded.

Lalum continued to move grocery items around on the table. "She owes the River Lord. I am not allowed to. He was QUITE clear on that when I pulled her out of the Springs."

Isolde listened to the words and looked over at Lalum. She pursed her lips and set her shoulders. "The River Lord tried to trick me into having his child..." Isolde stated flatly.

Kault hissed at the words and looked at Lalum. "Lalum! "they replied indignantly. "Mother will be SO displeased..."

Lalum simply shrugged their shoulders.

Kault turned back to Isolde and walked over to her. They reached out and took Isolde's hands into theirs.

"Child of the Wandering Lord, I can help you. But, as with all things, there will be hardship that you must endure, in exchange. Such is the pact the Anuket have made. Such was the price of our creation."

Isolde took Kault's hands in her own and met the strange creature's almost emotionless eyes. Tulok's short description of a wise, but bickering pair of teachers seemed aptly accurate.. It had been their guidance that had helped him to find the path that led him to his faith. Isolde smiled warmly at Kault and squeezed their hands.

"I need to find him Kault – not to just let him know I'm alive, but we are bound by an Oath. My Lord will guide my feet, so I will accept any aid that you can lend," Isolde said.

"A mount that you may reach your destination, but neither arms nor armor nor supplies to reach your destination. Or supplied, I can send you on your way afoot into the sands that no one afoot has ever crossed alone and lived. The choice is yours."

Isolde pondered the choices set before her. Neither was ideal and either could well result in her meeting a painful death under His Everwatchful Eye. The broken compass that hung around her neck vibrated gently.

"Tulok will have my gear, or gear that I can use when I find him. I'll take the mount." Isolde nodded firmly as a large black scorpion crept back under the door.

~~~

Smoke rising from the camp in the desert had been a beacon for her as she crossed the sandy wastelands. There was nothing for leagues in any direction, the dark column of smoke had been easy to see, even from how far out she had been. As her eyes focused on the dark beacon in the distance, her heart fell into her stomach. She grasped her
~~~

amulet and prayed to the Wandering Lord that she be mistaken and that the concerns that welled up in her were wrong. The Knight Wanderer, was, among other things, a God of Courage. He was known to encase the hearts of his people in an almost impenetrable shield that prevented fear from ever taking root. It often made His followers foolhardy as they were known to leap into circumstances with their iron-clad hearts and not their minds. Without the buffer that fears provided, caution was abandoned and danger all-too-often embraced. More than this, this shield of courage that He provided often also disconnected his Knights from emotions that might cause worry. At the discovery of the charred remains within the encampment, the protective shield that sheltered Isolde's heart fell away.

"No No No No No" she pleaded as she smoothly dismounted the Korser that Kault had given her. The creature groaned and grunted and bellowed at her in displeasure at both its treatment, and the smell.

Ignoring the heat of the sand on her wrapped feet, her boots had been left behind on the boat when she had entered the Iteru, Isolde scrambled over to the body and carefully reached out to examine it. The body was roughly her height, thin of frame, and slight in bone. No tusks protruded from the jaw. This was not an orc. A sense of ease washed over Isolde for a moment. She leaned back on her heels and looked up into the sky, offering a silent prayer of thanks, followed by a wish for the departed to be set to rest. A golden glint caught her eye and drew it toward the chest of the remains.

"Forgive me," she said to the corpse and carefully reached for the item that had drawn her attention. Covered in soot, flesh, and sand, was a round, golden medallion; in the center of the medallion was an ornate depiction of a stylized eye. The symbol of The Radiant Lord the Ever-watchful.

Isolde gasped and dropped the medallion, covering her mouth with the back of her hand.

"Bengt..." she whispered, naming the dead.

That strange strangled feeling washed over the Knight once more as she began to scan the area for another body – one far larger than this. She pushed herself up out of the sand and began to walk through the remains of the encampment. Packs had been opened and emptied, blankets and supplies were strewn across the area. Whoever had done this had not taken their goods, but instead had left them to the desert.

A statement?

A sacrifice?

Who would have done this? Why?

Her toe caught something hard under the sand. She swore, stumbled, and lost her balance to sit firmly in an uncontrolled flomp. She reached to rub her foot, a tiny trickle of blood oozed out of the bandage and into the sand. She frowned and stretched to dig her hand into the area that had tripped her. Her fingers caught the edge of something hard and familiar. Heart racing, Isolde began to dig frantically as she attempted to free what was buried. Slowly the outline of a section of armor came into view. It was the shoulder pauldron of her suit. Tulok HAD kept it. Hope sprung into her heart, replacing the well of fear that danced around its edges. Slowly she was able to uncover several parts of the suit she had carried with her from Avalon and was replaced with cured leather in Tarf-qua. It was not complete. She had cuisses, but no greaves. Pauldrons and their attached leather hauberk, but no breast or backplate. A left elbow cop. A right vambrace. And a single boot.

No ornate box sealed with runes and carvings.

Isolde spent a very long time searching the remains of the encampment until she found the bag, she had kept the box in. It had been opened and cast aside. Singed now, its contents were missing. Someone had taken it.

Throughout it all, no body of a very large orc priest was found.

Sitting in the sand, Isolde slowly fitted her body with the remains of her armor. She pulled a section of unburned tent out of the buried sand and wrapped her head in it, to offer some small protection from the severity of the sand. She sat in the remains of the encampment, knees pulled up, arms wrapped around them, contemplating.

The Korser that Kault had given her lowered and nudged her. Korsers were a strange breed of creature, much like all the creatures of Setesh as far as Isolde was concerned. It was as if someone had managed to cross-breed a camel with a draft horse. Large, suited for long distances without water, with strong, solid bodies. They smelled nominally better than camels, but still frothed and drooled and spat. She reached up and scratched the great beast's chin. It drooled on her. It was warm and slimy. She ignored it.

"Where did you go, Tulok?" Isolde asked, chewing on her bottom lip in thought. She flexed her toes and realized that she only had protection for one foot. Her eyes scanned the area again, hoping that her other boot might miraculously appear. Instead, her eyes fell on the body of Bengt, charred and abandoned.

"No, you can't," she said to herself and tore her eyes away.

Something crawled across her bare foot. She twitched and looked down. A long-bodied black scorpion crept over the top of her foot and continued its trek across the sand. Isolde pursed her lips and frowned at the creature.

"You bastards killed Safar. I should return the favor." she glowered and watched the insect continue skittering skillfully across the sand. She ran her tongue over her teeth, her mouth was parched. She was not going to survive very long out here unless she could discover where Tulok had been taken. She assumed he had been taken. His body was too big to simply be overlooked out here and there were no signs of carrion birds gathering anywhere that she had not checked. Someone had him. The fires that had consumed the encampment were still smoldering, so they could not be too far away.

Isolde's eyes traced back over to Bengt's body. She shook her head once more.

"You don't even know if he wore the same size boot, Isolde. Are you really going to defile the dead to find out?" she spoke to herself.

The korser lowed and nudged her again. "Stop it." She said to the animal. It huffed hot breath on her and wuffled at her head. She waved her hand at it.

The black scorpion continued to move across the white sands, it was impossible not to see. Isolde lay her cheek on her knee and watched as it crawled away on its nightly hunt. It did not seem interested in Bengt's dead body, which seemed odd. Isolde looked over at Bengt and then at the scorpion again. It was clearly walking away from a source of food. Isolde narrowed her eyes and pushed up, keenly aware of sand on one foot and not the other. She was going to have to do something about it. She continued to watch the scorpion as it made its way away from the body. As she followed its movements, she became aware of a mound of earth she had overlooked before. The scorpion crawled atop the mound and then disappeared into the sand, burying itself out of sight. Isolde carefully approached the area and looked down at it. Several small lumps were covered in sand. They seemed to form a pattern. Isolde squatted down and gently brushed at the sand that covered one of them, revealing a dark, smooth stone.

A map weight.

Excitedly, she carefully brushed the rest of the little mounds off to reveal what appeared to be a directional indicator. Isolde looked off in the direction the stones pointed. There was nothing that she could see, but one of them, either Tulok or Bengt, had clearly placed these here. They must have stopped to rest, and left them in case they needed to get bearings when they woke. Isolde closed her eyes and wrapped her hand around the broken compass that hung around her neck.

When it's important, they work.

The magic that protected Sanctum from the eyes of chaos and destruction also masked the magnetism that loadstones required to function. No compass could ever glean a true direction and so they were relegated to icons and artifacts of old worlds, now long gone and destroyed. They were nothing more than symbols of the Knight Wanderer and their unending Quest.

"Please," Isolde whispered. "Please help me find him."

The wind blew gently across the sands, the dunes dancing softly in the night. Safar had told her once about how they could sing or sound like drums, like the beat of a heart, alive and full of grace. They could share their stories in the ripples of the wind on their pale skin. A solace and a curse.

"Please..." Isolde entreated once more as she stood in her mismatched gear, one foot booted and the other bare, without gear or weapon, under the predawn sky of a foreign land. As she had come to this land, alone, but filled with purpose, and hope.

There was warmth in her hands. Isolde opened her eyes and looked down at her amulet. The compass arrow beneath the glass bobbed and spun and bobbed once more. Isolde focused on the tiny amulet and fixed her very being on its existence.

The arrow stopped and held a single direction.

Isolde's heart beat fast. She looked at the arrow on the compass and adjusted her position, the arrow continued to point in a specific direction. She lifted her eyes to follow the direction indicated. It ran parallel with the arrow in the sand. Dawn's light slowly began to creep over the horizon. Isolde looked at the horizon, where the light was soon to emerge, and oriented herself to be able to know where the sun would be, in relation to the direction she was to travel in.

"That direction." She nodded and bent down to scoop up the map weights that had been left behind. The edge of a boot top revealed itself as she did so and a black-bodied scorpion crawled out of the sand, assumed a position of defense, and then darted off.

"My boot!" Isolde exclaimed and fished her other boot out of the sand.

The knight mounted her korser, taking her bearings once more. She tucked her head and urged the creature into swift action as the Sun God's sleepy eye cast His Ever-watchful gaze across the desert once more.

Chapter 38

There was no Ghal. There was fire, and pain, and passion, and anger, and hate. Tulok strained against the ropes and chains that bound his massive frame. His hands were wrapped with leather bindings, his fingers woven together to prevent their movement. His arms were outstretched and held upward, straining the muscles of his shoulders. He was held at a height that required he stretch his legs and calves to take the tension off of his shoulders and arms lest they be pulled from their sockets. Even so, leg muscles could only stay active for so long before demanding rest.

Sleep was an impossibility, for the moment he lost consciousness, his body would slump and the muscles of his arms and shoulders would begin to tear. The only blessing Tulok could be thankful for was that the ruins offered shelter from the unmerciful gaze of the Everwatchful Lord of the Skies. In this place, the blinding light did not beat down on his bare flesh or sear his skin. Even so, there was something else. Beneath the earth within the shelter of the ruins, something prevented the Sun God's light from touching the soul of His priest. Devoid of sleep and rest, subjected to the heat and thirst of the sands, bound in pain, away from the gaze of his God, Tulok had but one companion.

Rage.

The priest of The Radiant Lord railed against his bindings, against the darkness, and against the injustice of his situation. The muscles and tendons on his arms, neck, and back, stood out like thick ropes of sinew and flesh. His veins bulged. His lips were dry and cracked, victims of the desert heat and lack of water. He tried to focus his mind, but waves of emotion crashed down on him, drowning reason with their frenzy.

Shadows moved and undulated at the corners of his eyes. He could not be certain if there were figures present, or if it was the heat and the rage calling forth figments of his exhaustion. Something cool and wet was placed against his mouth. He sucked at it greedily out of instinct. Suddenly his mouth was filled with pain and tingling that trailed down his throat and into his stomach; but also, a feeling of strange euphoria. He was dizzy and nauseous. The cool, wet item was pulled away from him.

"I was always fascinated by your people." the familiar voice of the Vidria merchant, Arman spoke in the darkness.

Tulok bristled at the sound of the voice. Images of Bengt's lifeless figure leaped forward. He growled and pulled at his bindings.

"A people given reason by the Lord of Knowledge Himself...and yet there is still so much anger in your souls."

There was a sound of splashing somewhere close to Tulok.

"So much Chaos."

Arman stood before Tulok, gazing upward at the giant figure. Rage pulled at Tulok, demanding violence as he glared downward. It would take no effort for him to smash the little man's body against the wall of the underground cavern and paint the rocks with his blood. He strained against his bindings.

Arman smiled.

"Finding one of your people in the desert is easy. You populate like locusts," he said with disdain. "But finding one like you..." Arman gazed up at Tulok, eyeing him as one might a prize bull. "Yes, I think you will do nicely."

"Don't poison it, Arman, we still need it." a woman's voice echoed. Tulok recognized the voice as belonging to the dark-robed woman who had helped kill Bengt and take him, prisoner. He pulled at the ropes once more.

"He will be fine, Nebiyre," Arman assured as he continued to gaze at Tulok. "He's a fine, strong specimen. He's withstanding the elixir well."

"It is no good to us dead." She hissed.

Arman smiled, not looking at Nebiyre. "I know what I'm doing, woman!" he snapped, still watching Tulok. "Yes, you feel it, don't you? That fire in your belly that's making your head swim? Keeping you on that line, that razor's edge. The heat and the dry make you need the water to survive... but the water takes away your reason...what a terrible dilemma for you..."

"Quit toying with it, we have work to do." Nebiyre scolded and turned to leave the room.

"As you will." Arman sighed and shrugged. He took a step back, out of Tulok's line of sight. The priest tried to raise his head to follow the movement and could not. He blinked, trying to focus.

"Oh, Your Radiance, I *did* want to apologize for your woman." Arman's voice commented from the other side of the room. "She was never the target, but ... she was in the way...and the river does need to be fed. I'm sure you understand."

Rage and Grief crashed down on Tulok at the mention of Isolde's demise. He howled in anger, his muscles bunching and straining as he pulled at the bindings. His red eyes were almost black with Gurkh.

"Interesting..." Arman mused, then disappeared in the darkness.

~~~

Light danced off of the walls of the cavern. Blues and greens, mixed with yellows and oranges. Fire and magic, flame, and bio-organic moss granting light to a lightless world. There was no light from the heavens. No warmth of the sun that touched this forbidden and cavernous womb. Water dripped from stalactites into colorful pools beneath them, gathered for centuries. Generations of eyeless fish dwelled in these waters, their only companions the colorless worms and insects that had also been cut from the surface for an unknown period of time. At the back of the cavern stood an altar, shaped from the earth and sand itself. Its crystalline green structure spoke to its Vidria origins. The crystals of the altar gathered the lights and reflected them back into the chamber in a dazzling, dizzying display of brilliance.

Behind the altar, carved into the wall were five niches. The niches were roughly two feet tall and a foot wide. Neatly tucked inside each was a jar sculpted of stone. Each jar was unique, made of different material, and topped with a unique figurehead.

The robed figure of Nebiyre gently caressed one of the jars. Her long, nimble fingers traced the smooth and flawless lines of the jar and then very carefully touched the figure that adorned its top. A bird's head, its pointed beak aimed at the heavens, delicate plumage sat atop its regal brow and flowed down its neck like liquid fire. Topaz gems the color of the sun at first light served as the eyes of the carved phoenix creature. They sparkled in the provided light, hungry for something more. Nebiyre smiled and gently set the jar into its niche.

She closed her almond-shaped eyes and rested her
~~~

hands on the Vidria crystal altar. A single tone sounded from her throat. The crystal altar vibrated at frequency, and the sound echoed out to the cavern, bouncing off of hundreds of crystals embedded in its walls. She smiled, feeling the sound as it rode up her body and touched her very bones. It was the sound of creation. And destruction. It was the creeping chill of water that had never known the touch of the sun, but still created and hosted life in its dark depths. It was the sound of the lightless sky at night. It was the lesson contained in the fear of a nightmare. It was the beauty of the earth as it reclaimed the fallen.

"In the beginning, there was only Chaos..." she spoke. The words of the priestess danced on the crystals of the cavern and light flowed within their dark earth-born hearts. "And from Chaos, Darkness and Silence were born, the first lives of the Universe; born without union, immaculate and pure." Nebiyre ceased speaking. Ceased moving. The vibrations from the crystals faded into nothingness. Lights in the cavern faded. Quiet fell over the cavern like a gentle blanket. All was silent. Straining, one could hear the still-beating of a heart, Nebiyre's. Her dark robe hung from her skeletally thin frame, concealing her body from the view of the world, obscuring her from casual view. Her smile stretched across tight skin that revealed thin lips and parchment-like flesh.

"Yes, yes, yes...and the scream of the Creator, risen like the phoenix from the darkness destroyed the sanctity and purity of the Universe and so was Silence forever broken." Arman's voice echoed from the back of the cavern. His booted feet tromped toward the altar and the tall skeletal woman.

Nebiyre turned anger-filled eyes on the dwarf and hissed her displeasure at the small man.

"You... dare..."

"I dare a great deal, my dear" Arman countered. "And

you would do well to remember that if it were not for me, this.... wondrous place of dedication to our shared... confidence... would not exist."

Nebiyre eyed Arman suspiciously as he approached. The dwarf paused, a respectful distance from the altar, closed his eyes, and inclined his head.

"From Chaos was Creation Born" he intoned reverently.

"The Balance is a lie," Nebiyre replied.

The Vidria opened his eyes, peering upward at Nebiyre. She was a strange creature; Arman had never truly been able to identify exactly what people she belonged to. She was tall and skeletal of frame and feature. Her eyes were wide and large. At times they seemed lidless. Other times they appeared as though they were windows into a bottomless void. Arman had seen desiccated corpses that resembled the strange priestess, but never one that walked the earth as she did. Nebiyre moved with an unnatural and unearthly grace that seemed to imply some otherworldly heritage, but who's he could never fathom. She was a terrifying visage to behold, and the dwarven merchant was always silently thankful that Nebiyre seemed to prefer covering her figure and features to displaying them for others to gaze upon.

Arman stepped up to the altar and reached out to lay his hand on its crystalline surface. He closed his eyes and paused for a moment allowing his Vidria nature to connect with the stone. He concentrated and then nodded.

"It is withstanding the vibrational field." He commented, opening his eyes.

Nebiyre watched the dwarf from behind the altar, her strange eyes assessing him. "It will channel what is needed from the Orc?" she asked simply.

Arman nodded and pulled his hand back. "It will serve its purpose. Are you certain that your little trinket will be able to siphon from him? He's a big boy."

Nebiyre chuckled darkly and nodded. "As it has in the past. Yes."

Arman frowned and reached up to rub his bare chin. "Have you been able to open the box yet?" he asked.

Nebiyre snarled a little and shook her head. "No. The Wanderer's former master was able to find someone with skill enough to lock it solidly away. I need more time." She looked down at Arman. "We could have used her. Your actions were not well thought out."

Arman held his arms wide, 'Well forgive me, your Eminence, for trying to eliminate an obstacle without obtaining your permission." he replied in a snide tone. He dropped his arms.

"Besides, the woman would have been more trouble than she was worth."

"She was Danuae." Nebiyre countered. "We could have used that." she waved her hand back at the jars that sat quietly in their niches.

Arman shook his head. "No. The woman was a Wanderer, Danuae, true, but..." he paused thinking, then continued. "No. She was not of the Folk, and her Divine Spark was not The Mother's." He looked back up at Nebiyre. "You'll just have to figure out how to open that little box, so you can recover that trinket. I didn't pay the exorbitant amount that I did to have it chauffeured across two continents to gather what you needed only to have you decide it's too much effort to pry open the oyster to obtain the pearl."

The strange woman glared down at the Vidria. "If my efforts are insufficient, then I welcome you to make every effort to do so on your own," she spoke coolly.

Arman chuckled and waved her off, "I am certain your skills are more than up to the task, Nebiyre. Unless the box is made of stone, mine will be of little use." he gestured around. "I have given..." he paused. "Our shared confidence..." he said carefully as if attempting to avoid speaking a name. "A place of hallowed ground that you may prepare Their way. That is what was asked of me." he folded his arms across his broad, squat frame. "Are my actions found wanting in this?"

Reluctantly the woman shook her head. "No. You have done what has been asked and answered the demands that have been presented to you. You will find reward." she inclined her head.

He inclined his head. "Excellent. We have an understanding once more." he watched her and sucked on a tooth, regarding the woman, and said nothing more.

"Did I understand correctly? Safar is dead?" the woman asked. Her hands rested on the altar gently.

Arman shrugged. "It certainly appears so." he held up a warning finger. "Not my doing."

Nebiyre pursed her lips and nodded, accepting both statements. "Unfortunate."

Arman queried an eyebrow at Nebiyre, "Why? He posed a significant threat if he ever found out about..." he waved his hand around, indicating the cavern.

Nebiyre nodded. "Mmmm. Yes. But with him alive, we at least knew where he was and thereby, where his Sire's attention would be."

"Ahhhh," Arman said, "And if the sands truly have claimed his life..." he rubbed his bare chin in thought. "Hrmph." he mused. "Maybe I'm old and superstitious, but ... I'll have someone go check the area when I get back, to ensure the truth of the matter."

Nebiyre conceded the point with a casual nod. "Have your contacts been successful in locating the other vessels?" Nebiyre inquired.

Arman nodded and shrugged, both in noncommittal agreement. "I have heard that there was a Skald who recently booked passage from Ophir to the great Library in Litharge. I have eyes on them, but no confirmation otherwise. Once we are done here, I will contact a caravan and make my way there."

"And the others?" Nebiyre inquired.

Arman turned irritated eyes on the priestess. "These aren't herbs and spices that I can go to market for." he chided. "What you are seeking...what...THEY...need...takes time....and unless you'd like me to tip our very carefully curated hand because you have suddenly lost the patience to wait..." he trailed off.

Nebiyre considered his words carefully as she regarded him from her position. Finally, she gave a gesture that seemed like blinking. "No. You are correct. They must have ONLY what They need. Nothing less will suffice." she stretched her neck from side to side, it seemed impossibly long to be considered either natural or normal. Closing her seemingly lidless eyes, she turned her face toward the cavern ceiling and outstretched her arms, and resumed her observations.

Arman felt a chill run across his body, the lights dampened slightly, shadows undulated in the recesses of the cavern. At the head of the altar, Nebiyre's figure seemed to grow slightly, shadows surrounding her skeletal frame. Soft voices seemed to echo from nowhere and everywhere all at once. The crystals in the cavern hummed.

From his place, two steps down before the altar the Vidria merchant looked up at the priestess and smiled widely at her.

"Good. Now figure out how to open the damned box." He commented, turned, and walked away.

Nebiyre hissed at Arman as he departed, shadows creeping and undulating like serpents in the darkness.

Chapter 39

The Sun Lord's Everwatchful gaze was neither kind, gracious, nor merciful. The sands here were an endless wasteland of pale dunes whose white sands reflected the heat of the sun back onto any so unfortunate to be traveling under its heated scrutiny. Isolde pulled a scrap of cloth from across her face and lifted a charred leather water purse to her lips. In her time searching through the ruins of the encampment, she had been able to locate what few items had not been left to fire or scavengers. It had not been much, but it was enough. Her korser grunted and bellowed in displeasure. While they were hardy creatures, even they had their limitations. She pulled out her tiny silver compass and looked at it once more. The arrow bobbed and swirled for a moment or two and then slowly settled in one direction. He was still showing her a path, which meant there was still hope. She looked at the arrow and at the horizon behind her, then the sun, then back at the horizon searching desperately for landmarks of any kind that might aid her in her travels. She looked down at the compass once more, then out in the direction that it pointed.

The dune she had been climbing crested a few yards ahead. Clucking at her mount, she directed it to kneel so she could dismount, then slowly scrambled up the edge of the dune. It would have been easy to ride the animal to the top, but caution was her friend at this moment, and she did not know what the downward slope of sand might reveal. The animal remained where it was, nestled into the hot sand like an egg in a nest as she made her way to the top. Peering over the edge she saw the sharp descent of the dune and the gentle rain of sand that caressed the sandstone formations that erupted from its rippled surface, like swirls of pale taffy.

She lay down on her stomach quickly and scanned the area. In the distance appeared to be a larger rocky outcropping of some sort. Tents had been erected around the area. This had to be what she was looking for.

"Alright...you've found them...now what are you going to do?" Isolde spoke into the dunes and the wind. Her eyes took in the valley below. There were several larger sandstone structures between her and the encampment. "Fossil Dunes," she whispered, as she recalled the term that Tulok had used when describing them to her on their journey from Tarf-qua. She chewed a little on her bottom lip, ignoring the sand and grit that coated her tongue. "I might be able to slide down that way and hide behind those..." she mused.

Something moved out of the corner of her eye. She froze and slowly turned to focus her gaze. A large black scorpion had crawled out of the sand next to her. It raised its tail and pincers defensively clicking at her.

"You are irritating me," she said to the scorpion, and with a quick motion of her hand, dug under the sand and scooped it and the sand up, casting it aside. The insect flew head over tail several feet away from her and landed on the leeward side of the slope. It slid several inches before stopping and righting itself. Isolde returned to looking at the area and attempting to assess the situation.

"That thing could kill you if you are not careful you know," she said to herself. "Yup" she replied to no one, "...THAT be ironic...make it all the way here and die on this damned dune, less than a quarter league from your destination."

Below her, the korser grunted and wuffled. "What was that, Cheniy?" she asked of the animal, "Oh...no...I suppose I should be more careful. I do have your life to consider, after all, you are right." She continued as she gazed out at the area below her. There was no movement along the tents, save for the flapping of canvas walls in the breeze.

"They are all inside, out of the heat..." she mused. "No one on guard..."

A black creature skittered along the leeward side of the dune six inches from her face.

"Oh, what the hell do you want?" she said to the scorpion. It stopped its movements, raising tail and pincers at her once more. She stared at it.

"We have had this conversation, and I am not impressed. Move along," she stated. The creature snapped its pincers at her and walked slowly sideways along her field of vision, then turned and darted down the dune, skittering and sliding.

"You are talking to scorpions, Isolde. You have lost your damn mind..." she shook her head, but her eyes followed the movements of the insect, and then looked beyond it. There, barely visible from her vantage point was a sand-colored escarpment, that dropped off and out of view. She furrowed her brow.

"What is this now?" she asked and slowly scramble-crawled her away across the dune, ducking her head back behind the windward side, to mask her progression. Struggling against the slipping sands, she slowly managed the distance and pulled herself back up. Peering over the edge once more, she saw what had been hidden before. A narrow passage that seemed to tunnel its way back into the sand and under the earth. Sandstone walls held the shifting sands around it away from the dark opening. These were not crafted by the will and whim of the wind. Mortal hands. Vidria hands had crafted this area.

"Ahsal..." she whispered.

Closing her eyes, she rolled over onto her back and clutched the compass around her neck.

"Thank you, my lord." She intoned. She draped her arm across her eyes to shield them from the sun. "And don't you worry, I'll get him back for you," she said to the blazing ball of fire in the sky. "Ok... you have to think about this, Isolde," she spoke to herself again. "The camp is not the destination, the archway is...but there will probably be people IN the camp, and there are more of them than there are of you."

Cheniy lowed and rested comfortably in the sand a few meters away. Isolde looked over at the korser. She nodded. "And... like him...they are all going to be taking a nice little nap right now...." She rolled back over and looked down at the area once more. "They will see a lone figure walking down these dunes...so...." she looked over at the fossil dunes. "Use the fossils for cover, make your way to one of the tents...." she took a breath. "Then what?" her eyes searched the small encampment. "Hope you either find Tulok, or whoever is in the tent is a deep sleeper..."

She stretched her neck and looked down at the korser. "Sorry Cheniy, you gotta stay here. I am not certain I can hide myself, and I KNOW I cannot hide you." She looked skyward.

"I am doing the best with what I have here, can you maybe, I dunno, keep an eye on him until I get back?" in her mind she whispered *Please don't leave, please don't run into the camp, please don't get eaten.* She pulled her scarf across her face again, and slowly scrambled back along the windward side of the dune, hands and feet and knees struggling to keep her from sliding down the surface of the sand. After what she guessed was 50 meters or so, she slowly crept back up to the top of the dune and peered over once more. Below her, a series of fossil dunes emerged from the sands and wove an indirect path toward the base of the dune. She glanced toward the tents once more, and seeing nothing and no one, crested the top of the dune and slipped skidded down its sandy surface to the sandstone below.

Isolde's heart beat hard and fast against her ribs, pounding and almost threatening to break free. She pressed herself against one of the upright structures, keeping it between herself and the camp. Taking a breath, she peeked out and around its edge quickly. Six tents, anchored on the sandstone, entrance flaps open to vent heat and allow airflow. No one was moving around. She ducked back. There were three more fossils between herself and the nearest tent, and the grouping provided shade at present. If she kept low, she should be able to creep close enough to get a better visual of things. Silently, she cursed her parentage and their very tall lineage, wishing for once that she was slighter in frame and height. She took another breath, blew it out quickly, and ducking down, quickly made her way along the line of the formation, offering silent words of prayer as she did. As she reached the edge of the fossils, she pressed herself low and peered out at the tents. She could faintly make out the outline of what appeared to be persons sleeping in two of them. The other four appeared empty.

Or they could have women in them.

She reminded herself of the Seteshi tendency to separate their men from their women in their desert sleeping quarters. Isolde reached up to rub her face with her calloused hand. *Think. Think. Think.* She peeked out once more, trying to assess the camp. A gentle breeze blew through the valley, lifting the flaps of one of the larger tents. The sounds of animals grunting in displeasure sounded in the distance.

That's where their mounts are. She identified. *That is... two sleeping tents and one for the animals. That leaves three. At least one of them should be supplies.* She paused in her thinking. *Extra gear maybe?* She chewed on her upper lip. *Maybe enough to replace items she was missing? No. Maybe enough for her to make herself look like one of them.*

She rolled her eyes toward the heavens.

"Ok, so, maybe being this tall will be a good thing," she muttered to herself. She looked back out at the three tents that she had not yet been able to identify. *One of them was closer than the other two. I can probably get around the backside, and in through there... I hope.*

Her hand drifted to her belt and she pulled out the small knife that she had been able to find in the wreckage of the camp. *We all started somewhere* she remembered, feeling the weight of the weapon in her hand. She longed for the protection of her sword. *OK Isolde, now or never.* She whispered to herself and darted for the backside of the tent.

Avalonian tents were constructed of solid walls of firm canvas that was often coated in oil to protect them from cold weather and wet rains. Seteshi tents served other needs. As she had observed in her time with the caravan, these tents were crafted from several different sections of cloth, each easily lifted from the bottom to allow venting of heat and airflow. Those separate sections also allowed one to pull a section away briefly and peer inside. This venting design allowed the foreign knight to quickly make her way around to the tents and view their occupants. As she suspected, two of the tents contained sleeping persons, and one contained animals resting outside of the heat of the day. She counted half a dozen dark robed people of mixed races. Two of the remaining tents contained what appeared to be supplied, and the other stood empty save for a table, rugs, and cushions. A meeting tent of some kind, but Tulok was nowhere to be seen.

Isolde's heart sank. He had to be here. Her eyes drifted across the valley to the narrow passage that led beneath the sands. They must have taken him below. She was going to have to go into the ruins of Ahsal herself to find him. What was supposed to have been a mission to obtain information for the Temple of Ophir was now a mission to rescue Tulok from the very group that was not supposed to exist. She closed her eyes and swore softly, then quickly clapped her hand over her mouth. She held her breath and stopped and listened. Animals rustled in the tent next to her, but nothing else. She nodded and exhaled slowly.

Supply tent. Maybe there would be something she could use there. Slowly separating one of the rear panels, she slid inside. The darkness of the tent was a welcome relief from the merciless sun above. She felt herself relax almost instantly and with that relaxation came a wave of exhaustion.

No No No No. She chided herself. *Stay awake, stay up. You have to do this.* She nodded and quickly crossed to the other side of the tent to drop one of the open flaps and conceal her presence.

You don't have much time; you don't know their patterns. Look Look Look. She started going through the bundles and bags that were piled up. Personal belongings, foodstuffs, items she did not recognize. Water skins, which she happily grabbed and sampled. *Careful, not too much, your stomach will cramp. Remember what Tulok taught you.* After pawing through several bundles, she was able to cobble together what appeared to be a robe and a long black scarf with multiple colors woven through its weft. She scowled at the thought of having to don colors that reminded her of the ones worn by the group that had assailed her home. *You are in another section of the world, Isolde. It cannot be the same group. Stop it.* She scolded herself.

As she wrapped the scarf around her head and face, she made certain to wrap it in the fashion that Safar always wore, instead of the way the women in Tarf-qua. She pulled it across her face hiding everything but her eyes. As she tucked some of the items back and away, a small medallion fell out of one of the bundles. It was Vidria crystal, shaped in the form of two elegant feathers. Isolde picked up the medallion and stared at it. She remembered this symbol. Arman had carved it into the back of the medallion of The Radiant Lord that he had gifted her. The stylized etching on the feathers bore the same patterns that the merchant Arman had used. She held the item in her hand, a cool sense of dread and suspicion rose in her stomach. She swallowed down her gorge and stretched her neck, then tucked the medallion away into her robes. She would deal with the merchant, and whatever his involvement when she saw him again.

Keep your wits about you, Isolde. You are too close to mess this up now. She reminded herself. She grabbed one of the short blades from the pile and tucked it into her sash. *Please let me have remembered how to wear this, at least well enough to get me inside...*

Opening the back of the tent, she skirted the rest of the tents and carefully made her way to the entrance to the ruins.

Chapter 40

Ahsal was a place that should never have existed according to Tulok. Buried under the sands in the wastelands on the far side of Setesh it was an ancient and abandoned place of heresy and lies. At least that was what the faithful of the Sun God said. The entrance to the ruins had been excavated and the Seteshi sands held away from the entrance by ancient Vidria magics and stone crafting. This was not the work of a handful of misguided cultists whose existence could be swept under the proverbial rug and whose deeds could be denied. Isolde stepped out of the open air and into the carved stone edifice and knew immediately that she was standing in a place of ancient and forgotten stories.

This is new

The voice in the back of her head whispered.

Thanks, but I do not have time to take notes right now. She replied internally.

Part of her tugged at her mind, seeking to examine the carvings on the walls and stones that made up the passageway.

You are a Witness

I am going to be a dead Witness if I cannot stay focused. She argued with herself.

Her eyes slowly adjusted to the absence of the sunlight. She blinked rapidly, squinting and trying to get her bearings as the light faded. In the distance, and along the walls were groupings of crystals and phosphorescent lichen. They glowed softly, providing a gentle light along the way.

Lichen? That must mean water.

Of course, there is water, Isolde. They would not have built this out in the middle of the wastelands if there was no water.

The walls of the entrance were easily twenty feet high, the entranceway a carved, rectangular open doorway. The passageway was impossibly smooth to the touch and cool. Ripples of color ran through the stone, like multicolored waves of petrified sand. It was beautiful. Isolde's steps echoed slightly as she walked. She stopped her movements and quickly wrapped her boots in strips of cloth to help muffle the sound. It made her gait awkward, but she no longer sounded like a farm horse on cobblestone.

The narrow passageway ended abruptly, in a set of carved stone steps that entered an open room.

No hiding now. She thought to herself.

Glancing around she tried to get a feel for the area without looking too much like she had no idea where she was.

I want more time here! Her mind screamed at her.

Not now, you have a priest to save, and then have to figure out how to get out of here alive.

Crystals jutted from the walls here and there, offering their strange glow.

I have no idea where you get your light from, but I know it is not from the sun. Isolde thought to herself.

There was some sort of carving along one wall, but it was faded and caked in what appeared to be mud or stone as if someone had tried to cover it all up ages ago.

There is no god of the sun but the Radiant Lord. Tulok's

voice echoed in Isolde's memory. *There are no challengers to His power.*

Oh boy.

She took a deep breath, wondering how much of this was known, and moreover, how much she was going to be permitted to remember once they got out of here.

This is why none of the Wanderers ever come out here. They are going to murder me when they find out I know about this.

Worry about that later, Tulok needs you.

She focused once more on the task at hand. Braziers had been hung, but instead of being filled with embers and fire, they were filled once more with strange glowing crystals.

So strange.

The silence of the chamber was broken by the sound of a deep howl of rage. It seemed almost animalistic in its tones. Isolde's stomach tightened in a knot as she recognized the voice. It was Tulok.

Isolde looked back and forth, trying to judge which direction the sound had come from. Whispering a quiet prayer to her Lord, she set her shoulders and picked a path. There was little in the way of cover here. If she encountered anyone, she would have to meet them head-on.

She placed her hand on her short blade and headed down the left-hand corridor out of the main room.

She could feel the damp of the air here. Where there had been a distinct absence of moisture at the entrance and even in the main room, where there was cool almost humid wetness hanging in the air. It smelled musty and earthy here, like forgotten life. She remembered this smell from the islands when she and her friends would defy their parents and go exploring the old caves outside the village. They had had the bad fortune of encountering a hibernating cave bear one year and had been lucky that they were swifter scared than a sleepy bear had been.

Interesting

Sounds of feet on stone ahead of her. Her heart quickened. She rested her hand on the hilt of her blade and lowered her eyes as she continued to walk. A figure clad in an identical robe approached from down the hall. It did not pause and gave no indication that her presence was out of place. It tapped two fingers to its chest and nodded its head. Isolde repeated the gesture and the figure passed by her and toward the main room.

Another howl of anger issued from down the hallway. Several of the crystals seemed to brighten as the sound bounced off of them and around the area. Small pebbles fell from the ceiling and danced on the floor. Isolde looked up, her eyes tracing tiny cracks in the stone. A second howl followed the first. Closer now.

Brighter light emanated from a room ahead of her. Shadows danced on the floor of the doorway. She could hear what appeared to be the sound of a scuffle and metal on metal. Steeling herself for the potential of combat, she rounded the corner.

A dark-robed figure struggled with a chained and bound orc. His arms were held up and back, affixed to chains that were lodged in the ceiling. One of these had come loose, and the robed figure was trying desperately to re-secure the combatant. A heavy iron cuff encircled the orc's bare wrist and the chain led up to the ceiling but had become slack, allowing him more reach and greater purchase. The robed figure struggled with a rope tied to the other end of the chain that he used to pull the chain taught. The knot in the rope had worked its way free.

"Help me with the rope before he breaks free and kills us all!" the figure called.

Isolde blinked, realizing the figure was asking her for help. She nodded and quickly made her way across the room.

Tulok roared again and attempted to swipe at Isolde, unaware that she was there to help him. Sweat covered his bare skin that glistened in the crystal light of the ruin. Tulok, no longer clad in either armor or robes flexed his bare massive muscles and growled in anger and rage. His eyes, normally a reddish hue were black as night. There was nothing left of the peaceful healer who had saved her life. All that was left was the monster.

Isolde's breath caught in her throat as she realized what she was staring at. Sorrow crashed down on her in a tumultuous wave, but in its wake, there was the clarity of purpose.

Sorry, Tulok.

Stepping up beside the other figure she reached out to grab hold of the rope and looped it around her hand, wrist, and forearm. Bracing her leg, she leaned back into the rope. Her right shoulder screamed in burning pain as she pulled.

"Good! Just like that!" the other figure called and stepped backward toward her and out of Tulok's reach.

Isolde nodded, watching the figure.

One more step.

She let the rope go slack. Tulok's arm swung free.

"What are you doing!?" the figure yelled.

Isolde flipped the rope and grabbed the slack, wrapping it around the man's neck and twisting it tightly. He struggled against her, reaching for his throat, and then balled up his fist and punched backward at Isolde's face and head. She ducked her head to protect her eyes and face and buried it between the man's shoulders as she twisted the rope tighter. Tulok's struggles only tightened the rope more, pulling both Isolde and her quarry off the ground suddenly.

There was a sickening *snap* and the robed figure went limp.

Isolde loosed her hands from her grip and stepped back quickly. The body fell to the floor in a heap. Tulok yanked at his bindings once more, the round eye in the ceiling that held them in place quivered under his strength.

"Hang on, Tulok." Isolde managed and quickly darted to the other side of the room and began to fight with the knotted rope that held his other arm in place. It was too tight, and her hands could not work it loose. She reached for her short blade and with several sharp blows, cut the orc priest free.

Isolde began to turn to face the big priest, lowering her hood, and was suddenly lifted from the floor and slammed into the wall. Tulok's massive hand wrapped itself around her throat holding her in place. Her feet dangled above the floor.

"Tulok....no..." she gasped, clawing at his hand.

The orc snarled at his quarry, muscles rippling and veins bulging. His dark eyes were glassy and without reason.

"Tulok..." she pleaded once more. There was a pain as he squeezed and shoved her harder into the stone wall.

"You are not her!" the savage creature managed to snarl at the woman. He pulled her body away from the wall and slammed it against the stones once more. Precious air escaped Isolde's lungs.

"You are...hurting...me..." she pleaded, as she tried to wrap her hands around his thumb and pull it free. It slipped slightly. She took a deep breath. He closed his hand around her neck once more.

"You KILLED HER!" he roared at the woman in his

grasp. To him, she was nothing more than an impossible phantom. Another trick of the mind that the Vidria and his people were inflicting upon him.

Hot wet tears escaped Isolde's eyes as she stared at the creature who had been her boon companion. The healer who had saved her life. The gentle librarian of Tarf-qua, who had been pulled from his books and his maps and carried across the sands to this place out of legend. If she did not stop him, he would kill her; and everything would be for naught. Fumbling with his hand and struggling, she reached for her blade; only to discover it was no longer in her belt. It must have fallen free when Tulok slammed her into the wall. She was not strong enough to pull herself free from his grasp. The room began to swim before her eyes – it would be over soon.

"Ha..mula..." she whispered.

A single word that carried the weight of a lifetime cut through the fog of black rage that engulfed Tulok's mind. He blinked. His hand loosened on Isolde's throat. She gasped deeply, continuing to struggle. Tulok narrowed his eyes and leaned in closer to the phantom in his grasp, inhaling deeply, then felt her hand on his face, cupping his cheek gently.

"Hamula." Isolde managed to say once more. She tugged at Tulok's hand with her other hand, trying to pull herself free. "We...are...hamula..." she forced out.

Tulok dropped Isolde and stepped back quickly, clutching the hand he had used to hold her against the wall to his chest as if it were suddenly burned. He frowned and shook his head.

"...no..." he whispered. He took another step backward, his legs failing him. He collapsed to his knees, staring at Isolde in both horror and awe.

Chapter 41

Isolde swallowed hard and scrambled across the floor over to the orc priest. She pushed herself up onto her knees and looked up into his face. Tears streamed down her dirt and blood-covered cheeks.

"My poor bookworm...what have they done to you..." Isolde wept softly. She reached for

Tulok and he pulled away from her, shaking his head.

"This cannot be..." he managed.

"It can....it is..." she offered. She reached for his hand and guided it to her face. "It's me."

Tulok's thumb gently traced the broken bridge of Isolde's nose, finding the areas that he had once mended. He stared down at the Island woman, the darkness in his eyes slowly retreating as reason once more came to his mind.

"Isolde..." he whispered.

She smiled up at him then, her emerald green eyes filled with joy and hope once more. She nodded. Huge arms engulfed her frame and pulled her in, pressing her against his chest. Tulok buried his face in her hair and breathed deeply, taking in her scent and holding her tightly. Isolde tensed for a moment, uncertain if the great priest was going to crush her, but then relaxed and wrapped her arms around him in an embrace. She leaned her head against his massive chest and for a moment, there was nothing else in the world but them.

After a moment, she gently tapped Tulok on the ribs and pulled reluctantly away.

"We have to get out of here," she stated, bringing them both back into the danger of the situation.

Tulok nodded, clearing his throat and releasing her. "Yes, of course." allowed her to use his shoulder to push herself up to a standing position. He stopped. "No. We cannot..." he corrected.

"What?" Isolde asked, turning a shocked face toward him. "There are two of us. I don't have my weapon or most of my armor. You are..." she gestured at Tulok who was largely devoid of attire of any kind. "Well..."

Tulok blinked and took a moment to assess his current state of affairs. At that moment he was once again the proper and reserved Librarian of the Temple of Tarf-qua. He blushed furiously.

"Ah. Yes. Well then..." he cleared his throat as his hands drifted to hang before him. He looked askance, avoiding looking at Isolde.

Isolde furrowed her brow for a moment and then her eyebrows rose.

"Oh! Right!" she exclaimed and pulled the hooded cape off of her shoulders and held it out to him. "For your... dignity... Father." she grinned a little at him.

Tulok snatched the helpless piece of cloth out of Isolde's hand and wrapped it around his waist in what amounted to a makeshift loincloth and stood. Isolde gave the priest an appreciative glance and winked at him.

Tulok scowled at her. "I feel like a side of beef," he muttered.

"Don't worry, Father, your honor is safe with me."

Isolde chuckled a little. She looked down at the deceased figure on the floor and tapped them with her booted foot, she rolled them over and knelt to search the body.

"Robes, belt, belt knife, feels like he's wearing leather under..." she pulled the neck of the robe down to look inside. "Yup." she stood. "Nothing else."

Tulok had stepped away from the area and was searching shelves for anything that might be of use. He stopped at the bucket of liquid they had been feeding to him. His lip curled up in disdain.

"What do you have?" Isolde asked, walking over to his side.

"Sun Viper venom," Tulok replied. "Fermented. They were feeding it to me." he continued and then reached out to kick over the bucket. The liquid spilled across the sandy floor.

"They were poisoning you?"

Tulok shook his head. "No, they were stripping me of my sanity. They wanted the raw fire...the rage in my blood...." he set his shoulders and clenched his jaw.

"But... why?" Isolde asked.

Tulok shook his head. "I don't know, but it was important. I apparently have something they want..." he looked at the doorway, "and I think they were planning to give it to someone...or someTHING else..."

Isolde bristled at that and her eyes followed Tulok's gaze to the doorway. "I see."

"We cannot leave until we know what they were looking for." The big priest looked down at Isolde.

Isolde contemplated Tulok's words. This was not going to be easy. "They are going to notice you are not bound up here in short order." She offered.

Tulok nodded.

"Do you have any idea how many there are here?" She asked

Tulok reached up to rub the back of his head with a massive hand. "Maybe four more here, not counting the priestess and ...Arman..." he said the name carefully.

Isolde swore in her native tongue. "He really is part of this?" she asked.

Tulok nodded. " I am afraid so."

Isolde shook her head, "So... ten guards, a Vidria stone shaper and a... priestess of some kind?"

Tulok nodded. "I did not recognize her symbols or colors. I have no idea what we are dealing with." He leaned carefully against the wall and looked down the hallway. "We need .... something...more to go on..."

Isolde walked to Tulok and rested her hand on his forearm.

"Normally, I would be all in on this, my friend... but... if we fail to get out of here, then no one will know what is happening here, and we lose any chance of stopping them."

Tulok's eyes rested on Isolde's hand on his arm then lifted to her face. "They have the scarab," he said plainly.

Isolde's eyes went cold, and her jaw set. "Gods damn them." She swore.

"Mmm... my thoughts exactly." Tulok agreed and looked back down the hall.

Isolde pulled her hand away and rubbed her face. She stretched her neck, wincing a little from the bruising that was coming to the surface.

"Which way is the way out?" Tulok asked.

Isolde pointed down the hall, the way she had come in. "I came in that way. Passed one guard on the way in."

Tulok nodded. "That makes sense." he looked back down the other way and then pulled his head back in. "I only ever saw Arman and the woman going in the other direction. Whatever they are doing...whatever we are looking for...it is down the other way." he looked down at her. "Six outside, you passed one on the way in, "he pointed at the dead guard on the floor with his chin, "One more there...."

Isolde nodded. "That leaves two guards...potentially...down the other way... and our two guests of honor."

"I like those odds better," Tulok commented.

Isolde chewed on her lip in thought, "I have an idea..."

Tulok cocked an eyebrow and looked at Isolde. "Am I going to like this idea?" he asked.

"Probably not... I am going to need that cloth back."

~~~

"I resent the enforced stereotype Isolde," Tulok muttered quietly. His loosely bound hands hung in front of him, a section of cloth draped over them and down, to afford him some modesty.

"Well next time we are taken prisoner, you can rescue me, and I will wear the chains..." she whispered back as she looked quickly down the hall both ways. She adjusted the robes and tugged at the pieces of ill-fitting leather armor they had managed to cobble together for her. She pulled the hood up over her head and turned back to Tulok.

"How do I look?" she asked quickly.

"Clothed." came the curt reply.

"Does His Radiance have a BETTER idea?" the woman asked the priest.

Tulok sighed audibly. "No. I concede the point."

Isolde walked up to Tulok and looked up into his eyes which had resumed their normal reddish hue. "I do not like this either. The entire concept rankles... but THEY" she hitched a thumb toward the hall, "...probably will not think twice about seeing you bound and chained and escorted somewhere... besides which..." she looked over at the
~~~

deceased guard, now mostly stripped of his gear. "Nothing he had was going to fit you. So you were going to be in a state of..." she paused searching for words...

"Disarray?" Tulok offered uncomfortably.

She nodded. "Exactly... regardless of what we chose to do... I think your gear must be in the tent outside. Maybe?"

"Marvelous." Tulok scowled.

"The sooner we get whatever information you need, the sooner we can try to get out of here. Can you get free of the bindings?" She asked

Tulok tested the manacles on his wrists, they came open with a quick tug. "Yes."

Isolde nodded. "All right then." taking a deep breath she looked back up at Tulok. "Let's go."

The priest nodded and lowered his head. His shoulders slumped and his body hunched over slightly, giving him the appearance of someone either deep in their cups or drugged. Isolde picked up the length of the chain and gave it a tug. Tulok's hands jerked forward slightly.

"Sorry." she apologized softly.

He grunted in reply.

Looking in either direction once more, Isolde stepped into the hall and began to walk down the corridor, Tulok's massive figure in tow.

The ruins were quiet, sound did not seem to carry well here for some reason. Isolde looked up at the walls of the hall, coated in the strange crystals from before. They glowed softly, providing light. She wondered if the crystals were responsible for the lack of sound. It was odd.

The hall was maybe 20 feet long and then turned sharply to the right. The floor began to slope gently downward.

Behind Isolde, Tulok shuffled his feet on the sandy surface of the floor. This place should not exist. The ruins of

Ahsal were supposed to have been buried centuries ago. A combined effort by the Temples of The Radiant Lord and The Scribe was to have seen to this location, and its heretical influences were eradicated. He bristled at the thought of walking here and being exposed to such a place. The crystals and their non-sunlight source of radiance were of particular concern. He'd read of the talents of the Vidria stone shapers, that some of them had the ability to craft the sands into truly unique crystals capable of almost magical qualities. These could be sound stones – stones with the ability to take in, channel, and store sound as energy. Such things were not only considered rare, but extremely dangerous. In the right frequency and combination, sound stones could be used as weapons to channel sound vibration and generate fantastic but deadly amounts of pure light. They could illuminate several leagues with such terrible, destructive light, but without the blessing of the heavens.

Or at least that was what the stories said.

From his position of assumed submission, Tulok glanced around briefly, trying to get a better idea of the surroundings. Crystals coated the walls and ceiling.

This was not just a cache of found sound stones – this was a mine! This should not exist.

The implications of this discovery sent the big priest reeling. This was no longer a matter of a heretical cult having been reborn. This was a matter of safety and security for the realm. This group had to be stopped, this mine destroyed, and the Temple of Ophir needed to be advised.

He pulled on the chain that Isolde was holding, yanking her backward slightly.

"Oof!" she exclaimed and stumbled slightly.

"Sorry," Tulok muttered softly. "I have seen what I need to see. We need to get out of here," he whispered. The stones around them glowed gently in response to his voice.

Isolde frowned a little inside her hood. "We haven't found anything..." she hissed quietly in return. Once more the stones glowed.

Tulok brought his hands up and put his finger to his lips and gestured for Isolde to be silent. Then he pointed to the crystals in the walls. He made a gesture with his hands that meant "bad".

Isolde scowled and looked around. She pointed at the crystals all around them.

Tulok nodded and lowered his hands once more.

Isolde stood there looking at him, she held her hands out as if to say "and?"

Soft sounds in the distance and fluttering lights in the hall alerted Tulok. He gestured behind Isolde and resumed his downtrodden position. Isolde quickly turned back around and jerked on the chain that held the orc. They began to move again.

A lone figure emerged from down the hall, another robed guard – taller and broader than the others that Isolde had seen. The figure paused, seeing the approaching duo.

"Where are you taking him?" the guard demanded. "Ceremony is not until tomorrow." he stepped forward quickly.

Isolde stopped and held her position. "Arman wants him," she replied, remembering that the Vidria merchant was supposedly here.

The figure cocked its head to the side cautiously. His hand slid toward the hilt of the blade at his hip. "You have a strange accent, sister..."

"I told you this would not work," Tulok stated and stepped up quickly to grab the guard and pin him against the wall. His meaty hand pressed against the guard's mouth, silencing him.

"Sorry about this...well...not really..." Isolde apologized and deftly removed the ropes and chains from Tulok's wrists and reached for the guard's hands. He kicked at her as she approached, connecting with her knee, and struggled against Tulok's grasp.

Isolde inhaled sharply as pain shot through her leg. She staggered back for a moment.

Tulok's eyes narrowed and he glared at the guard. "That was a mistake," he spoke softly, but the tone was not kind.

Inside his hood, the guard's eyes widened with fear. He screamed against Tulok's hand. The muffled cries were swallowed by the stones that surrounded them and they glowed brighter.

"May you find peace in His Grace and Mercy..." the priest whispered and with a wrenching motion quickly turned the guard's head farther than his neck would allow. The body went limp and slumped to the ground.

"You are terrifyingly good at that..." Isolde commented as she quickly searched the body of the guard and pulled his hooded cowl off. She handed it to Tulok, who once more covered his person as best as he could in a show of decency.

"It is not something that I am proud of..." he muttered apologetically.

"Efficiency over pride right now, I think..." she commented.

Tulok nodded.

"That should be it for the guards, so we just have Arman and the priestess...and the scarab..." Isolde said. "What about the crystals?"

"Sound stones," Tulok replied, keeping his voice low. "They... like the whole of this place...should not exist. They store the energy from sound which can be used to create light..." he gestured, "in large enough quantities... they can be harnessed for concussive force."

Isolde's eyes widened.

"Like... an... explosion?"

Tulok nodded.

"So, we are..."

"Standing in the middle of a Vidria shard bomb...yes." The priest nodded.

Isolde scrambled to gather whatever they could off of the body of the guard. "You just said things that I do not understand...and probably do not WANT to understand... "She offered him the length of chain. "It is not a mace..."

Tulok wrapped the chain around his right hand, allowing part of it to dangle. He swung it a couple of times and nodded. "No, but it will do."

Angry voices came from the hall behind them. They looked at each other.

"They found the other guard," Isolde commented.

Tulok nodded. "Here is hoping this corridor turns back on itself, otherwise we are about to be quickly outnumbered." he looked down at the Knight Wanderer and extended his hand. "If we do not make it out of here, it has been my honor to have known you."

Isolde duAvalonne looked at the extended hand and back up to the big orc. She reached to grasp his forearm in her hand and then raised herself to place her lips on his cheek. It was gentle, filled with both admiration and adoration. The orc priest's eyes widened in shock and surprise. His entire frame blushed with color.

"I... ah...ahem..." he cleared his throat.

"Never leave something undone that could weigh on your heart, right?" she asked and smiled up at him.

Tulok blinked and stared down at Isolde. "No... you are...correct..." he stammered, uncertain and confused. He cleared his throat and regained his composure. "Of course." he nodded. "We can... discuss this...once we are...not...here..."

Isolde patted Tulok on the shoulder "More reason for us to survive." She smiled and pulled her blade from her belt, headed down the hall at a quick trot, a notable limp from her left knee.

"Assuredly..." Tulok replied as he watched Isolde head down the hallway, deeper into the ruins.

Chapter 42

Arman rubbed his face with his hands and leaned back from the table. He closed his eyes. Before him lay several stacks of paper and papyrus, along with various round leather tubes containing even more of the same. Painted on the far wall of his room was a massive map of the realms of Sanctum. The entirety of the Knowne Worlde stretched from corner to corner and ceiling to floor. Several of the sections of the map had broken off and fallen to the floor over the centuries, leaving the world incomplete. Nonetheless, it was the most complete record of cartography that the Vidria had ever seen.

Five thousand years ago the peoples of Sanctum had been brought here from their various homes, to save them from the Reaping. Five thousand years of isolation, bickering, and wars had kept the nations from unification of any kind. Five thousand years of carefully guarded secrets and borders. Five thousand years of fear.

While the map on the wall was woefully outdated and did not bear any of the modern cities and settlements, what it did hold was a slice of history. History of origins. Nebiyre could have her sound stones and her precious cavern. This was what he was here for. Information that even the Librarian of Litharge and the Keepers of the Dead may very well not have. This was information and power.

Arman opened his eyes and stared at the wall. The continent of Sanctum that stretched from the farthest northern mountains to the deepest barren deserts in the south... and the island continent of Avalon. He rolled his tongue across his blunted teeth and stared at the island. There was something so very different about those lands. The people of the mainland made up various cultures and civilizations. Realms. Many were an attempt at preserving what they had left behind, what had been taken from them or lost. Six realms contested for power on the main continent. But alone across the water, and almost two-thirds the size of the mainland, Avalon was power in and unto itself. How they prized their isolation and secrets. It had taken him years of research and bribery to trace the lineage of the Magister of Deneb-aal. The little Folk man whose family had originally hailed from the Avalonian city of Brede.

All Folk were tied to The Mother, the life-giving protector of Avalon. They were Her chosen people, crafted from the very soil and bones of the continent itself. Finding one whose lineage traced back to the founders of Sanctum; that had been the challenge. While there were historians on the island that kept carefully curated records of familial lineages, this was not information that had been easy; nor cheap, to come by. The Islanders had no use for coin.

Making alliances with persons who carried enough *leug* in the community to obtain the information had taken years to cultivate. To compound the difficulty, the Lords of Sanctum who were native to the faith of the island seemed to take a more vested and personal interest in their people. Many of the lineages Arman had been able to trace had occurrences where family trees simply seemed to spring from the ether; as they no doubt truly had – when the divine chose to sire a child. The Vidria was convinced that one could not swing a dead cat in a group of Islanders and not strike one that was descended from a deity somewhere down the line. This was why the contents of the scarab were priceless. The sacred spark of a direct and traceable descendant of a founding family of Avalon could be absorbed – violently, from their body.

Arman stretched his neck and pushed himself away from the table. The orc had been another matter, easier to trace, but harder to get his hands on. The orcish people prided themselves on their Clan structure. Maintaining bloodlines to ensure intermarriage did not occur was important to them. Prying the Radiant Father away from the sacred Temple of Tarf-qua had been something that Arman had only just begun planning when the Knight Wanderer had shown up with the scarab in her possession. When she had vanished into the desert, he wrote her and the scarab off for lost. It had been luck to have her wander back into the picture again. To have both within his grasp...and Tulok eager to assist her in her Quest – it was perfect.

The gullibility of innocence.

The flickering of lights in the doorway caught Arman's keen eye and he glanced in that direction. Frowning, he put the stopper in his inkpot and reached for a bladed dagger that lay crosswise on the surface of the table. He narrowed his eyes and took several cautious steps in the direction of the door. Others not trained as himself might have overlooked the sound of feet on the sand in this area of the ruins. The stones glowed and faded and glowed and faded as if in response to the sound of someone running. Concentrating for a moment, Arman tried to pick out a telltale sound that should be audible, even from this distance. The sound of the orc priest in chains.

There was nothing.

A moment of panic and concern flooded across Arman's mind. The priest was unarmed and without protection, but he was a devout follower of the Sun Lord and more than this... he was still an Orc. Armed or not, Arman understood what it took to take the priest into custody from the start, and what it took to keep him under control. If he were loose in the underground...

The dwarf moved quickly to his work table, and grabbing his satchel, deftly began to shove leather cylinders into its mouth. The objects disappeared into the opening of the satchel, but it did not seem to reach its fill. He was not about to attempt to go head to head with a creature three times his size. He had recruited the guards for this reason. Let them cast their lots and see how well they fared. The Vidria had not come this far to fall at the hands of some Sandborn zealot. As much as he would regret losing the priest for the ceremony, he was intimately more familiar with the lineages of Setesh. The orc could be replaced. The research could not.

Shoving the last of the documents into the satchel, Arman took one final look at the map on the wall and sighing a regretful sigh, darted down the hall in the opposite direction of the sound.

~~~

"How many?!" Isolde called back as she ran down the hall.

"I saw three!" Tulok replied from behind her.

"Get in front of me!" She ordered and moved to press herself against the wall, to allow the big priest to get ahead of her.

"Isolde...no." Tulok pleaded. He paused for a heartbeat to look down into her face. Her green eyes offered gentle support as she looked up at him. She nodded.
~~~

"I'm armored, you're not. GO!" she replied and with a hard shove pushed his massive frame ahead of her.

Tulok stagger stumbled to regain his footing. His chest tightened with pain and anxiety. Had he come this far only to lose her again? He let out a groan of exasperation and frustration.

The stones around him lit up brightly in response to the sound. Gravel fell from the ceiling as several of the stones glowed brightly and began to vibrate. Tulok's eyes widened to see it. An idea began to form.

Three dark-robed figures rounded the corner behind Isolde and Tulok. Two carried sharp-looking short blades. The third brandished a long whip with cruel-looking barbs on the end.

Oh, this is going to hurt. Isolde thought upon seeing them.

"Go, go, go!" She yelled at Tulok and ran backward presenting the guards with a shield between them and their quarry. She knew the orc was what they wanted. She looked behind her quickly. Tulok's much longer legs afforded him the ability to distance himself from both the guards and Isolde. She nodded and looked at the approaching guards.

Oh boy.

Turning back around, she ducked her head and forced herself to sprint forward. Her left knee screamed in agony as she pushed herself forward. It would only be a matter of time before it gave way. She only hoped it would be enough.

"I have an idea!" Tulok yelled as he ran. Stones around him lit up from his voice.

"Less thinking, more running, Father!" Isolde replied.

"Do you trust me?" the orc called as he approached another corner.

Air burned in Isolde's lungs, she tasted copper. Steeling

herself, she reached down deep to find the strength of will to continue her pace. Her heart pounded in her head.

"You are asking me this now?!" she yelled.

Suddenly there was searing, ripping pain in her right shoulder as the barbed hooks of a long-reaching whip found purchase in her flesh. She was pulled up short. A pained cry escaped her lips. Stones all around her lit up like they were powered by the sun. Three dark figures closed in on her.

Tulok stopped at the sound and looked back to see the Knight Wanderer surrounded by the enemy. The glow of rage fired in the orc's stomach, kindled by the venom that still flowed in his veins.

"Isolde!" he yelled. Stones in the walls rattled around him and vibrated through the ceiling and floor.

The woman reached back and grabbed hold of the whip, then twist-turned, wrenching it free of the grasp of the guard who had lodged the barbs into her. Blood flowed freely down her shoulder and back. She turned to face the three guards. Two of them raised their weapons to bring them to bear on her, while the third staggered back, off-balance from losing his weapon. In her right hand, Isolde held the hilt of her short sword, in her left she swung the end of the whip.

One of the guards lunged forward, she countered his swing with her blade, forcing it down and toward the floor. She rode the momentum up his arm and slammed the knuckle-guard of the blade into his face.

Stones around the group began to glow and vibrate. The guard who once held the whip stepped away, looking around quickly.

The second blade wielder moved to engage Isolde.

"Let. There. Be. LIGHT!" The deep and commanding voice of Radiant Father Tulok bellowed from behind

Isolde. He held his massive arms outstretched and then pulled them together in a loud and thunderous clap. The sound of his powerful voice coupled with the concussive force of his clapping palms echoed down the hall. Around them all, the stones glowed as if powered by the light of the sun itself.

Suddenly the hall was filled with shards of broken crystals flying out of the walls, as the stones around them began to explode one by one. The area of destruction started at the priest and extended in both directions from him like a wave.

Isolde's eyes caught the sudden brilliance and felt the vibrations around her.

Vidria shard bomb.

Her eyes widened and she dropped to the floor as the wave of exploding stones reached the group. She scrambled to cover her head and face, as the bodies of the guards were suddenly riddled with knife-like shards from the ceiling and walls. They screamed in both pain and fear. The Knight was not spared from injury, she winced as sharp crystals sliced through her mismatched armor and into several places on her torso and legs. The injuries were noticeable, but not lethal.

The cries from the guards slowly faded with the ending of the shard explosion. Isolde rolled quickly to one side and pushed herself to stand. Her left knee buckled. She collapsed.

"Ugh!" she exclaimed as her hand reached out to steady herself. Instead of broken shards of the wall, she found purchase on the firm hand of the massive priest.

"I have you." the priest's soothing voice spoke gently as he offered her support.

Isolde nodded. "It would appear so."

"Can you walk?" Tulok asked her, concern flavored his deep voice.

Isolde paused and performed a quick mental assessment of her injuries. She shook her head. "Not without difficulty."

"If we can get you out of here and back to the sunlight, I can heal you." Tulok urged. "Can you try?"

Isolde looked up at the orc, noting the deep concern and worry in his face, his voice, and his eyes.

If I can bring the light of hope to a single soul suffering despair, then I have done my duty.

She nodded. "Because you inspire me to do so, Good Father." she smiled a pained smile and squeezed his hand. "Lend me your arm to lean on?"

"Of course," he replied and helped her to stand.

The pair stared at the guards laying on the floor in a pile of blood, shredded flesh, and broken bones. Isolde leaned on Tulok's arm for support. She nodded.

"I understand now. This is too dangerous to allow in the outside world," she replied. "You said you had an idea?"

"Now she listens to me." he chided, but there was no malice in his tone.

"Knights are a stubborn lot," she replied as she limped down the hall at his side. "Blood and injury usually work to get our attention." She smiled a little.

"I have noticed."

Isolde looked up and around. The section of the ruins they were in had changed in formation. The stones and crystals here were larger, some of them almost the size of a small child. Given the destruction of the smaller stones farther up the hall, she wondered what the destructive properties of these might be.

Tulok noted her attention. He nodded. "Hrmm. Yes. Precisely."

"You think we could bring it down?" she asked quietly.

Tulok took a breath and shrugged a little. "Possibly."

An open passage on the left gave them pause. Tulok stopped their progress and moved to let Isolde find balance on the wall. "I will look. Stay here."

"Oh ho, he has humor now," she quipped through the pain and then shooed him away.

Tulok scowled at her and then moved toward the opening. There was no sound and there were no lights from glowing stones to indicate sound. The priest ducked his head and peered quickly around the corner, and stopped short.

Isolde watched from where she had been left. Blood oozed from her shoulder and down her back.

Not good

Chapter 43

Tulok turned and stepped quickly back to Isolde. He reached for her and helped her to stand and lean on him once more.

"You need to see this," he whispered and half carried her to the doorway.

Soft smokeless candles lit the room, no doubt remnants of magic left behind from the previous occupant. The room was roughly fifteen feet on a side. Three of the walls had been shaped into low tables. In the center of the room was another low table with various writing supplies strewn about. The height of the tables seemed to imply they were for a child. Or a dwarf. The shaped stonework was clearly the result of the Vidria. Arman must have been here.

Tulok followed Isolde's gaze as she took in the room. He shook his head. "Not the stonework... over there..." he pointed across the room to the far wall.

The Knight Wanderer's eyes widened as she saw the map. Her face paled with both shock and awe. Her heart beat quickly against her chest.

"Take me to it." She managed.

Tulok nodded and helped her across the room.

Isolde's eyes widened as she stared at the ancient artifact. So much history displayed before her. She instinctively reached out to touch it but stopped herself as she realized her hand was covered in blood. Her blood.

Tulok's eyes widened. "Isolde!" he exclaimed and reached for her.

She waved at him, her eyes searching the map with a passion he had not seen before. "I will be fine," she murmured. "This..."

"Has to be buried with the rest of it." the priest said carefully.

Isolde turned almost panicked eyes to Tulok. "No... we can't... this..."

"Is the honey in the center of a pitcher plant." he countered.

Isolde shook her head in defiance and looked back at the map. Her eyes quickly searched the whole of it. "No. No. No." she whispered.

Tulok shifted from allowing her to lean on him to sliding his arm around her waist to give her more support. Tears welled up in Isolde's eyes. She knew what he was saying was true, but the loss of this magnitude pained her in the pit of her soul.

"I am so sorry..." she whispered as she closed her eyes. Tulok knew the words were not meant for him. He hugged her gently against his side. "Another reason to survive. A memory for a well." he offered softly.

The Holy Witness of the Lord Wanderer nodded simply and opened her eyes once more to take in the marvel that was displayed before her. Maybe they could just seal it off. Maybe it could be preserved. Maybe they could excavate it later. So many maybes. All of which hinged on their survival and her carrying the information out of here.

She nodded. "A memory for a well." She reluctantly agreed.

"Let me bandage you." Tulok finally said and pulled her away from the wall.

The woman did not fight the healer this time. She nodded and allowed him to guide her to the table. Sitting her down, he quickly began to rip at the robe that she had been wearing and make pressure bandages for her wounds. It was not his best work, but it would keep her from bleeding out at least until they could get out of here. He grabbed hold of the small wooden stool at the edge of the table and broke the legs off quickly to use for a splint on her knee. She continued to stare at the map while he worked, her lips moving in silent prayer.

"There is not much time. They are going to find those dead guards very soon." Tulok spoke. He looked around the room. "I am going to assume that Arman heard the commotion and is already ahead of us. It looks like he cleared out in a hurry."

Maybe he copied the map

Tulok's words brought the Knight back to the conversation. "We need to find him."

Tulok took Isolde's face in his hands and pulled her focus over to him. "One thing at a time. We need to get out of here. We need to get back to civilization. We need to tell our respective Orders about what is here. No chasing after Vidria right now. Agreed?"

Isolde met Tulok's eyes, unflinching.

"Agreed, Isolde?" he said once more. "Neither of us can see this through if we are dead. Agreed?"

Isolde reluctantly nodded. "Agreed."

The priest took a deep breath and relaxed. "Good." He stepped back from her and offered her his hand. "Stand up then, and let's get the hell out of here."

She reached out and grasped his hand firmly in hers and pulled herself up to a standing position. She wobbled slightly. He offered her his arm for balance. She shook her head, then wiped the back of her hand across her cheeks, clearing the tears away. Deep smears of dirt mixed with blood covered her face. For all the kindness and light in her heart, the Knight looked a horrific mess.

"Lead on. Let's go," she said with a voice rough with sorrow. Casting a look back over her shoulder one final time, she followed Tulok out of the room.

Two more poorly lit corridors led them to the very depths of the ruins. The walls and air became damp with moisture. There was clearly an underground spring here somewhere. Small pools of water could be seen here and there as the corridor began to widen and take on a more natural feel. Tulok marveled at the life that a place of this nature could support here. Yet the stones reminded him of the dangers of allowing it to be discovered. There was clearly a lesson to be learned in the existence of this place, but there was no time to discover it. The Librarian's heart ached just as surely as that of his companion's for the loss of knowledge that was going to have to happen to keep these ruins out of the wrong hands.

Soft green and blue light filled the area ahead of them. Tulok could tell that the narrow hall opened into a much wider chamber. He held out a hand of caution to Isolde. Holding his right finger to his lips, he pointed at the enormous crystals that jutted from the walls and ceiling. The light that illuminated the area came directly from them. The light that was not from the grace of the sun.

It was not right.

Isolde nodded at his cautionary gesture and moved slowly to approach his side and look beyond him. Her eyes widened and she reached for her compass.

Hollowed from the stones and shaped from the sands that surrounded the area was an enormous cavern. Crystals the size of men gathered in groups and glowed softly, giving light to a place that would otherwise be locked in darkness. Water dripped from the ceiling and along with their tapered bodies, falling into pools beneath them. There was a soft sound of running water from somewhere. At the far end of the cavern stood a smooth altar shaped and carved from the crystals themselves. It sat atop an elevated dais. Behind the altar, five arched niches held what appeared to be jars with strangely shaped stoppers. The jars appeared to be a little over two feet tall each. Above these niches was a large carving of a female figure bound in chains, one chain from each niche seemed to run to the figure, holding it in place symbolically.

The priest and the knight both swore softly and made signs against ancient forces, in an attempt to ward off evil.

"Who is that?" Isolde whispered.

"I have no idea," Tulok replied.

The crystals around them immediately lit up and a soft humming could be felt. Tulok's eyes widened and darted toward the altar. It glowed faintly.

Glancing inside, the pair made their way carefully inside. There appeared to be another entrance on the other side of the cavern. Isolde tapped Tulok's arm and pointed. He followed her direction and nodded, trying to carefully step through the cavern.

Melodic singing drifted across the air and the cavern came to life.

Tulok and Isolde froze, eyes searching around them for its source.

The vocalist continued her reverent hymnal tones, calling the stones around them to power. The hairs on Tulok's bare form stood on end as he felt both the vibration of the crystals and the divinity of the area. This was a sacred space, but the figure on the wall was not The Silent One. What had they uncovered?

The altar at the end of the cavern began to glow with a sickly green cast. From behind it a thin shadow of a woman emerged. She was almost emaciated in appearance. Any signs of racial descendancy had long disappeared, leaving behind only a mummified corpse-like being.

At her throat hung an ornate golden scarab covered in multi-faceted jewels. It glowed faintly with the light of the cavern. The figure stared down at the priest and the knight from her position of power. Her lips parted to reveal a broken and rotted smile.

"Thank you for coming so willingly..." she spoke in velvet tones. Her fingers began to dance in the air as her arms and hands wove arcane symbols.

"Run." Tulok hissed at Isolde and shoved her toward the door.

Nebiyre flicked her fingers in their direction, "Stop" she spoke. Both Isolde and Tulok felt their feet rooted to the ground. "This is my holy place, priest." She stared at Tulok. "You and your overbearing God does not give orders here."

Isolde looked over at Tulok. She was frozen in place. Shaking her head she stared at the orc indicating she could not move.

Tulok strained against the force of the priestess' magic, trying desperately to call on the power of his faith to free him. Devoid of sunlight, and cast only in the false light of this unholy place, he was powerless.

The creature that was Nebiyre stepped slowly away from the altar and began to approach the pair. She moved with a terrible grace and purpose. Her dark, sunken eyes fixated on Isolde. Her lips curled in a half snarl.

"Do not worry... Father..." she spoke in melodic tones. The crystals seemed to sing back to her and glow brighter.

"I promise not to play with my food..." she said as she stepped past Tulok and approached Isolde.

The Knight Wanderer met Nebiyre's eyes with unbowed courage and defiance. Refusing even now to let the power of the darkness smother the light in her soul.

"So much faith, in such a false path." the priestess purred. From the ether and shadows, a dagger appeared in Nebiyre's hand. "Tell the bitch at the crossroads I said hello."

The movement was swift and executed with the expert skill of someone well versed in the art of sacrifice. The knife's blade glittered quickly in the crystal's green glow and then found its sheath beneath Isolde's ribs. The Wanderer's eyes widened at the shock. Her body folded over Nebiyre's hand as her lifeblood began to spill out and onto the sand-covered floor. She slowly slumped to the ground, the magic holding her in place now gone.

Pain and anguish crashed onto Tulok, as he stood, helpless once more to save the woman who had become so important to him in such a short span of time. Once again, he was standing on the deck of the ship, unable to save her. The hollow pit of his stomach filled with a chill cold as he stared at Nebiyre standing over Isolde's fallen figure. His chest constricted, but this time it was not despair that the orc priest felt.

This time it was rage.

The Gurkh of his people flooded Tulok's senses, filling him with a singular purpose. Unlike the poisonous rage brought upon him by the pain of the venom, this was a clear and calculating thing with a clear and defined goal. His muscles flexed and his tendons stretched even as his very being called for His God to bless Him with His Holy vengeance.

Nebiyre turned to face the priest, her smile falling quickly away.

Tulok's lips pulled back from his teeth, baring his great tusks as his face took on a war-like visage. Something touched his heart, and the power of the priestess fell away.

The sound that emanated from the orc priest was filled with not only the rage of the Gurkh of his people but also powered by the desire for unbridled vengeance from his heavenly sponsor. It was less a bellow and more a roar. Less a shout and more a declaration that could not be disputed. A single syllable. A single word. A statement of intent and defiance.

"No!"

The sound echoed off of the surface of the chamber walls. Crystals erupted with light unlike any that Nebiyre had ever seen. She reached for the scarab at her throat and backed away in fear as the sound chamber began to vibrate. It was a vibration that could be felt in her very bones.

"You have killed us all," she whispered and stumbled backward.

The massive figure of Father Tulok ripped himself from his position and closed the distance between himself and the woman. With a single smooth swipe of his meaty hand, he struck the side of Nebiyre's head and sent her slight frame flying across the cavern and into one of the crystals. She bent in several unnatural angles and lay atop them, a strange liquid slowly oozing from her and onto the crystal. The humming vibration continued to build and grow.

Tulok turned his rage-filled eyes to the fallen figure of Isolde. With unimagined gentleness, he bent to scoop her broken and bleeding body from off the floor and cradled it against his chest. With a final snarl and roar, he set his shoulders and ran for the entrance as glowing Vidria shards reached their capacity and began to give way behind him.

Each concussive explosion added to the energy of the next. A chained wave of destruction following in his fury charged wake.

Chapter 44

Panic and disorder erupted in the ruins and the camp as the temple began to destruct from deep within. Sections of the ceiling began to fall in, crushing anyone unfortunate enough to be beneath them. The remaining scouts and guards scrambled for gear and mounts as sounds of death and destruction spewed forth. The dunes themselves began to rumble and the ground to shake. Foul-smelling air belched forth from the entrance to the ruins of Ahsal as it coughed out shards of stones and smoke. Through this hellscape the figure of the priest of Tarf-qua emerged, carrying the limp form of the Avalonian Knight. The camp was consumed in chaos. Less than a handful of men remained to defend their goods and gear.

As Tulok emerged from the darkness and false light of Ahsal, he felt the warm and invigorating caress of the presence of his Lord of Light. He stumbled slightly, taking a knee suddenly, but careful not to drop his precious cargo. Two guards approached him; swords bared. He turned teeth and tusks on them and snarled with the rage and vengeance of his people and his God. The earth rumbled beneath them again. The guards stepped back and away from the creature that was clearly possessed by a power greater than they were paid to address.

He looked down at the island woman, her pale face covered in dirt, tears, and blood. Dark liquid continued to ooze from the wound under her ribs.

Tulok's eyes softened slightly and he turned his face toward the sky and howled his anger, rage, and despair.

"Father!" he cried. "Hear me!" he pleaded with the skies. His eyes searched the heavens above him, even as he held the knight's body. "Father!" he called again. "I left my Library and children for you." he began, "I crossed the wastelands for you." he continued. "I defended your name to my people" he choked slightly on his words as his throat tightened. "I gave you Ahsal..." he closed his eyes and hung his head.

"Please let her live." the priest whispered his prayer to the oft unforgiving heavens.

The Sun Lord's Mercy was not often considered kind. Setesh was a place of harsh truths and harder lives. His people were tested on a daily basis, for the weak would never survive. Sacrifice without reward however would only result in resentment. The bowed figure of the orc priest felt the warm hand of His Lord's blessing course through his body in answer to his prayer. The healing light of the Everwatchful Lord touched the body of the fallen Knight of the Wandering Lord. The blood that flowed from her side stopped and slowly color returned to her cheeks. Her eyes fluttered.

Air caught in Tulok's lungs as he felt the healing power of the heavens on his soul. He leaned forward and gently placed his lips to Isolde's forehead and held her to him for a moment.

"Thank you, Father," he murmured.

~~~

The travois finally collapsed just as he dragged them both into the remains of the burned campsite where Bengt
~~~

had been murdered. The wandering sands had claimed most of what had been left behind. Tulok was able to patch together enough protection from the sun for them both, but precious little else. The ruins had collapsed in on themselves as the sands reclaimed that which they had hidden for centuries before. Survivors, both human and korser alike had run off into the desert in hopes of escape.

He sat next to her prone body, looking out from the shelter. Nebiyre and Arman had stripped him of his vestments and clothing and left it behind when they had taken him, prisoner. Digging through the sands, he found enough clothing to cover his body once more. Buried far from the camp he had unearthed his holy sigil. It had clearly been flung from the encampment by Nebiyre's people. A long black scorpion had burrowed down into the sand next to the sigil, revealing its chain. He held it in his hand and stared at it as he sat, watching and waiting. He was exhausted and not terribly certain what would befall them now.

Isolde stirred next to him. His heartbeat quickened a pace and he turned his focus to the injured woman.

"Isolde?" he asked anxiously.

She moaned softly.

"Be careful, you are still injured." he cautioned.

Slowly, her eyes opened. She tried to lick her lips, but they were parched and her tongue felt like sandpaper.

"Here. I was able to find one canteen." Tulok offered. He opened the hardened leather bottle and placed it to her lips. He wet them gently, careful not to spill any of the life-preserving liquid.

"This is all there is," he commented.

She nodded in understanding. Her eyes focused and unfocused trying to look around.

"We are where I was taken," he replied to her unanswered question.

"Ru-ins?" she croaked in question.

Tulok lowered his eyes and shook his head. "Reclaimed by the sands."

She nodded slightly. "For...the...best." she managed.

The priest nodded in agreement.

"What. Next?" she asked him, rolling her head to the side to look at him. She carefully flexed her fingers and began to assess her injuries. She had lost a lot of blood. Movement was only barely possible. She blanched at the effort.

"Stay still, woman!" The healer chided and scowled at her.

Isolde stopped moving and just looked at Tulok. "Better?" she asked.

He harrumphed at her in response. He looked up at the sky for a moment and then back over at her. "We have, most of a single bottle of water, no korsers, camels, and the travois is broken. Also, your injuries are beyond my ability to heal without the appropriate supplies." he finally replied.

She lay next to him, staring at him, and listened. She nodded again slowly. "Oh. Is that all?" she looked over at him, forced a smile and an attempted wink.

He scowled at her. "How can you find humor in this?" he asked in an exasperated tone.

Isolde squinched her face up into a pained and exhausted smile. She slowly lifted her right arm and held out her hand to him.

Tulok looked at her with a confused stare but reached out to take her hand in his.

"Because...you inspire me... to continue." She said softly.

Tulok's red eyes softened as he stared down at the broken woman lying in the sand next to him. There was a warmth in his chest when he looked at her and he instinctively felt the corners of his lips curving into a smile. He held her hand a little tighter.

Isolde blinked sluggishly and smiled gently up at him and squeezed his hand in response. She pulled his hand to her and placed parched lips on his knuckles. She kissed it gently. Tulok stared at her in both wonder and confusion as she did so. His eyes searched her face, trying to understand something he desperately wanted to know. She smiled gently and held his hand to her cheek for a moment and closed her eyes. She felt him pull their joined hands away from her face and then felt him unfold his hand from hers and press her fingertips to his cheek. She opened her eyes and looked up at him to see him staring down at her. He covered her hand with his and pressed it to his skin. Gently cupping his cheek in her rough hand, she caressed it with her thumb. A simple gesture that conveyed emotions beyond the reach of words.

"Should I come back later?" a voice disturbed the moment as the silhouette of a figure stepped up to their shade. Their hands were held up with palms facing outward. The sun on his back, his face was covered in shadows; but the voice was familiar.

Tulok jerked away from Isolde in response and reached for the broken tent pole at his side in defense. He tried to stand, but exhaustion was too great, forcing him back into a seated position. Isolde cried out in pain at the sudden motion.

"Ah! You are going to kill her, Tulok!" the deeply accented voice cautioned. "I thought priests were supposed to be healers!"

Tulok narrowed his eyes and held the pole between him and the dark figure. He edged close to Isolde, trying to interpose himself between the intruder and his patient. Eyes the color of golden honey stared back at him from a deeply tanned face, accented with a black mustache and beard. A single black curl escaped the headscarf that wrapped around his head and tangled in his beard.

Tulok blinked.

"Safar?" he asked in astonishment.

The lean figure of the Reysis smiled broadly down at them both. "That is the name my mother blessed me with, yes." he replied.

Tulok pointed the end of the tent pole at him and readied to battle the figure. "Be gone apparition. You assume the face and form of a fallen friend, the Reysis is dead."

The man hummed slightly and looked at Isolde. "Yes, and so was she I believe," he nodded at her injuries, "Yet here we are."

Tulok frowned and lowered his weapon slightly. "I buried you."

Safar pursed his lips and held up a warning finger. "No. You blessed the sands under which I was dragged."

"After being stabbed by Swammerdami." Tulok protested.

Safar once again gestured at Isolde's prone figure. "She at least tried to pull me out of the sand," he said of Isolde. "Thank you, by the way." he nodded in her direction.

The Knight carefully tilted her head back to look up at the figure. She raised her arm slowly to shade her eyes and examine him.

"If .. you... really are... Safar..." Isolde spoke then.

The man turned his golden gaze to her. His smile faltered for a moment and his eyes suddenly filled with compassion and concern. "Yes, Island?" he asked her.

"What... do I... have... under my robes?" she asked.

Tulok turned shocked eyes to Isolde. She did not look

at him but held Safar's gaze from her position in the sand.

The man laughed once uncomfortably and then chuckled. He nodded as he laughed. "Ah. Yes." he cleared his throat. Tulok continued to stare at them both aghast in disbelief.

"Armor. You had a chest plate." he looked over at Tulok's shocked face. "What did you think she meant?"

Isolde shrugged as best as her position would allow and nodded and lowered her hand, satisfied.

Tulok continued to look between the two.

"Did you find them, Reysis?" a young male voice called out.

Safar looked back in the direction of the voice. "Yes, boy! Go tell the others. We set camp here. The Islander cannot be moved just yet!"

Isolde could not be certain, but when Safar turned away, she thought she saw the ink of a tattoo peeking out of the collar of the shirt of the handsome Sun Guide.

A black scorpion.

Chapter 45

The coastline of Setesh was a mixture of tall cliffs that fell off into the water and lazy sands that sloped into the surf. It was only around the Delta of Iteru where that landscape differed. Kef-aal was a small coastal city on the far end of the continent. A small trade center where caravans on both land and sea made their final drops of goods and merchandise. Most of the travel that left this city consisted of travelers heading north to Ophir, or merchants departing with lists that needed filling once more. The only trade good that Kef-aal had an abundance of, was salt. The salt capital of Setesh, caravans departed from Kef-aal on a regular basis across the desert and up the coast to exchange the needed commodity for more diverse cargo.

Reysis Safar stood on the elevated walkway that ran the length of the cliff face looking out across the ocean and the docks below. Two ships were currently moored and being loaded with crates of salt, animals, and people. He folded his arms across his chest, closed his eyes, and breathed in deeply, taking in the damp sea air. He would soon be surrounded once more by the sea of sands that made up the majority of the realm. It was his comfort and his home.

Heavy footfall alerted him to the presence of another

person approaching him. He smiled without opening his eyes.

"Your Radiance." he greeted the priest.

"Are my footfalls that noticeable?" Tulok asked as he stepped up next to the Sun Guide.

Safar turned to look up at the orc. "There are less than a handful of orcish people in Kef-aal at present, none of the others have business with me." Safar lifted his right hand and scratched at his beard. "You are also very loud, my friend."

Tulok nodded and took a place at the side of the Reysis, turning to look out at the ocean. He nodded and said nothing.

Safar turned to look back at the men loading the boats below. "How is she?" he asked.

Tulok took a deep breath and folded his great arms across his massive chest. "Better. Ready to travel, or so she insists."

Safar shook his head. "Stubborn woman, there are people who could help her..."

Tulok nodded. "She knows... but..." he sighed once more. "I think she must be punishing herself for the loss of Ahsal."

Safar uttered a comment in a strange language that could only be swearing.

Tulok nodded. "I agree." the orc looked over at the dark man. "Did you know? About Ahsal?" he asked him.

Safar pursed his lips and looked at the sky then and over at the priest. "I would not be Reysis if I did not."

Tulok sniffed disapprovingly at the reply, "You could have said something."

Safar sucked on a tooth in thought. "Mmmm... yes... if I had known that was what you were looking for..." he looked at Tulok. "And I would have told you not to go."

"And now?" the orc asked.

Safar turned away to look back out at the docks once more. "I've advised the other Sun Guides to keep clear of the area. Word will reach them all soon. We will simply have to bury information on the location once more, just as the sands did."

"And if there are those who go searching?"

Safar shrugged. "Sun Vipers kill a lot of lost travelers in that area of the wastes."

Tulok regarded Safar carefully, searching for the validity in his words. The Reysis looked over at the orc priest and met his assessing gaze with his own. "You will tell your people, if they come for Ahsal, they come to me, or not at all... Your Radiance."

Father Tulok nodded in both understanding and agreement and held out his hand. "I will tell them. I do not know they will agree."

Safar took the big orc's hand with his own. "Then I will have that conversation with whatever Champion or Halsa member they send should the time come."

The two men stood, hands clasped, staring at each other; neither willing to relinquish their grasp first.

"I hope I am not interrupting?" Isolde asked, clearing her throat from a few feet away.

Safar continued to hold Tulok's gaze, "If I said yes, would it alter your actions?" he replied.

"Probably not." she smiled, repeating the exchange that he and Tulok had had weeks ago when this had all begun.

Safar rolled his eyes at that and released his grip on Tulok. "I do not know why either of you even bothers to ask that question sometimes..." he muttered and turned to look at Isolde.

The Knight was once more dressed in sand-colored trousers and tunic that concealed her haphazard armor.

Her hair was covered in a colorful headscarf, a length of which hung down on the right side, to be pulled up and across her face. She leaned heavily on a finely crafted cane, which aided her as she walked to both of them.

Tulok cleared his throat and stepped a little to the side to make room for her. Safar stepped away from the priest and opened his arms wide to embrace the woman warrior warmly. He pulled back and rested his hands on her shoulders and gazed into her face. "You are feeling well today, yes?" he asked of her.

Isolde nodded and patted Safar gently on his shoulder as she leaned on her cane with the other hand. "Better and better, yes."

"Excellent!" he smiled brightly. "I will confirm with the Captain that we will be traveling with him to Ophir then."

"A boat?" Isolde asked cautiously. She looked up at Tulok.

"It is the fastest way to Ophir from here, along the coast, yes," the Sun Guide replied.

Isolde and Tulok exchanged glances.

Safar frowned and then his eyes lit up. "Ah, yes. Your...incident...in Nahral. I heard all about it. You have nothing to worry about. The River Lord governs the Iteru, not the coast...despite what He may think. "

Tulok shrugged and nodded. Isolde relaxed.

Safar squeezed Isolde's shoulders gently, "Your life is safe in my hands, dear Lady." he offered sincerely.

"Knight." Tulok corrected.

Safar frowned and looked over to Tulok.

"Ser Knight. She's a Knight, Reysis, in service to the Wandering Lord. She's earned her honorific just as surely as you or I. You should use it."

Safar lifted his hands off of Isolde's shoulders and

inclined his head, placing his hand over his heart as he did so.

"I am corrected."

Safar raised his eyes to Isolde's once more, "If you would please excuse me. I will tend to our travel arrangements." He bowed his head in respect and stepped away.

Tulok watched the Reysis depart and rubbed the back of his head in thought. Then became aware of Isolde's presence next to him as she bumped her hip against his.

"Ophir then?" she asked.

Tulok nodded.

"I need to advise my order of what happened. I think there may also be a shrine or a small memory well there to the Wanderer."

Isolde leaned slightly against the big priest, who lifted his arm and wrapped it around her shoulders. "Will you return to Tarf-qua from there?"

"I... I am not certain?" Tulok answered. "It will depend on where they need me, I suppose." he looked down at her. "Why do you ask?"

"I owe a life debt yet, to the people of Tarf-qua." the Knight replied. She turned to look up at Tulok. "I have to pay it back."

Tulok frowned, "I am sure they will understand..."

Isolde shook her head. "I am sure they would, but my *leug*...my...value among my people...demands it. If I break my word to them in this, then...what value is my word?"

Tulok dropped his arm from around her. "So, you will leave then?" he asked, his voice filled with confusion and pain.

"Tarf-qua is only a three-day journey by camel from Ophir...and it is only for a year." she offered. "Letters are carried often, the village is on a regular trade route every fortnight. I could travel with the caravans and ensure the goods make it back and forth...we would still see each other, frequently," she reasoned.

The priest stood on the walkway looking down at the knight. This was the crux of it all then. Obligations that were greater than the both of them. He swallowed hard and clenched his jaw. Duty and obligation were things that his faith knew well. The Lord of the Everburning Sun was a demanding God. What Isolde asked and offered was not an unreasonable thing, but reason had no place here and now.

He nodded and took a step away. "Of course." he managed to say.

"Tulok..." Isolde pleaded and reached for him.

The priest shook his head and held up his hands. "I need... to think...please...excuse me," he managed. Turning away, he left her standing on the walkway overlooking the docks and the city below, as The Radiant Lord's fading light gently colored the horizon.

~~~

She did not have much to pack or ready for her trip from Kef-aal to Ophir. Little more than the clothes on her back was all she had left to her name. Standing at the window of the small room that Safar had secured for her she stared out at the darkness of the sky and the dancing lights of the city below. On the small table behind her were several letters to be sent to various locations on the morning tide. The Sun Guide had assisted her in understanding where and how to accomplish what needed to be done. She had gone looking for Tulok but had been advised by one of the Acolytes at the Temple that the Radiant Father was in sequestered prayer and had asked not to be disturbed. Isolde was not certain which had hurt more than, being denied access to seeing him, or the realization that she was the reason he had locked himself away for the evening before their departure.
~~~

Resting her hands on the windowsill, she let her head hang as she closed her eyes and simply took a moment to be one with her thoughts. She dare not dwell on them, for in that lay the path to despair, but neither could she deny their existence. She had a duty and a promise to uphold. A story to be recorded, a history to be witnessed.

If Safar could rise from the sands of Setesh, then it was possible that Arman and the priestess were still out there... somewhere. Tulok had the whole of his faith to lean on for research and aid in this endeavor. She was not so blessed. The eyes and ears of the caravans would be her best source of tales and information. She would just have to explain it to him.

A pounding at the door interrupted her thoughts. She stood up and grabbed her cane, then walked slowly to the door.

"Who comes?" she asked from her side of the door.

There was a pause.

"A great fool." Tulok's deep voice answered.

Isolde's eyebrows shot into her hairline and she quickly unlatched the door and let it swing wide.

Radiant Father Tulok stood in the doorway. In one hand he held a basket and in the other a colorful glass lantern. "Permission to enter?" he asked uncomfortably.

"You never need to ask," she replied and stepped aside to allow him passage.

He crossed the threshold and she closed and latched the door behind him as he did. Stepping to the small table he set his items down gently. "I was not certain if you had eaten yet..." he said.

She shook her head. "I have not."

"Writing home?" he asked of the letters.

Isolde shrugged and hobbled back toward him. "Among others, yes."

"Isolde, I..." Tulok began, but she held up her hand to stop him.

"You do not have to explain." she countered.

He was silent and stared at the table, saying nothing. Then, "I... I found something for you..." he reached for the lantern. "I remembered that I made a promise to buy you one..."

Isolde smiled warmly at him and accepted the gift. It was a masterfully worked glass lantern made of three different colors. Reds, oranges, and golds. The colors of sunrise and sunset. "Nice color choices..." she mused.

"I... thought...you might enjoy something to remind you..." the orc stammered and stumbled over his words.

"Of you?" she asked looking up at him.

Tulok's brows knit together, he looked away. All at once, he was the shy and reserved Librarian and Healer who had saved her life from the cruelty of the desert. He nodded uncomfortably.

She smiled and nodded and set the lantern aside carefully then looked up at the big priest. Isolde was a tall woman. Even so, the orc was almost a head taller than she was. She reached out and placed the flat of her palm on his chest, over his heart. "I could never forget you," she replied. Beneath her hand, she could feel his heart beat strong and fast. His chest rose and fell under her touch.

"You said something, at Ahsal..." Tulok said quietly.

Isolde nodded and reached to lean her cane against the table beside them both. "We both said a great many things. It was a busy day."

"About not leaving things undone..." Tulok spoke.

She nodded.

"The burden of a weighted heart..." He looked down at her.

The Knight Wanderer nodded and lifted her hand from

Tulok's chest to place it on his cheek once more. His eyes closed then and he leaned in to her touch. "I... don't know how ...this ...works?" he blushed and stammered. He gently wrapped one arm around her still injured frame and held her to him.

Isolde smiled up at him, a smile that lit up her entire face. She shook her head. "I don't either," she replied softly. "I guess we will just have to figure it out as we go along."

~~~

The sand sled creaked and groaned as she climbed into it. She carefully hung the ornate lantern on the end of the sled and then set her walking cane beside her.

"You are being..." she began

"Careful. Careful is the word you are looking for, Island," Safar chided as he helped to secure her and flipped the shade up. "You insist on traveling by sand instead of water, fine. I make accommodations, yes? Even if it means we are a solid fortnight behind The Radiant Father. You refuse healing, fine, I will respect your wishes. But you are not well enough to ride a camel for this journey yet. So, until then, you get to ride behind the arse end of my mount and hope he does not decide to relieve himself on your palanquin...Ser Knight."

Isolde rolled her eyes at the Reysis and looked off toward the docks. A ship bound for Ophir cleared its moorings and its sails unfurled, catching the wind and snapping full. A tall figure clad in the white and gold robes of the priesthood of the Everburning Sun stood at the stern of the vessel, looking in their direction. He raised his hand in salute.

Isolde raised her hand to him in return, eyes locked on him and his vessel as it sailed away.

Safar looked at the ship in the distance and back at the knight.
~~~

"He would have come with you, if you had asked him to, Island," Safar told her.

The Holy Witness continued to watch the vessel as the wind filled her sails and carried her out of sight. She slowly lowered her hand and then pulled her scarf across her face.

"I know."

Lexicon - Deities

The Mother - Avalonian	Mother of Life and Goddess of Avalon's Pantheon
Lord Wanderer - Avalonian	God of Adventuring Souls, Courage and Lost Stories
The Radiant Lord - Seteshi	God of the Sun and Skies, Lord of the Seteshi Pantheon
The Grim Lord - Seteshi	God of the Dead & the Underworld, Shepherd of the Dead
The River Lord - Seteshi	God of Rivers and Water in Setesh
The Changebringer - Seteshi	God of Storms and Violent Change
The Scribe - Seteshi	God of Knowledge and Wisdom
The Healer - Seteshi	Goddess of Healing Arts and Medicine
Silent One - Seteshi	Legendary Rival God of The Radiant Lord
Starmaiden - Agalian	Goddess of Justice and Stars

Lexicon - Unique Races of Sanctum

The Anuket	A reptiloid race of people native to Sanctum (Seteshi desert) created by The Star Maiden.
The Avalonian	The name for a person from the continent of Avalon. One of the 5 realms of Sanctum. Rumored to be descended of the Fey.
The Folk	A small race of people native to Avalon and created by The Mother on Sanctum. They are helpers, and healers.
The Orc	Survivors of the Reaping saved by The Scribe. An often brutal race of people governed by the Gurkh and the Ghal – Rage and Reason.
The Seteshi	The name for a person from the mainland continent's Southern desert realm of Setesh. One of the 5 realms of Sanctum.
The Sobekite	A reptiloid race of people native to Sanctum (Seteshi rivers and waters) created by The River Lord
The Vidria	A race of beardless dwarfs native to Sanctum. Gifted with the ability to stone shape sand and raw earth.

Lexicon - Towns and Terminology

Ahsal	Ancient ruins – home to the Lost Temple of Silence
Deneb-aal	A trading town on the Northern Coast of Setesh
Djad-aal	A trading town in Setesh
Eydafu	A legendary city in Setesh, supposedly buried under the sand
Ghal	Gift of Reason bestowed upon the Orc People by The Scribe
Gurkh	The Power of Rage that churns in the heart of all Orc people
Kas-qua	A village in Setesh, known as the Twin Springs for its two large oasis pools
Kef-aal	A trading town on the coast of Setesh – known as the Salt Capital of Setesh
Lan-Not	Bat Clan of the Orc People
Leug	A measure of worth unique to Avalonian culture. Used instead of coin
Litharge	The City of the Dead. Necropolis of Setesh. Home of the Grand Library
Mukt-aal	A trading town in the south desert. Also known as The Veiled Oasis.

Mya-tal	Serpent Clan of the Orc People
Nahral	The River City. Large city located on the Iteru between Ophir and Litharge
Obor-qua	A village in Setesh with a dedicated Temple to the Radiant Lord
Ophir	Capital City of Setesh. Largest city and home to the grand Temple of Radiance
Reysis	Also known Sun Guides – desert guides in charge of a caravan
Sha-brd	Raptor Clan of the Orc People
Sik-iln	Great Cat Clan of the Orc People
Tarf-qua	A village in Setesh with a dedicated Temple to the Radiant Lord
The Halsa	The governing body in charge of the Temple of The Radiant Lord
The Morpheum	A place of dreams that some Avalonians can traverse

Epilogue

Sands parted before him like waves before the bow of a boat. They solidified on either side of him as he slowly made his way down into the depths of the dunes. His hands trailed along the edges of the passageway that formed beneath his fingertips as he exerted his will over the earth.

Patches of broken stone emerged as he moved onward, step by careful step. How many years had he spent pin-pointing the exact location of this sacred space? He could navigate these sands without the aid of any Sun Guide.

It had taken him four days to recover the jars that had once occupied the niches of the Temple. If they had all been empty, he would not have bothered, but two of them were already filled with the sacred sparks of their lineages. Arman had not relished the idea of beginning everything from the start once more, and he was nothing if not persis-tent. One thing yet remained to be found.

As the sands and stones slowly moved away from him, revealing their hidden treasures beneath, the Vidria stone shaper began to feel a sense of anxiousness. What if Nebiyre had survived and escaped the cave in? Perhaps the old witch had managed to make her way out of the tunnels some other way.

At the end of day five, Arman was ready to resign him-self to needing to find another Danuae to serve as a sacrifice when the sands gave up an emaciated arm. He began to giggle gleefully as he shoved the sand and broken shards out of his way. Slowly the broken figure of Nebiyre was unearthed. Around her neck hung his prize. The selfish bitch had not even bothered to tell him that she had managed to open the box. He reached for the scarab.

Nebiyre's eyes fluttered. Her almost lipless mouth moved in a silent plea for aid.

Arman's fingers closed around the sacred scarab and ripped it free from her throat.

"May someone at the Crossroads take pity on you," he spoke. Turning away from Nebiyre's exposed body, Arman made his way out of the cleared area and returned to his mount. Buzzards circled above.

-The end?-

About the Authors

C.S. Kading – She is a poet, playwright, and a storyteller, whose love for writing began in 3rd grade when she won a district writing contest. Her love for fantastical forces motivates her to create stories of heroes, villains, gods and monsters that often have a foundation in Old World mythology and legends.

Tony Fuentes – Whether it is taking up a child's toy and creating a world around it, or giving the epic history of a cocktail that he made up five minutes ago, Tony's imagination borders on the fantastic and sometimes the inane. A storyteller, gamer, and part-time occultist – he gives the weird and wondrous things a place in our world for all to enjoy.

Map of Sanctum

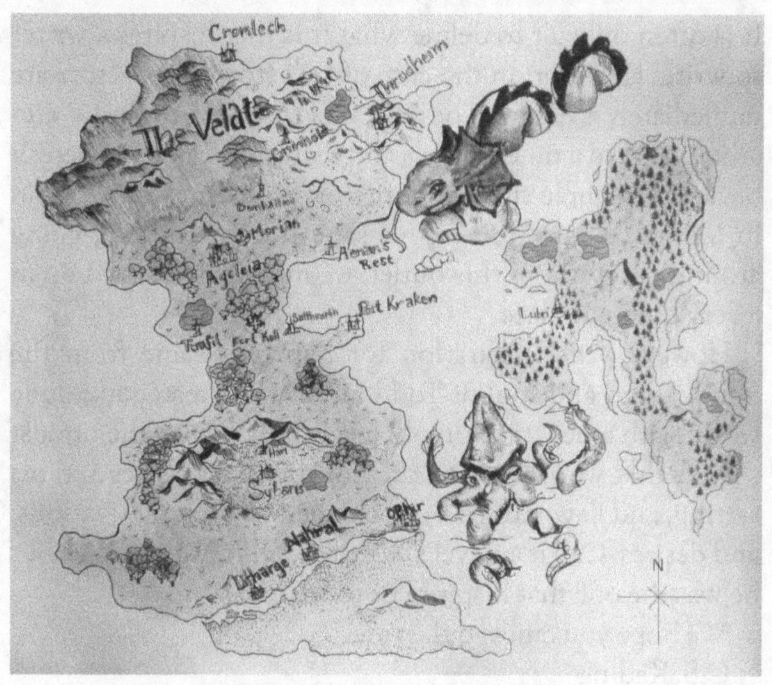

Acknowledgements

It is often difficult to define what it is that inspires a writer to write. However; in the case of this story, two factors are immediately evident. The first was the need to find a creative outlet in a time of crisis and seclusion. Sands of Setesh began as a simple shared short story that Tony and I began in March of 2020, to keep us sane from everything going around us. Without this outlet, we might have ended up in a very different place.

However; the inspiration for Sanctum came from the mind, heart, and soul of Todd Filek; who created a unique world with a new take on old legends. It is with the utmost thanks that we are able to present this story , placed in his setting, and flavored with our characters, their motivations, and desires. Call it a novel's worth of fanfic, we suppose; but he was the one that inspired us to write.

We hope you enjoyed the ride.

C.S. Kading

Tony Fuentes

www.ingramcontent.com/pod-product-compliance
Lightning Source LLC
Chambersburg PA
CBHW010747310726
48980CB00004B/398

* 9 7 8 0 5 7 8 7 5 6 9 8 1 *